DADDY SANG LEAD

DADDY SANG LEAD

The History and Performance Practice of
White Southern Gospel Music

Stanley Heard Brobston, Ph.D.

VANTAGE PRESS
New York

Cover design by Susan Thomas

FIRST EDITION

Copyright © 2006 by Stanley Heard Brobston, Ph.D.

Published by Vantage Press, Inc.
419 Park Ave. South, New York, NY 10016

Manufactured in the United States of America
ISBN: 0-533-15353-0

Library of Congress Catalog Card No.: 2005908508

0 9 8 7 6 5 4 3 2 1

Contents

Figures

Foreword

Gospel music studies are often found in music literature, listed in CD catalogs, and even may be viewed on television programs. Gospel music group research, however, rarely has been pursued.

Using his familiarity with local citizens and knowledge of his native South Georgia, Stanley Brobston has been able to locate, interview, and document family gospel singing groups. Even with the universal acceptance of television and other media, these family singing gospel groups still meet musically in their homes, in churches, or in local gospel music festivals.

Because the field of gospel music is so diverse racially and culturally, Brobston restricted his study to family groups of Anglo-Saxon heritage.

The songs of these family groups, largely unadulterated by today's media, bring a uniqueness to Brobston's research. He used oral history techniques to interview and record some of these family groups in action.

Oral historians, folk music enthusiasts, and music researchers should welcome this unique contribution to the field of music research.

It is gratifying to see this study in print form. The musical and general public will benefit from Brobston's study.

—Roger P. Phelps
Professor Emeritus
New York University

(Dr. Phelps is the coauthor of *A Guide to Research in Music Education*, 5th ed. (Lanham, MD, Scarecrow Press, 2005). His *A Guide to Research in Music Education*, now in its fifth edition, is the definitive text for scholars in the field of music education. Dr. Brobston's study is cited on pp. 217, 218 of the 5th Edition as an example of oral history research.)

Acknowledgments

The field research for this book took place during the summer of 1975 and the summer and fall of 1976 in South Georgia. The writer introduced himself to literally thousands of people. With the rarest of exceptions, everyone met was courteous, open, warm, hospitable, and helpful. The writer was a guest in the homes of many persons met on short acquaintance. Many others freely allowed the use of their personal offices, telephones, and extended other courtesies. Even a partial listing of these persons would take far too many pages, although each unique memory is cherished.

A special debt of gratitude, however, is owed to the writer's brother, Henry Brobston, and his wife, Charlotte, who not only suggested the topic for the book, but made their home a center of operations during the field research.

The following persons also contributed in some substantial way to the completion of this undertaking: Theron and Elizabeth Aldridge, James and Bess Beckworth, Jim Black, Norma L. Boyd, Don Butler, Dr. David Crawford, J. William Denny, Howard Gallimore, Dr. John C. Gilbert, Beverly Greer, Connor B. Hall, Raymond Hamrick, Lou Hildreth, Wayne and Cindy Hilliard, Dr. John Huxford, Reggie and Flo Jackson, Dr. Robert John, Dr. Kathryn Mahan, Ray Melton, Ray Douglas Moore, Jim Myers, Norman Odlum, Dr. Ted Phillips, Martha Powell, Joe Pritchard, Ed Robbins, Dr. Norma H. Thompson, Claudius and Carolyn Thurmond.

Special thanks are due to Dr. William Jensen Reynolds, of the Church Music Department of the Sunday School Board of the Southern Baptist Convention, for his broad knowledge of the subject of gospel music, and for his insightful suggestions. Books from his personal library were of immense value in the writing of the historical chapters of this work.

The writer also acknowledges with gratitude the specific and positive suggestions of Dr. Roger P. Phelps. The writer considers it a privilege to know him not only as a professor and adviser, but as a friend.

Joan Lange, teacher of English and personal friend, examined the manuscript in minute detail. Her many perceptive comments regarding grammar and English usage are greatly appreciated. Errors that remain should be attributed to the writer's stubborn refusal to follow her advice.

In the course of the acquisition of data, the writer visited a number of libraries. The assistance afforded by the library personnel, whether in prestigious institutions or in small county libraries, was uniformly courteous and helpful. To the best of the writer's memory, each library that was visited is listed below:

Library of Congress, Washington, D.C.
Andrew College, Cuthbert, Georgia
Brewton Parker Junior College, Mt. Vernon, Georgia
Columbia Presbyterian Seminary, Decatur, Georgia
Columbus College, Columbus, Georgia
Emory University, Atlanta, Georgia
Fort Valley State College, Fort Valley, Georgia
Georgia Historical Society, Savannah, Georgia
Georgia Southern College, Statesboro, Georgia
Mercer University, Macon, Georgia
University of Georgia, Athens, Georgia
Valdosta State College, Valdosta, Georgia
Georgia County Libraries of Bulloch County, Chatham County, Jenkins County, Pulaski County, Upson County, Wayne County, and Worth County
Asbury Theological Seminary, Wilmore, Kentucky
Southern Baptist Theological Seminary, Louisville, Kentucky
Country Music Foundation Library and Media Center, Nashville, Tennessee
Dargan-Carver Library and Historical Commission of the Southern Baptist Convention, Nashville, Tennessee

Joint Universities Library, Music Library, Nashville, Tennessee

Lee College, Cleveland, Tennessee

Elmer H. Bobst Library, New York University, New York, New York

Columbia University Libraries, New York, New York

Library and Museum of the Performing Arts, New York, New York

New York Public Library, New York, New York

State University of New York, Stony Brook, New York

Union Theological Seminary, New York, New York

Special mention should be made of the music library of the Southern Baptist Theological Seminary in Louisville, Kentucky. This library, with its Mary B. Converse Collection of Hymnology, and its Janet T. Ingersoll Collection of Gospel Music, was that which the writer found most beneficial in his quest for information.

Thanks are also due the University of Georgia Library and the Dargan-Carver Library, mentioned above, for providing much-needed carrel space for extended periods of time.

Acknowledgments would not be complete without recognizing in some way the sacrifices of the writer's wife, Sandra (Sandy), and sons, Stanley and Stephen. It is difficult for a wife and children to have an absentee husband and father for over three years, and the writer wants them to know, in writing, that he appreciates the unselfish contributions they made.

DADDY SANG LEAD

1

Introduction

The present book was originally conceived as an examination of one facet of gospel music, the amateur family singing groups. A brief historical chapter was planned in order to acquaint the reader with the background of the subject matter. In the process of acquisition of data it became more and more apparent that a history of white southern gospel music had yet to be compiled. Soon the main thrust of the book became that of compiling historical material. The Field Research became not the primary focus of the book, but a separate study.

Statement of the Problem

The problem was to document the antecedents of gospel music singing, and to describe its present performance practice as exemplified by selected amateur family gospel music singing groups [hereinafter called groups] in rural Georgia.

Subproblem I. The objective of the first subproblem was to document the antecedents of gospel music singing. This was accomplished by compiling information from primary and secondary sources. In general, information was obtainable from public and academic libraries. The several libraries utilized by the writer are enumerated in the Acknowledgments. Personal libraries of individuals interested in gospel music were also valuable sources of information. Many of these individuals are also named in the Acknowledgments. Additional information was obtained by interviewing many present-day leaders in the field of gospel music. Names of persons interviewed are cited in the Bibliography. Unfortunately, a multitude of additional persons who

1

were helpful in the compilation or verification of isolated bits of data have not been named. The many contributions of these unnamed persons are again gratefully acknowledged.

Subproblem II. Identification and selection of amateur family gospel music singing groups in rural Georgia was the focus of Subproblem II. The methodology for this portion of the book is delineated in Chapter 6. The characteristics of the selected groups are summarized in Chapter 7. Detailed information concerning each selected group is contained in Appendix A.

Subproblem III. The objective of the third subproblem was to analyze the words and music of selected compositions. The methodology used in this analysis is delineated in Chapter 6. The characteristics of the words and music of the selected compositions are summarized in Chapter 7. The songs, themselves, are reproduced in Appendix A.

Subproblem IV. The purpose of the fourth subproblem was to determine differences between the performance of the music and its published notation. The methodology utilized to identify these differences is delineated in Chapter 6. The characteristics of these differences, that is, the performance practices of the groups, are summarized in Chapter 7.

Definition of Terms

Several terms used by the writer may need clarification. For purposes of this study the following definitions will apply.

Amateur: Performing groups were considered amateur if they earned less than fifty percent of their gross income from performing, composing, or arranging music; or from revenue from recordings and sheet music sales.

Family Group: A music performing group was considered a family group if it had three members related by blood or marriage.

Gospel: According to Webster's Dictionary, "gospel" originally meant "good news." The term now represents "the teachings of Jesus and the Apostles" or "the history of the life and teachings of Jesus."[1]

Gospel Song: According to Davidson, a gospel song is:

A simple harmonized tune in popular style combined with a religious text of an emotional and personal character in which the individual and/or the individual religious experience is usually the center rather than God. The text . . . is usually subjective in nature, developing a single thought instead of a line of thought. . . . The melodic, harmonic and rhythmic style is often associated with the style of secular music, often drawing attention of itself and away from the text.[2]

Gospel Music Singing Group: Any musical organization considering itself to be a gospel music singing group was considered the same without verification.

Rural: Counties in which a large proportion of the economy is based upon agriculture. All counties in Georgia Congressional Districts One, Two, Three, and Eight were considered rural.

Home Church: The church in which the adult members of the group had placed their membership was considered their home church. In most cases this was a church in close proximity to present place of abode.

Evangelism: According to *Webster's Dictionary,* evangelism is "a preaching of, or zealous effort to spread, the Gospel, as in revival meetings."[3]

Evangelistic Music: According to Davidson:

Characteristically, evangelistic music is more testimonial than instructional, and personal rather than collective. It emphasizes the now and today and the importance of the decision for Christ. Its emotional content is comparatively high. Evangelistic music may be instrumental or vocal or both. If instrumental, it will be based on a tune that readily will recall a familiar gospel text.[4]

Delimitations

For the Field Research portion of the study the following delimitations were imposed.

The Field Research was concerned with only family performing groups.

Groups were not considered for inclusion in the study unless they had performed at least once outside the confines of their home church within the previous calendar year. The purpose of this delimitation was to establish minimum competency.

Only amateur groups were considered. Amateur groups who received occasional remuneration for their performances, however, were not excluded.

Only white groups were considered for the study.[5]

No attempt was made to compare the quality of the songs or of the performances with one another or with any predetermined standard.

Significance and Need for the Study

The term gospel music[6] has been used to identify the words and music of popular religious hymnody in America for more than one hundred years. The amount of music composed and published in this musical genre is quite substantial. The number of persons who could be considered adherents or aficionados of this music is also considerable. Yet this music has been almost totally neglected in scholarly writings. When the music has been studied it has, with few exceptions, been denigrated. Examples of writings concerning gospel music are detailed in the Review of the Literature which follows. The need for a separate history of gospel music is self-apparent.

To the writer's knowledge, the present study is the first attempt to record the history of white southern gospel music into a scholarly document. In addition, the writer's Field Research represents the first known study of gospel music to use an objective method for the selection of representative performers or for the selection of the music to be examined.

Review of Related Literature

Historians who attempt to record the total spectrum of American music must, of necessity, limit the amount of space allotted to various types of music. Musical "firsts" are generally awarded more space than other music of a similar nature and music with outstanding historical significance is also given more weight. However, it does seem that some historians have been less than matter-of-fact in their documentation of gospel music and other popular hymnody, with the notable exception of the Negro spiritual. Howard, for example, admits that gospel songs have undeniable value in swaying crowds and states that some have shown amazing endurance. But his terminology betrays a lack of respect for the music as he calls it, "music better fitted to the dance hall."[7] He describes "Moody and Sankey songs" as "representing to many musicians the lowest depths to which music could descend."[8]

Howard and Bellows take a more sympathetic approach to folk hymnody but their lack of familiarity with the genre leads to erroneous statements such as, "One of the leading latter-century composers was Ira David Sankey";[9] or, speaking of the two forms of shaped note notation, "However, the point to bear in mind is that the music *itself* was the same, whether printed in four shapes or seven. The same large body of American song appeared in both notations as the years went on. . . ."[10] Clarification of the errors contained in the above statements will be presented in the text which follows.

Hitchcock, in *Music in the United States*, discusses gospel hymnody in his chapter on "The Vernacular Tradition, 1820–1920"[11] Hitchcock also wrote the "Introduction" to the Da Capo Press reprint of *Gospel Hymns Nos. 1 to 6 Complete.*[12] His choice of words to describe gospel hymnody can hardly be considered neutral, however, when he states:

> Its musical background was the correct, bland style of Mason and Hastings, but its harmony tended to be more chromatically engorged, its texts more sentimentally swollen.[13]

He accuses the gospel hymn writers of being "intent on engaging large masses in cathartic songfests."[14] He does, however, recognize the strength and suitability of gospel music. He writes:

> Bliss's *Pull for the Shore* may have a text as metaphorically exag-

5

gerated as a seventeenth-century Italian opera aria and as artfully homespun as the doggerel of Edgar Guest, but its chorus is an almost irresistible march, perfectly suited to its soul-stirring evangelistic purposes.[15]

Robert Stevenson, writing on "Church Music: A Century of Contrasts" in Lang's *One Hundred Years of Music in America,* describes gospel singing as follows:

Whether in tent or tabernacle, minor mode hymns are never sung, women have the congregational lead, chromatically altered chords often sentimentalize the harmony, the third of a chord is never omitted, and wearisome successions of thirds and sixths are the rule.[16]

His sentence following the above quotation uses "treacly mannerisms" as a further descriptive term.[17]

Barzun does not discuss religious music at all, yet he gives a warning that might be applicable to the present study:

What is clearly inadmissible is to pass judgment on contemporary music culture by singling out one of its elements which happens to be popular, or by illicit comparisons of things unlike—the mediocre of today with the best of the past, or again, the total impression of the present—necessarily vague, with the total impression of the golden age—necessarily imaginary.[18]

Sablosky, also, does not discuss religious music. In a chapter entitled "A Question of Taste," he offers some insight into the difference between European and American tastes. This difference in tastes could explain some of the apparent dichotomy between historical European hymnody and the American gospel songs. Brief mention of folk hymnody is made in the following quotations:

Thomas Jefferson's lament over his country's musical shortcomings in Revolutionary days was echoed by newcomers a half century later with a new note of derision. Mrs. Trollope saw barbarism not only in the camp meeting but in the theater as well.[19]

Religious folk music was apparently not too different from the other popular music of the time:

> The minstrels and the sentimental song represented two aspects of the American musical taste of the time. Neither was notable for its sophistication, but both were remarkable for the extent of their prevalence in a country already far-flung and diverse.[20]

This reference to the "sentimental song" and its prevalence is interesting in light of both Hitchcock's and Stevenson's references to the sentimentality of the gospel songs.

Edwards and Marrocco have an eight-page chapter on "The Minority Sects And Their Music,"[21] and their brief chapter on "Fasola, Doremi, and Revivalism" summarizes George Pullen Jackson's research on white and Negro spirituals.[22] They describe the songs sung at post Civil War revival meetings as:

> Simple and attractive tunes in verse and refrain form, composed over simple tonic and dominant harmonies usually in major keys and often employing the dotted eighth and sixteenth note pattern of a marching song.[23]

Ritter, whom Sablosky identifies as the author of the first historical account of *Music in America,*[24] discusses Hastings, Mason, and Gould in a chapter entitled, "Last Representative Psalm-Tune teachers."[25] Ritter's last chapter discusses "The Cultivation of Popular Music," in which he laments America's lack of a true folk art. He goes into some detail on "the songs of the colored race," and briefly discusses the music of Stephen Foster.[26]

Mathews has one chapter on "Psalmody and Popular Music After the [Civil] War," in which he discusses the music of William B. Bradbury, Phillip P. Bliss and other composers of hymns and hymn-tunes. He mentions the origin of the term "Gospel Songs" as coming from the evangelist, Dwight L. Moody:

> Two other names are particularly well known in this department, yet neither is strictly appropriate to the present work. Ira D. Sankey is a popular singer, who has a large following, drawn to him by his originally beautiful voice, and the sincerity and depth

of expression with which he interprets his "Gospel Songs," to use the appropriate term, originated, it is believed, by Mr. Dwight L. Moody. Mr. Phillipp [sic] Phillipps [sic] occupies an analogous position in the Methodist denomination, but he has devoted his talents to commercial uses, and is neither a musician nor an evangelist.[27]

Mathews stated that all of these men "suffered from insufficient professional preparation."[28] He apparently considers them an exemplification of the democratic ideals upon which this country was founded. Mathews observes that "they represent the average musical consciousness of this country, self-developed by the influences of rural environment, and undisturbed by imperfectly assimilated musical training."[29]

Elson does not mention a folk-hymn singing style except in his first chapter on "The Religious Beginnings of American Music."[30] His chapter on "The Folk-music of America" discusses American Indian music, Afro-American music, and the music of Stephen Foster.[31]

Lowens does not discuss music created after the Civil War, and therefore does not go into the "gospel songs." But his chapters on the *Bay Psalm Book;* John Tufts's *Introduction to the Singing of Psalm-Tunes;* Andrew Law; Little and Smith's *The Easy Instructor;* and John Wyeth's *Repository of Sacred Music, Part Second;* (chapters 2, 3, 4, 6, and 7, respectively)[32] were particularly helpful in the historiography of the antecedents of gospel music. In his chapter on "The American Tradition of Church Song," Lowens describes church song as America's national folk song:

In England, the catalyst appears to have been the national folk song. In America, may not the catalyst well be our native church song, which encompasses that portion of the Anglo-Celtic heritage of folk music that took root here, and adds to it something more?[33]

In describing America's native church song he is not too concerned about the way it is supposed to sound to a listener:

This music was experienced rather than heard because it was not written for an audience's appreciation or to tickle an ear—it was written to be experienced in performance by performers. How it "sounded" to a non-participant was of very little importance. This is no novel concept; it is one of the essential pre-conditions of genuine church song.[34]

Ewen, other than a brief recognition of jazz and folk music, is more concerned with opera, orchestral music and other forms of classical music.[35]

Of the more well-known historians, Chase[36] is probably the most sympathetic to religious folk music. His chapters on "The Fasola Folk" and "Revivals and Camp Meetings" give excellent information and musical examples of this rustic music that apparently led to gospel music being sung after the Civil War. In describing the difference between the written music and its performance practice, he states:

There is one aspect of revival singing that cannot be reconstructed from the printed music and that can be but inadequately described with words. That is the practice of taking familiar, conventional hymns and ornamenting the melodies with . . . "numberless little slurs and melodic variations."[37]

Unfortunately, Chase does not continue tracing this music into the late nineteenth and early twentieth centuries.

American gospel music is mentioned by at least one European historian. Scholes states, "A few of the hymns and tunes of this class are genuinely touching and stirring, but the bulk of them are commonplace reiteration of one or two sentimental ideas set to fitting music."[38] Scholes does recognize the relationship between the camp-meeting songs and the history of gospel song. He writes, "When its history comes to be studied it will probably be found that behind Sankey and Moody lies the powerful influence of the American Camp Meeting."[39]

When they have not ignored it, historians of Church Music, even more so than historians of American Music, have been harsh on gospel music. Breed, in his chapter on "Gospel Songs and Singers,"[40] states six criticisms of the music. These criticisms are long and detailed, and will not be enumerated here. Breed is in turn criticized by Lorenz for not really having an understanding of gospel hymnody at all.[41] Lorenz, who does not consider himself a historian, presents a strong argument in favor of the gospel song as he writes:

> Better that literary unskillfulness and mediocre musical talent shall continue to write, better to have ephemeral, shallow, and unsatisfying songs written by the thousands, than that the impulse to express spontaneously the vital godliness within should be entirely lost.[42]

According to Lorenz, the gospel song evolved from the "spiritual":

> We have seen that the Sunday-school song is a hybrid produced by crossing the "spiritual" with the American hymn tune. It had the harmonies and the major scale of the latter with the freedom, vigor and in part the form of the sacred folk song. The Gospel song while affected by the same influence that produced the American hymn tune, was the direct outgrowth of the "spiritual."[43]

Foote, whose opinion of gospel songs is not very high ("If they helped to draw the ignorant and untrained to Christianity, they also served to repel the more intelligent and experienced"),[44] makes a comparison between the spirituals and the gospel songs:

> Deeply moving as the words of many of the "spirituals" are, as utterances of the depths of human suffering and sorrow, their great power lies in their music. Almost without exception the melodies possess dignity in their simplicity and breathe the spirit of a deep religious experience. It is in this respect that they stand out in marked contrast to the gospel songs, which too often represent a deliberate cheapening of literary and musical standards in an effort to cater to a popular taste.[45]

George Pullen Jackson, however, is convinced that the Negro spiritual and the white spiritual grew up together and have very much in common. He discounts those who would say that the Negro spiritual is the unique contribution of the Afro-American.[46] Howard agrees with Jackson:

> Those who know the gospel songs of the white folk are in accord with this view. It is known that the Negro did adopt many scores of his religious tunes and texts from the white people, especially the Baptist white people. He resang them with the perfect freedom which led to much unconscious revision . . . (just as all real folk singers do).[47]

Jackson's *White Spirituals in the Southern Uplands,*[48] published in 1933, provided more specific information on the subject of southern gospel music than any other one source the writer was able to find. Yet even Jackson mentioned the subject only in the final chapters of his first book. He touched upon the subject again in his article for the *Musical Quarterly* of the same year.[49] Thereafter, Jackson apparently began to devote his attention exclusively to earlier music written in four-shape notation. An excellent summary and perspective of Jackson's pioneering musicological studies is presented by Yoder as an Introduction to the Folklore Associates reprint of *White Spirituals* (1964).[50] Unfortunately, this Introduction does not appear in the more readily accessible Dover Publications reprint of the same work (1965).[51]

Hooper has a well-written summary of gospel music to approximately 1900.[52] He avoids arguing about the merits of the music and presents a concise history of the musical style. His eight-page bibliography was a valuable source of titles.

Routley, the English church musician, has written several books on church music, most of which can be counted upon to say something derogatory about gospel music. For example:

> And we must say that the music content of much of the Sankey-type hymnody is so low as to be infantile. The pretentious and succulent rhythm of Mrs. Knapp's *Behold Me Standing,* for example, is frankly nauseating to any musician of sensitiveness. The puerile technique of most of the work of Bliss (1838–1876) arouses the wrath of the most tolerant critics.[53]

11

But even Routley reluctantly bows to the durability of gospel music when he states:

> The interest shown in the 1960s in church music affecting the style of secular popular music must not make anybody forgetful that the church itself has had a "pop" section in its music which has had a continuous vogue at any rate since the days of Sankey, and possibly since the days of Wesley.[54]

Ellinwood recognizes some of the controversy and some of the significance of gospel songs when he states:

> In no facet of American life has the cleavage, social or otherwise, been so sharply drawn as between those familiar with historical hymnody and those who know only the so-called "gospel songs." The latter songs form such a distinctive lore, and at the same time such a large segment of the field of religious music in this country that some attempt should be made to describe them.[55]

Ellinwood does not truly describe them in the five pages he allots to the subject. Instead, he spends much space on the history of shaped note notation and concludes with "... none of them [gospel songs] deserve to survive the cheap wood-pulp on which they are printed."[56]

Benson, who has been called "the foremost hymnologist that America has produced,"[57] provided several insights into the beginning of gospel hymnody in his important book, *The English Hymn.* In 1915 Benson stated:

> The time has come when it is perceived that all songs called Gospel Hymns are not a homogenous mass, and that they should be judged like other hymns upon their individual merit.[58]

Benson's later book, *The Hymnody of the Christian Church* (1927), however, states:

> The *Gospel Hymns* occupy a far background now. Most are forgotten. Those once popular are staled by repetition. The few that may find a place in church hymnals convey no covert threat of an

"era of Gospel Hymns" and may or may not prove an addition to church song of some permanence.[59]

He is highly critical of what he calls "The Later Degeneracy":

The more pressing problem is how the Church is to deal with the evangelistic and popular song that has taken the place of the *Gospel Hymns,* appropriating their name and now rivaling their popularity.[60]

Reynolds also provides perceptive information concerning the beginnings of the *Gospel Hymns* series. Instead of deprecating subsequent gospel music, he provides a brief résumé of later southern gospel hymnody in his three pages entitled "Expansion of Southern Shaped-Note Singing."[61] He states, "The many collections of 'convention' songs which have appeared in recent decades have escaped the attention of most hymnological writers."[62]

Information concerning southern gospel music was, for the most part, available only from unpublished or popular sources.

Eskew provides detailed information concerning early music published in the Shenandoah Valley.[63] Unfortunately, Eskew's research was limited to the time span 1816–1860. The majority of southern gospel music was published after that time.

Fleming's study of James D. Vaughn, Music Publisher,[64] and Reed's study of A.J. Showalter and his publishing company[65] were invaluable in tracing the later history of southern gospel music. Beary's study of the Stamps-Baxter Music and Printing Company[66] was also helpful. As Beary's dissertation was still in its final stages, her willingness to mail copies of portions of chapters and to answer questions posed over the telephone is gratefully acknowledged.

Gentry's *A History and Encyclopedia of Country, Western, and Gospel Music*[67] consists mainly of reprints of selected articles on the respective subjects. Gospel music does not command a great deal of space in the first edition (1961), and even less in the "completely revised" second edition (1969).[68]

Racine's popular biography of the Blackwood Brothers Quartet[69] contains quite a bit of historical information regarding

13

professional gospel performing groups. Much the same can be said about Blackwood and Martin's biography of James Blackwood,[70] and Becker's story of the Speer Family.[71] Other popular biographies of gospel performers offer some insights but little historical information.

The review of the literature would be incomplete without mention of Burt and Allen's *The History of Gospel Music.*[72] This 205-page paperback publication can best be classified as a "folk document." George Pullen Jackson's description of James's *Brief History of the Sacred Harp* could easily apply to Burt and Allen's *History*:

> James's *Brief History of the Sacred Harp* is poorly organized, its language is often hard to understand, and in the few instances where I have been able to check up on his data, I have found a considerable number of errors. But, until further investigations are made in this field, we shall have to take James's findings for what they are, namely, the only attempt at a history of the *Sacred Harp* in existence, indeed the only historical attempt that has ever been made in any angle of the shape-note field. And we shall have to be grateful for this as the work of one who was on the inside, one who was boundlessly enthusiastic. . . .[73]

Insofar as known, Burt and Allen hold an analogous position as the first historians of southern gospel music. Despite the illogic, erroneous information, internal contradictions, and naïveté of Burt and Allen's *History,* included is a great deal of information regarding the history of gospel music as viewed by those active in professional performance. The outline biographies of gospel musicians, which occupy approximately one-half of the book, provide a listing of many past and present leaders in the field.

Past and present gospel music periodicals, such as the *Musical Million,*[74] *Vaughan's Family Visitor,*[75] *Gospel Music News,*[76] *Gospel Singing Journal,*[77] *The Singing News*[78] and *Concert Life,*[79] provided occasional articles of usefulness. In general, historical information published in these periodicals was not considered reliable.

A great many sources were utilized other than those enu-

14

merated in the above Review of the Literature. Where appropriate the additional sources are cited in footnotes and also included in the Bibliography.

Notes

1. "Gospel," *Webster's New Twentieth Century Dictionary of the English Language* (unabridged second ed.; USA [sic]: Collins World, 1975), p. 788.
2. James R. Davidson, *A Dictionary of Protestant Church Music* (Metuchen, New Jersey: Scarecrow Press, 1975), pp. 135–136.
3. "Evangelism," *Webster's Dictionary,* op. cit., p. 632.
4. Davidson, op. cit., p. 118.
5. The musical concepts and practices of Afro-American gospel musicians differ in such magnitude from white gospel music practices that in actuality they constitute separate genres. Cf. page 114 below.
6. In most cases used synonymously with "gospel hymn" or "gospel song."
7. John Tasker Howard, *Our American Music* (New York: Thomas Y. Crowell Co., 1965), p. 663.
8. Ibid., p. 668.
9. John Tasker Howard and George Kent Bellows, *A Short History of Music in America* (1957; New York: Thomas Y. Crowell Company, 1967), p. 324.
10. Ibid., p. 66; emphasis in original.
11. H. Wiley Hitchcock, *Music in the United States: A Historical Introduction* (2nd ed.; Englewood Cliffs, New Jersey: Prentice-Hall, Inc., 1974), pp. 96–106.
12. Ira D. Sankey [et al], *Gospel Hymns Nos. 1 to 6 Complete* (1895; New York: Da Capo Press, 1972), n.p.
13. Hitchcock, *Music in the United States,* op. cit., p. 104.
14. Ibid.
15. Ibid., p. 105.
16. Paul Henry Lang (ed.), *One Hundred Years of Music in America* (New York: G. Schirmer, 1961), p. 88.
17. Ibid.
18. Jacques Barzun, *Music in American Life* (Garden City, New York: Doubleday and Co., Inc., 1956), p. 70.
19. Irving Sablosky, *American Music* (Chicago: University of Chicago Press, 1969), p. 56.
20. Ibid., p. 58.
21. Arthur C. Edwards and W. Thomas Marrocco, *Music In the United States* (Dubuque, Iowa: Wm. C. Brown Company, 1968), pp. 20–28.
22. Ibid., pp. 29–37.
23. Ibid., p. 37.
24. Sablosky, op. cit., p. 83.
25. Frédéric Louis Ritter, *Music in America* (New York: Charles Scribner's Sons, 1883), pp. 157–180.
26. Ibid., pp. 390–401.

27. W.S.B. Mathews, *A Hundred Years of Music in America* (Chicago: G.L. Howe, 1889), p. 95.
28. Ibid.
29. Ibid.
30. Louis C. Elson, *The History of American Music* (New York: The Macmillan Co., 1904), pp. 1–25.
31. Ibid., pp. 123–139.
32. Irving Lowens, *Music and Musicians in Early America* (New York: W.W. Norton and Company, Inc., 1964), pp. 25–88, 115–155.
33. Ibid., p. 286.
34. Ibid., p. 283.
35. David Ewen, *Music Comes to America* (New York: Allen, Towne and Heath, Inc., 1947).
36. Gilbert Chase, *America's Music from the Pilgrims to the Present* (rev. 2nd ed.; New York: McGraw-Hill Book Company, 1966).
37. Ibid., p. 224.
38. Percy A. Scholes, *The Oxford Companion to Music* (ninth ed.; London: Oxford University Press, 1955), p. 508.
39. Ibid.
40. David Riddle Breed, *The History and Use of Hymns and Hymn Tunes* (New York: Fleming H. Revell Co., 1903), pp. 331–342.
41. Edmund S. Lorenz, *Practical Church Music* (New York: Fleming H. Revell Co., 1909), p. 105.
42. Edmund S. Lorenz, *The Singing Church: The Hymns It Wrote and Sang* (Nashville: Cokesbury Press, 1938), p. 99.
43. Edmund S. Lorenz, *Church Music: What a Minister Should Know About It* (New York: Fleming H. Revell Co., 1923), p. 342.
44. Henry Wilder Foote, *Three Centuries of American Hymnody* (1940; rpt. Hamden, Connecticut: Archon Books, 1968), p. 270.
45. Ibid., pp. 274–275.
46. George Pullen Jackson, *White and Negro Spirituals, Their Life Span and Kinship;* Tracing 200 Years of Untrammeled Song Making and Singing among our Country Folk, With 116 Songs as Sung by Both Races (1944; New York: Da Capo Press, 1975).
47. Howard, op. cit., pp. 682–683).
48. George Pullen Jackson, *White Spirituals in the Southern Uplands;* The Story of the Fasola Folk, Their Songs, Singings, and "Buckwheat Notes" (1933; Hatboro, Pennsylvania: Folklore Associates, Inc., 1964).
49. George Pullen Jackson, "Buckwheat Notes" *The Musical Quarterly,* XIX (October, 1933), 393–400.
50. Jackson, *White Spirituals,* op. cit., pp. I-XV.
51. Jackson, *White Spirituals in the Southern Uplands* [etc.,] (1933; New York: Dover Publications, Inc., 1965).
52. William Lloyd Hooper, *Church Music in Transition* (Nashville: Broadman Press, 1963), pp. 79–101.
53. Erik Routley, *The Church and Music* (rev. ed.; London: Duckworth & Co., Ltd., 1967), p. 189.
54. Erik Routley, *Twentieth Century Church Music* (London: Herbert Jenkins, Ltd., 1964), p. 196.

55. Leonard W. Ellinwood, *The History of American Church Music* (rev. ed.; New York: Da Capo Press, 1970), p. 101.

56. Ibid., p. 105.

57. Henry van Dyke, quoted by Morgen P. Noyes, "Louis P. Benson, Hymnologist" *The Papers of the Hymn Society,* XIX (New York: The Hymn Society of America, 1955), p. 3.

58. Louis F. Benson, *The English Hymn: Its Development and Use in Worship* (1915; Richmond, Virginia: John Knox Press, 1962), p. 491.

59. Louis F. Benson, *The Harmony of the Christian Church* (1927; Richmond, Virginia: John Knox Press, 1956), pp. 267–268.

60. Ibid., p. 268.

61. William J. Reynolds, *A Survey of Christian Hymnody* (New York: Holt, Rinehart and Winston, Inc., 1963), pp. 113–116.

62. Ibid., p. 115.

63. Harry Lee Eskew, "Shape-Note Hymnody In The Shenandoah Valley, 1816–1860" (unpublished Doctoral dissertation, Tulane University, 1966).

64. Jo Lee Fleming, "James D. Vaughan, Music Publisher, Lawrenceburg, Tennessee. 1912–1964" (unpublished Doctoral dissertation, Union Theological Seminary, 1972).

65. Joel F. Reed, "Anthony J. Showalter (1858–1924): Southern Educator, Publisher, Composer" (unpublished Doctoral dissertation, New Orleans Baptist Theological Seminary, 1975).

66. Shirley Beary, "The Stamps-Baxter Music and Printing Company: A Continuing American Tradition, 1926–1976" (Doctoral dissertation-in-progress, Southwestern Baptist Theological Seminary).

67. Linnell Gentry, ed., *A History and Encyclopedia of Country, Western, and Gospel Music* (Nashville: McQuiddy Press, 1961).

68. Linnell Gentry, ed., *A History and Encyclopedia of Country, Western, and Gospel Music* (2nd ed., completely revised; Nashville: Clairmont Corp., 1969).

69. Kree Jack Racine, *Above All: The Life Story of the Blackwood Brothers Quartet* (Memphis: Jarodoce Publications, 1967).

70. James Blackwood with Dan Martin, *The James Blackwood Story* (Monroeville, Pennsylvania: Whitaker House, 1975).

71. Paula Becker, *Let the Song Go On; Fifty Years of Gospel Singing with the Speer Family* (Nashville: Impact Books, 1971).

72. Jesse Burt and Duane Allen, *The History of Gospel Music* (Nashville: K & S Press Inc., 1971).

73. Jackson, *White Spirituals,* op. cit., p. 82.

74. *Musical Million* [Dayton, Virginia, 1870–1914].

75. *Vaughan's Family Visitor* [Cleveland, Tennessee].

76. *Gospel Music News* [Dallas, Texas, 1927–1975].

77. *Gospel Singing Journal* [Powell, Missouri].

78. *The Singing News* [Pensacola, Florida].

79. *Concert Life* [Mechanicsburg, Pennsylvania].

2

Historical Backgrounds

Biblical Basis for Religious Music

Music for religious purposes has been a significant part of the Judeo-Christian religious life since its beginning. As early as the fourth chapter of Genesis it is recorded that Jubal "was the father of all such as handle the harp and organ."[1] It is interesting to note that King David, the writer of many of the Psalms, did not alter his unabashed love of music when he achieved political power. One of the first committees he assigned upon ascending his throne was for the creation of music. The Levites were appointed ". . . to be the singers with instruments of musick, psalteries and harps and cymbals, sounding, by lifting up the voice with joy."[2]

In the King James Version of the Bible angels do not sing. For example, the often-set-to-music chorus of angels at Jesus' birth is recorded: "And suddenly there was with the angel a multitude of the heavenly host praising God, and *saying,* Glory to God in the highest, and on earth peace, good will toward men."[3] Other versions of the Bible, such as *The New English Bible,* translate the italicized verb as "singing."[4] Since the word "gospel" means the "good news"[5] about Jesus Christ, this could conceivably be considered the first instance of "gospel music." This Annunciation to the Shepherds anticipates many of the later gospel songs by being presented in the form of a solo and chorus.

Music apparently was an integral part of Jesus's religious life although little information is available. In the only recorded instance of His involvement with music, Jesus and His disciples sang a hymn immediately after the Last Supper and before going to the Mount of Olives for His betrayal.[6] This hymn, in all proba-

18

bility, was part of the Hallel (Psalms 113–118), which was sung at festivals such as Passover, Tabernacles, and Hanukkah.[7]

The early Christian missionary, Paul, was an ardent promoter of vocal music. Music was such a fundamental part of his ministry that he and Silas, his partner, were able to sing praises even while imprisoned in a Philippian jail.[8] Paul's advice to the Ephesians to speak to themselves "in psalms and hymns and spiritual songs, singing and making melody in your heart to the Lord,"[9] indicates his concern that music, especially singing, be a part of the worship experience in the church. The above passage is often quoted by those who need to cite a Scriptural foundation for the inclusion of music in the church.[10]

Religious Music in America

Music has also been important in religious life in America from its beginning. Ritter, whom Chase calls the first historian of music in America,[11] was inaccurate[12] regarding secular music when he stated that "the Puritans, who landed in 1620 at Plymouth Rock, brought with them their psalm-tunes and their hatred of secular music."[13] He was more correct when he wrote:

> From the crude form of a barbarously sung simple psalmody, there rose a musical culture in the United States which now excites the admiration of the art-lover, and . . . justifies the expectation and hope . . . of an American school of music.[14]

Virtually every historian of music in America has written on the subject of these New England psalm singers, and it would be redundant for this writer to reiterate what they have stated so well. Much less is known about the music of those who settled in Jamestown, Virginia, in 1607. Possibly the best reason for this lack of information is given by Howard and Bellows, when they say, ". . . music was obviously so much a part of daily life, no one took the trouble to mention it."[15] It is undeniable, however, that the music of the Southern colonies did not exert as great an influence on American religious music as did that of the New England colonies. Covey states it this way:

Church-musical practice for early America as a whole was set by New England, which first resorted to lining out and first undertook to overthrow it; which led in psalm- and hymn-book publishing and in the establishment of singing schools; and which inaugurated both fugal tunes and standard hymns—even the first folk-hymns—and produced the first sacred-musical composers of English-speaking America. Not only was New England first; it also generated the most songbooks, the most singing schools, the most hymns and hymn-writers, and the most discussion of every church-musical matter.[16]

Proof of the importance of religious music to the early settlers is that the *Bay Psalm Book*[17] is given credit for being the first book published in the English-speaking colonies of North America.[18] The ninth edition of the *Bay Psalm Book,* published in 1698, is considered to be the first book containing music notation published in the English-speaking colonies.[19] This ninth edition of the *Bay Psalm Book* will be mentioned in more detail later in this chapter.

Religious music may well be America's native folk song. Whereas Ritter, in 1890, once asked how it was possible to account for the "utter absence" of American folk song,[20] Lowens suggests that our national folk song is that tradition which stems from the psalmody of the early American settlers; that which "encompasses that portion of the Anglo-Celtic heritage of folk music that took root here, and adds to it something more."[21] Cecil Sharp, in his "Introduction to the First Edition, 1917," of the monumental *English Folk Songs From The Southern Appalachians,*[22] gives unintentional support to this concept. When the rural singers were asked to sing folk songs, their first response was to sing religious music. Sharp says:

> Very often they misunderstood our requirements and would give us hymns instead of the secular songs and ballads which we wanted; but that was before we had learned to ask for "love-songs," which is their name for these ditties.[23]

But what is gospel music? What makes gospel music unique or different from other forms of religious music? Where did the term gospel music originate? Who was the first to use the terminology in the way it is used today? Is it still in use today, or was it a historical curiosity that vanished or attenuated with the passing of time? What does the music sound like? Are there different forms of gospel music which sound differently although their various advocates use the term to indicate their particular form to the exclusion of the others? Are there organizations for the promotion and advancement of gospel music? These questions and others will be answered by the study which is to follow.

First Use of the Term Gospel [Music]

Ira David Sankey, the song leader for the internationally known evangelist, Dwight Lyman Moody, is generally given the credit for originating the term "gospel music"[24] with his co-publication[25] in 1875 of *Gospel Hymns and Sacred Songs*.[26] Sankey was not the first to use the term, however. Another member of the Moody and Sankey organization, Philip Paul Bliss, in 1874, used a similar phrase in the title of his collection, *Gospel Songs*.[27] Still another popular compiler, Philip Phillips, had published a collection, also in 1874, entitled *The Gospel Singer*.[28]

Two recent authoritative commentaries on religious music make reference to first usage of the phraseology "gospel" in titles of song collections. Reynolds' *Companion to Baptist Hymnal*[29] states that Edward Mote made "first use of the term, 'gospel hymn'" in his *Hymns of Praise, A New Selection of Gospel Hymns*, published in London, 1836.[30] Davidson's *Dictionary of Protestant Church Music*[31] cites a collection of songs in 1821 with the title *Gospel Melodies*.[32] The writer, however, has been able to find three additional published collections with the title *Gospel Hymns*.[33] Each of these was published well before 1875. The earliest of these was published in 1811, and is undoubtedly a reprint of an earlier edition.

Lorenz, emphasizing his point that the date of the first use of the term in a title does not necessarily prove innovation, cites Homes' *Gospel Musick* of 1644.[34] He writes:

Dr. Breed's statement in his book on "Hymns and Hymn tunes"[35]

21

that the Gospel song was born in Newcastle, England, in 1873, is distinctly amusing. He might almost as truthfully say that it was born in 1644, because a book was issued in that year entitled "Gospel Music."[36]

Sankey, in his autobiography, states that "the first gospel-song I had ever composed"[37] was written in Edinburg, Scotland, in November 1873. This was the song, "Yet There Is Room," with words by Horatius Bonar.[38]

Sankey collaborated with P.P. Bliss to publish the first two versions of *Gospel Hymns [And Sacred Songs]*.[39] After Bliss' death, Sankey collaborated with James McGranahan and George Coles Stebbins to publish four more versions. In 1894 all of the versions were combined into *Gospel Hymns Nos. 1 to 6 Complete (Without Duplicates) for Use in Gospel Meetings and Other Religious Services,* which, as Hitchcock says, "not only symbolizes the gospel-hymn movement of the later nineteenth century, but virtually embodies it between two covers.[40] A more detailed discussion of Sankey and the *Gospel Hymns* series is presented in Chapter 3.

But gospel music was not the product of one man. The songs, as a distinct style of religious music, did not appear overnight. Lorenz is correct when he states that "the songs that won the earnest heart of England in 1873, with but few exceptions, had been written years before by Bradbury, Lowry, Doane, Root, Bliss and others."[41] He further states:

> It is difficult to define the exact period when the "spiritual" became a Gospel song but the transition occurred between 1850 and 1865. Dadmun, Horace Waters, Asa Hull, Hartsough, Philip Phillips, O'Kane—all helped in the change.[42]

By "spiritual" Lorenz apparently refers to the white, generally rural, folk-like hymnody which evolved from the camp meeting. This will be discussed later in this chapter. More discussion of the immediate precursors of gospel hymnody will be postponed until the beginning of Chapter 3.

It is highly probably that the confluence of two strong factors in the music of rural church life in America, both of which occurred in approximately the early 1800s, can be shown to have produced the climate and conditions necessary for the growth and development of the gospel songs. These two factors were the religious camp meeting and the introduction of shaped notes into music teaching.

Camp-Meeting Songs

Early Camp Meetings

As with gospel music itself, it is difficult to be sure exactly when the first camp meeting was held. Several revivalist preachers claim to have been first; but according to Bruce, "it is likely that the first camp meeting, lasting several days and complete with camping out, was held in Kentucky in July, 1800."[43] Although "camp meeting" is almost synonymous with Methodism,[44] the Presbyterian minister, James McGready, is credited with being the leader of this first camp meeting, a revival of the Gasper River congregation in Logan County, Kentucky.[45]

Revivals had been held in America before 1800. The "Great Awakening" is the term given to an earlier revival, in the middle 1700s, led by Jonathan Edwards and aided by the English preacher, George Whitefield. The music of that revival was characterized by the fervent singing of the hymns of Isaac Watts and those of the Wesleys, John and Charles.[46] Some aspects of gospel music, especially the texts of some of the hymns and even some of the tunes, may be traced to this revival. The term "Dr. Watts Hymns," for example, has become almost a generic term for many hymn favorites, not necessarily all by Watts, of Afro-American gospel singers.[47] The hymns of Watts and the Wesleys are discussed in greater detail in Chapter 3.

But the Kentucky camp meeting revival that began in 1800 and swept in five years to include Tennessee, Virginia, North and South Carolina, Georgia, Ohio territory, Western Pennsylvania, and Maryland,[48] was different. According to Weisberger:

Holy enthusiasm among the squirrel hunters of Kentucky, western Virginia, the Carolinas and Tennessee was something special. They had concepts of pious experience that went with braining bears and battling Indians. Theology was presented to them by men whose faith was strong but who "murdered the king's English about every lick." They received it with tears and shouts and such wild dances as David performed before the Ark of the Lord.[49]

The camp meetings took place in outdoor settings. As suggested in a later *Camp Meeting Manual,*[50] great care needed to be taken in selecting a site. Because of hecklers and drunken outsiders it needed to be near a religiously sympathetic community and have adequate water and sufficient open pasture land to accommodate the large crowds. Enough large trees to form an outdoor canopy was also considered an asset.[51]

Crowds at camp meetings often numbered in the thousands. The largest, and most thoroughly documented, camp meeting was at Cane Ridge, Bourbon County, Kentucky in 1801. Various accounts give the attendance as being between twelve thousand and twenty-five thousand, "entirely possible for this region of Kentucky," according to Boles.[52] Others suggest a number somewhere between the extremes as being more realistic.[53]

This Cane Ridge meeting was atypical in its size and in its chaotic character. Johnson suggests that it should not be taken as the norm for a camp meeting although many lurid descriptions of the services were documented by participants and spectators.[54]

Accounts of the kinds of activities that took place at some of these meetings, especially the Cane Ridge meeting, are very interesting. Under the hysteria of the preaching and exhortation, persons would become afflicted with various "exercises," such as the "falling exercise," or the "jerk," or the "shout," or the "singing ecstasy."[55] Elder Barton Stone described the "singing exercise," which may have been similar to the "singing ecstasy," by writing:

This is more unaccountable than any thing I ever saw. The subject in a very happy state of mind would sing most melodiously, not from the mouth or nose, but entirely in the breast, the sounds issuing

24

thence. Such music silenced every thing and attracted the attention of all. It was most heavenly. None could ever be tired of hearing it.[56]

Due to the size of the crowds it was often impossible for one preacher to address everyone at once. The result was described as chaotic. According to Sweet, sometimes there would be several sermons taking place simultaneously, "a dozen different hymns or songs would be sung at once," or many people would be praying in loud voices all at the same time.[57]

Music of the Camp Meeting

Although the camp meetings were begun by the Presbyterians, they were eventually taken over enthusiastically by the Methodists.[58] All three of the strongest denominations in the South at that time, Baptist, Methodist, and Presbyterian, participated equally in the meetings. Since these denominations had not yet a clearly established denominational hymnody, there was no fixed body of song material that everyone knew. Due to the fact that the majority of the congregation was illiterate, even the few published works, available in words only, were of limited value.[59] It is only a logical conclusion that many favorite hymns were altered by faulty memory and that many new songs were created to satisfy the need for music which everyone could sing. George Pullen Jackson, writing in *Grove's Dictionary of Music and Musicians,* says:

> In the free-and-easy atmosphere of such meetings and along with an entire absence of song-books and of any wish to use them, song became little more than the common denominator of the crowds' memories.[60]

In this manner, fragments of one song would sometimes become wedded to a fragment from another. The verse-and-refrain pattern became almost a necessity for ensuring that the crowd would join in with full-voiced enthusiasm. Jackson, in his *Spiritual Folk-Songs of Early America,* states, "At the camp meetings it was not a question of inducing every one to sing, but of letting

25

every one sing."[61] He details the "progressive simplification" of texts which allowed the singer to sing a tune without letting the words "interfere with it." The chorus of "On Jordan's Stormy Banks" is one example:

I'm bound for the promised land,
I'm bound for the promised land;
O who will come and go with me?
I'm bound for the promised land.[62]

Jackson cites even simpler examples until:

The last word in brevity of text is where simply one short phrase or sentence [such as "Death, Ain't You Got No Shame?"], sung over and over, is made to fill out the whole tune frame as a stanza.[63]

Benson also tells how many of the camp-meeting songs originated:

Spontaneous song became a marked characteristic of the camp meetings. Rough and irregular couplets or stanzas were concocted out of Scripture phrases and every-day speech, with liberal interspersing of Hallelujahs and refrains. . . . Hymns were also composed more deliberately out of meeting and taught to the people or lined out from the pulpit.[64]

Although the above can give some idea of how and why the songs were constructed, it is still difficult to conceive of how the songs sounded. Chase says that, unfortunately, there are few written accounts of exactly how the singing sounded, although all accounts agree that it was loud.[65]

Both Chase and Sablosky cite Samuel E. Asbury's description of camp-meeting singing. Although Asbury, a relative of the Methodist circuit-riding Bishop Henry Asbury, is recalling the camp meetings of his youth, not those of the "Great Revival," he writes:

There was no instrument, not even a tuning fork. . . . Some

26

brass-lunged relative of mine pitched the tune. If he pitched it in the skies, no matter. The men singing the leading part with him were as brass-lunged as he. As for the women, they placed an octave over the men's leading part, singing around high C with perfect unconcern because they didn't realize their feat. The immediate din was tremendous; at a hundred yards it was beautiful; at a distance of half a mile it was magnificent.[66]

Negroes were allowed to participate in the camp-meeting services, although they were delegated to the rear of the area.[67] They had their own preachers and "exhorters," ones who encouraged the sinners to repent. They also participated enthusiastically in the singing. The slave curfew was generally suspended during the revivals and often the Negroes would continue singing long after the whites had closed the services.[68] Johnson quotes B.W. McDonald's description of this singing:

When a thousand negroes keeping time with foot and hand, with arms and body, poured out their souls upon the night air in a camp meeting chorus . . . the weird and solemn grandeur and grotesqueness were indescribable.[69]

Later Camp Meetings

According to Boles, the intensity of the "Great Revival" began to decline after approximately 1805.[70] Smith, however, states that when the religious fervor of the camp meeting was beginning to decline in the location where it started, it was just "hitting its stride" in the Middle Atlantic and New England states.[71] It would be a mistake to conclude that the camp-meeting tradition had vanished simply because it had ceased to be a religious novelty. It is still a very vital part of religious life in America, not confined only to the South. In the July, 1975 issue of *The Herald,* the latest issue to contain listings of camp-meetings prior to a format change, eighty-one camp meetings are scheduled to be held in twenty-four different states.[72] This should by no means be considered a complete listing of camp meetings in the United States, only those known to the edi-

27

tors of the publication. It does, however, give some indication of the permeation of the camp meeting as a place in the contemporary religious life of America. In some respects, even the large denominational encampments such as those at Falls Creek Baptist Assembly (Oklahoma), Ridgecrest (North Carolina), and Glorieta (New Mexico), of the Southern Baptist Convention; Lake Junaluska (North Carolina), and Ocean Grove (New Jersey), of the United Methodist Church; and Montreat Assembly (north Carolina), of the Presbyterian Church in the U.S., could be considered continuations of the camp-meeting concept of religious enclave.[73]

The music and singing style of the camp meeting is closely reflected in much of the gospel music of today. J.D. Sumner, one of the leaders in present-day quartet-style gospel music, states that he received his impetus to become a singer at the camp meetings of his youth. He writes:

Camp meetings looked like tent cities. Most people lived in tents that they made themselves by stretching wire from tree to tree or from pole to pole (if all the trees were taken) and pegging their canvas, or whatever they used for a tent, across the wire and to the ground on either side. They draped blankets on the inside to divide one sleeping area from another. Everybody cooked on open fires outside their tents. Sleeping was accomplished however a family preferred, or could afford. Some were fortunate enough to have cots, many of the World War I variety. I slept on the ground, quite comfortably, too, for camp meeting was an Occasion with a capital "O."

The music at camp meeting was gospel, of course, not nearly as refined as it is now and certainly in no way as commercial. . . .

I am sure it was at camp meetings that I got my first encouragement to become a singer.[74]

It is quite possible, however, that the many spontaneous hymns and folk-like melodies of the early camp meetings would have been lost forever if it had not been for the phenomenon of the singing school and the shaped note tradition. George Pullen Jackson states it thusly in his characteristic style:

. . . if the matter of recording those tunes had been left solely to

28

the camp-meeting people, that recording would probably never have been done. . . . But here is where the fasola singing-school folk came in.[75]

Singing School and Shaped Notes

Early Singing Schools

The singing school movement has a long history in American musical life. It was instituted in order to improve the quality of psalm singing in the churches because singing had deteriorated markedly in the New England colonies.[76] The date of the earliest known singing school in America has been set at 1720, in Boston,[77] although Cheek suggests that singing schools may have been held earlier but no written record was made of them.[78] In what is believed to be the earliest reference to attendance at a singing school, Britton cites the four short entries from the diary of William Byrd of Virginia, in 1710 and 1711. Britton summarizes Byrd's entries by saying:

> He mentions a sequence of events which, in epitome, characterizes the entire history of the subject, from the arrival of the singing master with his instruction books, through the quarrels which immediately developed, to the day when "we began to give in to the new way of singing Psalms."[79]

Because of its origin as a means of improving the music in the churches, hymns and religious songs were a major portion of the singing school's musical literature. In the rustic environment of the time, however, the singing school also afforded a valuable means of entertainment and social exchange.[80] Britton states that the question of whether the singing school was a sacred or a secular institution may be answered by saying that it was both.[81] In fact, besides its social role, it provided a triple function of combining education, art, and religion.[82]

Once it was initiated, the singing school soon became a ubiquitous institution with the "Yankee Singing Masters,"[83] to use

Jackson's term, venturing to the farthest reaches of the expanding nation.[84]

At first the singing school teachers earned their income from occupations other than music and taught their schools in the evenings. By the early 1800s, however, some teachers were able to earn enough to teach on a full-time basis.[85] Aside from their fees for teaching music and conducting choral groups, many of the singing masters supplemented their income by compiling and editing their own tune books, to which they contributed many of their own compositions. According to John, this became "a very lucrative concomitant side line for Singing School masters."[86]

These tune books generally contained a section on the rudiments of music, a collection of psalm and hymn tunes, and a collection of extended works suitable for advanced classes and singing societies.[87] Sometimes secular songs were included in a separate section.[88]

From the beginning, these tunebooks compilers and teachers endeavored to simplify musical notation and theory. This was done in order to help their students learn to read music at sight more quickly and thus become eager consumers of the teacher's musical materials. The first music textbook published in America,[89] John Tuft's *An Introduction to the Singing of Psalm-Tunes,*[90] for example, does not contain notes. Instead, it substitutes on the staff letters representing the four solmization syllables, *fa, sol, la,* and *mi,* which were in common usage at that time. Use of four syllables rather than the seven commonly used today will be explained further in this chapter.

For the most part, each of these simplified methods was extremely short-lived. Ritter had this to say about these typically American short cuts:

> Numberless attempts have been made since [Tufts] in this direction in America; but after a little while the amateurish inventions, failing to realize the expected business profits and economy of time, have always sunk into a justly deserved oblivion.[91]

30

Shaped Notes

One of the simplest and most unique of these methods has endured. This was the creation of differently shaped note heads to indicate the diatomic scale degrees in a "movable do"[92] solmization system. These shaped notes have been called variously "character notes," "patent notes," or derisively, "buckwheat notes."[93] They were introduced into the singing schools as a means of simplifying the thought processes necessary to the reading of music at sight. The unique advantage of this system is that it does not alter the placement of notes on the staff or change the conventional notation of rhythm. According to Reynolds, the significance of this system lies in its reinforcement of the aural signal to the brain in coordination with an unambiguous visual signal.[94] It shows at a glance the function of a note in its relation to the major or minor scale. All other aspects of standard musical notation remain intact. According to Lowens and Britton:

> Had this pedagogical tool been accepted by "the father of singing among the children," Lowell Mason, and others who shaped the patterns of American music education, we might have been more successful in developing skilled music readers and enthusiastic amateur choral singers in the public schools.[95]

The effectiveness of teaching music by the shaped note system has been dramatically demonstrated by Kyme in his experimental study with California fourth and fifth grade students.[96] Not only could the students trained on shaped notes read music more easily than their counterparts, they could also note their own compositions and harmonize accompaniments on the autoharp.[97] Most impressively, when transferred to junior high school, sixty-three percent of these students chose to elect music, a before-school course. The average enrollment from the other schools[98] was approximately twenty percent.[99]

As an implication for future research, it is suggested that the above study, which is almost seventeen years old, could well be replicated, perhaps in a comparison with the British Tonic Sol-Fa[100] system.

First Shaped Note Publications

Two obscure northerners, William Little and William Smith, are now generally accepted as being the first[101] to have published a shaped note tunebook, *The Easy Instructor, Or A New Method Of Teaching Sacred Harmony.*[102] Little, with another historically unknown personage, Edward Stammers, copyrighted a title page in Pennsylvania in 1798, but as it was not necessary at that time to produce a document in order to obtain a copyright, it is doubtful if that particular version was ever printed. At least no copy has ever been found.[103] Stammers may have died[104] sometime prior to the publication of the first edition because, for this, Little collaborated with a William Smith. Smith is another person about whom practically nothing is known.[105] According to Lowens, what is apparently "the genuine first edition"[106] of *The Easy Instructor* was published in Philadelphia sometime prior to August 22, 1801.[107]

In 1803, Andrew Law, whom Crawford calls "the most ambitious American psalmodist of the eighteenth century,"[108] published the fourth edition of his *The Art of Singing*[109] in shaped notes and without staff lines.

The shapes of Andrew Law and those of Little and Smith were identical: circle, square, right triangle, and diamond. The difference between the two systems lay in which shape was assigned to which scale degree. Law used fa:■, sol:●, la:▲, mi:◆. Little and Smith used fa:▲, sol:●, la:■, mi:◆.

According to Britton, it is still somewhat of a mystery why a lawsuit was never instituted. In those days it was almost second nature to go to court,[110] and Andrew Law waged almost continuous legal battles in the protection of his real and imagined rights.[111] Crawford presents evidence that Law did contemplate suing Little, the sole copyright owner at that time, but abandoned the idea after advice from his friend, Nathan Jones.[112]

Britton also states that it is curious, in light of the fact that Little and Smith were apparently the first to obtain a copyright for the use of the shaped notes, that Law, who was a "highly educated and devoutly religious man"[113] never admitted to plagiarism. Law, however, did repeatedly stress that the "new plan" of his publication was the absence of the staff lines and not the shape of the notes.[114]

Regardless of whatever controversy there may have been at the time, it is the shaped notes of Little and Smith, and not those of Law,[115] which still survive in the few four-shape tunebooks still being published today.[116]

An example of a major scale in the Little and Smith four-shape notation is shown in Figure 1 below. Note that the seventh scale degree, *mi,* represented by a diamond shape, is the only shaped note that does not designate more than one scale degree. Apparently the ambiguity of the other notes was not a cause for concern among the adherents of the fasola system of solmization.

fa   sol   la   fa   sol   la   mi   fa

Figure 1. Major scale in four-shape notation.[117]

Four-syllable Solmization (Fasola)

The reason for the use of only four shapes, representing the solfeggio syllables *fa, sol, la,* and *mi,* has its own history. It is perhaps most clearly explained in the definition for "Solmization" in *Grove's Dictionary of Music and Musicians.* Here it is stated that the concept of the tetrachord, or four-note scale, dates back to the ancient Greeks, where syllables were assigned to each scale degree and rules were made for their function.[118]

In the eleventh century, Guido d'Arezzo substituted hexachords for the tetrachords of the Greek system. He assigned his own syllables, based upon the words to successive lines of a hymn to Saint John the Baptist. These syllables were *ut, re, mi,*

33

fa, sol, and *la.*[119] Rockstro states that "the definite use of a seventh syllable cannot be traced back to an earlier date than the year 1599. . . ."[120] But a seventh syllable is not applicable to the present narrative. For some undefined reason, in England the use of the syllables *ut* and *re* died out completely before the middle of the seventeenth century. Recurring changes of only four syllables, *mi, fa, sol,* and *la,* were all that were used for the solmization of melodies.[121]

To underscore that the "Fasola" method of reading music was the accepted practice in colonial America, it should be pointed out that the ninth edition of the *Bay Psalm Book,* which has already been stated as the first book containing music to be published in the English-speaking colonies,[122] contains the letters *f, s, l,* and *m,* beneath the notes to assist in the identification of the scale degrees.[123]

Spread of Shaped Note Usage

Although *The Easy Instructor* had been copyrighted in 1798, it was not until after 1805 that it achieved widespread usage. Apparently William Little, stated previously as the sole copyright owner at this time, sold or assigned his copyright to an Albany, New York trio of printers, Charles R. and George Webster, and Daniel Steele.[124] According to Lowens and Britton:

> In Albany *The Easy Instructor* really hit its stride. . . . A veritable flood of editions, the first in 1805 and the last in 1831, poured from the presses. Tens of thousands of copies were sold, and the tune book became celebrated throughout the country, extending its influence far beyond its Albany base.[125]

It may be appropriate at this point to remind the reader that the camp-meeting movement, discussed previously, was also "hitting its stride,"[126] throughout America in 1805.

When, in 1816, the copyright to *The Easy Instructor* was due to expire, the owners of the copyright, represented by George Webster, applied for and received a patent for the casting and use of the shaped note types.[127] The 1817 edition of *The Easy In-*

structor contains this information: "The Music Types used in printing this Book are secured to the Proprietors by Patent Right,"[128] and it is undoubtedly from this and similar notices that the term "patent notes" was derived.[129]

American Music Bias of Shaped Note Tunebooks

From the time William Little and Edward Stammers submitted the title page of *The Easy Instructor*. For copyright in 1798, until the time it first appeared in print in 1801, something happened. According to Lowens and Britton, the original tune book was to have included new songs from Europe as well as those by American composers. This, apparently, was due to the influence of Stammers. When the Little and Smith 1801 edition emerged, it contained only songs by American composers, except for five European songs that had become established American favorites.[130] Lowens and Britton conclude: "The European musical bias of Stammers had been transformed into the thoroughly American one of Smith, with Little serving as a bridge between the two musicians."[131] This "thoroughly American" bias of the first shaped note tunebook has remained a marked characteristic of almost all subsequent shaped note publications. This helps to account both for the success of these publications among the "plain folk," and their obscurity in the eyes of those who have based their musical heritage upon more sophisticated European traditions.

Migration of Shaped Notes to the South and West

In the earlier years of the singing school movement, the schools were attended by all, in the North as well as the South, in the cities as well as in the rural areas.[132] In the beginning of the nineteenth century, this pluralism began to change. The cities along the eastern coast, and particularly in the northeast, were growing rapidly; the hallmark of the times was "science" and "progress."[133] Champions of the "better music" used words like "scientific" and "improvement" in describing their works, and they were strongly partisan to European influences.[134]

The music written in shaped notes was decried by these "Better Music Boys,"[135] as Jackson calls them, and the singing masters were pushed further back from the centers of musical culture. They took their tunebooks and their instruction books west of the Appalachians and to the south.[136] There they were readily accepted and there the tradition has remained. Jackson gives the often quoted statement of the reasons for the acceptance and continuance of the singing school and the rural music in the South:

> The factors . . . which alienated the northern masses from their own naive form of song fostering were not active in the rural South. Economic prosperity, European musical influences, urban-continental-Nordic immigration, the growth of cities—from all of these the upland southerner was, naturally, exempt. . . . So when the singing schools came into the South, they stuck.[137]

Seven-Syllable Solmization (Dorayme)

Nevertheless, some of the European musical ideas did come into the South, and the one which has had the most direct bearing on the published gospel music of the south today is the seven-syllable system of solfeggio.

The first American reference[138] to this seven-syllable system was in 1763, when Francis Hopkinson, in his *A Collection of Psalm Tunes,*[139] urged the adoption of the European seven syllables using round notes.[140] The acceptance of this system by the advocates of better music, and the increasing immigration of those who had been trained in this system in Europe, meant that by the early 1800s this newer system had begun to rival the old English fasola system. Some publishers began to devise means of making the shaped note system of notation compatible with a seven-syllable concept of solmization.

Kaufman, in his study of the history of seven-shaped notation, cites several examples of what he calls "transitional systems" devised by Andrew Law, Chapin and Dickerson, Jeu de

Berneval, and David Sower, Jr.[141] None of these achieved any degree of popularity.

It was not until 1846 that Jesse B. Aikin arrived at the system which is still in use. Adding to the four shapes of Little and Smith, he devised three more shapes for *do, re,* and *ti,* the latter called *si* at that time. The complete system is shown in Figure 2.

do   re   mi   fa   sol   la   ti   do

Figure 2. Major scale in seven-shape notation.[142]

Aikin's system first appeared in *The Christian Minstrel*[143] and this compilation went through 171 editions! Many other notational systems were tried by various authors, each of whom retained the basic "fasola" shapes, and added their own shapes for the other three syllables. Jackson shows seven different systems,[144] exclusive of the systems using numbers and all of *their* various combinations. Edwards and Marrocco show Jackson's seven systems, plus five others, for a total of twelve.[145] Gradually, however, the superiority of the Aikin shapes was realized and soon after 1876 this was the only system in use.[146]

This universal turning to Aikin's system did not come about by tacit mutual acceptance as some accounts[147] would lead one to believe. Aikin apparently undertook to ensure its happening. Jackson relates the story of how the Ruebush-Kieffer Company, a highly influential southern organization, discussed in greater detail in Chapter 4, came to accept Aikin's shapes:

"But one day in the early fall of 1877,"[148] Daniel F. Blake, who was then a typesetter in the Funk plant, told me in a letter, "our mail carrier deposited at the office (in Singer's Glen) a personage whose age must have been close to seventy years; gray hair, almost white, and a Van Dyke beard covered his head and face. He was dressed in a Prince Albert coat and vest, gray trousers, shoes with spats and a high-crowned derby hat; he carried a light over-coat on his arm, a gold-headed cane in one hand and a light travel-ing grip in the other. That person was JESSE B. AIKIN.

"There had been some correspondence previously, about stop-ping the printing of books in the Funk shapes, but it had not been satisfactory to either of the interested parties. Now Prof. Aikin had come for a 'show down.' Kieffer told me that it was a hot, con-tinuous word battle, but he knew from the beginning Funk's shapes would lose. After practically an all-day session had been held, Prof. Aikin got to his feet and said: 'Well, I will go home and have my lawyer get a restraining order forbidding any one using the Funk shapes,' and in a hasty, hasty way, started to leave the room.

"They stopped him and in the next hour an agreement was reached, that as fast as the printed books on hand were sold, they would discontinue printing certain books, no longer selling, and would have those old ones that were still selling, using Aikin's shapes, and having the plates made . . . by Armstrong [Aikin's electrotyper] in Philadelphia."[149]

Joseph Funk, Ruebush, and Kieffer may have been intimi-dated into converting to Aikin's shapes but they were alert to see the advantage of having a unified system of notation and became verbal champions of it in their publication, *The Musical Million*. These writings in *The Musical Million* became, as Jackson says, "the greatest single factor in the unification of notation."[150]

Seven-shape Notation Supplanting Four-shape Notation

By this time, the seven-shape system of musical notation had gradually supplanted the traditional four-shape system. Af-ter the Civil War no new books were published in the four-shape notation.[151] The tradition of singing from the four-shape books did not die, however. It continues to thrive in the republications and revisions of such books as *The Sacred Harp*[152] and *Southern Harmony*.[153]

The change from four to seven shapes was not accomplished

without some inner turmoil on the part of some of those who had grown up in the earlier tradition. The prime example of this is the frequently quoted statement of William Walker. Walker's *Southern Harmony,* published in four shapes, was so popular that he used the initials, A.S.H. (Author, *Southern Harmony*) after his name.[154] He explains in "Seven-Syllable Character-Note Singing. [sic] The quickest and most desirable method known," which follows the "Preface" of his *The Christian Harmony,*[155] why he finally decided to change over to the seven shapes. The statement, originally made in jest, was so logical that it has persisted, even today, as the most valid reason for "dorayme" solmization:

> To those who are in favor of four-note singing, and think it is the best way, we would remark that we were for many years opposed to any other,—delivered many lectures on the subject, and were not convinced of our error till we taught our first *normal school.* There we saw clearly that, as we had *seven distinct sounds* in the scale, we needed and must have, to be consistent *seven* names; we tried many names, but finally agreed on the Italian as the most euphonious. During the discussion, the question was asked, Would any parents having seven children ever think of calling them by only four names? The question caused a good deal of merriment; there the discussion ceased, all were convinced, all prejudice against seven-note singing was gone; and our opinion from experience is, that a school will learn nearly twice as many more tunes in the same time in the latter way than in the former.[156]

There is more than a difference in typography between the singers of the four-shaped-note music and proponents of the seven-shaped notation, however. The difference goes beyond the mere difference in number of shapes. The four-shape singers were those who chose to "ask for the old paths and walk therein," as Jackson puts it.[157] They carry their conservatism over into their choice of music. They do not consider themselves singers of gospel music. For this reason, the present study will deal only superficially with the remnant of four-shape singing extant today. This remnant has been more thoroughly covered by writers such as Cheek,[158] Ellington,[159] and Horn.[160]

Apparently, perhaps because it was an innovation at the

time, the seven-shape system attracted the less conservative singers, composers, and compilers. They did not feel bound to the more traditional songs and were a great deal more receptive to the influences of secular music, instrumental accompaniment, and major tonality, which are some of the characteristics of early gospel hymnody.[161] An example of this can be found in *The Olive Leaf*,[162] which is the last of the oblong tunebooks published in the South.[163] It was published in seven-shape notation and already, according to Jackson, its songs show many of the characteristics of the gospel songs.[164]

Summary

Thus far it can be seen that the groundwork for the emergence of gospel music lay in the consistent demand for a folk hymnody suitable for the religious needs of the common man. This demand was intensified in the camp meeting and revival service tradition that swept the country during the 1800s and which persists today. The songs of those camp meetings and revivals were notated and published by rural singing school masters who had learned their skills by way of the simplified method of shaped note notation. Because of this unique notation a rustic musician did not need to have extensive preparation before he was able to notate and harmonize his own creations or to record those which were the spontaneous outpourings of a religiously inspired congregation.

But it should also be mentioned that natural regional differences caused by limitations in modes of transportation were exacerbated by the psychological wounds caused by the Civil War. These differences were not helped by the scorn of shaped note writing by those in the urban centers of the North and East. These regional differences, although ameliorated somewhat, persist today.

After the midpoint of the nineteenth century, gospel music, as a form of popular music set to religious texts, was emerging under a variety of names. Some of these were "Spiritual Songs," "Sunday School Songs," "Y.M.C.A. Songs," and "Soldier Songs."

What remained was for this music to come to some kind of focus. This focus was provided by the revivalism and the publications of the evangelistic team, Dwight L. Moody and Ira David Sankey.

Notes

1. Genesis 4:21
2. Chronicles 15:16.
3. Luke 2:13–14; emphasis added.
4. *The New English Bible, With The Apocrypha* (Cambridge: Oxford University Press, 1970), "The Gospel," p. 71.
5. *Webster's New Twentieth Century Dictionary of the English Language* (unabridged 2nd ed. USA [sic]: Collins World, 1975), p. 788.
6. Matthew 26:30; Mark 14:26.
7. "Hallel," *The New Westminister Dictionary of the Bible* (Philadelphia: The Westminster Press, 1970), p. 359.
8. Acts 16:25.
9. Ephesians 5:19; Colossians 3:16.
10. An expansion of the above directive is exemplified by the appointment, in at least one denomination, of "music missionaries." In 1970 the Southern Baptist Convention is reported to have had forty-six music missionaries serving in eighteen mission stations; cf. Marion Fred Ellerbe, "The Music Missionary of the Southern Baptist Convention: His Preparation and His Work" (unpublished Doctoral dissertation, The Catholic University of America, 1970), pp. iv, 11.
11. Gilbert, Chase, *America's Music from the Pilgrims to the Present* (2nd ed.; New York: McGraw-Hill Book Company, 1966), p. xvi.
12. Percy Alfred Scholes, *The Puritans and Music in England and New England* (New York: Russell & Russell, 1962), presents impressive evidence that the Pilgrims were quite musical and enjoyed both sacred and secular music.
13. Frédéric Louis Ritter, *Music in America* (1890; rpt. New York: Johnson Reprint Corporation, 1970), p. 6.
14. Ibid., pp. 3, 4.
15. John Tasker Howard and George Kent Bellows, *A Short History of Music in America* (1957; New York: Thomas Y. Crowell Company, 1967), p. 9.
16. Cyclone Covey, "Of Music and of America Singing," Chapter 9 in *Seeds of Liberty: The Genesis of the American Mind,* by Max Savelle (1948; Seattle: University of Washington Press, 1965), p. 548.
17. Richard Mather, Thomas Welde, and John Eliot, *The Whole Booke of Psalmes Faithfully Translated Into English Metre* (Cambridge, Massachusetts: The press of Stephen Day[e], 1640), popularly called the *Bay Psalm Book.*
18. Howard and Bellows, op. cit., p. 15.
19. Ibid., p. 20.
20. Ritter, op. cit., p. 424.

21. Irving Lowens, *Music and Musicians in Early America* (New York: W.W. Norton and Company, Inc., 1964), p. 286.
22. Cecil Sharp and Maud Karpeles, *English Folk Songs from the Southern Appalachians* (1917; London: Oxford University Press Humphrey Milford, 1932). "Introduction" by Sharp alone.
23. Ibid., p. xxvi.
24. William Loyd Hooper, *Church Music in Transition* (Nashville: Broadman Press, 1963), p. 99.
25. An explanation for Sankey rather than Bliss receiving such credit is given in Chapter 3.
26. P.P. Bliss and Ira D. Sankey, *Gospel Hymns And Sacred Songs By P.P. Bliss And Ira D. Sankey, As Used By Them in Gospel Meetings* (New York: Biglow & Main; Cincinnati: John Church & Co., 1875).
27. Philip P. Bliss, *Gospel Songs; A Choice Collection of Hymns And Tunes, New And Old, For Gospel Meetings, Prayer Meetings, Sunday Schools, Etc.* [sic] (Cincinnati: John Church & Co., 1874).
28. Philip Phillips, *The Gospel Singer, For Sabbath Schools, Etc.* [sic] (Philadelphia: Published by Lee and Walker, 1874).
29. William Jensen Reynolds, *Companion To Baptist Hymnal* (Nashville: Broadman Press, 1976), p. 386.
30. Cited in ibid.
31. James Robert Davidson, "Gospel Song," *A Dictionary of Protestant Church Music* (Metuchen, New Jersey: Scarecrow Press, 1975), p. 139.
32. Ibid., apparently Davidson refers to [Burton?], *Gospel Melodies; By The Author Of Several Fugitive* [sic] *Pieces* (Petersburg, Virginia: Printed and Published by Stith E. Burton, Intelligencer Press, 1821). In this work "Melody" is used synonymously for "poem"; the book contains poems without music.
33. These collections are: James H. Brooks, *Gospel Hymns* (St. Louis: Published by the Old School Presbyterian, 1871); also John Kent, *Gospel Hymns.* [sic] *An Original Collection.* [sic] *To Which Is Added, An Appendix, Containing A Number of Select Hymns* (1803?; Boston: Reprinted [sic] and Published by Lincoln & Edmands, 1811); also Thomas Salwey, *Gospel Hymns* (London: J. Hatchard And Son, 1847). Each of these collections is published in words only.
34. Nathaniel Homes, *Gospel Musick. Or the Singing Of David's Psalms, & c. in The Publick Congregations* (London: Printed for H. Overton, 1644). This defense of the use of Psalm singing contains no music.
35. David Riddle Breed, *The History and Use of Hymns and Hymn Tunes* (New York: Fleming H. Revell Co., 1903), p. 331. Footnote not provided by Lorenz.
36. Edmund Simon Lorenz, *Practical Church Music* (New York: Fleming H. Revell Co., 1909), p. 105.
37. Ira David Sankey, *Sankey's Story of the Gospel Hymns and of Sacred Songs and Solos* (Philadelphia: The Sunday School Times Company, 1906), p. 25.
38. Ibid., pp. 22, 25; yet Sankey did not call this a "gospel song" in 1873; it was one of the songs included in his publication *Sacred Songs and Solos,* discussed in greater detail in Chapter 3.
39. Only the first version was entitled *Gospel Hymns and Sacred Songs.*

40. H. Wiley Hitchcock, "Introduction" to *Gospel Hymns Nos. 1 to 6 Complete,* by Ira D. Sankey, James McGranahan, George C. Stebbins, Philip P. Bliss (1894; rpt. of 1895 ed.; New York: Da Capo Press, 1972), n.p.
41. Lorenz, op. cit., p. 105.
42. Ibid., p. 106.
43. Dickson Davies Bruce, Jr., *And They All Sang Hallelujah: Plain-folk Camp-meeting Religion, 1800–1845* Knoxville: University of Tennessee Press, 1974), p. 43.
44. Charles Edwin Jones, *Perfectionist Persuasion: The Holiness Movement and American Methodism, 1867–1936* (Metuchen. New Jersey: the Scarecrow Press, Inc., 1974), p. 16.
45. Bruce, loc. cit.
46. Chase, op. cit., pp. 46–48; also William Jensen Reynolds, *A Survey of Christian Hymnody* (New York: Holt, Rinehart and Winston, Inc., 1963), p. 87.
47. Tony Heilbut, *The Gospel Sound: Good News And Bad Times* (New York: Simon and Schuster, 1971), pp. 20–22.
48. John B. Boles, *The Great Revival, 1787–1805* (Lexington: The University Press of Kentucky, 1972), p. 70.
49. Bernard A. Weisberger, *They Gathered At The River: The Story Of The Great Revivalists And Their Impact Upon Religion In America* (Boston: Little, Brown and Co., 1958), p. 20.
50. B.W. Gorham, *Camp Meeting Manual, A Practical Book For The Camp Ground* (Boston: H.V. Degen, 1854), p. 121, cited by Bruce, op. cit., p. 70.
51. Ibid.
52. Boles, op. cit., p. 65.
53. Charles A. Johnson, *The Frontier Camp Meeting: Religion's Harvest Time* (Dallas: Southern Methodist University Press, 1955), p. 63.
54. Ibid., pp. 62–63.
55. Frederick Morgan Davenport, *Primitive Traits In Religious Revivals: A Study In Mental And Social Evolution* (1905; rpt. New York: Negro Universities Press, 1968), pp. 76–78.
56. John Rogers, *The Biography Of Eld. Barton Warren Stone, Written By Himself: With Additions And Reflections By Elder John Rogers* (Cincinnati: Published for the Author by J.A. & U.P. James, 1847), pp. 41–42.
57. William Warren Sweet, *Revivalism in America* (Gloucester, Massachusetts: Peter Smith, 1965), p. 143.
58. Bruce op. cit., p. 52.
59. John N. Sims, "The Hymnody Of The Camp Meeting Tradition" (unpublished Doctoral dissertation, Union Theological Seminary, 1960), p. 100.
60. George Pullen Jackson, "Spirituals," *Grove's Dictionary of Music and Musicians,* ed. Eric Blom (5th ed.; New York: St. Martin's Press, Inc., 1966), VIII, p. 9.
61. George Pullen Jackson, *Spiritual Folk-Songs of Early America: Two Hundred and Fifty Tunes And Texts With An Introduction And Notes* (1937; New York: Dover Publications, Inc., 1964), p. 7.
62. Ibid., p. 8.
63. Ibid.

64. Louis Fitzgerald Benson, *The English Hymn: Its Development and Use in Worship* (London: Hodder & Stoughton, 1915), p. 292.

65. Chase, op. cit., p. 222.

66. Samuel E. Ashbury and Henry E. Meyer, "Old-Time White Camp-meeting Spirituals" (Austin: Texas Folklore Society Publications, 10:169–185, 1932), quoted by Irving Sablosky, *American Music* (Chicago: University of Chicago Press, 1969), p. 38. Both Sablosky and Chase op. cit., p. 223, cite Asbury alone as author of the above quotation.

67. Bruce op. cit., p. 75.

68. Johnson, op. cit., pp. 114–119.

69. B.W. McDonald, *The History of the Cumberland Presbyterian Church* (Nashville, 1888), p. 434, quoted by Johnson, ibid., p. 117.

70. Boles, op. cit., p. 183.

71. Timothy L. Smith, *Revivalism and Social Reform in Mid-Nineteenth-Century America* (New York: Abingdon Press, 1957), p. 9.

72. "Camps," *The Herald* (a publication of Asbury Theological Seminary), LXXXVII (July, 1975), 22–23.

73. Benson, op. cit., p. 298; Benson does not cite the examples given.

74. Bob Terrell, *J.D. Sumner: Gospel Music Is My Life* (Nashville: Impact Books, 1971), pp. 24–25.

75. George Pullen Jackson, *White Spirituals In The Southern Uplands: The Story Of The Fasola Folk, Their Songs, Singings, And "Buckwheat Notes"* (1933: New York: Dover Publications, Inc., 1965), p. 237.

76. Edward Bailey Birge, *History of Public School Music in the United States* (1928; Washington, D.C.: Music Educators National Conference, 1966), p. 4.

77. Curtis Leo Cheek, The Singing School and Shaped-Note Tradition: Residuals in Twentieth-Century American Hymnody" (unpublished Doctoral dissertation, University of Southern California, 1968), p. 99.; also Alan Clark Buechner, "Yankee Singing Schools and the Golden Age of Choral Music in New England, 1760–1800" (unpublished doctoral dissertation, Harvard University, 1960), p. 112, cited in Cheek, ibid.

78. Cheek, ibid.

79. Allen P. Britton, "The Singing School Movement in the United States." *Report Of The Eighth Congress of The International Musicological Society* (New York: Bärenreiter, 1961), p. 91.

80. Birge, op. cit., p. 22.

81. Britton, op. cit., p. 96.

82. Ibid.

83. Jackson, *White Spirituals,* op. cit., p. 15.

84. Edward Everett Dale, "The Singing School," *Dictionary of American History,* V, ed. James Truslow Adams (2nd ed. rev.; Charles Scribner's Sons, 1946), pp. 82–83.

85. Robert W. John, "The American Singing School Movement, 1720–1780," *Journal of the American Musicological Society,* VII (Summer, 1954), 165.

86. Ibid.

87. Jackson, *White Spirituals,* op. cit., p. 349.

88. Ibid.

89. John, loc. cit.

90. John Tufts, *An Introduction to the Singing of Psalm-Tunes, in a Plain &* [sic] *Easy Method. With a Collection of Tunes in Three Parts,* facsimile rpt. of 5th ed. 1726 [earliest located edition], Foreword by Irving Lowens (1721?; Philadelphia: For Musical Americana by Albert Saifer: publisher, 1954).

91. Ritter, op. cit., p. 34.

92. Apel, Willi, "Movable do(h)," *Harvard Dictionary of Music* (1944; 2nd ed.; Cambridge, Massachusetts: The Belknap Press of Harvard University Press, 1969), p. 547; this means that the names and shapes of the notes are transposable to any key.

93. George Pullen Jackson, "Character Notation," *Grove's Dictionary,* op. cit., II, p. 185.

94. William Jensen Reynolds, Chairman, Church Music Department of the Baptist Sunday School Board, Southern Baptist Convention, personal interview, Nashville, Tennessee, November 22, 1976.

95. Irving Lowens and Allen P. Britton, "*The Easy Instructor* (1798–1831): A History and Bibliography of the First Shape Note Tune Book," *Journal of Research in Music Education,* I (Spring, 1953), 32.

96. George H. Kyme, "An Experiment in Teaching Children to Read Music with Shape Notes," *Journal of Research in Music Education,* VIII (Spring, 1960), 3.

97. Ibid., p. 8.

98. No other information is given concerning these schools.

99. Kyme, loc. cit.

100. "Tonic Sol-Fa," *Grove's Dictionary,* op. cit., VIII, pp. 504–511.

101. Lowens and Britton, op. cit., p. 31.

102. William Little and William Smith, *The Easy Instructor, or a New Method of Teaching Sacred Harmony* (1798; Philadelphia: n.n., 1801), cited by Lowens, op. cit., p. 125, with a reproduction of the title page shown on p. 308.

103. Lowens and Britton, op. cit., p. 35.

104. Ibid., p. 34 footnote.

105. Ibid., p. 36.

106. Lowens, op. cit., p. 124.

107. Ibid., p. 125.

108. Richard Arthur Crawford, *Andrew Law, American Psalmodist* (Evanston, Illinois: Northwestern University Press, 1968), p. xv.

109. Andrew Law, *The Art of Singing; In Three Parts: To Wit, I. The Musical Primer, II. The Chistian* [sic] *Harmony, III. The Musical Magazine. Fourth Edition with Additions and Improvements. Printed Upon a New Plan* (4th ed., 1803; Cambridge: W. Hilliard, 1805). Part I was published in 1803; Parts II and III were not published until 1805, according to p. 102 and the title page of Part Third (unpaginated). Copy viewed courtesy of Raymond Hamrick, Macon, Georgia. Lowens, op. cit., p. 80, states that Part II was published in 1804, Part III, in 1805.

110. Britton, op. cit., p. 97.

111. Lowens, op. cit., p. 61.

112. Crawford, op. cit., p. 173.

113. Britton, op. cit., p. 97.

114. Lowens, op. cit., p. 85.

115. Because of the prominence of Law and the relative obscurity of Little and Smith, it is understandable that early historians, such as Birge, op. cit., p. 25; and Frank J. Metcalf, *American Writers and Compilers of Sacred Music* (New York: The Abingdon Press, 1925), p. 68; would credit Law with the invention of shaped note notation. In view of recent research, however, similar credits by Davidson, op. cit., pp. 120, 137, and 138; should be considered serious errors and corrected at the first opportunity.
116. The Little and Smith shapes also form the basis for the Aiken seven-shape notation, which is another story in itself; see pp. 36 ff., below.
117. This scale is shown in the key of Eb in order to emphasize that this is a "movable do" system. Also, NB the up-stem and down-stem shapes for *fa*. This is seldom mentioned in related literature, and is shown incorrectly in Leonard Ellinwood, *The History of American Church Music* (1953; Rev. ed.; New York: Da Capo Press, 1970), p. 104.
118. W.S. Rockstro, "Solmization," *Grove's Dictionary,* op. cit., VII, p. 879.
119. Ibid.
120. Ibid., p. 881.
121. Ibid.; see also Percy A. Scholes, *The Oxford Companion To Music* (1938; 10th ed.; London: Oxford University Press, 1970), pp. 563–564, who names this method of solmization "Lancashire Sol-fa" or "Old English Sol-fa."
122. See p. 20 above.
123. Richard G. Appel, *The Music of the Bay Psalm Book: 9th Ed (1698)* (Brooklyn: Institute for Studies in American Music, 1975); contains facsimiles of the original tunes with transcriptions in modern notation.
124. Lowens and Britton, op. cit., p. 38.
125. Ibid.
126. Smith, op. cit, p. 9; cited on p. 27 above.
127. Lowens and Britton, op. cit., p. 43.
128. Ibid.
129. Ibid.
130. Lowens and Britton, ibid., p. 37.
131. Ibid.
132. Cheek, op. cit., p. 128.
133. Chase, op. cit., p. 153.
134. Ibid., pp. 154–155.
135. Jackson, *White Spirituals,* op. cit., pp. 16–17.
136. Hugh Wiley Hitchcock, *Music in the United States: A Historical Introduction* (2nd ed.; Englewood Cliffs, New Jersey: Prentice-Hall, Inc., 1974), p. 97.
137. Jackson, *White Spirituals,* op. cit., p. 22.
138. Lee Jack Kaufman, "A Historical Study Of Seven Character Shaped Note Music Notation," (unpublished Doctoral dissertation, University of Virginia, 1970), p. 17.
139. Francis Hopkinson, *A Collection of Psalm Tunes* (Philadelphia: 1763), cited by ibid., p. 19; also cf. Arthur C. Edwards and W. Thomas Marrocco, *Music in the United States* (Dubuque, Iowa: Wm. C. Brown Company Publishers, 1968), pp. 32, 37, who say in 1753. Neither source gives full citation.

140. Kaufman, op. cit., pp. 17, 19.

141. Ibid., pp. 21–37.

142. This scale is shown in the key of D in order to emphasize that this is a "movable do" system. The shapes and names would be the same for any key.

143. Jesse B. Aikin, *The Christian Minstrel: A New System of Music Notation* [etc.] (1846; 104th ed.; Philadelphia: T. K. Collins, Jr., 1858).

144. Jackson, *White Spirituals,* op. cit., p. 337.

145. Edwards and Marrocco, op. cit., p. 32.

146. George Pullen Jackson, in "Buckwheat Notes," *The Musical Quarterly,* XIX (October, 1933), 398, states, "soon after 1873;" however, later research indicates that it was not until after the Ruebush-Kieffer Company had accepted Aikin's shapes in 1876 [cf. p. 38 below] that unification of notation was achieved.

147. O.F. Morton, "The Ruebush-Kieffer Company," *The Musical Million,* XLII (August 1911), 85.

148. This date is incorrect by more than a year; the correct date of the Aikin visit was in May of 1876 according to Kaufman, op. cit., pp. 97–99. This is confirmed by Grace I. Showalter, *The Music Books of Ruebush & Kieffer 1866–1942; A Bibliography* (Richmond: Virginia State Library, 1975), p. ix.

149. Jackson, *White Spirituals,* op. cit., pp. 352–353.

150. Jackson, *White Spirituals,* op. cit., p. 354.

151. Jackson, "Buckwheat Notes," op. cit., p. 397.

152. Benjamin Franklin White, *Original Sacred Harp; Denson Revision, 1971 Edition* (1844; Kingsport, Tennessee: Kingsport Press for the Sacred Harp Publishing Company, 1971).

153. William Walker, *Southern Harmony, and Musical Companion* (1835; rpt. of 1854 ed. in facsimile; New York: The Federal Writers Project, Works Progress Administration, 1939), cited in Chase, op. cit., p. 689.

154. Chase, ibid., p. 191.

155. William Walker, *The Christian Harmony: In the Seven-Syllable Character Note System of Music;* [etc.] (1866; rev. ed., 1873; Philadelphia: E. W. Miller Company, 1901), p. iv.

156. Ibid.; emphasis in original.

157. Jackson, *White Spirituals,* op. cit., p. 313.

158. Cheek, op. cit.

159. Charles Linwood Ellington, "The Sacred Harp Tradition Of The South: Its Origin And Evolution" (unpublished Doctoral dissertation, Florida State University, 1969).

160. Dorothy Duerson Horn, *Sing To Me of Heaven; A Study of Folk and Early American Materials in Three Old Harp Books* (Gainesville: University of Florida Press, 1970).

161. Jackson, *White Spirituals,* op. cit., pp. 345, 351.

162. William Hauser and Benjamin Turner, *The Olive Leaf: A Collection of Beautiful Tunes, New and Old; The Whole of One or More Hymns Accompanying Each Tune* (Wadley, Jefferson Co., Ga.: Wm. Hauser, M. D., and Benjamin Turner, 1878).

163. Jackson, *White Spirituals,* op. cit., p. 323.

164. Ibid., p. 336.

3

Gospel Music: Its Beginning in Evangelism

Before discussing in detail the contributions to gospel music of the evangelist, Dwight L. Moody, and his soloist and song leader, Ira D. Sankey, it is perhaps necessary to examine some additional historical precedents for a popular type of religious hymnody.

Biblical Basis for Informal Hymnody

The Apostle Paul's injunction to the Ephesians[1] to speak to one another in "psalms, and hymns, and spiritual songs," although far from being specific, was similarly repeated in his letter to the Colossians.[2] This had led to suppositions that the three types of sacred vocal music he named were distinct entities. It has also been suggested that the "spiritual songs" were the least formal and most personally oriented of the three types. Hooper theorizes that:

> In all probability "psalms" referred to the Old Testament psalms, while "hymns" and "spiritual songs" were Christian creations. . . .
> It would seem likely that New Testament "hymns" are expressions of praise and adoration to Jehovah. The more subjective, personal expressions of religious experience would be embodied in the "spiritual songs."[3]

Paul's citation was used by Martin Luther during the time of the Reformation in Germany, in the sixteenth century, as Biblical authority for the cultivation of hymn singing among the congregation. But this could not be considered a real influence on the later gospel hymnody. According to Hooper, "The immediate background of the gospel song lies in England."[4]

Music in Early Evangelism

Isaac Watts

The acknowledged "Father of English hymnody,"[5] Isaac Watts, was born in Southampton, England, in 1674. While a young man, Watts wrote hymns which retain their vitality today. According to Reynolds, "Watt's [sic] basic philosophy was founded on the conviction that the song of the New Testament church should express the gospel of the New Testament. . . ."[6]

It is said that Watts began writing hymns after having complained to his father about the poor quality of the psalms sung in his church in Southampton. His father informed him that if he could write better ones, he should do so. Although the statement was made in jest, the young man began to write. His first hymn, when submitted to the congregation, was so well liked that he was asked to supply a new one each Sunday, which he did.[7] According to Fountain,[8] that first hymn was "Behold the Glories Of The Lamb," and it appears as the first hymn in Book 1 of Watts' *Hymns and Spiritual Songs*.[9] This was the beginning of a hymn writing career that has been unsurpassed. Bishop, who recently compiled a bibliography of over 755 different editions of Watts's *Hymns And Spiritual Songs* published in England and America since the original edition of 1707, did not include over 300 editions that varied too much from the original to meet her criteria. She states, "Watts was second only to Wesley in numbers and second to none in greatness. . . ."[10]

Watts intended for his hymns to reach all levels of Christianity, and they have done just that. According to Hooper, it would be unthinkable for a modern hymnal "of distinction" not to include at least one Watts' hymn;[11] and on the other hand, Bishop states, "It has been generally admitted that of all Hym-

49

nists Watts is most likely to make all the hymnbooks used by evangelical congregations."[12]

Although Watts's influence in hymnody was of the greatest magnitude,[13] he was not a composer. His hymns were set in the metric patterns to which the psalms had been set; and therefore, could be sung to any appropriate tune. These texts provided words for many of the folk-hymns that emerged in America during the middle 1700s and were used in the revivalism called the "Great Awakening." Sometimes these hymns would be set to tunes taken from secular songs and ballads appropriated for religious purposes.[14] At other times the texts would be set to anonymous hymn tunes,[15] such as that one normally associated with John Newton's "Amazing Grace."[16] Watts's hymns were later set to some of the spontaneous tunes that were generated at the camp meetings and revivals discussed earlier, and many were recorded in the shaped note tunebooks.[17]

John and Charles Wesley

Another influence upon the emergence of gospel hymnody may be seen in the music of John and Charles Wesley. While students at Oxford, England, the brothers formed a religious group that was so methodical in their habits that they became known as the "methodists."[18] Although the brothers did not intend to establish a denomination separate from the Church of England, of which they were members, the American congregations to whom they had preached as Anglican missionaries insisted. Much of this was due to the intense feelings that followed the Revolutionary War. The Methodist Episcopal church was formed as a separate organization in America in 1784,[19] fifty-two years before a similar organization in England, long after the Wesleys' deaths.[20]

Coming to America in the middle of the "Great Awakening," the term given to the period of revivalism in America from approximately 1725 to 1750,[21] the Wesleys were quick to see the value of congregational singing. They began a series of meetings which Alford terms the "Wesleyan Revival."[22] According to Alford, "If John Wesley may be rightly called the preacher of the Wesleyan revival, then Charles Wesley can be called its poet and song writer."[23] The Wesleys published sixty-three collections of hymns,[24] including in their collections many which had been written by Watts. Charles Wesley, himself, wrote as many as six thousand five hundred hymns.[25]

The Wesleyan hymns differed from the Watts' hymns in that they were more personal and direct. Benson says:

> In the quiet of his study Watts had aimed to improve the character of the Service of Praise. The Wesleys struck a new note,—the proclamation of an unlimited atonement and free gospel. . . . They sounded it in revival hymns, directly addressed to sinners, and glowing with the exhorter's excitement. They aimed to bring the unchurched and unsaved within the sound of the gospel, and to use song as a means of his conversion and upbuilding.[26]

By the latter part of the nineteenth century, precedent for a popular hymnody in revivalism was well established. As has been stated, the revivalism of the early part of the eighteenth century, led by the preachers Edwards, Whitefield, and Wesley, was called the "Great Awakening."[27] The camp-meeting revivalism of the early nineteenth century was called the "Great Revival"[28] or sometimes, the "second Great Awakening."[29] In both of these spontaneous religious upheavals, music performed the vital task of unifying the congregations psychologically and emotionally for the spoken message. The texts and tunes of the hymns that were sung were immediately accessible. They were appropriate for the multitudes who were relatively unacquainted with the more staid psalmody and hymnody of the established churches.

The music used by Dwight L. Moody and Ira D. Sankey in their revivals, however, had different characteristics than even the folk hymns and revival songs. Several immediate influences presaged this newer style of religious music. The two most important were the Young Men's Christian Association hymns and the Sunday School songs.

Y.M.C.A. Hymns

The Young Men's Christian Association which was organized in 1844 in London, reached Boston in 1851, and was soon established in cities throughout the country, and indeed, throughout the world.[30] According to Benson, "The rendering of familiar church hymns by male voices in a then strange atmosphere of 'Union' was the first novelty of its Hymnody."[31] In the beginnings of the organization, and as shown in the Y.M.C.A.-sponsored hymnbooks published during the Civil War, the hymns that were sung at first were mainly those which were already familiar to the men. After the Civil War, however, the collections published or used by the Association began to make greater use of the more evangelistic-type hymns. Many Sunday School songs, those appropriate for use in the Y.M.C.A. services, were included in these compilations.[32]

The Y.M.C.A. movement was influential, not so much because their song collections were innovative, but because so many of the men who were influential in the spreading of gospel music throughout the nation, and Europe, were affiliated with the organization. Dwight L. Moody and Ira D. Sankey were each Y.M.C.A. presidents in their own localities. Later they went into evangelistic work full-time. Eben Tourjée, president of the Boston Y.M.C.A.,[33] organized "Praise Services," which were a kind of forerunner to the Moody and Sankey services.[34] Philip Phillips, the "Singing Pilgrim,"[35] another influence on Moody and Sankey, was also active in the organization's activities.[36] Even Moody and Sankey first met at a Y.M.C.A. convention—but that will be told later.

Sunday School Songs

The most immediate influence on the gospel hymn was the Sunday School song. Many songs later published as "gospel hymns" had, in fact, appeared first in Sunday School collections.[37]

The Sunday School had been introduced into American society in 1786,[38] and the American Sunday School Union was founded in 1824.[39] But most of the early Sunday School songs were ill-adapted to the needs of the children for whom they had been compiled or composed. The first collection of songs to break with tradition was Horace Waters' *Sabbath School Bell*.[40] Describing this book, Lorenz states:

> But now appeared a new force. . . . It was a fairly complete departure from the hymn tune ideal of Sunday-school music, as its preponderating material consisted of arrangements of popular secular melodies, more or less sentimental in character, and of arrangements of "spirituals" gathered up from among the people. The sentimental and stirring rhythmical elements overshadowed the sedater hymn tunes completely.[41]

Waters was not a composer, however, and did not create a new style of music. He simply compiled the already existing secular and religious folk song and arranged it for the Sunday School. Nevertheless, the popularity and suitability of his book was influential in changing the style of writing of William Batchelder Bradbury.[42]

Bradbury was a well-trained musician, having spent two years in England and Germany studying with leading teachers. He was able to compose music at various levels of difficulty, from primary songs to extended anthems.[43] He had previously brought out a Sunday School book, *Oriola*,[44] but in his leading of singing conventions Bradbury was in a position to observe group reaction to the songs that Waters had included in his collection. In 1861 Bradbury brought out the first of his publications to reflect the new tastes and needs. This book, *Golden Chain*,[45] was even more widely approved than Waters' collection had been.[46] Bradbury continued to publish collections containing many of his own compositions and each received an enthusiastic welcome. According to Reynolds, during the years between 1841 and 1867 Bradbury was associated with the publishing of fifty-nine collections of sacred and secular music.[47] After his death, his work was continued by Robert Lowry and W. Howard Doane. They published *Pure Gold*[48] in 1871, which, according to Lorenz, "was superior in literary and musical value to anything that had appeared before. . . ."[49] It sold over a million copies.[50]

Many more collections of Sunday School songs appeared. Some of the more prominent composers and compilers, other than those previously mentioned, were Philip Phillips, William J. Kirkpatrick, John R. Sweeney, and George F. Root.[51] Sunday School collections continued to be published, but the phenomenal success of *Gospel Hymns and Sacred Songs,* mentioned in the previous chapter,[52] soon eclipsed them. The above collection was often purchased for use in the Sunday Schools. Later editions of the *Gospel Hymns* series[53] included many of the most popular compositions originally written for Sunday School collections. The use of the term "gospel" to identify the music of popular hymnody unquestionably derives from this title of the hymnbooks used in the Moody and Sankey evangelistic campaigns of 1871 to 1899.

Popularization by Moody and Sankey

Moody and Sankey

There are many reasons to help explain the success of the *Gospel Hymns* series and no small credit is due to the personalities and revivalism of Dwight Lyman Moody and Ira David Sankey. Sankey's account of how the two met shows some of the character and temperament of the two men:

In 1870, with two or three others, I was appointed a delegate to the International Convention of the Association, to be held at Indianapolis that year. It was announced that Moody would lead a morning prayer meeting at 7 o'clock. I was rather late, and therefore sat down near the door with a Presbyterian minister, the Rev. Robert McMillan, a delegate from my own county, who said to me, "Mr. Sankey, the singing here has been abominable; I wish you would start up something when that man stops praying, if he ever does." I promised him to do so, and when opportunity offered I sang the familiar hymn, "There is a fountain filled with blood."

54

The congregation joined heartily and a brighter aspect seemed to be given to the meeting.

At the conclusion of the meeting Mr. McMillan said to me: "Let me introduce you to Mr. Moody." We joined the little procession of persons who were going up to shake hands with him, and thus I met for the first time the man with whom, in the providence of God, I was to be associated for the remainder of his life, or nearly thirty years.

Moody's first words to me, after my introduction, were, "Where are you from? Are you married? What is your business?" Upon telling him that I lived in Pennsylvania, was married, had two children, and was in the government employ, he said abruptly, "You will have to give that up."

I stood amazed, at a loss to understand why the man told me that I would have to give up what I considered a good position. "What for?" I exclaimed.

"To come to Chicago and help me in my work," was the answer.

When I told him that I could not leave my business, he retorted, "You must; I have been looking for you for the last eight years."

I answered that I would think the matter over; but as yet I had no thought of giving up my position. Mr. Moody then asked me if I would go with him and pray over the matter, and to this I consented—out of politeness. After the prayer we parted, and I returned to my room, much impressed by Mr. Moody's prayer, but still undecided.[54]

Moody continued to press and finally, after a delay of over six months, Sankey accepted the offer and they began working together in 1871. This was only shortly before the great Chicago fire of the same year and Moody lost everything he had except, as he put it, ". . . my Bible, my family and my reputation."[55] It did not take Moody long to recover, however, and after one previous trip by Moody alone, it was decided that the two of them would take their revival campaign to England. They were ill-prepared for this trip. According to Goodspeed:

In the spring of 1873, Messrs. Moody and Sankey left Chicago for England. They had been invited by three gentlemen to hold meetings in that country. No one else had joined in the invitation, and

no one else was interested in their visit. They had no appoint-
ments. No arrangements were made for them. No compensation
was promised. No one knew of their intention to come. They were
persuaded that God sent them, and therefore they went. Mr.
Moody carried his Bible, Mr. Sankey his organ and singing book.[56]

Apparently Goodspeed doesn't think it important enough to
mention that both men were accompanied by their families.[57]
Nevertheless, after a rather inauspicious beginning, their campaign picked up momentum until suddenly they were in great
demand and were attracting large crowds. The "singing book"
that Sankey used was a collection of hymns by Phillip Phillips,
called *Hallowed Songs,*[58] and some other songs brought from
Chicago in manuscript form. The intense demand for these latter
songs prompted Sankey to request the publishers of *Hallowed
Songs* to include them as a supplement. Although Sankey and
Phillips were good friends, the publishers were unable to contact
the latter for permission and, therefore, refused publication. A
London publisher, R.C. Morgan, of Morgan and Scott, hearing of
the refusal, offered to publish them. Sankey clipped the songs
from his scrapbook, rolled them up, and wrote on the outside,
"Sacred Songs and Solos, sung by Ira D. Sankey at the meetings
of Mr. Moody of Chicago," and delivered them to Morgan.[59] This
small pamphlet of sixteen pages[60] enjoyed huge success. In time
it grew to a volume of 1,200 songs, and it is still being published
in England under the same title.[61] Moody's son wrote that the
proceeds from the sale of this book amounted to £7,000 ($35,000)
before Moody and Sankey left England, and that this money was
not accepted but turned over to an organization for the furtherance of their work in that country.[62] Not knowing what to do with
that sum of money, the committee turned it over to another committee to help rebuild Moody's church in Chicago.[63]

Sankey's major influence on gospel music was not as a composer. Although Howard and Bellows state that Sankey was
"One of the leading latter-century composers,"[64] they are mistaken. His actual output was slight and few of his songs have
survived. According to Lorenz:

Sankey's contributions were negligible. . . . He never became a full-fledged composer. He furnished a crude outline of a melody and Hubert P. Main, musical editor of Biglow and Main's publications . . . did the rest.[65]

Gospel Hymns Series[66]

It must have been Sankey's unique ability to sense what was needed, regardless of its source, that accounts for the success of the compilations with which he was associated. Speaking of the consolidated edition of all six *Gospel Hymns* publications into one book, Hitchcock writes:

> If Sankey and Bliss wrote a new chapter in American popular hymnody, they did not entirely reject the past. *Gospel Hymns* includes pages from virtually every earlier chapter in the history of Protestant congregational song, from Luther . . . on to Handel and Haydn. . . . Read . . . Holden . . . Mason and Hastings. . . . Whenever tunes or texts, or both, struck their fancy . . . they cheerfully turned them into gospel hymns.[67]

The initial publication of this series had Philip Paul Bliss as the senior editor.[68] Bliss was already an established composer of Sunday School songs and in fact, had only recently published his book called *Gospel Songs*[69] in 1874. He was engaged in revival work similar to that of Moody and Sankey, in conjunction with the evangelist, Major D.W. Whittle. (Both Bliss and Whittle had been enlisted into evangelistic work at the urging of D. L. Moody.) When Moody and Sankey returned to America in 1875, it was suggested that the two books, Bliss's *Gospel Songs* and Sankey's *Sacred Songs,* be combined into one for use by the entire force doing evangelistic work under Moody's auspices.[70]

It was this combination that can also be considered a major factor in the success of the resultant publication, *Gospel Hymns And Sacred Songs.*[71] Bliss had been affiliated with the Cincinnati and Chicago-based firm, John Church Company, and Moody and Sankey established connections with the New York and Chicago-based firm of Biglow and Main. This brought together the combined copyright sources of the two largest publishers of popular sacred music in America.[72] According to Reynolds:

> The combination of the two compilers, Bliss and Sankey, and the two publishers, Biglow and Main and the John Church Company, explains to a large degree the dominant role played by this series. ... No better plan of merchandising and promoting this book could have been available for Bliss and Sankey.[73]

The book was immediately successful. Lorenz describes its acceptance this way:

> The sale of this book swept America from ocean to ocean and across the waters to foreign lands. These songs had already won England, now they passed over the Continent in translations and were widely used in Protestant Europe. Even sedate Germany had its own edition. ... Missionaries all over the world translated the hymns into the language of the peoples for whom they were working, and so the tide of Gospel Song encircled the globe.[74]

Of course, simply because the book was used in the Moody-sponsored revivals did not guarantee this enormity of its popularity. As was previously mentioned by Hitchcock, it had drawn upon the most appropriate and appealing sources in the history of Protestant hymnody. The music was infectious. According to Benson:

> The new melodies penetrated even the music halls and were whistled by the man on the street. . . .
> They [were] "easy," and "catchy" and sentimental, swaying with a soft or martial rhythm and culminating in the taking "refrain"; calling for no musical knowledge to understand and no skill to render them; inevitably popular with the unfailing appeal of clear melody.[75]

The immediate commercial success of the initial compilation spawned a flood of imitators.[76] The number of song collections published after 1875 that include the term "gospel" in their titles or subtitles is overwhelming.

It may have some significance for the regional differences in gospel music, however, to point out that at least one influential southern publisher, the Ruebush-Kieffer Company, did not immediately adopt the "gospel song" typification. This company, discussed in greater detail in Chapter 4, did not use the term as a description for any of its publications until 1881.[77]

Bliss continued to be senior editor for *Gospel Hymns No. 2,* published in 1876.[78] Unquestionably Bliss would have had a greater share in the later gospel song movement if his life had not ended in the tragic train wreck at Astabula, Ohio, in 1876. In this wreck at least one hundred persons were killed. Bliss was thrown clear of the train, but perished when he re-entered the burning wreckage in a futile attempt to save his wife.[79]

After Bliss's death, Sankey collaborated with James McGranahan and George Coles Stebbins in the compilation of *Gospel Hymns* nos. 3, 4, 5, and 6; and in the culminating volume, *Gospel Hymns Nos. 1 to 6 Complete,* published in 1894.[80] According to Reynolds, the *Gospel Hymns* series "remained unchallenged to the end of the century."[81]

It was mentioned previously that the sales of the collections with which Sankey was associated were phenomenal. Moody's son, William R. Moody, stated in 1930 that "seventy million copies [of *Sacred Songs and Solos* alone] have been sold since the first edition appeared."[82] The books published in America sold equally well. When one realizes that the books were sold for as little as two cents each[83] at the Moody and Sankey meetings (although the cover price was stated at thirty cents each), the following report is even more impressive. In an earlier biography of his father, Moody quotes the chairman of the American trustees of the song book sales[84] as saying:

The sale of the first editions of the books greatly exceeded our expectations, and, although the royalty was, on a single copy, small, as trustees we received up to September, 1885, the large sum of $357,388.64. All of this was carefully distributed among various religious and educational institutions.[85]

Subsequent Gospel Hymnody in Evangelism

Moody Bible Institute

Funds from the sale of these books had a more direct effect on subsequent gospel hymnody when another religious and educational institution was established in 1886. This was the Moody Bible Institute.[86] This institution has had, and continues to have, an enormous impact on the development of gospel music.

Moody had organized two previous institutions in Northfield, Massachusetts, his childhood home. These were the Northfield Seminary for girls and Mount Hermon School for boys.[87] A Chicago Evangelization Society was chartered in 1887, and this later organization's Bible Institute was renamed the Moody Bible Institute in 1900, shortly after Moody's death.[88]

The music program at the Bible Institute was begun in 1889, with H.H. McGranahan as the first director of music. According to Getz:

> The aim of this department was to train students "to become singers, leaders or organists" who could "assist evangelists and pastors, and do a work on the mission fields, both at home and abroad."[89]

The Institute's musical leadership increased when Daniel Brink Towner became the director of the Musical Department in 1893.[90] According to Reynolds:

> In this position he exerted an unusual influence in church music throughout the midwest as he trained evangelical church music leadership and evangelistic singers.[91] Towner remained as head of the department until his death in 1919.[92]

The Institute's influence in music has been exceptional. Hustad cites more than thirty musical leaders who have been associated with Moody Bible Institute.[93] Among these are Charles Alexander, whom Hooper calls "the forerunner of the evangelistic song leader,"[94] and Isham E. Reynolds, the first music faculty

60

member of a Southern Baptist seminary.[95] The Institute was also a pioneer in the radio broadcasting of religious programs and religious music as early as 1925. It began transmitting under its own call letters, WMBI, in 1926.[96]

Perhaps John W. Peterson, the recipient of the SESAC[97] International Gospel Songwriting Award for 1975,[98] and composer of one of the songs performed by an amateur gospel singing group in the Field Research portion of this study, captures some of the atmosphere of Moody Bible Institute when he writes:

> If there is any metaphor adequate to express what it was like to be at Moody in those days, I don't know it. I thought I was in heaven. . . . Moody was a paradise of all that fed my soul and nourished my spirit. To sit in Monday morning chapel and hear a thousand kids sing the majestic old hymns of faith . . . to listen to the Moody Chorale, unable to prevent tears of happiness from forming in my eyes. . . . I was like a sponge, soaking up all the richness of the experience. I knew now that I had not misread God's intentions; this was where He wanted me to be.[99]

Fanny Crosby

Almost as great an influence as Moody, Bliss, and Sankey in the establishment of gospel hymnody was the "Queen of American hymn writers,"[100] Fanny Jane Crosby (Mrs. Alexander Van Alstyne). Fanny Crosby, who was blind from infancy, wrote a prodigious number of poems for the Sunday School song collections which preceded the *Gospel Hymns* phenomenon. She also provided lyrics for the mainstream of gospel hymnody which followed. Quite accomplished as a performer on the guitar, piano, and harp, she refused to allow more than a few of her own musical compositions to be published. Apparently she felt that the difficulty or sophistication of her compositions would be above the heads of the masses of the humble people she wanted to reach. Choosing to maintain a living standard bordering on poverty, she also deliberately wrote poems that would appeal to unsophisticated tastes. Her influence on the publications of the publishing firm of Biglow and Main was considerable. Ruffin, whose recent biography of Fanny Crosby deserves to be read, states:

> [Main] and Biglow were primarily businessmen, and they generally left the work of producing hymns to the various poets and musicians who were associated with the firm. Of these Fanny Crosby rapidly became the most prominent, and in many ways was responsible more than any other person for setting the style of the hymns that the new company produced for the next half century. Although she seldom wrote the music, the fact that she pronounced on the suitability of the numerous tunes that were submitted to her for lyrics made her influential even in that area.[101]

Reports of the number of hymns Fanny Crosby wrote vary from the 3,000 figure recorded on the grave marker erected forty years after her death,[102] to the "around nine thousand hymns—more than anybody else in recorded Christian history . . ."[103] cited by Ruffin. It is said that she used over two hundred pen names and Ruffin lists forty of them, stating:

> So prolific was her writing that the editors had to induce her to use pen names in order to disguise the fact that they depended to such a large extent on one person to supply the lyrics.[104]

Fanny Crosby outlived the associates who had helped make "gospel music" a household word, and after dictating one final poem only hours before, died of a heart attack at the age of ninety-five. This final poem reads:

In the morn of Zion's glory,
When the clouds have rolled away,
And my hope has dropped its anchor
In the vale of perfect day,
When with all the pure and holy
I shall strike my harp anew,
With a power no arm can sever,
Love will hold me fast and true.[105]

As Hitchcock states, the gospel hymn movement of the late

nineteenth century was an urban phenomenon.[106] Although the background for its acceptance may have been prepared by the camp-meeting movement, and the verse-and-refrain pattern of the songs may have been a direct result of that movement, the Moody and Sankey revivalism took place in the metropolitan centers of America. The composers of the Sunday School songs and of the *Gospel Hymns* were not those who had learned the shaped note songs by way of the rural singing school. They had been trained in the music schools of the northeast, where shaped note hymnody was undoubtedly forgotten if it ever had been known.

Before returning to the more rustic and rural form of gospel hymnody, however, some mention of the continuance of gospel music in urban revivalism should be made.

Alexander, Torrey, and Chapman

Whereas Sankey had swayed his audiences by singing earnest solos and leading the congregation to sing by merely stating, "Let us all rise and sing heartily,"[107] Charles Alexander, who was previously mentioned in connection with Moody Bible Institute, used a more dynamic approach. Alexander was song leader for two outstanding revivalists, Reuben A. Torrey and J. Wilbur Chapman. According to McKissick:

Charles Alexander, song leader for Torrey and Chapman, was responsible for making a vital contribution to the new techniques of mass evangelism. He substituted the piano or a horn accompaniment for the church organ and was the first to combine the personality of a master of ceremonies with the vivaciousness of the leader of a community songfest. His method of "warming up" an audience brought back something of the social significance of religious life which had played such a large part in the frontier camp meetings. This aspect of revivalism was of great importance to the city dwellers who felt lost and overwhelmed by the complexity of urban life.[108]

Rodeheaver and Sunday

Modeling his style of songleading after Alexander rather than Sankey, Homer Alvan Rodeheaver served for over twenty years as song leader for the revivalist Billy Sunday, beginning in 1910.[109] Sunday was the energetic former professional baseball player who maintained in his retinue an athletic trainer to keep himself in shape.[110] Rodeheaver's style of songleading was equally dynamic. Comparing Rodeheaver to other revivalist song leaders, McKissick states:

> Sankey usually played his accompaniments on a small, pump organ. . . . But in the Sunday and Rodeheaver campaigns brass bands and drum and bugle corps were often employed for the tabernacle meetings. Rodeheaver often played trombone solos in the Sunday meetings and usually used his instrument to "set the pace" of the song service.[111]

Rodeheaver also conducted enormous choirs in the singing of hymns and gospel songs, and occasionally had them perform larger works such s Handel's "Hallelujah Chorus" or Mozart's "Gloria,"[112] Rodeheaver was also alert to the potentialities of recordings and radio. He made recordings using the label "Rainbow Records" as early as 1916.[113] He also began a program of gospel music over KDKA, Pittsburgh, one of the first two commercial radio stations in the United States,[114] as early as 1922.[115]

After World War I, interest in revivalism waned in America but not so interest in gospel music. Rodeheaver had begun a publishing firm in Winona Lake, Indiana, with Charles H. Gabriel as music editor.[116] This company became highly influential in promoting gospel music. Rodeheaver, himself, was also an influence in the southern gospel hymnody which will be discussed in Chapter 4. Although Rodeheaver died in 1955, the Rodeheaver Company continues today as a subsidiary of Word, Incorporated, in Waco, Texas.[117]

Graham Crusades

It was not until after World War II, and as late as 1949, that a revivalist of the statue of a Moody or a Sunday emerged in America again, and that was in the personage of Billy Graham. Graham, who continues to be an active force in the religious life of America, achieved nationwide attention with the dramatic conversions of singer Stuart Hamblen, ex-convict Jim Vaus, and athlete Louis Zamperini, in Los Angeles, California, in 1949.[118]

Similar to Moody and Sunday, Graham uses a soloist, George Beverly Shea, and a song leader, Cliff Barrows, as an integral part of his services. Graham met Barrows on an occasion reminiscent of the Moody and Sankey meeting. Shea tells it this way:

> Billy had run into Cliff at Ben Lippen Bible Conference in North Carolina in 1945. Called in to speak on youth night, he had discovered that he had no song leader. Conference officials suggested that he use a young man from the audience, a twenty-two-year-old Californian who was on his honeymoon. Expecting the worst, Billy accepted the volunteer. To his pleasant surprise, Cliff took charge and soon had the auditorium ringing with enthusiastic song. In addition to a warm personality and a good voice, Cliff's assets also included a well-played trombone he "just happened to have along" and a talented, piano-playing wife.
>
> "Inside of five minutes I knew I had found a prize," Billy recalls.
>
> Whenever I hear Billy tell about finding Cliff, I think of the story of Dwight L. Moody's discovery of Ira D. Sankey—song leader and soloist. The circumstances have strong parallels.[119]

The Graham revivalism has produced very little in the way of new music, however. The *Billy Graham Song Book*[120] contains, with rare exceptions, only tried and true favorites from the gospel songs of the early twentieth century. According to McKissick:

> Very little really "new" music is used. Just as the gospel message from the Graham pulpit resembles the message of preceding evangelists, so, the music of the choir and congregation sounds

strikingly familiar. Barrows is not a song writer, and Shea has written only a very few gospel melodies.[121]

A more recent discussion of the Graham revivalism says much the same thing. Peterson writes:

Following Billy Sunday as America's noted evangelist is Billy Graham, who along with his song leader Cliff Barrows and his soloist George Beverly Shea, has continued to rely upon the old gospel songs in mass evangelistic programs. With this reliance upon hymns written before 1914 very little new music has emerged. . . .
With the great popularity of the crusades and the musical talent made available to them it is surprising that more new hymns have not been forthcoming.[122]

In comparing the revivalism of Moody, Sunday, and Graham, McKissick again observes:

. . . each of the three revivals used large choirs and a single soloist. . . . In each revival movement one man was used as principal soloist. Congregational song has been a vital part of almost every religious revival.[123]

The last statement by McKissick may not hold true regarding the Graham crusades. In these meetings, although the congregation is allowed to participate to a limited extent, the majority of music performed is accomplished by the Crusade Chorus or by featured soloists and ensembles.

Two other present-day evangelists have utilized congregational singing even less than Graham. Yet the music associated with their services has had a professed impact and influence on the amateur gospel singers who comprise the Field Research portion of this study. These two evangelists are Oral Roberts and Rex Humbard.

Oral Roberts

Oral Roberts began his ministry as a faith healer in 1956[124] but has gradually expanded his outreach to include sermons and special programs broadcast to a wide television audience. He is also founder of a highly acclaimed university in Tulsa, Oklahoma, Oral Roberts University. Morris describes Roberts' distinctions:

> Since the early 1950s, the name Oral Roberts has been synonymous with faith-healing for millions of people in the United States and countries all around the world. Many became his supporters because of Roberts' far-flung network of radio and television faith-healing programs. In more recent years he has reached out to other millions with his more modern television specials, hour-long programs which skillfully blend religion with musical entertainment provided by many of American's leading motion picture and television performers. More than faith healer and television star, Roberts is known also as educator, banker, college president and Chamber of Commerce director. After more than twenty years in the religious spotlight, it is safe to say that except for Dr. Billy Graham, Oral Roberts is better known to the general public than any other preacher in America.[125]

In his television programs, Roberts' son, Richard, and daughter-in-law, Patti, perform solos and duets accompanied by a choreographed ensemble of ostensibly Oral Roberts University students, the World Action singers. Their "Now" sound[126] is comprised of standard hymns and gospel songs performed in modern, rock-oriented, musical settings.

Rex Humbard

Rex Humbard, who operates a worldwide television ministry of more than 425 television stations[127] in the United States and overseas, claiming to reach "more than thirty-two million people,"[128] has always included gospel music as a fundamental part of his ministry. He, with his family, sang as the Humbard Family gospel singing group when his father was preaching from a small tent in back alley areas in the early 1950s.[129] His family still forms the majority of the Cathedral Singers who appear each Sunday on his Cathedral of the Air program. He feels that the music is what initially attracts the majority of listeners to his television broadcasts,[130] and this is supported by the statements of the Field Research sample.

Although the music used by Graham, Roberts, and Humbard in their evangelistic services does reflect some of the performance practice of gospel music today, it would be erroneous to consider the music of their services to be the mainstream of gospel music activity. The music which incorporates the major field-of-interest of the present-day Gospel Music Association has origins more closely related to the shaped note hymnody and camp-meeting tradition discussed in Chapter 2, than that of Moody and Sankey and the later revivalists. These origins will be detailed in Chapter 4.

Summary

Gospel music had its origin in the need for a popular style of hymnody that would attract large numbers of people to evangelistic meetings. Early evangelistic movements in America were the "Great Awakening" in the second quarter of the eighteenth century, and the "Great Revival" in the early 1800s. These and other revival movements in America were, and are, accompanied by the performance of music, whether performed by the congregation or by soloists and ensembles.

Another form of evangelism was manifested in the Sunday School movement, which produced many compilations of attractive and unsophisticated songs for use in its services.

The evangelistic movement that brought about the widespread usage of the term "gospel" to designate popular hymnody was that headed by Dwight L. Moody and Ira D. Sankey in the late 1800s. The music of the Moody and Sankey services was, for the most part, a product of urban composers and lyricists; but the overwhelming success of the *Gospel Hymns* series made the name "gospel" a generic term for any personal, unsophisticated, popular religious song. This name was soon adopted by the southern composers and compilers of religious music whose traditions had progressed along different lines.

Notes

1. Ephesians 5:19.
2. Colossians 3:16.
3. William Loyd Hooper, *Church Music in Transition* (Nashville: Broadman Press, 1963), pp. 21–22.
4. Ibid., p. 80.
5. William Jensen Reynolds, *A Survey of Christian Hymnody* [hereinafter referred to as *Survey*] (New York: Holt, Rinehart and Winston, Inc., 1963), p. 49.
6. Ibid., p. 48.
7. Hooper, op. cit., p. 81.
8. David G. Fountain, *Isaac Watts Remembered* (Worthington, England: Henry E. Walter, Ltd., 1974), p. 34.
9. Isaac Watts, *Hymns And Spiritual Songs. In Three Books* (1707; London: Printed by J. H. for M. Lawrence, 1716); cited in Selma L. Bishop, *Isaac Watts' Hymns And Spiritual Songs (1707) A Publishing History And A Bibliography* (Ann Arbor: The Pierian Press, 1974), p. 1; this, apparently, is the first edition extant.
10. Bishop, cited ibid., p. x; apparently Bishop did not include the writings of Fanny Crosby (see p. 61) in the comparison of the numbers of hymns written.
11. Hooper, op. cit., p. 81.
12. Bishop, op. cit., p. xxi.
13. Louis F. Benson, *The English Hymn* (London: Hodder & Stoughton, 1915), p. 218.
14. George Pullen Jackson, *Spiritual Folk Songs of Early America* (1937; rpt. New York: Dover Publications, Inc., 1964), p. 6.
15. Hugh Wiley Hitchcock, *Music in the United States: A Historical Introduction* (2nd ed.; Englewood Cliffs, New Jersey: Prentice-Hall, Inc., 1974), p. 98.
16. William J. Reynolds, "Amazing Grace," *Companion to Baptist Hymnal* [hereafter referred to as *Companion!*] (Nashville: Broadman Press, 1976), p. 165.
17. Harry Lee Eskew, "Shape-note Hymnody In The Shenandoah Valley, 1816–1860" (unpublished Doctoral dissertation, Tulane University, 1966), p. 150.
18. Hooper, op. cit., p. 135.
19. Ibid., p. 139–140.
20. "Methodism," *Encyclopaedia Britannica* (1768; Chicago: Encyclopaedia Britannica, Inc., William Benton, Publisher, 1971), XV, 302.
21. "Revivalism," *Encyclopaedia Britannica,* op. cit., XIX, 247.
22. Delton L. Alford, *Music in the Pentecostal Church* (Cleveland, Tennessee: Pathway Press, 1967), p. 41.
23. Ibid., p. 42.
24. Wesleyan hymnody may not have been as popular among folk congregations as is generally alleged. George Pullen Jackson states, "The only piece among the Wesley-borrowed and specially composed songs which enjoyed long currency among American country singers in the mass was

'Old German [?]." He further acknowledges, "This is precisely the opposite view held by most authorities. . . ." He states that he had previously sanctioned the "authoritative" view until he found out the facts for himself. Cf. George Pullen Jackson, *White And Negro Spirituals* (1943; New York: Da Capo Press, 1975), pp. 19, 24-footnote.

25. Benson, op. cit., p. 245.
26. Ibid., p. 248.
27. Cf. p. 23 above.
28. John B. Boles, *The Great Revival 1787–1805: The Origins of the Southern Evangelical Mind* (Lexington: The University Press of Kentucky, 1972), p. ix.
29. "Revivalism," op. cit., p. 248.
30. "Young Men's Christian Association," *Encyclopaedia Britannica,* op. cit., XXIII, 909–910.
31. Benson, op. cit., p. 483.
32. Ibid., pp. 483–484.
33. Tourjée was also founder of the New England Conservatory of Music in 1867; this was "the first large institution of its kind in America," according to John Tasker Howard and George Kent Bellows, *A Short History of Music in America* (1957; New York; Thomas Y. Crowell Co., 1967), p. 137.
34. Benson, op. cit., p. 484.
35. Ibid., p. 301; the appellation stems from Phillips's travels as a soloist and from the title of one of Phillips's song collections.
36. Ibid., pp. 484–485.
37. Reynolds, *Survey,* op. cit., pp. 104–105.
38. "Sunday Schools," *Compton's Encyclopedia* (1922; Chicago: F. E. Compton CO., Division of Encyclopaedia Britannica, Inc., William Benton, Publisher, 1971), XXI, 516.
39. Ibid.
40. Horace Waters, *The Sabbath School Bell: A New Collection of Choice Hymns and Tunes, Original and Standard; Carefully and Simply Arranged* [etc.] (New York: Published by Horace Waters, 1859).
41. Edmund S. Lorenz, *Church Music: What a Minister Should Know About It* (New York: Fleming H. Revell Company, 1923), p. 330.
42. Ibid., p. 331.
43. Ibid.
44. William B. Bradbury, *Oriola; A New and Complete Hymn and Tune Book. For Sabbath Schools* (1859; 30th ed., enl.; Cincinnati: Wilstach, Baldwin & Co., 1871).
45. William Bradbury, *Bradbury's Golden Chain of Sabbath School Melodies* (New York: Ivison, Phinney & Co., 1861).
46. Lorenz, loc. cit.
47. Reynolds, *Companion,* op. cit., p. 272.
48. Robert Lowry and W. Howard Doane, *Pure Gold for the Sunday School: A New Collection of Songs, Prepared and Adapted for Sunday School Exercises* (New York and Chicago: Biglow & Main, (successors to William B. Bradbury), [sic], 1871).
49. Lorenz, op. cit., p. 333.
50. Ibid.
51. Ibid., pp. 332–338.

52. Cf. pp. 21 ff.

53. The basic editions of this series are cited on p. 71 in footnote 66.

54. Ira D. Sankey, *Sankey's Story of the Gospel Hymns; and of Sacred Songs and Solos* (Philadelphia: The Sunday School Times Company, 1906), pp. 5–6.

55. Dwight L. Moody, quoted by Sankey in ibid., p. 16.

56. E.J. Goodspeed, *A Full History of the Wonderful Career of Moody and Sankey, in Great Britain and America . . . and Everything of Interest Connected with the Work* (1876; rpt. New York: AMS Press, 1973), p. 60.

57. James Findlay, Jr., *Dwight L. Moody: American Evangelist 1837–1899* (1969; Grand Rapids: Baker Book House, 1973), p. 150.

58. Philip Phillips, *Hallowed Songs, (harmonized) for Prayer and Religious Meetings, Containing Hymns and Tunes Carefully Selected from All Sources, Both Old and New, and of the Most Spiritual Character* (rev. ed.; New York: Harper Brothers, [etc.,], 1871).

59. Sankey, op. cit., p. 20; although the above narrative is that which generally appears in most secondary sources, Moody's son gives a different version. He states: "Moody turned to Messrs. Morgan and Scott and asked them if they would undertake the publication of a book to be known as *Sacred Songs and Solos*. They too were unwilling to risk a possible loss. [The publishers of *Hallowed Songs* had been asked first.] Then Moody asked Mr. Sankey to share with him a guarantee against any loss to the publishers. But Sankey too was not convinced that such a venture would be safe and declined to assume any responsibility.

Moody returned to Messrs. Morgan and Scott and guaranteed personally a sum not exceed sixteen hundred dollars any loss incurred. This guarantee was the total amount of Moody's sayings [sic]; he offered it with the knowledge and concurrence of Mrs. Moody. . . ." See William R. Moody, *D.L. Moody* (New York: The Macmillan Company, 1930), p. 199.

60. Benson, op. cit., p. 486; Cf. Reynolds, *Survey,* op. cit., p. 105, which says 24 pages; the smallest edition (no date) which the writer has viewed contains 32 pages and 31 musical selections.

61. *British Books in Print, 1976* (London: J. Whitaker & Sons Ltd., 1976), 2, p. 3719.

62. William R. Moody, The Life of Dwight L. Moody by His Son William R. Moody, The Official Authorized Edition [etc.] (New York: Fleming H. Revell Company, 1900), p. 172.

63. Ibid.; This was the Chicago Avenue Church, constructed at Chicago Avenue and LaSalle Street as a replacement for Moody's Illinois Street Church, destroyed by the 1871 fire.

64. John Tasker Howard and George Kent Bellows, *A Short History of Music in America* (1957; New York: Thomas Y. Crowell Co., 1967), p. 324.

65. Lorenz, op. cit., p. 346.

66. The basic editions of the *Gospel Hymns* series are as follows: *Gospel Hymns and Sacred Songs* 1875); *Gospel Hymns No. 2* (1876); *Gospel Hymns No. 3* (1878); *Gospel Hymns Combined* [(1, 2, 3] (1879); *Gospel Hymns No. 4* (1881); *Gospel Hymns Consolidated* [1, 2, 3, 4] (1883); *Gospel Hymns No. 5 With Standard Selections* (1887); *Gospel Hymns No. 6* (1891); *Gospel Hymns Nos. 5 and 6 Combined* [With Selections From

Nos. 1–4] (1892); *Gospel Hymns Nos. 1 to 6* (1894); *Gospel Hymns Nos. 1 to 6,* Brevier, and Excelsior Editions (1895).

67. Hugh Wiley Hitchcock, "Introduction," *Gospel Hymns Nos. 1 to 6 Complete, by Ira David Sankey, James McGranahan, George C. Stebbins, Philip P. Bliss; New Introduction by H. Wiley Hitchcock* (1894; rpt. of 1895 "Excelsior" ed.; New York: Da Capo Press, 1972), "Introduction" unpaginated.

68. Bliss should receive more credit than he is generally given for the beginnings of the gospel hymn movement. Although it is beyond the scope of this study to do so, it is certain that an analysis of Bliss' contributions, compared with those of Sankey, would confirm this. Such a comparison, combined with Bliss' first real use of the term to identify this particular style of religious music, should make a strong case for Bliss, not Sankey, to be considered the "Father of the Gospel Song." Bliss' untimely death and Sankey's association with the more widely known evangelist, Dwight L. Moody, account for a great deal of the credit accorded the latter musician.

69. Philip P. Bliss, *Gospel Songs; A Choice Collection of Hymns and Tunes, New and Old, for Gospel Meetings, Prayer Meetings, Sunday Schools, etc.* [sic] (Cincinnati: John Church & Co., 1874); that this book of 128 pages was larger than Sankey's 16-page *Sacred Songs and Solos,* and also larger than the resultant *Gospel Hymns and Sacred Songs* (112 pages) has been neglected in all secondary sources viewed by the writer.

70. Lorenz, op. cit., p. 347.

71. Philip P. Bliss and Ira D. Sankey, *Gospel Hymns and Sacred Songs, by P.P. Bliss and Ira D. Sankey, as Used by Them in Gospel Meetings* (New York and Chicago: Biglow & Main; Cincinnati and Chicago: John Church & Co., 1875).

72. Lorenz, loc. cit.

73. Reynolds, *Survey,* op. cit., p. 106.

74. Lorenz, op. cit., pp. 347–348.

75. Benson, op. cit., pp. 487, 488.

76. Ibid., p. 490.

77. Grace I. Showalter, *The Music Books of Ruebush & Kieffer, 1866–1942: A Bibliography* (Richmond: Virginia State Library, 1975), pp. 6, 32, 38; two undated publications, however, do contain the word "gospel" in their titles.

78. Philip P. Bliss and Ira D. Sankey, *Gospel Hymns No. 2 by P.P. Bliss and Ira D. Sankey, as Used by Them in Gospel Meetings* (New York and Chicago: Biglow & Main; Cincinnati and Chicago; John Church & Co., 1876).

79. D.W. Whittle, *Memoirs of Philip P. Bliss* (New York: A.S. Barnes & Company, 1877, pp. 65–71. (Title should more accurately read Memories of . . .)

80. Ira D. Sankey, James McGranahan and George C. Stebbins, *Gospel Hymns Nos. 1 to 6 Complete (Without Duplicates) for Use in Gospel Meetings and Other Religious Services* (Chicago: Biglow & Main Company; Philadelphia: The John Church Company, 1894); The 1895 "Excelsior" edition of this publication, cited on p. 97 above as Hitchcock, "Introduction," was reprinted by Da Capo Press in 1972; also, the basic editions of the *Gospel Hymns* series are itemized in on p. 71 in footnote 66.

81. Reynolds, *Survey,* loc. cit.
82. William R. Moody, *D. L. Moody* (New York: The Macmillan Company, 1930), p. 209.
83. Bernard Ruffin, *Fanny Crosby* (Philadelphia: United Church Press, 1976), p. 115.
84. As a means of avoiding scandal, Moody delegated the financial details of song book sales to trustees, both in America and in England; See Moody, *D. L. Moody* (1930), op. cit., pp. 199–203.
85. William E. Dodge, quoted in Moody, *The Life of Dwight L. Moody* (1900), op. cit., p. 174; the same quotation appears in Moody, *D. L. Moody* (1930), op. cit., p. 202.
86. Gene A. Getz, *MBI, The Story of Moody Bible Institute* (Chicago: Moody Press, 1969), p. 30; the rather arbitrary nature of 1886 as a beginning date for MBI is thoroughly discussed by Getz in his pp. 30–46; he provides a "Time Line of Events Leading to the Origin of Moody Bible Institute" on his p. 45.
87. James F. Findlay, Jr., *Dwight L. Moody: American Evangelist 1837–1899* (1969); rpt. Grand Rapids: Baker Book House, 1973), pp. 308–310.
88. Getz, op. cit., pp. 37, 46.
89. Ibid., p. 140.
90. Ibid., p. 141.
91. Reynolds, *Companion,* op. cit., p. 447.
92. Reynolds, *Survey,* op. cit., p. 107.
93. Donald P. Hustad, "Moody Bible Institute's Contribution to Gospel Music," *Founder's Week Messages,* (1968?), pp. 281–294. Copy made available to the writer by Moody Bible Institute does not contain bibliographic information.
94. Hooper, op. cit., p. 100; Alexander is discussed in greater detail on p. 63.
95. Reynolds, *Companion,* op. cit., pp. 409–410. Reynolds began the Department of Gospel Music of the Southwestern Baptist Theological Seminary, Fort Worth, Texas in 1915.
96. Martin J. Neeb, Jr., "An Historical Study of American Non-commercial AM Broadcast Stations Owned and Operated by Religious Groups, 1920–1966" (unpublished Doctoral dissertation, Northwestern University, 1967), pp. 436–438.
97. Society of European Stage Authors and Composers. The name no longer reflects its main function, which is as an American performing rights organization.
98. John W. Peterson with Richard Engquist, *The Miracle Goes On* (Grand Rapids: Zondervan Publishing House, 1976), p. 220.
99. Ibid., p. 129.
100. Ruffin, op. cit., p. 14.
101. Ibid., p. 100.
102. Ibid., p. 240.
103. Ibid., p. 16.
104. Ibid., p. 105.
105. Ibid., p. 237.
106. Hitchcock, *Music in the United States,* op. cit., p. 100.
107. Ruffin, op. cit., p. 115.
108. Marvin McKissick, "The Function of Music in American Revivals since

1875," *The Hymn*, IX (October, 1958), 112; the above quotation is a paraphrase of William G. McLoughlin, Jr., *Billy Sunday Was His Real Name* (Chicago: University of Chicago Press, 1955), pp. 41–42.

109. McLoughlin, op. cit., p. 75.
110. Ibid., p. 76.
111. McKissick, op. cit., p. 116.
112. Homer Rodeheaver, *Twenty Years with Billy Sunday* (Winona Lake, Indiana: The Rodeheaver Hall-Mack Co., 1936), p. 76.
113. McLoughlin, op. cit., p. 86.
114. Neeb, op. cit., p. 2.
115. Harlan Daniel, "From Shape Notes to Bank Notes: Milestones in the Evolution of White Gospel Music," (unpublished chronology presented at the Sixth Annual Meeting of the Popular Culture Association, session on white gospel music and the country tradition, Chicago, April 24, 1976), n.p. (Mimeographed.)
116. Lorenz, op. cit., p. 351; this publishing company was begun [in Chicago] in 1910, according to McLoughlin, op. cit., p. 84.
117. "Word, Inc. Celebrates 25 Years," *The Singing News* [Pensacola, Florida], December 1, 1976, p. 2B, col. 4.
118. James Morris, *The Preachers* (New York: St. Martin's Press, 1973), p. 374.
119. George Beverly Shea with Fred Bauer, *Then Sings My Soul* (1968: Old Tappan, New Jersey: Spire Books Fleming H. Revell Company, 1971), pp. 98–99. See also Moody and Sankey meeting quoted on pp. 54 ff.
120. Cliff Barrows, comp., *Billy Graham Song Book* (Minneapolis: The Billy Graham Evangelistic Association, 1969).
121. McKissick, op. cit., p. 115.
122. Robert Douglas Peterson, "The Folk Idiom in the Music of Contemporary Protestant Worship in America" (unpublished Doctoral dissertation, Columbia University, 1972), pp. 69–70.
123. McKissick, op. cit., p. 116.
124. Morris, op. cit., p. 61.
125. Ibid., p. 59.
126. Ibid., p. 114.
127. Rex Humbard, *To Tell The World* (Englewood Cliffs, New Jersey: Prentice-Hall, Inc., 1975), p. 21.
128. Ibid., p. 205.
129. Ibid., pp. 3, 54–55.
130. Ibid., pp. 136–137.

4

Gospel Music in the South

Although the *Gospel Hymns* of Bliss, Sankey, McGranahan, and Stebbins were as popular in the South as in any other location, it has already been pointed out that this music did not originate in the South or in a rural milieu.

The South had its own tradition of popular religious hymnody. The similarity in concept of its music with the music of the *Gospel Hymns* inevitably brought about an adoption of the term "gospel music" to designate the southern musical style.

But the indigenous popular hymnody of the South predates the *Gospel Hymn* phenomenon by at least several decades. To understand better the southern religious music traditions it will be necessary to discuss these traditions from the standpoint of the three separate forms of group activity, aside from use in worship services, in which this music was, and is, used. These group activities are: four-shape singing conventions, seven-shape singing conventions, and gospel sings. The use of the term "shape" refers, of course, to the shaped note-heads discussed in detail in Chapter 2. Music written in shaped notes is one of the most distinctive features of southern gospel music, especially in its written form.

Singing Conventions

The concept of singing conventions did not originate in the South. According to Cheek, who offers documentation for the statement, "The first singing society was established in Boston in 1720, possibly as an outgrowth of the first singing school."[1] Whether or not it can be fully substantiated that this was a genuine "first," nevertheless singing societies were formed as an outgrowth of the singing schools and were eventually established throughout New England.[2] According to Howard and Bellows, "the oldest singing society in America" is the Stoughton Musical Society formed at Stoughton, Massachusetts in 1786, from a singing class of William Billings.[3]

Many of these societies, however, soon outgrew the limitations of their singing school tunebooks, and undertook to perform more extended works by European composers. Chase states:

> The singing school, as an institution, developed in two directions. In the cities it prepared the way for the formation of choirs and choral societies, such as the celebrated Handel and Haydn Society of Boston, [founded 1815[4]], devoted chiefly to the performance of music imported from Europe. In the rural areas, mainly in the South and Middle West, it formed the foundation for a homespun hymnody and for a communal type of singing that kept alive many of the old New England tunes along with the later "revival spirituals" and camp-meeting songs that were a distinct product of the American frontier.[5]

Four-shape Singing Conventions

In Chapter 2 it was mentioned how the itinerant singing school master was crowded out of the burgeoning cities of the Northeast and into the frontiers of the South and Middle West. Due to the social isolation in the rural areas, the singing schools and their adjunct singing conventions were a welcome opportunity for social contact. Almost all of the songbooks used in these schools and conventions were published in the shaped note notation first appearing in Little and Smith's *The Easy Instructor* in 1801.[6]

Southern Musical Convention (Sacred Harp)

The first Southern singing society has been stated as being

76

the Southern Musical Convention, formed in Upson County, Georgia in 1845 by Benjamin Franklin White.[7]

There had undoubtedly been other informal singing conventions in the South before the formation of the Southern Musical Convention.[8] These could have been unstructured social and musical occasions, perhaps prompted by a church or family homecoming. Reynolds suggests also that the economic necessity for circuit-riding ministers, and other shared-time clergy, for rural churches may have been a primary factor in the origination of singing conventions. Sundays without a preacher afforded opportune moments for rural musicians to gather for group singing. "Fifth Sundays," that is, the last Sunday of a month containing five Sundays, were even better opportunities for several congregations to join for informal music activities.[9] Before the establishment of denominational hymnals, many times the only songbooks available for these informal singings were those which had been used in the singing schools.

The Southern Musical Convention was quite unique, however. It was organized on a formal basis, with elected officers, recorded regular meetings, and adopted constitutional regulations.[10] This convention became a model for many of the other formal conventions which were subsequently formed.

A unique aspect of the Southern Musical Convention, one which separated it from the earlier northern singing societies and from many of the southern conventions, was its adoption of a single book as the official songbook for the organization. This book was *The Sacred Harp*.[11] Conventions devoted exclusively to the singing of music from *The Sacred Harp* have continued to the present day. The survival of this book from among the numerous four-shaped tunebooks used in early singing conventions can be attributed directly to its singular usage in the organizations founded by Benjamin F. White.[12]

The Southern Musical Convention became the largest and most influential of the southern singing societies, and remained so until 1867, when its policy of adhering to only one tunebook was changed. Jackson states:

> In 1867 the tendency toward separatism which was inevitable among such individualists as these appeared in the ranks of the

Southern Convention singers. It was all started, as it seems from James's account, by E.T. Pound of Barnesville. Being himself author of a number of song books he saw in this convention a fine sales opportunity. So he and his friends got the convention to give up its *Sacred Harp* "closed shop" policy and to allow the use of "other books" as well. Pound was elected president. The intransigent Sacred Harpers, "after wrangling for some time," deserted the Southern, and went over to the Chattahoochee Convention [which had been organized in 1852[13]].[14]

The subsequent history of the Southern Musical Convention is not clear from secondary sources. According to Jackson, B.F. White may have been re-elected President of the Convention at a later date,[15] and if so, the Convention may have returned to *The Sacred Harp* as its official tunebook. Ellington, in 1970, stated that the Original B.F. White Interstate Sacred Harp Singing Convention claimed to be the continuation of the Southern Musical Convention, "and in 1964 was reported to have held its one hundred and twentieth annual session."[16] Neither the Southern Musical Convention nor the Interstate Convention is listed in the *Directory and Minutes of Annual Sacred Harp Singings 1975–1976.*[17]

Other Four-shape Tunebooks

The Sacred Harp was not the only four-shape tunebook used in the South. Jackson published in 1933 what he considered "as complete a list as [could] be made at present" of song books appearing in the four-shape notation.[18] This list is shown as Figure 3. The asterisks indicate those books compiled by southerners.

To the writer's knowledge there has been no attempt to update Jackson's list in its entirety, although several studies have been made of individual books that he listed. Eskew documents fifteen tunebooks which were printed in shaped notes before 1816. All of these were published in the North. Eskew's list is shown as Figure 4, with the asterisks indicating three books also shown in Jackson's listing.

Year of Publication	Name of Book	Author	Author's Home	Place of Printing
1798......	Easy Instructor	Wm. Little & Wm. Smith	?	Albany.
1803......	Musical Primer	Andrew Law	Cheshire, Conn.	Cambridge, Mass.
1810......	Repository of Sacred Music	John Wyeth	Harrisburg, Pa.	Harrisburg, Pa.
*1815(?).....	Kentucky Harmony	Ananias Davisson	Virginia	Harrisonburg, Va.
*1816......	Choral-Music	Joseph Funk	Mountain Valley, Va.	Harrisonburg, Va.
1816......	Columbian Harmonist	Timothy Flint	?	Cincinnati, O.
*1817......	Kentucky Harmonist	Samuel L. Metcalf	Lexington, Ky.	Cincinnati, O.
*1820......	Suppl. to Kentucky Harmony	Ananias Davisson	Virginia	Harrisonburg, Va.
*1820......	Missouri Harmony	Allen D. Carden	St. Louis, Mo.	Cincinnati, O.
*1820......	Songs of Zion	James P. Carrell	Lebanon, Va.	Harrisonburg, Va.
1821 or 1822	Methodist Harmonist	Printed by Waugh and Mason	?	New York.
1822......	Sacred Music	Seth Ely	Germantown, Pa.	?
*1824......	Western Harmony	Allen D. Carden & Samuel J. Rogers	Nashville, Tenn.	Nashville, Tenn.
*1825......	Columbian Harmony	William Moore	Wilson County, Tenn.	Cincinnati, O.
*1826......	Western Harmonic Companion	James W. Palmer	Lexington, Ky.	Cincinnati, O.
1829......	Union Harmony	John Cole	?	Baltimore, Md.
*1831......	Virginia Harmony	James P. Carrell and David S. Clayton	Lebanon, Virginia	Winchester, Va.
1831......	Western Lyre	Wm. B. Snyder & W. B. Chappell	?	?
*1831......	American or Union Harmonist	Wm. R. Rhinehart	Maryland	Chambersburg, Pa.
*1832......	Genuine Church Music	Joseph Funk	Mountain Valley, Va.	Winchester, Va.
1832......	Sacred Harp	James H. Hickok	Lewiston, Pa.	?
*1832......	Lexington Cabinet	Robert Willis	Lexington, Ky.	?
1834......	Evangelical Musick	J. H. Hickok & G. Fleming	Carlisle, Pa.	?
1834......	Ohio Sacred Harp	Lowell Mason and Timothy Mason	Boston, Mass. and Cincinnati, O.	Cincinnati, O.
1834......	Church Harmony	Henry Smith	Chambersburg, Pa.	Chambersburg, Pa.
*1835......	Southern Harmony	William Walker	Spartanburg, S. C.	New Haven, Conn.
1835......	Introduction to Sacred Music	Amos S. Hayden	Ohio	Pittsburgh, Pa.
*1836......	The Valley Harmonist	J. W. Steffey	New Market, Va.	Winchester, Va.
1837......	The Harmonist	(Printed by Mason & Lane)	?	New York, N. Y.
*1837......	Union Harmony	William Caldwell	Maryville, Tenn.	Maryville, Tenn.
*1838......	Knoxville Harmony	John B. Jackson	Madisonville, Tenn.	Madisonville & Pumpkintown, Tenn.
*1844......	Sacred Harp	B. F. White and E. J. King	Hamilton, Ga.	Philadelphia, Pa.
1844......	Western Harp	Samuel Wakefield	?	Pittsburgh, Pa.
*1845......	Southern and Western Harmonist	William Walker	Spartanburg, S. C.	?
1846......	Southern Melodist	George Hood	Massachusetts	?
1848......	Sacred Harmony	Samuel Jackson	?	New York, N. Y.
*1848......	Hesperian Harp......	William Hauser	Wadley, Ga.	Philadelphia, Pa.
*1855......	Social Harp	John G. McCurry	Andersonville, Ga.	Philadelphia, Pa.

Figure 3. Song books in four-shape notation as listed by G.P. Jackson in *White Spirituals in the Southern Uplands*, p. 25.

79

William Little and William Smith, *The Easy Instructor* (Albany, 1802)*

Andrew Law, *The Art of Singing* (Cambridge, 1803);* and *Harmonic Companion* (Philadelphia, 1807)

Charles Woodward, *Ecclesiae Harmonia* (Philadelphia, 1807)

Andrew Adgate, *Philadelphia Harmony* (Philadelphia, 1807)

Nathan Chapin and Joseph Dickerson, *The Musical Instructor* (Philadelphia, 1808)

Joseph Doll, *Der Leichte Unterricht* (Harrisburg, 1810)*

John Wyeth, *Repository of Sacred Music Part Second* (Harrisburg, 1813)

Robert Patterson, *Patterson's Church Music* (Cincinnati, 1813)

Freeman Lewis, *Beauties of Harmony* (Cincinnati, 1814)

Joseph Doll, *Der Leichte Unterrich* Vol. 2 (Harrisburg, 1815)

John M'Cormick, *Western Harmonist* (Cincinnati, 1815)

Figure 4. Shape-note tunebooks published before 1816 as listed by H.L. Eskew.[19]

Annanias Davisson, *An Introduction to Sacred Music* (Harrisonburg, Virginia, 1821); and *A Small Collection of Sacred Music* (Mount-Vernon, Virginia, ca 1826)

Wheeler Gillet, *The Virginia Sacred Minstrel* (Winchester, Virginia, 1817)

James M. Boyd, *The Virginia Sacred Musical Repository* (Winchester, Virginia, 1818)

George Hendrickson, *The Union Harmony* (Mountain Valley, Virginia, 1848)

Levi C. Myers, *Manual of Sacred Music* (Mountain Valley, Virginia, 1853)

Figure 5. Additional four-shape notation tunebooks as cited by H.L. Eskew.[20]

Eskew's dissertation presents a detailed examination of six of the 1816 and later tunebooks listed by Jackson in Figure 3. He also discusses six additional tunebooks published in the South after 1816 which were not included in Jackson's list. These latter six tunebooks are listed as Figure 5.

For the most part, however, these books are of interest only as historical documents. Very few are currently used as standard musical materials by any viable musical organizations.

With the exception of the "Big Singing" at Benton, Kentucky, which continues to use William Walker's *Southern Harmony;*[21] the University of Georgia sing, which uses John Gordon McCurry's *The Social Harp;*[22] and the North Georgia-Tennessee Sacred Harp Singing Convention, which includes singings from William Walker's *Christian Harmony,*[23] printed in seven-shape notation, most of the four-shape "fasola" singing today is from *The Sacred Harp.*

Ellington, in 1964 and 1965, made an attempt to document the major Sacred Harp conventions in the South. Due to the fact that he does not tabulate them but incorporates the data into his text, it is difficult to ascertain exactly how many conventions are extent in the various states. The Georgia descriptions will serve to illustrate:

Sacred Harp singings in Georgia were less numerous than in Alabama, but Georgia singers took pride in the eighty to one hundred singings held each year within their state and were concerned about the quality of their singings. In addition to the Cooper book sings held in the southwest corner of the state, there were four other groups of Sacred Harp singers in Georgia. The smallest of these was the North Georgia-Tennessee Sacred Harp Singing Convention which had only about four Sacred Harp singings each year. The remaining seven or so singings of this group were from *Christian Harmony,* a seven-shape book compiled by William Walker, White's brother-in-law. A second group was closely associated with the Original B.F. White Interstate Sacred Harp Singing Convention and with the Stone Mountain Sacred Harp Singing Convention. The former of these claimed to be a continuation of the old Southern Musical Convention and in 1964 was reported to have held its one hundred and twentieth annual session. These two conventions, in addition to the eight other annual sings and twenty-four Tuesday night singings, used the

James L. White (1911) revision of the *Sacred Harp*. A third group of active singers was centered in west-central Georgia and to the north in the counties of Carroll, Cobb, Coweta, Douglas, Fulton, Haralson, Heard, Paulding, and Polk. The Denson revisions were used by these singers, and a number of persons from this area were important in Denson revision activities, including the Sacred Harp Publishing Company. Two of the more than forty singings in this area were the Georgia State Sacred Harp Convention held in March on the "fourth Sunday and Saturday before" and the Chattahoochee Sacred Harp Musical Convention, so important in the history of the Sacred Harp singing movement, on the "first Sunday and Saturday before" in August. The fourth singing group functioned primarily from within the south Georgia Sacred Harp Singing Convention held on the first Sunday in November. The approximately fifteen annual singings of this group used the James (1911) book and the Denson revisions. The membership of this group was small but it was composed of singers from all over south Georgia and northern Florida, who were firm in their resolve to remain true to their beloved old songs, sung in the same spirit they had been for over one hundred and twenty years.[24]

Ellington does provide a summary, however:

In summary . . . there were an estimated one hundred and fifty Cooper book singings in Alabama and Florida, twenty-four other Florida singings; fifteen South Georgia and thirty west-central Georgia Denson revision singings; thirty-four White book singings in the Atlanta area; four other singings in north Georgia; seven Tennessee and fifty-eight Mississippi singings utilizing the Denson revision; three hundred and eight Alabama singings from the Denson revisions; and twenty-four Texas sings from the Cooper book. These totaled six hundred and fifty-four Sacred Harp singings for the year.[25]

Sacred Harp as a Generic Term

To a certain extent, the term "Sacred Harp" has come to mean not only the music from any of the several editions of the tunebook by that name, but also inclusive of singings from any of the remaining four-shape books. This is demonstrated in the *Proceedings* of the South Georgia Sacred Harp Singing Convention, where the By-Laws state that only *The Sacred Harp* is to be used as a songbook for the convention;[26] but one of the scheduled sings is at the University of Georgia where McCurry's *Social Harp* is used.[27]

In an even broader sense, "Sacred Harp" is used as an inclusive term for *a cappella* singing from even the early oblong seven-shape tunebooks, such as Walker's *Christian Harmony*[28] or Joseph Funk's *Harmonia Sacra.*[29]

Sacred Harp Singings

Sacred Harp singing, using the term in the larger sense, has many unique characteristics. Many of these characteristics are social as well as musical. Ellington describes a "typical" Sacred Harp singing:

Sacred Harp sings of the 1960s resembled those of many years ago. The faces and modes of transportation and dress were changed but the songs and friendly spirit remained the same.

A typical singing of the sixties began at nine o'clock in the morning with singers arriving, bringing their own books, and exchanging greetings and brief bits of news. The interior of the church, schoolhouse, or other meeting hall had been put in readiness with an ample number of chairs, pews, or benches arranged facing each other in a hollow square.

Promptly the "class" was called to order by the Chairman of last year's singing. He led two or three songs, and called for an opening prayer. After this the election of officers was held for the choosing of a Chairman, a Secretary-Treasurer, and a Chaplain.

The newly elected Chairman then appointed members to the Arranging Committee, whose job it was to assure that all attending felt welcome and had an opportunity to lead if they so desired. A Finance Committee and a Memorial Committee to plan a service for Sacred Harp singers and relatives who died during the previous year were also appointed.

The "business session" thus having been disposed of, the group began the real business of the day, the singing of Sacred

Harp songs. The chairman of the Arranging Committee called in pairs the names of successive leaders, mixing personalities to insure a balance of men and women of varying ages and of leaders who were known to be partial to specific types of songs. Each person in turn led a "lesson," usually two songs of his own choosing. If he was an experienced singer, he could "key" his own song; otherwise he would ask someone else, usually appointed by the Arranging Committee, to "hist" the pitch for him.

The rather coveted position of "Keyer" was particularly important to the success of the singing. The person appointed needed not only a good sense of pitch but also a thorough knowledge of the songs and the singing capabilities of the group at differing times of the day. Many pieces were not sung at the pitch level at which they were written but were adjusted for singing comfort.

In some singings the first songs were led by the elected officers followed in turn by appointed members of committees. The remaining people then led as they were called. Thus the singing progressed through the morning, with only a brief recess, until noon when the group was dismissed for one hour to have "dinner on the ground." This traditional meal was usually spread in picnic fashion on tables in the adjoining yard.

Sacred Harp women took great pride in the food they provided for these occasions and their results presented a culinary repast of quality, quantity and variety.

Despite the sumptuous nature of the lunch, a Sacred Harp sing was primarily an occasion for singing, and all eating and the friendly chatter which accompanied it were concluded in time for the ladies to put away their things and be ready to return to the building when the Chairman called the "class" back into session with the singing of another Sacred Harp song.

Shortly after the afternoon session began the Chairman called for the Memorial Service or "Memorial Lessons." These were usually led by close relatives or friends of the departed ones and often consisted of a brief word of eulogy and one or two songs which were favorites of the deceased.

The remainder of the afternoon was given to more singing in much the same manner as it had been done for decades. The leader announced the number of his selection and a pitch was given; the voices sounded a hearty "Fa," "Sol," or "La"; and all parts launched into the singing of the notes using the four syllable

84

names so much a part of the Sacred Harp tradition. After this the text was sung.

As the four o'clock hour approached the Chairman stood and announced number sixty-two "Parting Hand," and the "brothers" and "sisters" performed a custom of long standing in the Sacred Harp movement. As the piece was sung the members of the group circulated and shook hands with one another in a sign of farewell and affection.[30]

The above description is important as a reference point for comparison with the later gospel singing conventions and gospel sings. The social aspects are quite similar. The music is very different, however, and it is beyond the scope of this study to detail the unique characteristics of Sacred Harp music. For purpose of this study, the most obvious difference between Sacred Harp sings and gospel singing conventions is that Sacred Harp music is performed *a cappella* and gospel music is almost always accompanied.

Transition from Four-shape to Seven-shape Singing Conventions

It was previously mentioned that the Southern Musical Convention was unique in its adherence to only one publication as its official songbook. Other conventions were not as strict.

An interesting sequence of newspaper accounts, discovered in the writer's field research,[31] serves to illustrate how the transition from four-shape singing to seven-shape singing may have come about. These accounts are in reference to the Fourth of July singings in Upson County, Georgia.

As stated earlier, many singing conventions in the South were begun in conjunction with church or family homecomings. Other favorite opportunities for "singings" were, and are, national holidays. The Fourth of July singing at Shiloh Baptist Church in Upson County may be one of the oldest continuing activities of this sort.[32]

The first mention of the Shiloh Fourth of July singing occurs in *The Thomaston Herald* in 1872. This anonymous[33] account

85

gives a detailed description of how a singing was conducted over one hundred years ago:

FOURTH OF JULY SINGING: It is well known, especially by the singers of the county, that it has been the custom to have a singing on the 4th of July at Shiloh Church in this county. It was our pleasure to listen to the good music last Thursday. Although the weather looked threatening there was a good turnout—more than could get in the church at the same time. . . .

The first session was opened and led by Allen Reid, 30 minutes, and T.J. Blasingame, 30 minutes. Recess 10 minutes.

The second lesson led by John M. Harp, 25 minutes, and Joel Reid, 30. Recess 10.

The third by James A. Chambers, 30 minutes.

Dinner then being in order, all attention was diverted that way until half past one, when Isaac Jones led 30 minutes and C.A. Bishop 30. Recess 10, and Mr. Story and John Chambers led 30 minutes each. James A. Chambers then led 20 minutes and closed at half past four o'clock.

The occasion was one of singing pleasure with nothing to mar it except an occasional shower, which run [sic] the traders in love from their buggy retreats into the church. A little electioneering; a little love making; a little religious discussion; much good eating and a deal of singing was the order of the day.[34]

The similarity of this sing with the typical twentieth-century Sacred Harp sing previously described by Ellington is readily apparent. The items listed above as the "order of the day" have changed very little in subsequent years of southern singing conventions.

The next newspaper account, three years later, not only mentions Judge E. T. Pound, who was cited earlier in Jackson's quotation in connection with the Southern Musical Convention; it also indicates that the *Sacred Harp* was displaced by the *Gem* in the afternoon session:

THE SINGING AT SHILOH.—It has been a custom for the last ten years among the lovers of good singing to meet at Shiloh church, on the 4th of July of every year, for the purpose of having an all day singing. In pursuance of this custom it was understood

86

that last Sunday, the 4th inst., was to be celebrated in the usual way. So early in the morning, of that day, this reporter together with a friend, Mr. W.J.Z., left town for Shiloh church, where we arrived in due season. A vast crowd had already assembled, but before the exercises begun [sic] it had swollen to an almost incredible number.

About 10 o'clock it was announced that the singing would begin and in a few minutes the house was crowded to overflowing. One familiar face, however, seemed to be missing, that of Judge E.T. Pound, of Barnesville, who, heretofore, has been the leader of the singings at Shiloh. Notwithstanding his absence, his place was well filled by Mr. Chambers, of Hampton, Ga., who lead the first lesson. The class seemed to be a little "rusty" at the beginning, but soon brightened up and sung [sic] very well.

Each lesson would consume thirty minutes. So at the expiration of that time, a recess of ten minutes was given. Upon the reassembling of the class Mr. J. H. Pickard took charge and led it during the next thirty minutes. Mr. Pickard was followed by Judge Thomas J. Blasingame, the worthy Ordinary of Pike county, who soon manifested the same ability to conduct a singing that he does in administering the affairs of his county.

A respite of about two hours was then allowed for the purpose of refreshing the inner man. The good people of the surrounding country had come prepared with a bountiful supply of every thing that goes to make up a first class dinner, which seemed to be enjoyed by all with a keen relish. Dinner being over all repaired again to the church where the singing was again conducted by Mr. Chambers. The "Sacred Harp" was laid aside for the present and the "Gem," a sabbath School [sic] song book, was taken up and the hour following was devoted to singing Sabbath School songs. The young ladies from town accepted a kind invitation to join in. These songs were well rendered, the splendid bass voices of the gentlemen corresponding so well with the silvery soprano of the ladies. Mr. Wm. P. Franklin familiarly known as uncle Billy, took charge of the class for the next lesson and led them through in his usual happy style. He seemed to enjoy it better than he did his dinner. Several lessons followed this one led respectively by Messrs. Bussey, Sanders and others.[35]

The above article, again anonymous but obviously by the same author, shows that the "Sabbath School"[36] song book had gained a foothold in this particular singing convention by 1875. It will be remembered that this was the year in which Bliss and Sankey's *Gospel Hymns and Sacred Songs* was published. The *Gem* could have been a songbook with that title published by the Ruebush-Kieffer Company in 1873.[37] If so, it would have been printed in the Funk seven-shape notation.[38]

Although the above article states that the Shiloh singing had been continued on a regular basis for ten years, this one espoused by Judge E.T. Pound says EIGHTEEN:

> REGRET we did not have the pleasure of attending the Singing Convention at Shiloh on the 4th. We are informed by our old friend Judge E.T. Pound, that there was quite a large concourse of people in attendance and that it was indeed "a most enjoyable occasion." This is the eighteenth annual singing at that church. The good citizens who live near furnished more nice barbecue & c., than their visiting friends could dispose of—quite a feast.[39]

Based upon the above newspaper articles, the beginning of this singing could have been from as early as 1859.[40]

Other than the question of whether this can be considered a "First" Fourth of July Singing Convention, a point to be made from the above discourse is that whereas many Sacred Harp conventions were "closed shop,"[41] as Jackson put it, others in the same locality[42] enjoyed using a wider variety of singing materials.

Decline of Four-shape Singing Conventions

The Civil War was a turning point in many ways in the South and it also had its effect on the singing conventions. To a great extent it marked the end of the four-shape books and their singings although, as has been shown, the "fasola" tradition still has a large number of strong adherents. Jackson acknowledges, however, that "those books . . . and individuals, though *in* the present age are not *of* it."[43]

As was mentioned in Chapter 2, no more new compilations in the four-shape format were published after the Civil War. The

War came just at the time when the four-shape notation was giving way to the seven-shape notation and this, combined with the fact that almost all of the older books had been printed in the North, served to hasten their obsolescence.[44] Jackson describes the new era:

> With the close of the Civil War a new era dawned in the singing practices of the rural South, an era that might be termed that of the gospel-hymn-tinged religious music in shape notation.[45]

Jackson deliberately uses the term "gospel-hymn-tinged" rather than "gospel hymn" because the indigenous southern music had different characteristics from the popular hymns of the Sankey and Bliss genre. The main difference was that the music was created for those who had learned to read music by means of the shaped note singing schools and these singers wished vitality and variety in all of the voice parts in order to challenge their reading skills.

Southernization of Northern Choral Writing

Northern songs which had failed to have this variety in the harmony parts had become "southernized,"[46] a term first used, it is believed, by William Hauser in his *Hesperian Harp*.[47] Jackson shows the effect of "southernizing" in the alto part of "Prescott" which appears in the *Christian Minstrel*,[48] a northern publication. This northern alto part is shown in Figure 6.

Figure 6. A northern alto part. (*Christian Minstrel*, p. 283.)

Hauser's "southernizing" of the same song's alto part, depicted in Figure 7, shows the difference:

89

Figure 7. "Southernizing" of a northern alto part. (*Hesperian Harp*, p. 347.)

Jackson summarizes the change:

It will be noticed that the ... northern alto has become southernized into a sequence that sounds like a fairly good independent tune. What violence such changes may have done to the harmony seems to have been looked upon as a secondary matter. The first rule was to make each part melodically interesting.[49]

This southernizing was a necessity for the songs used in the singing schools, and their corollary singing conventions, in order to keep adequate numbers of people interested in each of the four parts. The southern publishing company that became the leader in supplying this need in the post-Civil War tunebooks was the Ruebush-Kieffer Company, located in the Shenandoah Valley of Virginia.

Influence of Ruebush-Kieffer Company

Ruebush-Kieffer Company: Early History (Joseph Funk)

The history of the Ruebush-Kieffer Company dates back to 1816 when Joseph Funk, whose grandfather had emigrated from Germany in 1719, published his first book. This book was entitled *Choral Music*[50] and was printed in German with the Little and Smith four-shape notation.[51]

It was not until sixteen years later that Funk was to publish his second book, which he named *Genuine Church Music.*[52] This was printed in English but still continued to use the four-shape notation. With the fifth edition of this book in 1851, the title was

90

changed to *Harmonia Sacra, Being a Compilation of Genuine Church Music*.[53] This was published in seven-shape notation. Funk had devised his own three additional shapes. According to Eskew, this book was still in print in 1966.[54]

Quickly nicknamed the "Hominy Soaker,"[55] this book was widely used, not only in the South, but as far north as Canada. According to Wayland, Funk's books were sold in Virginia, Georgia, Illinois, Ohio, Maryland, North Carolina, Indiana, Pennsylvania, Iowa, Missouri, and Canada West.[56] Wayland adds, "Apparently, the best individual buyer of the Funk music from 1856 to 1858 was Charles Beazley, of Crawfordville, Taliferro County, Georgia."[57]

Although *Harmonia Sacra* contained exclusively religious materials it was never used as a church hymnal. Noah D. Showalter, a descendant of Joseph Funk, in his preface to the twentieth edition, states:

> It has always been a singing school book and was used by all denominations, and was never adopted by any church as a Hymnal, although it was made up of the very songs that were used in the various Church Hymnals.[58]

Joseph Funk, Senior, died in 1862. After a hiatus during the Civil War, his sons took over the family business. They were not successful, however, and were eventually forced to close it in approximately 1876.[59]

Ruebush-Kieffer Company

But Funk's legacy was not to pass away. It was taken up by his grandson, Aldine S. Kieffer. Kieffer, with his brother-in-law Ephraim Ruebush, was to become the leading force in the perpetuation of shaped note hymnody in the South.

These two men, interestingly enough, had fought on opposite sides during the Civil War. Apparently there was no personal animosity between the two of them because Ruebush was instrumental in getting Kieffer released from a Union prisoner of-war camp,[60] and they remained in business together until 1901 when Kieffer retired.[61]

This Ruebush-Kieffer Company, as it eventually came to be known,[62] revived two of the elder Joseph Funk's ideas that were to have enormous impact on the future of gospel music in the South. These were the publication of a periodical, the *Musical Million,*[63] and the formation of a Normal Music School for the purpose of training singing school teachers.

The Musical Million Periodical

The *Musical Million* was, as Kieffer called it, the "foster-child"[64] of the short-lived *Southern Musical Advocate and Singer's Friend,*[65] which had been begun by Joseph Funk and Sons in 1859. According to Morton, the newer publication put out its first issue on New Year's Day of 1870 and within a year the subscription list had grown to twelve hundred.[66] By 1911, Morton could state: "The 'Musical Million' has now a regular circulation of 10,000 copies, and goes into Canada as well as into all states of the Union."[67]

Hall, who examined the history of the publication in detail, writes:

> The *Musical Million* became the most popular Southern journal for the following reasons. First, its huge subscription list outclassed all its competitors. . . . Second, the quality of its journalism was unmatched. . . . Third, its longevity outlasted its competitors. The *Musical Million* was published continuously from January, 1870, to December, 1914, a total of forty-five years.[68]

Kieffer was editor of the *Musical Million* for thirty of these years and was, according to Morton, "no half way advocate of the shaped note, and his critics were very liable to shatter their lances on his shield."[69]

Because of Kieffer's unrelenting championing of the shaped note system over that of the "round note knights" and their "monkish customs," as he called them,[70] it is unquestionable but that this magazine was greatly significant in the perpetuation of shaped notation in the music of southern rurals. Jackson considered the *Musical Million* to be "the one journal that was, so to speak, the official organ of rural music [and] the greatest single factor in the unification of notation."[71]

Virginia Normal Music School

The second of Joseph Funk's ideas, the normal music school,[72] may actually have been more influential in subsequent years than was the *Musical Million*. Funk and Sons had opened a boarding school for the training of singing school teachers in 1859. It will be remembered that this was also the first year of Funk's *Musical Advocate*. In fact, an advertisement describing the new boarding school appeared in the first issue of that magazine.[73] Later, Ruebush and Kieffer determined to begin a normal school themselves. In August 1874, they opened the Virginia Normal Music School in New Market, Virginia.[74] Benjamin C. Unseld was the principal, with P.J. Merges assisting. The course of study included: harmony, thorough bass, piano, organ, voice building; reading of round notes, tonic sol-fa and seven-shape notes; practice in church psalmody, glee singing, and oratorio.[75] The reading systems other than from shaped notes were dropped after the first session at the insistence of Kieffer.[76]

Unseld maintained his position as principal for eight years, and after leaving the Ruebush-Kieffer school, taught other normal schools in North Carolina, Kentucky, Tennessee, and Missouri. He spent the last eleven years of his life at the Vaughan Conservatory, Lawrenceburg, Tennessee.[77] C. C. Stafford, a highly revered gospel music teacher himself, states, ". . . it can be just [sic] claimed for Professor Unseld that he is the musical father or grandfather of nearly all the successful normal teachers of the South."[78]

Of the hundreds of music teachers who studied under Unseld, either in New Market, Virginia, or in other normal schools patterned after it, two especially deserve mention at this time. They were James D. Vaughan and Anthony Johnson

93

Showalter. These two men, who will be discussed in greater detail in Chapter 5, became successful teachers themselves. Each began his own highly influential publishing concern, patterned after the Ruebush-Kieffer model.[79]

Seven-shape Singing Conventions

Convention Songbooks

Singing conventions throughout the South used song books from these and other companies in ever-increasing quantities. The companies began publishing yearly "Convention Books" in paperbound upright volumes comprised of selected reprintings; and a large number of recently written songs by the publishers themselves, by singing school teachers, and by other rural composers. When that was not enough to supply the demand they would make twice-yearly issues, and occasionally would even release quarterly compilations. In 1933, Jackson made an attempt to estimate the number of new songs which were composed annually for these convention books:

> How many songs, produced thus, are published annually in the shape-note books? An estimate is all that is possible . . . Multiply the sixty (average) new songs in each book by twenty-five—the number of different books per year—and we have an estimated fifteen hundred new songs, all the music of which is made by southerners, appearing every twelve months.[80]

The appearance of the annual or semi-annual songbooks was an exciting event for rural musicians.

Informal Singing Conventions

A "typical" Sacred Harp singing convention was described previously by Ellington; and the transition from four-shape conventions to seven-shape conventions was shown in the newspa-

94

per articles previously cited. Becker, in a biography of the
Singing Speer Family, captures the atmosphere of an early gospel singing convention, sometimes called an all-day singing:

It was the first Sunday in August, and that meant all day singing
and dinner on the ground in Winston County, Alabama. . . . By
ten o'clock the church would be packed and children would be sit-
ting on window sills and all over the front steps. The straight
wooden pews would grow progressively harder as the day went
on. But that wouldn't matter. They had come to sing. . . .

The church hadn't been this full since last August. Families
crammed themselves tightly into rows and picked up the new convention songbooks that were already on the seats. It was fun to
look over the new songs, and see what some of the well-known
songwriters had come up with this year. Each man who wrote regularly for a certain publishing company had his own number, and
it never changed. A.M. Pace, one of the Vaughan Company's outstanding contributors, had number 110. Dad Speer's number in
the Vaughan books was 78.

Now Brother Harding [in charge of the singing on that particular Sunday] stepped to the platform. Singing time had started.
Each conductor on the list planned to lead one song. Often impromptu quarters organized on the spot. The conductor would
say, "Brother Miller, why don't you get a group together and sing
something special for us?"

So Brother Miller would leaf through the book to find a song
that looked interesting and ask three of his friends to join him. Of
course they had never seen the song before, but that didn't matter. Most of them had been to singing school, and sight reading
certainly was no problem. Often groups born at an all day singing
would stay together for years. . . .

By the time the afternoon was over, the crowd had sung their
way through a good share of the songs in the new convention
book. . . . Children might get fidgety and wander outside to play
around the wagons, but the grownups sang until they couldn't
sing any more.[81]

Not only does this account indicate the delight in the new
convention songbooks, it describes the formation of "special" ensembles. These "special" groups will be discussed in greater detail subsequently.

95

It was previously mentioned that *a cappella* singing was a distinction of Sacred Harp conventions. The use of an instrumental accompaniment, generally performed on the piano, is an equally distinctive characteristic of gospel singing conventions. In a description of a singing convention, similar in concept to Ellington's description of a Sacred Harp sing, Fleming mentions the role of the accompanist:

> As the accompanist approaches his instrument, the song leader announces the name of the book and the number of the selection which he plans to lead, the accompanist plays a short introduction taken from the theme of the song, and the singing gets underway. . . .
>
> The singing is done in four parts, with the accompanist doubling the voices, adding flourishes here and there as his skill may make possible; and frequently he will add a cadential formula between stanzas of the song. The sound of the group might impress the cultured listener as untutored, and the facts will bear this out. . . . One thing that they can do, though, and do well, is to sight-read music printed in shape-notation. . . . I have known a group of these singers to sing lustily, forcefully, and with amazing accuracy, song after song which has just appeared in a new publication, and of which they could have had no foreknowledge. . . . [82]

It should also be emphasized that the accompanist is sight-reading as well. The tempo at which the songs are taken is what Housewright calls "primarily upbeat."[83] This applies to the "slow" songs as well as to the "fast" ones. Although there are some rhythmic jazz elements to the songs and in their improvised accompaniments, the music could not be considered jazz. For want of a better term, Housewright calls this music "religiously fast."[84]

One additional occasional for informal singing conventions is New Year's Eve. Many of the sings on this date have evolved elaborate traditions, but the distinctive feature of most of these sings is the use of the "old books" until midnight, and the sight-reading from the "new books" in the early hours of the New Year. This can be a highly emotional experience, especially if composers are present. Edwards, speaking about himself, relates such an event:

96

Edwards states now that his greatest thrill in gospel music was not in singing before huge crowds, or publishing his own songbooks or sheet music, but in hearing Mr. Pace lead his song first when the new books were opened after midnight at the New Year's Eve singing at Pell City, Alabama, on January [sic] 31, 1944. That was really a proud night for him.[85]

State and Wide-area Singing Conventions

One of the earliest, if not the first, of the singing conventions to assume a state name was the South Georgia Singing Convention, now called the Old South Georgia Singing Convention. This was founded by William Jackson Royal in 1875.[86] Royal was also founder, in 1893, of the Royal [Family] Singing Convention in Mystic, Georgia, held annually in almost the same location in Irwin County since that time.[87]

The first state convention of seven-shaped singers[88] is generally considered to have been the Alabama State Convention which was originated in 1932 in Birmingham, Alabama.[89] Although the singings held in local churches in the rural areas often have their own formalities, the state and other wide-area conventions are marked by an even greater formality. Such associations have elected officers, usually a president or chairman, a secretary and a treasurer. Other officers may be elected as necessary. The chairman or president is not an honorary position. Upon him is placed almost the entire responsibility for the success of the convention. He has the power to appoint as many assistants as are needed to accomplish the tasks at hand. These tasks include ensuring an adequate supply of songbooks, arranging for lodgings for out-of-town singers, providing the meals and refreshments, ensuring that accompanists will be present, and arranging for public address systems if such are to be used. It is also the responsibility of the president or chairman to ensure that all visiting leaders and singers are allowed to appear on the stage or pulpit area at least once during the convention. At the larger sings this is accomplished by calling groups by community or county to appear and lead *en masse*.[90]

97

The By-Laws of the Georgia State Singing Convention[91] specifically state that no musical instrument is barred from being used as an accompaniment. At one time in the 1976 session two pianos, an electronic organ, and two accordions accompanied the singing of approximately 600 participants.[92]

At the time of this writing there appear to be state conventions in the following states: Alabama, Arkansas, California, Florida, Georgia, Louisiana, Michigan, North Carolina, New Mexico, Ohio, Oklahoma, South Carolina, Tennessee, Texas, and West Virginia.[93]

National Gospel Singing Convention

Plans for a national convention were made during the 1936 Alabama State Singing Convention; and the National Gospel Singing Convention was formally organized in 1937 in Birmingham, Alabama.[94] Adger M. Pace, referred to previously in both Becker's and Edward's quotations and composer of one of the songs performed by a group in the Field Research sample, was elected the first president of this Convention.[95] The National Convention differs from the state and wide-area conventions in that it is conducted primarily by the songbook publishers. Although officers are elected annually, a Supreme Council of publisher representatives has final authority. In order to ensure that each publisher is fairly represented at the Convention, the By-Laws delineate a strict procedure:

> Each publisher member shall be accorded equal showing in the convention, but to be represented on the floor of the convention in order, he must have at least three different leaders or three different groups of singers. *The same singer or singers shall not be permitted to occupy the floor twice in successive order.* In other words, if only one representative of a publisher be present, he or she must take his or her third turn around and the number of encores each singer or singers shall have shall be determined by the audience, at the discretion of the directors.[96]

In order to keep overt competition to a minimum, and also to

98

ensure that the Convention remain a group-singing activity, the By-Laws further state:

> . . . no two special singers or two groups of special singers shall immediately succeed each other without one or more intervening chorus numbers, unless such cannot be avoided. Personal introductions of special singers shall not be permitted by any one unless called for by the chair.[97]

Current Activity: Publishers

Although singing conventions are still very active and singing schools are still being taught, this aspect of gospel music can no longer be considered the area of paramount gospel music activity. For example, Jackson, in 1933, listed thirty publishers of seven-shape books. He says:

> This list includes all, as far as I have been able to ascertain, of those southern firms who put out such books. It does not, however, include the various denominational publishing firms or those northern concerns which send shape-note books into the southern territory.[98]

Of those thirty publishers listed in 1933, only five remain today. These are:

Benson Publishing, Nashville, Tennessee;
Hartford Music Company, Powell, Missouri;
Stamps-Baxter Music, Dallas, Texas;
James D. Vaughan, Music Publisher, Cleveland, Tennessee;
Winsett Music Company, Dayton, Tennessee.[99]

The Hartford, Stamps-Baxter, and Vaughan companies have been purchased by other publishing concerns who retain the former name to identify certain of their publications. The Benson and Winsett companies, although publishing music in shaped notes, do not publish the small convention books.

A total of seven[100] music publishers provided convention books for the 1976 National Gospel Singing Convention. These, therefore, can be considered the most active companies in this field. These are:

James D. Vaughan, Music Publisher, Cleveland, Tennessee;
Tennessee Music Company, Cleveland, Tennessee;
Leoma Music Company, Leoma, Tennessee;
National Music Company, Coleman, Texas;
Convention Music Company, Gallant, Texas;
Jeffress Music Company, Crossett, Arkansas;
Stamps-Baxter Music Company, Dallas, Texas.[101]

Besides these seven, two additional publishers of convention books are known to the writer. These are the Hartford Music Company, previously mentioned in reference to Jackson's 1933 list;[102] and the Watson Music Company, Heflin, Alabama.[103] Although both of these companies published convention books in 1975, apparently they were unable to provide books for the 1976 National Convention.

From all accounts, gospel singing conventions are not as large now as they were in the 1930s and 1940s; yet they are still well attended and their adherents are fierce supporters. Connor B. Hall, editor for both the Tennessee and Vaughan music companies, states that his companies' sales of convention books in the past year exceeded all previous records.[104] He attributes this increase in sales to the formation of numerous small conventions instead of the more conspicuous large conventions of previous years.

Current Activity: Shaped Note Singing Schools

As closely as can be ascertained, there are presently four permanently established music schools that teach shaped note hymnody. These schools would be the nearest equivalent of a continuation of the tradition begun by the Virginia Normal Music School of Ruebush and Kieffer in 1874. These schools are:

Gospel Singers of America School of Music, Pass-Christian, Texas;

Jeffress School of Music, Crossett, Arkansas;

National School of Music, Roanoke, Alabama;

National School of Gospel Music, Murray State College, Murray, Kentucky.

The last of the four schools shown above is more oriented to the stage performance aspect of gospel music than to the singing convention tradition. These schools run from three to four weeks in the summer. They combine musical instruction with a summer camp atmosphere and their students are generally college-age or younger.

Itinerant ten-day singing schools are still conducted by individuals in many areas of the South. This activity has decreased considerably from what it had been prior to the consolidation of county schools in the South. Consolidation into large school systems brought about many educational advantages for young southerners, including improved opportunities for musical training. Nevertheless, some teachers such as Hyman Brown of Commerce, Georgia can boast of teaching singing schools in various locations as often as fifty weeks out of the year.[105]

Current Activity: Singing Convention Periodicals

Insofar as known, there is only one gospel music periodical with a wide circulation that addresses itself to the needs of the singing convention folk.[106] This is *Vaughan's Family Visitor,* published by James D. Vaughan, Music Publisher, Cleveland, Tennessee.[107] This sixteen-page magazine is similar to the earlier Ruebush-Kieffer *Musical Million* in that it contains brief articles and columns pertaining to gospel singing, and includes news items of interest to its constituency. A listing of scheduled gospel singing conventions appears in each issue. The October-November 1976 issue, for example, lists a total of 155 singing conventions scheduled in fourteen states. The editor, however, is reasonably certain that this listing is indicative of only ten percent or less of the number of singings that actually take place.[108]

Gospel Sings

Becker's description of an all day singing, quoted earlier, pictured the formation of an impromptu quartet which was to provide "special" singing for the assembled "class." This formation of special music ensembles led to what can be considered the mainstream of gospel music activity today, the Gospel Sing. The term gospel sing is generally used to denote that gospel music activity in which the majority of those who attend act as an audience and do not participate in the singing.

In Sacred Harp meetings all singing is performed by the entire assembly of singers; no ensemble singing is allowed. In the majority of seven-shape singing conventions this is not the case, although individual organizations may choose to have stricter rules. In most singing conventions at least some time is reserved for special ensembles and soloists to perform. In the gospel sings all of the music, except for possibly a familiar congregational hymn, is provided by special ensembles.

Transition from Singing Convention to Gospel Sing

Karen Jackson's history of the Royal Singing Convention states, "During the 1920s, ensemble singing featuring duets, trios, and quartets became more popular and vocal class singing began to decline."[109] This, of course, was soon after commercial radio had become popular. The gospel ensembles that had been formed in the singing conventions began to sing over the radio. Soon the radio broadcasts attracted audiences more interested in listening than in singing.

In Becker's story of the Singing Speer Family, she summarizes the transition from singing convention to gospel sing:

When all-day singings first started in the South, they were purely a form of entertainment and socializing for the local community.

102

Churches would have homecomings once a year, and people who had lived in the neighborhood years ago might come back to get together with old friends and enjoy the good music and the good food. Or sometimes a community would make singing a regular monthly thing all summer long, moving from one church to another each Sunday, and choosing a different leader for every singing.

Then the singings began to grow and become more and more organized. Sometimes two or three counties would get together for regular singings. They would elect officers—a president, secretary, and treasurer—to handle the details which seemed to get more numerous by the month. The county meetings grew into statewide conventions which attracted thousands of people into places like Birmingham and Nashville. The little impromptu groups that got together in the little country churches became professional quarters that came to the big singing conventions as special added attractions to draw bigger and bigger crowds. . . .

Then some of the professional groups began to plan Saturday night programs where the quartets could perform for the entire evening and offset some of the expense involved in traveling to the all-day singings. Those in charge of the Saturday night programs would charge 25-for admission [sic] and give the performers their share of the profits. The Saturday night concert became a popular entertainment feature in many Southern communities.[110]

These concerts, which began as Saturday night preliminaries to all-day Sunday singing conventions, have since developed into one of the major activities in gospel music of the late twentieth century.

Professional Gospel Sings

A large number of professional gospel singers are able to make a career out of performing throughout the nation and even concertizing in other countries. Gospel sings combine many elements of religion, music, and family entertainment into a concert form that attracts large audiences. Buckingham's story of the "Happy Goodman Family" describes some of the mystique of a professional gospel sing:

103

Gospel singing is always big in Atlanta. The old city auditorium with its two tiers of balconies seating almost seven thousand is about two-thirds full. People from all walks of life are present. Men with jeweled tiepins and ladies with diamond necklaces sit beside folk wearing cotton pants and flowered dresses. . . .

Warren Roberts, manager of radio WYZE, is the master of ceremonies. He comes on stage dressed in white bucks and flashy sports jacket. After the welcome, he introduces a group known as the VII Romans who finish with a fast rendition of the popular song, "Jesus Is Coming Soon." The audience is alive, and there is good response to this lively instrumental group.

Next are the Kingsmen Quartet followed by the Downings. Both groups do their own rendition of "Jesus Is Coming Soon." The Florida Boys come on strong with an opening number and then swing into Tommy Atwood's popular fiddle arrangement of "Power in the Blood" and a humorous arrangement of "Daddy Sang Bass" in which Derrell Stewert mimicks the words with his mouth while the deep bass singer Billy Todd sings behind his hand.

Steve Sanders is next. He's a big favorite with the Atlanta crowd that is made up of many young people. Steve sings a few old numbers including "When the Roll Is Called Up Yonder." Stepping to the front of the stage, he motions for the audience to clap in unison. They oblige and approximately ten thousand hands can be seen clapping vigorously as Steve sings. . . .

Steve has finished, and the announcer brings on the Happy Goodmans. The ovation even before the Goodmans arrive onstage is proof of their popularity in Atlanta.

Howard hits the keyboard and the group moves into "O Happy Day." Flashbulbs puncture the darkness as people raise cameras to their eyes. All over the auditorium people begin clapping in spontaneous rhythm.

Howard turns to the mike. "There's gonna be a lot of people in heaven and I'm thankful I'll be there. Listen as Sister Vestel sings, 'This Is Just What Heaven Means to Me'. "

The song is over and Howard shouts, "All who want to go to heaven say 'Amen'."

There is a thunderous roar from the crowd. "Aaa-men!"

"Now folks, let's listen while Brother Rusty sings something that we've never done onstage before. It's become a favorite on our last album, and we want to do it for you."

104

All the lights go out except for a lone spotlight that picks up Rusty's head and shoulders onstage. The soft guitar and piano music form the backdrop as Rusty begins to recite softly, "Guilty of Love in the First Degree." The tears glisten from his face as he talks in meter with the music. He finishes and there is total darkness. Then a soft red spotlight picks out the form of a wooden cross on the far side of the stage. There are gasps from the crowd and then audible sobs as the full impact of the cross comes to the hearts of those present.

Almost immediately the tempo changes as the Goodmans swing into "The Sweetest Song I Know." The audience is clapping in rhythm and the beat increases. Finally, exhausted, they stop and leave the stage. The clapping continues and grows louder, and they emerge from the back curtains and take a bow. Warren Roberts calls them back for an unusual third curtain call. The audience just won't stop applauding, and finally Howard sits down at the piano, his coat hanging open like the flaps on a circus tent. The rest of the Goodmans join him at the microphones as they swing into "When Morning Sweeps the Sky."

Sam comes to the mike. "I want to tell you something. Had it not been for the grace of God the Goodmans wouldn't be here tonight. We'd still be back in the sand hills of Alabama living in dirt poverty. God had a purpose for us. He's carried us a long way, but we're the first to recognize that it's all because of His goodness and not because of any talent we might have. We've been blessed tonight, just by being able to tell you about God's goodness, grace, and wonderful love."[111]

The unique blend of skillful showmanship and religious sentiment, though varying in degree from group to group, is as much a part of the gospel sings as is the music itself. The professional groups are in great demand nationwide. A more detailed discussion of the activities of the professional gospel singers appears in Chapter 5.

Amateur Gospel Sings

Professional groups are not the only groups in great demand throughout the nation. Particularly in the South and Midwest, amateur and semi-professional groups also concertize year-round. The amateur gospel sings are generally patterned after the professional sings. The expertise exhibited by many of the amateur performing groups can be quite high. In more than a few instances groups with the skills and talent to perform as professionals do not do so because of a reluctance to accept payment for the conduct of what they feel to be a religious mission.

Most gospel sings take place in the evening, with Thursday, Friday, and Saturday evenings being the most popular nights. This has caused a revision of the traditional "Dinner-on-the-ground" event, a southern rural custom of long standing. During the evening non-professional sings a "break" is generally observed at the midpoint of the musical program and homemade refreshments are served. On rare occasions, generally in connection with a fund-raising promotion, a nominal charge may be made.

The gospel sing spectrum ranges from the completely amateur performances, through a complex assortment of semi-professional singing groups and singing events, to the fully professional groups who perform for a fixed fee or for a percentage of gate receipts at concerts. In some form or another gospel music is a ubiquitous phenomenon in the South. In the Field Research portion of this book, only two of the twenty-five South Georgia counties selected at random did not have a significant amount of gospel music performing activity. Each of these two counties were quite small in population and each adjoined larger counties where gospel music activity was quite strong.

Summary

Gospel music in the South, although certainly influenced to a great extent by the popular hymnody of evangelism, developed within the framework of two musical institutions established by and for rural musicians trained in the shaped-note singing schools. These institutions were the four-shape singing conventions generally called "fasola" or Sacred Harp, and the seven-shape singing conventions sometimes called "dorayme."

Because of differing musical and cultural concepts these two institutions existed, and continue to exist, as separate and discrete entities but with similar social customs and religious values. Later, from the seven-shape singing conventions, emerged a trend for small ensembles to be created to perform as entertainment for the larger assembly. This gradually developed into the entertainment and concerting activities usually termed gospel sings.

At present all three of these institutions, Sacred Harp, Singing Conventions, and Gospel Sings, remain viable organizations for the perpetuation of popular religious hymnody in performance practice other than as an adjunct to religious preaching services. The growth and popularity of the gospel sings, however, has made gospel music more widely known among larger audiences; especially since most concertizing performers also make phonograph recordings. The sale of gospel recordings and sheet music, in addition to concert admissions, has turned gospel music into a highly commercial entertainment industry.

Notes

1. Curtis Leo Cheek, "The Singing School and Shaped-note Tradition; Residuals in Twentieth-Century American Hymnody" (unpublished Doctoral dissertation, University of Southern California, 1968), p. 157.
2. John Tasker Howard and George Kent Bellows, *A Short History of Music in America* (1957; New York: Thomas Y. Crowell Company, 1967), p. 29.
3. Ibid., p. 56.
4. Ibid., p. 80.
5. Gilbert Chase, *America's Music from the Pilgrims to the Present* (1955; rev. 2nd ed.; New York: McGraw-Hill Book Company, 1966), p. 40.
6. Copyrighted 1798 but the first edition did not appear until 1801; see pp. 32 ff. above.
7. Cheek, op. cit., p. 161. Cheek states that this convention was formed in 1847. His cited source of information, however, was George Pullen Jackson's *White Spirituals in the Southern Uplands* (1933; rpt.; New York: Dover Publications, Inc., 1965), p. 100; the latter reference states 1845 as the correct date. Also, most secondary sources state that the Southern Musical Convention was begun in "Huntersville," Georgia in Upson County. Based upon the writer's Field Research in Upson County, it is safe to say that a town of such name never existed in that county. The town in question may have been the now extinct Hootonville.
8. Charles Linwood Ellington, "The Sacred Harp Tradition of the South; Its

Origin and Evolution" (unpublished Doctoral dissertation, Florida State University, 1970), p. 42.

9. William Jensen Reynolds, Head of Church Music Department, Sunday School Board, Southern Baptist Convention, Nashville, Tennessee, personal interview, December 15, 1976.

10. Ellington, op. cit., p. 47; the specific reference is to the Chattahoochee Musical Convention, second of White's organized singing societies.

11. Benjamin Franklin White and E. J. King, *The Sacred Harp,* facsimile of the 3d. ed., 1859, including as a historical introduction: *The Story of the Sacred Harp* by George Pullen Jackson (1844; 3d ed., 1859; Nashville, Broadman Press, 1968).

12. Ellington, op. cit., pp. 42–43; other cited factors, besides the music itself, were White's own personality and his ability to teach teachers. These teachers would also espouse White's book.

13. George Pullen Jackson, *White Spirituals in the Southern Uplands* (1933; rpt.; New York: Dover Publications, Inc., 1965), p. 101.

14. Ibid.

15. Ibid., p. 86.

16. Ellington, op. cit., p. 125.

17. *Directory and Minutes of Annual Sacred Harp Singings 1975–1976—Alabama, Florida, Georgia, Tennessee and Mississippi* (n.n., n.d.). Failure to be listed in the *Directory and Minutes* is in itself no absolute indication that these conventions no longer exist; for example, of the 15 Sacred Harp singings listed in the *1975 Proceedings of the Fifty-sixth Annual Session of the South Georgia Sacred Harp Singing Convention* [etc.,] (n.n., n.d.), n.p., only two appear in the *Directory and Minutes.* The *Directory and Minutes* does not even indicate that a South Georgia Sacred Harp Singing Convention exists.

18. Jackson, op. cit., p. 24; list is from p. [25].

19. Harry Lee Eskew, "Shape-Note Hymnody In The Shenandoah Valley, 1816–1860" (unpublished Doctoral dissertation, Tulane University, 1966), p. 18; asterisks indicate those books which also appear in Jackson's list in Figure 3 above.

20. Ibid., pp. vii–viii, 52–53, 61, 68, 127, 135.

21. William Walker, *Southern Harmony, and Musical Companion* (1835; 1854 new ed; rpt. ed. Glenn C. Wilcox; Los Angeles: Pro Musicamericana, 1966).

22. John Gordon McCurry, *The Social Harp, A Collection of Tunes, Odes, Anthems, and Set Pieces* [etc.] (1855; facsimile rpt. ed. Daniel W. Patterson and John F. Garst: Athens: University of Georgia Press, 1973).

23. William Walker, *The Christian Harmony: In the Seven-syllable Character Note System of Music* [etc.] (1866; rev. ed., 1873; Philadelphia: E. W. Miller Company, 1901).

24. Ellington, op. cit., pp. 125–126.

25. Ibid., pp. 130–131.

26. *1975 Proceedings of the Fifth-sixth Annual Session of the South Georgia Sacred Harp Singing Convention* [etc.] (n.n., n.d.), n.p.; the By-Laws of this Convention appear in Appendix B.

27. Ibid.

28. Walker, *Christian Harmony,* op. cit.

108

29. Joseph Funk and Sons, *The Harmonia Sacra* (1851; 13th ed.; Singers' Glen, Virginia: Joseph Funk's Sons, 1869).
30. Ellington, op. cit., pp. 131–135; separation into paragraphs by the writer; original is written as one paragraph.
31. The writer wishes to thank Dr. and Mrs. R. L. Carter of Thomaston, Georgia, for bringing these articles to his attention.
32. Jackson states that "perhaps the oldest" Fourth of July singing is that at Helicon, Alabama, which began in 1891; Cf. Jackson, op. cit., p. 113. The Shiloh Baptist singing could have begun as early as 1859; see p. 88 below.
33. Internal evidence suggests that this was the editor of the paper.
34. *The Thomaston Herald,* [Georgia], July 6, 1872, p. 3, col. 2.
35. *The Thomaston Herald,* July 10, 1875, p. 3, col. 2–3.
36. The immediate next article in the newspaper describes in detail a Sabbath School Festival.
37. Grace I. Showalter, *The Music Books of Ruebush & Kieffer 1866–1942; A Bibliography* (Richmond: Virginia State Library, 1975), p. 3; see also pp. 91 ff. below for additional information concerning the Ruebush-Kieffer Company.
38. Ibid., p. ix.
39. *The Thomaston Herald,* July 7, 1877, p. 3, col. 2.
40. Unfortunately, the minutes of the Shiloh Baptist Church, which have been preserved, do not mention this first singing convention, nor any of the other Fourth of July singings for that matter.
41. Jackson, op. cit., p. 101, cited on p. 78 above.
42. The Shiloh Baptist Church, in Upson County, Georgia, is in the same county in which B.F. White established the Southern [Sacred Harp] Musical Convention.
43. Jackson, op. cit., p. 127; emphasis Jackson's.
44. Ibid., p. 128.
45. Ibid., p. 345.
46. Ibid., p. 209.
47. William Hauser, *Hesperian Harp* (Philadelphia, 1848), cited and described by Jackson in ibid., pp. 72–73.
48. *Christian Minstrel* (Philadelphia, 1846), cited by Jackson, *White Spirituals,* op. cit., p. 210. Apparently this was not published in shaped notes for it does not appear on Jackson's list reprinted as Fig. 3, p. 79 above.
49. Jackson, op. cit., p. 210. Page numbers for the above musical examples are also from Jackson, ibid., pp. 209–210.
50. Joseph Funk, *Die Allgemein Nützliche Choral-Music* (Harrisonburg, Virginia: Laurentz Wartmann, 1816). A detailed description of this book is given by Eskew, op. cit., pp. 75ff, and the title page is shown on p. 78.
51. Both Morton and Wayland, who will be cited later, attribute the shapes to Law but they are mistaken.
52. Joseph Funk, *A Compilation of Genuine Church Music* [etc.] (Winchester, Virginia: Published at the office of the Republican, [J. W. Hollis, Printer.], 1832). A detailed description of this book is given by Eskew, op. cit., pp. 87ff, and the title page is shown on p. 88.
53. Joseph Funk and Sons, *The Harmonia Sacra, A Compilation of Genuine Church Music, Comprising a Great Variety of Metres, Harmonized for Four Voices; Together with a Copious Explication of the Principles of Vo-*

cal Music. Exemplified and Illustrated with Tables, in a Plain and Comprehensive Manner. By Joseph Funk And Sons (1851; 13th ed.; Singer's Glen, Rockingham Co., Virginia: Published by Joseph Funk's Sons, 1869). A detailed description of the first and subsequent editions of this book is given by Eskew, op. cit., pp. 140 ff., but no title page is shown.

54. Eskew, op. cit., p. 87.
55. William Jensen Reynolds, *A Survey of Christian Hymnody* (New York: Holt, Rinehart and Winston, Inc., 1963), p. 114.
56. John W. Wayland, *Joseph Funk. Father of Song in Northern Virginia* (Dayton, Virginia: The Ruebush-Kieffer Co., [1911?]), p. 11.
57. Ibid.
58. Noah D. Showalter, ed., *New Harmonia Sacra* [etc.] (20th ed.; Dayton, Virginia: Ruebush-Kieffer Company, 1942), n.p.
59. O. F. Morton, "The Ruebush-Kieffer Company. A Record of Seventy Years in the Publishing of Music," *Musical Million,* XLII (August, 1911), 84.
60. Jackson, op. cit., p. 346.
61. Morton, op. cit., p. 86.
62. According to Grace I. Showalter, op. cit., p. ix, the following is the sequence of imprints by which the company became known: 1866, Ruebush & Kieffer imprint added to Joseph Funk's Sons imprint; 1872, Ruebush, Kieffer & Company; 1891, The Ruebush-Kieffer Company.
63. Paul M. Hall "The *Musical Million:* A Study and Analysis Of The Periodical Promoting Music Reading Through Shape-Notes in North America From 1870 to 1914" (unpublished Doctoral dissertation, Catholic University of America, 1970), p. 2, states the accurate title as the *Musical Million and Fireside Friend.* Hall lists "Volumes and Numbers Available" and "Volumes and Numbers Unavailable" in his Appendixes A and B, respectively.
64. Weldon T. Myers, "Aldine S. Kieffer, The Valley Poet, and His Work," *Musical Million,* XXXIX (August, 1908), 231. Myers attributes the above quotation to Kieffer.
65. *The Southern Musical Advocate and Singer's Friend,* Vol. 1, No. I, July, 1859. Ran from 1859 to April, 1861. Resumed publication January, 1867 to August, 1869 as *The Musical Advocate and Singer's Friend.* Cited by Eskew, op. cit., p. 144; Eskew, in turn, cited Irvin B. Horst, "Joseph Funk, Early Mennonite Printer and Publisher," *Mennonite Quarterly Review,* XXXI (October, 1957), 278.
66. Morton, op. cit., p. 85.
67. Ibid., p. 87.
68. Hall, op. cit., pp. 2–3.
69. Morton, op. cit., p. 86.
70. Aldine S. Kieffer, "Editorial," reprinted in "Kieffer Memorial Number," *Musical Million,* XXXIX (August, 1908), 240.
71. Jackson, op. cit., p. 354.
72. "Normal School" was used to designate an institution for the training of teachers. The first public normal school in the United States was established in Lexington, Massachusetts in 1839. The time requirement for completion of the public normal schools was generally two years beyond

high school. See "Normal School," *Encyclopaedia Britannica,* op. cit., XVI, p. 575. Southern music normals were of much briefer duration.

73. *The Musical Advocate and Singer's Friend,* I (July, 1859), 16.
74. Hall, op. cit., p. 43.
75. *Musical Million,* VII (March, 1876), 58, cited by Hall, op. cit., pp. 43–45.
76. Jackson, op. cit., p. 356.
77. Ibid., p. 357.
78. Christopher C. Stafford. "B.C. Unseld (1843–1923)," *Vaughan's Family Visitor,* LXX (January, 1971), 10.
79. It is significant that two additional men whose influence, more than any others, can be seen in the gospel music of the South today were associated with Vaughan and Showalter. These two men were Virgil Oliver (V.O.) Stamps and Jesse Randall (J.R. "Pap") Baxter. Stamps and Baxter joined forces in 1926 to form the Stamps-Baxter Music & Printing Company, which will be discussed in greater detail in Chapter 5.
80. Jackson, op. cit., p. 379.
81. Paula Becker, *Let the Song Go On: Fifty Years of Gospel Singing with the Speer Family* (Nashville: Impact Books, 1971), pp. 43–46.
82. Jo Lee Fleming, "James D. Vaughan, Music Publisher, Lawrenceburg, Tennessee. 1912–1964" (unpublished Doctoral dissertation, Union Theological Seminary, 1972), pp. 28–29.
83. Wiley Housewright, Florida State University, Tallahassee, Florida, telephone interview, September 6, 1976.
84. Ibid.
85. Ernest N. Edwards, *The Edwards Album* (Bessemer, Alabama: The Ernest N. Edwards Music Company, 1955), p. 15.
86. Karen Luke Jackson, "The Royal Singing Convention, 1893–1931: Shape Note Singing Tradition In Irwin County, Georgia," *The Georgia Historical Quarterly* (Winter, 1972), p. 498.
87. Ibid., p. 499.
88. G.P. Jackson, op. cit., p. 394 states that "state conventions have practically disappeared from among the seven-shape activities." This intriguing statement, published in 1933, warrants additional investigation beyond the scope of this study.
89. *Alabama State Gospel Singing Convention [Program]* (Montgomery, Alabama: n.n., 1976), p. 8; this source does not state that the Alabama Convention was the first.
90. Observations and notes taken during 1975 and 1976 Georgia singing conventions, including the Georgia State Singing Convention, Commerce, Georgia, October 9–10, 1976.
91. By-Laws of the Georgia State Singing Convention, dated October 12, 1959. These By-Laws are included in Appendix B.
92. Observations and notes, loc. cit.
93. Extracted from advertisements in 1976 *National Gospel Singing Convention [Program]* (Roswell, New Mexico: n.n., 1976), p. 2, 10, 21; and names of states which have previously hosted the National Convention as listed in the 1969 *[Program]* (Cleveland, Tennessee: n.n., 1969), n.p. Also, Arizona, Indiana, Missouri, and New York were represented at the 1976 National Convention but did not seat a full slate of delegates, ac-

cording to letter from Talmadge Johnson, President of 1976 National Gospel Singing Convention, December 22, 1976.

94. Stella Benton Vaughan, Rupert Cravens and Oliver S. Jennings, "A Brief History of the National Singing Convention 1936–1968," *Souvenir Book of the 32nd Annual Session of the National Singing Convention* (Plainview, Texas: n.n., 1968), n.p.

95. Ibid.

96. "Constitution And Bylaws Of The National Gospel Singing Convention, Organized in 1936, From Revised Copy," 1976 [Program], op. cit., p. 57; emphasis in original. This Constitution and Bylaws are included in Appendix B.

97. Ibid., emphasis in original.

98. Jackson, op. cit., p. 367; list shown on p. 366.

99. *Gospel Music 1977 Directory & Yearbook* (Nashville: Gospel Music Association, 1976), pp. 121–122. Vaughan company does not appear in this reference.

100. The five which did not appear on Jackson's list referred to above are presumed to have been established more recently.

101. *National Gospel Singing Convention [Program],* op. cit., p. 29; the P.J. Zondervan Music Company, which also appears in this reference, did not provide a book according to Oliver S. Jennings, attendee, telephone interview, December 16, 1976.

102. This company is discussed in greater detail in Chapter 5.

103. According to Oliver S. Jennings, gospel singing convention devotee, telephone interview, December 16, 1976, Watson was killed by a robber in 1975 and it is not known if this company has been continued by his heirs.

104. Connor B. Hall, editor of Tennessee and Vaughan Publishing Companies, Cleveland, Tennessee, personal interview, Nashville, Tennessee, October 6, 1976.

105. Hyman Brown, shaped note singing teacher, personal interview, Commerce, Georgia, June 27, 1975.

106. *GMA Directory & Yearbook,* op. cit., p. 109, lists thirty-seven periodicals. Most of these would generally be considered "fan" magazines addressed to the professional gospel sing public.

107. This company and its periodical are owned by Tennessee Music Company, Cleveland, Tennessee, the music publishing arm of the Church of God.

108. Connor B. Hall, loc. cit.

109. Karen Jackson, op. cit., p. 504.

110. Becker, op. cit., pp. 46, 49.

111. Jamie Buckingham, *O Happy Day: The Happy Goodman Story* (Waco: Word Books, Publisher, 1973), pp. 43–45.

5

The Commercialization of
Gospel Music

To a great many persons, a number not limited to the adherents of fundamentalist religion in the South, the concept of commercial activities associated with religious music is distasteful, if not actually repugnant.[1] In many respects, however, the commercial aspects of religious music may have helped to foster the propagation of the music more so than would have a complete altruism, if such were possible. Many historical antecedents exist.

Reference was made in Chapter 2 to John's observation that the publishing of singing school compilations, which were predominantly religious music collections, was a "very lucrative concomitant side line" for the singing master.[2] One could question the adverb "very" in John's comment, but the remuneration did enable many of the singing masters to devote themselves to music rather than to other occupations. Britton's description is probably more accurate when he states:

> The economic position of the singing masters generally seems to have been more or less typical of that of musicians of every time and place, ranging from a polite poverty to a modest affluence.[3]

It should be stated from the outset that the writer's use of the term "commercial" is not intended to be derogatory. It is used to indicate that process whereby an increasingly greater number of persons have been able to earn their full livelihood by the production of that music. For the sake of convenience, this chapter is divided into sections entitled: Publishers; Radio, Recordings, and Television; Gospel Sings and their Promotion; and Gospel Music Association.

113

Rationale for Omission of Afro-American Gospel Music

Conspicuous by its absence is discussion of the history of Afro-American gospel music and musicians.[4] This is not an oversight. Afro-American gospel music may share some similarities with the music of the white gospel tradition, but by and large, the differences are of such magnitude that they constitute separate genres. Goldberg describes the basic difference between the two styles:

> It is impossible to discuss gospel music without specifying what kind. The only thing that the word "gospel" implies is a connection to any of the many Christian churches in this country. The field divides itself into two very separate entities differing from each other culturally and musically. One of them is black or "soul" gospel, which comes our [sic] of black churches and has influenced virtually every major r&b[5] artist. The music has the same African routes [sic]. . . .
> On the other side of the gospel spectrum is white or country gospel, corresponding in sound and appeal to the growing country market. There is scarcely a country artist who has not put out an album of hymns at one time or another. . . . Country gospel, aided by the fledgling Gospel Music Association is becoming a substantial field.[6]

It should be mentioned, however, that although the cultural backgrounds of white gospel music may be similar to those of country music, *these* two styles are also quite dissimilar. According to Green:

> Whatever the reasons, gospel music is in a world of its own, and despite its common origin with country music, its current sound, style, performance, and musical objectives are far different from those of country music.[7]

Publishers

Previous reference was made to the Ruebush-Kieffer Company and its rise to eminence in the field of publishing shaped note tunebooks after the Civil War. No small credit for this growth can be attributed to the company's publication of the journal, *The Musical Million,* and to the establishment of the first normal music school in the South.

A.J. Showalter

A student of this Virginia Normal Music School and a pupil of B.C. Unseld, mentioned previously, was Anthony Johnson Showalter. Showalter was to become another strong force in the propagation of gospel music.

Showalter's relationship to the Ruebush-Kieffer Company was stronger than that of merely being one of the students in the normal school. He was a close relative[8] of Joseph Funk, mentioned earlier as one of the founding fathers of southern shaped note hymnody. Showalter's first book was published in 1880 in collaboration with Aldine S. Kieffer.[9] Two years later he published the first of his three books on harmony and theory. In his own words, but written in the third person, Showalter states:

> . . . his *Harmony and Composition,* the first work of the kind by a southern author, was published at the age of twenty-three; his *Theory of Music,* published some years later, was the second work of the kind by a southern author, while his *New Harmony and Composition,* issued in 1895, made the third book upon this subject which he had written before any other southern author of works of this kind appeared. . . .[10]

Subsequent revisions of these books are still being used in at least one[11] of the gospel music schools named in the previous chapter.

In 1884 Showalter was sent to Dalton, Georgia, to establish a branch of the Ruebush-Kieffer Company. In this same year he severed relations with the parent organization and began his own company in the same location.[12] According to Stafford, "Mr. Showalter was known as a successful business man as well as musician and publisher."[13] In 1904 Showalter described the relative strength of his publishing operations:

115

The A.J. Showalter Co., Dalton, Ga., and the Showalter-Patton Co., Dallas, Texas, the two combined are larger than any other dozen publishing houses south of Mason and Dixon's line, outside of the large denominational publishing houses. . . .[14]

Showalter's most popular book was *Class, Choir and Congregation,* published in 1888.[15] According to Jackson, it had sold 400,000 copies by 1911.[16] This book, and another published two years earlier, *Work and Worship,*[17] were two of the earliest shaped note books to appear with the four voice parts condensed to two staves.[18] This, of course, made music reading more difficult for singers but much easier for keyboard accompanists.

Continuing the example set by Joseph Funk, Showalter published a periodical, *The Music Teacher and Home Magazine,*[19] and conducted numerous four-week normal schools, which he called S. M. N. I.[20] These initials stood for Southern Music Normal Institute.[21] Although Showalter sponsored and taught in a great many normal schools in various locations, secondary sources do not indicate a permanent school located in Dalton, Georgia. Apparently Showalter's many normal schools were conducted on an itinerant basis.[22]

James D. Vaughan

The Reubush-Kieffer Company also had an exceedingly strong effect on another publisher, James D. Vaughan. The specific basis for this is not apparent from available secondary sources. The most clear-cut evidence of influence is that Vaughan named his son Glenn Kieffer Vaughan. This was in honor of Aldine S. Kieffer, mentioned in the previous chapter, and for R.A. Glenn, a popular song compiler for the Ruebush-Kieffer company.[23] It is a striking coincidence that Glenn Kieffer Vaughan should be named for Glenn and for Kieffer whose only collaboration, *New Melodies of Praise,*[24] in 1877, was also the first publication by the Ruebush-Kieffer Company which incorporated Aiken's seven shapes instead of Funk's.[25]

James D. Vaughan evidenced an interest in music at an early age but did not publish his first book[26] until 1900, when he was thirty-six years old. Vaughan moved to Lawrenceburg, Tennessee, in 1902, but it was not until 1905 that he began publishing from his own office in that location.[27]

Stafford has only the highest praise for the character of Vaughan. He writes:

Mr. Vaughan was so kind and congenial to all until no one could help but love him. . . . In all my visits with Mr. Vaughan, I could never discover a fault in this great and good man of God. . . .

Being saved at the age of ten years, Mr. Vaughan started out early in life putting Christ first. His success as a composer and publisher can well be accredited to this religious background. He taught Bible and Sunday school classes from his young manhood to the close of his career. He was clean of the known bad habits, such as tobacco, any kind of intoxicating liquor, never used any type of by-words nor at any time in his life ever swore an oath. All who knew Mr. Vaughan would speak of him as being one of the cleanest Christian gentlemen they ever knew.[28]

Although Vaughan's public image may not have been the stereotype of a hard-headed businessman, nevertheless he was very successful. In addition to the establishment of the Vaughan School of Music in 1911,[29] and the publication of a periodical in 1912, which came to be known as *Vaughan's Family Visitor,*[30] Vaughan initiated three promotional concepts which were to have a profound effect on the later development of gospel music. These innovations were the use of vocal quartets to promote company publications, the broadcasting of gospel music over the radio, and the making of disc recordings of gospel music.

There are two "first" Vaughan Quartets. Fleming states that the very first was in "about 1882" when Vaughan would have been approximately eighteen years old.[31] He had recently attended two ten-day singing schools and felt himself fully capable of teaching his own singing school. He organized a quartet comprised of his three younger brothers and himself. Thus, in Vaughan's very first professional situation was germinated the concept of special music ensembles used in the promotion of gos-

117

pel music. This first group was not a commercial success, however, and disbanded in 1891 upon the death of one of the members.[32]

The next "first" Vaughan Quartet came into being after Vaughan was firmly established in the business of music publishing. Stella Benton Vaughan, the wife of Glen Kieffer Vaughan, narrates:

> It was in 1910 that the first Vaughan Quartet was organized. It was composed of Charles W. Vaughan who was manager [bass], George W. Sebren [lead], Joe M. Allen [baritone] and Ira T. Foust [tenor].[33] The quartet singing songs from the book of that year "Voices For Jesus" added to the sale of the books.
>
> From this first quartet many others were added until in the middle twenties there were sixteen quartets traveling for the Vaughan Company in all parts of the country. They sold over half a million books in one year.[34]

These quartets also sold subscriptions to *Vaughan's Family Visitor,* and the magazine published a list of those quartets which solicited the most customers.[35] Mrs. Vaughan also states that James D. Vaughan was the first to establish present-day quartet voicings:

> The quartet idea of four male voices singing gospel songs written for mixed voices originated with James D. Vaughan with one voice singing in the same register used by women singing alto. All the other quartets doing that today owe the beginning to the example of the first Vaughan Quartet.[36]

It might be interesting to see if the claim could be substantiated; but the implication for the expansion of gospel singing is that, by Vaughan's example, no longer did a male quartet need to rely on music published specifically for that performing medium.

There is one additional "first" Vaughan Quartet. This is the first gospel quartet to broadcast over radio. Here again it would take detailed investigation to substantiate the complete validity of such a claim;[37] nevertheless, this quartet is unquestionably the one with the widest influence in terms of southern gospel music. According to Stella Vaughan:

James D. Vaughan built, owned and operated the first radio Station in Tennessee—WOAN. He bought it in October and received the license from the Federal Communications Commission November 21, 1922.[38]

Fleming states, however, that Vaughan did not begin broadcasting until January 1923.[39] The members of this first Vaughan Quartet to perform over radio were: Kieffer Vaughan, lead; Hilman Barnard, first tenor; Walber B. Seale, baritone; and Roy L. Collins, bass.[40]

Information regarding the Vaughan recordings is more difficult to obtain. Fleming's dissertation makes no mention of recordings and the information presented by Stella Vaughan is not specific. Apparently the members of the above named quartet made recordings in 1924 in two locations. These were in New York for the Edison Company[41] and also in Richmond, Indiana for the Vaughan label.[42] Stella Vaughan states, without giving a time reference, that "Kieffer and another Quartet[43] spent several seasons at Winona Lake, Indiana [with Homer Rodeheaver]. . . . They were in Indiana to make records."[44] In the only reference to recordings on a major label, Vaughan states, "In August of 1929 Kieffer's quartet made recordings for Victor Co."[45]

It should be apparent from the above that a discography of the Vaughan Quartet recordings, though difficult to compile, would be most essential for future research in gospel music.

Three additional publishers of gospel music need to be mentioned at this point. None achieved the stature of the Vaughan Company nor that of the Stamps-Baxter Music and Printing Company, which will be discussed subsequently; nevertheless their publications were widely used and their influence was considerable. These are the Winsett Music Company, the Hartford Music Company, and the J. M. Henson Music Company.

Winsett Music Company

The Winsett Music Company, mentioned briefly in Chapter 4, was established by Robert Emmett Winsett whose first song book was published in 1903.[46] The company was located for a time in Chattanooga, Tennessee and Fort Smith, Arkansas before moving to its present location in Dayton, Tennessee in 1929.[47] According to the *Gospel Song Writers Biography,* Winsett died in 1952 and his widow continued the business. Mrs. Winsett re-married in 1954, and her husband, Harry J. Shelton, joined her in the business which retains her deceased husband's name.[48] This company is still active in gospel music although it did not provide a gospel songbook for the 1976 National Gospel Singing Convention.

Hartford Music Company/Albert E. Brumley and Sons

The Hartford Music Company was also mentioned briefly in Chapter 4. This company was established in 1918–1919 in Hartford, Arkansas by Eugene M. Bartlett, Senior, as an outgrowth of the Central Music Company.[49] Bartlett had studied under J.H. Ruebush and Homer Rodeheaver, among others.[50] Beginning in 1922, the company published a periodical, the *Herald of Song,*[51] and conducted twice-yearly normal schools of three weeks duration. These schools were called the Hartford Music Institute. In 1948, the company was purchased by Albert E. Brumley and the location changed to Powell, Missouri.[52]

Brumley had been a student under Homer Rodeheaver, James Rowe, and W.H. Ruebush, among others, at the Hartford Music Institute. He was, and still is, a prolific and popular composer, having composed over 600 gospel and folk-type songs.[53] Brumley's most popular song, "I'll Fly Away," has been recorded by almost every major gospel group,[54] and at least four major artists have recorded albums of exclusively Brumley songs on major recording labels.[55] Brumley and his sons continue to operate the Hartford Music Company in addition to their own company, Albert E. Brumley and Sons. According to Brumley's son, Bob, the two companies differ only in their respective catalogs of copyrighted songs. Both companies are under the same management.[56] The management [both companies combined] publishes a periodical entitled *The Gospel Singing Journal,* which has

120

been in continuous publication since 1971. In addition to sheet music, the management publishes one convention song book each year.[57] The company also sponsors the annual Albert E. Brumley Sundown To Sunup Singing, a three-night professional gospel sing, in Springdale, Arkansas each August. The 1976 session marked the eighth consecutive year of this sing.[58]

Albert E. Brumley still serves as a consultant to the company that bears his name, but the company is presently owned by his sons, Bill and Bob Brumley.[59]

J.M. Henson Music Company

The third previously mentioned company no longer exists under any of its former names. John Melvin Henson began his publishing career with the Parham-Morris Company in Atlanta, Georgia, then joined with Morris to found the Morris-Henson Company.[60] In 1937 Henson bought Morris' interest and the company became known as the J.M. Henson Music Company.[61] According to the *Gospel Song Writers Biography:*

> The Morris-Henson Company . . . was the first company to make two new song books each year and the J.M. Henson Company kept up the same practice, publishing about forty books during these years.[62]

In 1961 the company was sold to the Statesmen Quartet, and in 1974 the Statesmen Quartet sold the Henson catalog to the Lillenas Publishing Company.[63] Additional information concerning the Lillenas Publishing Company appears in Appendix A along with two of its copyrighted songs chosen by groups in the Field Research.

Stamps-Baxter Music and Printing Company

The next company to be discussed became such a leader in the field of southern gospel music that its name became a generic term for the music itself. The Stamps-Baxter [Music and Printing] Company became, in the minds of many persons,[64] the creator of the gospel singing style, the quartets, the radio programs, the concerts, and even of the shaped notes themselves.[65]

Virgil Oliver Stamps had evidenced an early interest in music and had taken positions with several music publishing firms. He worked for James D. Vaughan for several years before forming his own company in 1924.[66] The name of Stamps' first publication was *Harbor Bells,*[67] published in 1925. In Stamps' obituary sketch, the eulogist describes its acceptance:

> This first publication was an instant success, the sales not only far exceeding those of any similar book issued by a new concern, but also surpassing sales records made by many old-established [sic] publishing companies.[68]

Even this is somewhat of an understatement. In J.D. Sumner's more colorful terminology, "It blew Vaughan off the market!"[69] The reason for its success is due to Stamps having made friends with most of the best songwriters, each of whom in turn had saved for him their best songs.[70] This songbook is still in print in 1976, an unusual longevity for a paperback convention book.

Despite the success of *Harbor Bells,* Stamps needed additional financial backing for his grandiose plans. In 1926 he formed an alliance with J.R. Baxter, Jr., which was to propel gospel music to heretofore unheard of popularity and, eventually, to change its emphasis from group performance to ensemble performance.

Jesse Randolph Baxter, Junior, had attended normal schools taught by A.J. Showalter and T.B. Mosley. According to the *Gospel Song Writers Biography:*

> Without Mr. Baxter's knowledge of what was being done, these two teachers made some schools for him and he had to teach the schools or let his teachers down. Thus began the musical career of one of the foremost teachers of his day. . . .[71]

Baxter eventually went to work for Showalter and was manager of his Texarkana, Texas-Arkansas plant at the time of

Showalter's death in 1924. He and Stamps had met previously many times in singing conventions and, although representing competing companies, each recognized the leadership ability of the other. In 1926 it was decided that they would combine their holdings and their influence into one business.[72] This was the best possible combination of personalities that could have been formed at this time. Baxter was a serious and astute business-man who liked for all details to be in perfect order. Stamps was an aggressive, crowd-loving salesman with an overwhelming personal magnetism. According to Butler, it would have killed Stamps to have had to remain in an office to edit words and mu-sic, or to keep up with copyrights.[73] These same items of de-tail-work were exactly what Baxter enjoyed doing. Baxter, in fact, had quite a reputation for taking the often crude writings of many of the rural songwriters and creating songs of reasonable quality.[74] Baxter's editing served both as a means of establishing a loyal following and of maintaining a standard of quality for the company.

It was agreed then, that Baxter would establish an office in Chattanooga, Tennessee, to be in charge of company operations east of the Mississippi, and that Stamps would establish an of-fice in Texas, eventually Dallas,[75] to be in charge of the company activities west of the Mississippi.[76]

Stamps proceeded to take two of Vaughan's innovations and carry them to their zenith in the promotion of the new company's publications. These two areas of eminence were in the authoriza-tion of traveling quartets to represent the company, and in the use of radio broadcasting.

Stamps, as a general policy, hired only singers to work in the Texas organization, teaching them what skills were necessary in order for them to perform their publishing duties. All would work in the printing company during the day, and at night and on weekends would represent the company at singing conven-tions.[77] Each representing quartet would have a car filled with company publications for sale. These quartets would sing with the members of the convention and occasionally perform special numbers, always from the current Stamps-Baxter publication. Later, Stamps made arrangements with the better quartets,

123

those which had been operating independently, to affiliate with the organization. They were required to append "Stamps-Baxter" to their original quartet name. James Blackwood tells how the arrangement worked:

> Loosely, our business agreement with Stamps was this: Mr. Stamps would assist us with our booking arrangements and widen our field of operation; when needed, he would assist in securing and placement of personnel including pianists for accompaniment; he would immediately furnish a late model, dependable automobile for our business transportation as well as for our personal use and he did just that. We were given a brand new car. At last we had a car young enough, and good enough, to bear up under the punishment of extremely heavy road use.
>
> In return, we gave the Stamps [-Baxter][78] company a percentage of our gross income after it had passed a stipulated amount. It was a very fair arrangement. Financially, for the first time, we could flex our "money muscles" and breathe easier. This was a substantial aid to us, psychologically. Roy was already a family man with a wife and two children to support. Doyle and I were about to assume marital obligations ourselves.[79]

Thus was the Stamps-Baxter Company able to provide some measure of financial security for performers who had decided on gospel music for their life's work. In a later writing Blackwood goes into more detail on the actual financial arrangement:

> In addition to the automobile—and the first one he gave us was a 1939 Mercury—we profited by selling his song books. Each member of the quartet got to keep up to eighteen dollars and fifty cents a week, depending on how many song books we could sell.
>
> We'd never made that kind of money before. That was pretty good money for four country boys from Ackerman, Mississippi, who had been struggling along near starvation.
>
> Mr. Stamps was good to us. . . .[80]

It was also a mark of prestige to be affiliated with the company. It is difficult to learn exactly how many groups carried the Stamps-Baxter name, either at one time or in total. The number could have ranged from the fifteen cited by Blackwood[81] to the

124

"more than one hundred [at one time]" cited by Horstman.[82] In any event, Butler is reasonably certain that no more than six quartets were outfitted with automobiles at any one time. These quartets with Stamps-Baxter automobiles, then, would have been among the very best quartets of the time. Exactly which quartets these were remains to be documented.

V.O. Stamps was also enamored with radio. He sang bass with his own quartet, the Stamps Quartet,[83] and encouraged the other company quartets to perform over the radio. He was a good salesman through this medium. W.B. Nowlin describes Stamps' radio salesmanship:

American Beauty Flour sponsored most of the Stamps radio programs at that time; V.O. did the commercials. He'd read the copy one time before the program and throw it away. He was one of the best; he'd make you so hungry that you'd want to sop syrup with a biscuit halfway through the program.[84]

Blackwood indicates the magnitude of Stamps' sphere of influence by way of radio:

V.O. Stamps got a big break in radio back in 1936 when he got on 50,000-watt KRLD in Dallas during the State Fair of Texas. He landed two daily broadcasts on the station because the people liked the Stamps Quartet so well at the Fair.

Mr. Stamps also had a fifteen-minute program on a 50,000-watt[85] radio station in Mexico, just across the Rio Grande River from Del Rio. He sold hundreds of thousands of song books with the program on that station. . . .

. . . He had a listening audience in the millions by the late thirties. . . .

The announcers in Dallas referred to V.O. Stamps as "The Man With a Million Friends." He could have been elected governor of Texas if he had wanted to run, because he was so popular.[86]

Stamps is also credited with the origination of the all-night gospel sing, one of the favorite promotional formats since that time. According to Nowlin, who was making a songbook purchase from Stamps at the time, an elderly lady made the suggestion. Nowlin relates:

Her immortal words were, "Virgil, I could sit and listen to your quartet sing all night long and never bat an eye." Thus a seed was planted in the keen mind of V.O. Stamps; and the idea of the all-night singing was born.[87]

The first all-night singing was held at the close of the annual three-week Stamps-Baxter School Of Music on June 25, 1938. Legends surrounding this first event make accurate documentation difficult. For example, in a recent writing Nowlin recalls:

Ten thousand people jammed into the Dallas Sportatorium that night to pat their feet, clap their hands, and devour the good gospel singing of V.O.'s own Stamps Quartet; his brother's group, the Frank Stamps Quartet from WHO Radio in Des Moines, Iowa; the Melody Boys from Little Rock, Arkansas; and a group of young men who were destined to become as legendary as the Stamps, the Blackwood Brothers Quartet.[88]

Other documentation indicates that the first event was held at the Band Shell of the State Fair in Dallas,[89] that the Blackwood Brothers did not perform until 1939,[90] and that an estimated audience of 10,000 did not attend until 1940.[91]

Undoubtedly Stamps would have initiated many other promotional concepts for gospel music if he had lived longer. It was a shock to the entire world of gospel music when Virgil Oliver Stamps died of a heart attack on August 19, 1940.

After Stamps's death, Baxter and his wife moved to Dallas to take over operation of the company.[92] Although Baxter's personality was quite different from the personality of Stamps, the company continued to expand. It remained far superior to all others in the field. The memory of V.O. Stamps and the loyalty he had engendered remained almost palpably strong among those who had worked for him. The workers strove even harder to attain the goals to which he had aspired.[93] Baxter and his wife, in their unpretentious way, commanded their own loyal following. The use of quartets performing over the radio and representing the company at conventions; the publishing of the company periodical, *Gospel Music News;*[94] and the maintenance of the

Stamps-Baxter School of Music, continued stronger than before. Mrs. Baxter worked side-by-side with her husband and was considered an equal partner in the business.[95]

The Stamps-Baxter School of Music[96] has a unique place in history as the only school of gospel music, teaching shaped notes, to be authorized for Veterans to attend under the G. I. Bill.[97] During the time of this authorization the school operated on a year-round basis with the course being divided into four three-month sessions.[98] Competition with Frank Stamps, however, ultimately forced the discontinuance of the school except in the form of itinerant schools authorized by the company.[99]

Stamps Quartet Music Company

Frank Stamps, four years junior to V.O. Stamps, had a personality almost the equal of his brother's. He had been active in music from his early childhood and had studied at the Vaughan School of Music under B.C. Unseld and Adger M. Pace,[100] both of whom were mentioned in the previous chapter. Frank sang bass in a quartet, "Frank Stamps And His All-Stars," which is credited with being the first in the South to record gospel music for a major record company.[101]

In 1940, Frank Stamps had been persuaded by his brother to leave the Hartford Music Company, for which he had been working, to join the plant operations in Dallas. This was only a short time before V.O. Stamps's death. Apparently Frank Stamps and the Baxters were unable to operate in partnership because Frank left the parent company and formed his own company in 1945.[102] Calling his company the Stamps Quartet Music Company, he set up operations less than a block away. He also took fourteen of the better staff members and teachers with him.[103] Being an excellent teacher himself, and having a special propensity for the furtherance of gospel music through a school, he formed the Stamps Quartet School Of Gospel Music. It was conducted in the Bethel Temple, within eight blocks of the Stamps-Baxter school (which was conducted in the Tyler Street Methodist Church), and on the very same dates. To many this

127

may have seemed somewhat unethical, but it was a boon for students. By paying one tuition, but commuting between both schools, a student could learn from and be inspired by the very best teachers of the day.[104]

It was during the second year of Frank Stamps's school that the largest enrollment for a school of shaped-note gospel music was recorded. The 1946 session of the Stamps Quartet School Of Gospel Music had a total of 1,171 students enrolled. Mrs. Frank Stamps modestly states, "As far as can be ascertained, this is the largest school of its kind in history."[105]

The competition between the Stamps Quartet Music Company and the Stamps-Baxter Music and Printing Company was not looked upon as competition by the lay public. Many persons thought they were actually the same corporation.[106] This can be seen as another reason for the equating in the public mind of the Stamps-Baxter name with the music performed by the quartets who represented these two aggressive companies.

To summarize the remaining history of the two companies: Baxter died in 1960, and the operation of the company was assumed by his wife, Clarice, who was affectionally called, "Ma."[107] She was able to maintain the company as a viable organization until her death in 1972. After her death, the company was maintained by her heirs, Dwight Brock, Lonnie Combs, Videt Polk, and Clyde Roach; with Brock serving as president.[108] In 1974 the company was sold to the Zondervan Corporation of Grand Rapids, Michigan, but the name Stamps-Baxter Music [of the Zondervan Corporation] is perpetuated in publications originating from the Dallas plant.

In 1962 the Stamps Quartet Company was purchased by the Blackwood Brothers and J.D. Sumner.[109] This company no longer publishes convention books and the School of Music is now called the National School of Gospel Music, located at Murray State University, Murray, Kentucky. The Stamps Quartet name has been perpetuated by the performing group, "J.D. Sumner and the Stamps Quartet."[110]

Sheet Music

The publishing of shaped note gospel song books began to give way to the publishing of gospel sheet music in the late 1940s. Lee Roy Abernathy is apparently given credit in *The History of Gospel Music* for being the first to publish a "full size, color front gospel sheet music."[111] The name of this song was "I Thank My Savior for It All," published in 1943.[112]

The prospect of royalties for airplay and prospective income from sheet music sales of popular gospel songs made any songwriters reluctant to submit their songs to the convention book publishers if they thought the songs had 'hit" potentiality. These songs would be copyrighted and published at personal expense. Many times this would be the first step toward establishment of a separate publishing concern. The growth in the number of publishing companies is reflected in the *Gospel Music 1977 Directory & Yearbook* published by the Gospel Music Association. This directory lists a total of 135 gospel music publishers.[113] Only two of these listed publishers, however, were among those seven previously listed as providing gospel songbooks for the 1976 National Gospel Singing Convention.[114] The majority of the remaining companies listed in the *Directory* publish sheet music only. Few of these publishers maintain their own printing equipment. Almost all southern gospel sheet music is contracted on a job basis to private printers.[115] According to Marvin Norcross, the three main publishers of southern gospel music today are the Benson Company; Zondervan, Incorporated; and Word, Incorporated.[116]

Field Research Data

The diversification of publishing companies is reflected in the Field Research sample. Of the twenty-three songs chosen by amateur family gospel music singers in South Georgia, three were in the Public Domain; three were published by Journey;[117] two each by Benson, Hemphill, and Lillenas; and one each by Cedarwood, LeFevre-Sing, Lexicon, Lynn, Mannah,

Singspiration/Zondervan, Tennessee, and Vaughan. Information concerning these publishers appears with their respective songs in Appendix A.

Radio, Recordings, and Television

It has been intimated from the above that the utilization of the media of radio and recordings, was begun by gospel music publishers primarily as a means of advertising their own publications. Whereas this can be considered true for the earliest beginnings, it was not long before radio, recordings, concertizing, and later, television broadcasts, became independent activities with varying degrees of interplay and a multitude of permutations. For a gospel music performing group to maintain a full-time livelihood it was, and is, necessary to be involved simultaneously in the selling of music, making of recordings, performing over radio or television, and the giving of concerts. In actuality it is impossible to separate these activities, but for purposes of discussion the following pages will focus primarily upon the history of gospel music in its relationship to the broadcast media.

Early Radio

It was stated that James D. Vaughan is credited with having been the first to broadcast southern gospel music over the radio in 1923.[118] With the proliferation of radio stations in the 1920s, it was not long before gospel quartets and ensembles were performing over this medium throughout the South and in other parts of the nation as well. It was previously mentioned that Homer Rodeheaver had a program of gospel music over KDKA, Pittsburgh, as early as 1922,[119] and the Moody Bible Institute in Chicago had its own radio station, WMBI, in 1926[120] Undoubtedly, religious music was broadcast over many other radio stations throughout the country.[121]

In the South the popular times for gospel broadcasts were

early in the morning, at noontime, and on Sundays. As a general rule the gospel groups were not paid for their services, but were allowed to promote their sponsor and to advertise when and where their concerts would be held. James Blackwood describes some of the problems of gospel quartets during the 1930s:

> Our radio career was on the way.
> There was only one hitch. We were radio performers, but we didn't get paid for our singing—although we could announce our engagements and open dates on the show and make our bookings over the air. . . .
> Finally, we made the decision to go to Jackson, Mississippi—the capitol [sic] and the largest city in the state—and try for a spot on WJDX radio. It would be a full-time place, but we wouldn't get paid for our services there either. We auditioned for—and got—a daily rather than a weekly show.
> We were able to sing and witness every day. But a problem arose. We were committed to sing Gospel music, and the station wanted us to mix some country songs in.
> Although we didn't like it very much, we finally agreed to sing some of the popular country and folk songs. But we knew we were Gospel singers. God had called us to sing Gospel, not country music. After a few programs, we got the station management to put the matter to a straw vote by the listeners. . . .
> The response was tremendous. The vote was overwhelming. We went to an all-Gospel program. We never sang "pop" music again.[122]

In the early years of radio all music was performed "live" rather than from recordings or tapes. This was a distance-limiting factor for a group's personal appearances, especially if they had a daily show in the early morning. The use of transcriptions was an important innovation, but it was not until the late 1940s that these transcriptions became widely used. Blackwood describes the process and the role his quartet played:

> Transcriptions were necessary in the forties, and God arranged it for us to be the first in the Gospel music transcription service. . . .
> The transcriptions were sixteen-inch vinyl discs, very flexible

and unbreakable. We cut the songs and then had them pressed, just like our records were pressed.

The library records were available to radio stations, and were the things which bridged the gap between live shows and the disc jockeys. . . .

Cutting the big vinyl discs was a tricky process. We'd often be tired and trying to get through, but recording wasn't like it is today . . . Then you had to do the whole thing. There was no editing. If it was right, good. If it wasn't, you either had to do it over again or just let it go.[123]

Radio Today

Today, radio plays an all-important part in the career of a gospel music performing group. Although groups as a rule no longer make live appearances over radio, the airplay of their recordings is no small factor in their success or failure.

The *Gospel Music 1977 Directory & Yearbook* lists over 830 radio stations in forty-five states, Canada, and Puerto Rico, which program varying amounts of gospel music. Although many are listed as being "full-time" gospel stations, at the time of this writing there is no station which plays strictly gospel music[124] on a twenty-four hour basis. KSON, in California, was to have been the first,[125] and actually operated as such for a limited amount of time. Due to internal staffing problems it has since changed format.[126]

The record for the longest continuing radio program in America goes to that of a gospel music broadcast. Marion Easterling has hosted a gospel music program over WKLL in Clanton, Alabama seven days each week since December 2, 1947. He has never missed a broadcast and very rarely has he pre-recorded his show for later replay.[127] As of September 29, 1976 this added up to 16,168 hours of airplay. This information has been submitted to the Guinness Book of World Records for inclusion in their next issue.[128]

That radio airplay affects the sale of recordings and sheet music is nowhere more evident than in the "Official Hits" charts of *The Singing News*. These charts are compiled solely from re-

132

sponses to questionnaires sent by the publication to selected radio stations.[129]

In recognition of the part that radio plays in the promotion of gospel music, the Gospel Music Association presents an annual Dove Award to the "Gospel Disc Jockey Of The Year."[130]

Recordings

It was stated previously that to James D. Vaughan goes the credit for sponsoring the first southern gospel music recordings. The lack of documentation in support of such a claim was also mentioned.[131] Complicating the matter is the distinction usually made between having recordings made at one's own expense, to be sold at concert engagements; and those recordings made under contract with a major record company whereby the company arranges for the sale of the recordings through its own distribution procedures.

In almost all of the few secondary sources which mention the subject, "Frank Stamps and his All-Stars"[132] receives credit for being the first gospel music quartet to record for a major label.[133] This recording, mentioned previously, was entitled "Give The World A Smile" and was produced by RCA Victor in 1927.[134] However, this may not have been the "first." In *The History of Gospel Music* it is mentioned that:

> At the age of five, Lee Roy Abernathy was singing in his good father's "ATCO" Quartet. This was in 1918, the year World War I ended. The ATCO Quartet, with Lee Roy Abernathy, made its recording debut on the RCA label. When Lee Roy reached the age of eleven—1924—he and the ATCO Quartet, Lee Roy singing first tenor, were recorded by Columbia.[135]

Regardless of whether the Frank Stamps' 1927 recording can be substantiated as a legitimate "first," it is certain that his quartet served as a model for many subsequent quartets. Apparently very few gospel groups recorded on the major labels, however. Blackwood relates:

133

There was practically no Gospel singing on records in those days [the late 1940s]. People could buy classical and popular music, along with some country and western records, but about the only Gospel records we knew of were ones recorded by Frank Stamps and the All Stars in the twenties.

When we checked out the possibilities of recording our songs, we decided to use our own label. . . .

Those first records were big black 78-rpm discs.

"When we go into the record business, we are going to advertise our records everywhere we can," we decided just before we cut our first record.

We bought ads in every religious periodical across the country. The advertising costs [sic] hundreds of dollars, but we sold thousands of records through it.

We started carrying records to our concerts. Boxes and boxes and boxes of the heavy black discs.[136]

The gospel recording group with perhaps the greatest longevity[137] is the Chuck Wagon Gang. This group, comprised of Anna, Rose, Jim (Ernest), and their father, D.P. "Dad" Carter, made their first gospel recording for Columbia in 1937, although they had recorded country songs previously.[138] The Chuck Wagon Gang was sponsored by Bewley Mills Flour over radio station WBAP in Forth Worth, Texas. They acquired the name by being asked to assume the name of a previous group sponsored by that company.[139] According to Daniel, this group "became the first full time professional singers of gospel songs without a connection with a publisher, school or evangelist.[140] The Chuch Wagon Gang still records under contract to Columbia[141] and has recorded over 300 titles and sixteen Columbia albums.[142] Over forty Columbia album releases contain their songs[143] and they are believed to have sold more records than any other gospel group.[144]

Billboard magazine[145] did not begin reporting gospel music until 1964. The first gospel music chart of this publication was entitled "Best Selling Gospel LPs By Label." It appeared July 26, 1964. A copy of this first *Billboard* gospel music chart is included in Appendix D. On this chart all of the recordings were performed by white singers and the records were grouped under record label subheadings. By 1976, the "Billboard Best Selling

134

Gospel LPs" chart, which appears monthly, lists only recordings produced by Afro-American groups.[146] The obvious biases of both the all-black *Billboard* chart and the all-white *Singing News* chart,[147] both considered authoritative by their constituents, would present several problems to a researcher attempting to trace even recent history of recorded gospel music from an interracial standpoint.[148] In many respects, however, it may be more realistic to have two separate gazeteers. The difference between the two distinct types of gospel music was mentioned at the beginning of this chapter.

Distribution of recordings has been a persistent problem with gospel music. Stores that sell predominantly secular recordings are reluctant to stock gospel records due to the limited demand for the product from their clientele. Religious bookstores, on the other hand, are reluctant to stock a large inventory of gospel records because of competition with gospel performing groups who set up recording displays and sell records at their concerts. Currently, concert sales account for the majority of gospel recordings sold.[149]

The three major recording companies, RCA, Columbia, and Capitol, produce only a relatively limited number of religious music recordings. The largest producer of religious music records is Word, Incorporated, mentioned previously in conjunction with music publishing.[150]

Word, Incorporated

Word had its beginning in 1950, with an imaginary broadcast of a play-by-play football game between Christianity and Evil, prepared for a local youth rally.[151] The name of the imaginary radio station was WORD. Jarrell McCracken, creator of the script, was besieged by demands for the 78-rpm transcriptions he had made and he reluctantly made 100 additional copies. As McCracken was a ministerial student at the time, the $75 investment to make the copies was quite substantial. A friend suggested that the name of the imaginary radio station become that

135

of the record label. The name of this very first Word record was "The Game Of Life."[152]

The investment was a success, and after several partnerships, Word became incorporated in 1953. From this beginning, expansion of the company has been constant. At present the company's main interest is in religious recordings, but it also publishes religious music, Word Books, and a periodical entitled *Faith at Work.* In addition to its own Word recording label, the corporation owns the Canaan and Myrrh labels. As a general rule the Word label is reserved for traditional religious music, the Canaan label is used for southern quartet-style gospel music, and the Myrrh label is used for contemporary rock-oriented religious recordings. Word, Incorporated also distributes records for several other companies by various contractual agreements.[153]

Word, Incorporated cannot be considered to have a monopoly on the gospel music recording field, however. The *Gospel Music 1977 Directory & Yearbook* lists fifty-three recording studios and seventy-nine record companies.[154] Several names are duplicated within the two categories.

For a gospel music performing group to consider entering the field as a full-time vocation, apparently it is of the utmost necessity to make a recording. Bob Benson, Senior, gives some of the reasons for this necessity:

> The importance of records in the development of the career of a gospel group or artist can hardly be overemphasized. It is not only the hope of all beginning performers to record—it is really an absolute necessity. . . .
>
> Early religious records were largely "custom projects" in that it was assumed and usually true that the artists themselves would sell most of the product in their own personal appearances. If the label could distribute additional records to stores and rack-jobber-distributors, it would be so much the better.
>
> The recording scene is different today in that the companies that record religious music are making greater commitments to aid in the process of making their rosters of talent known in the marketplace. . . .
>
> For the new artist the record is a must. If a recording contract can be obtained that will provide know-how and resources, then so much the better. If it is only a custom record that will establish

136

a "track record" to interest the labels, the record is probably the most singularly important tool in the beginning. Songs and arrangements will establish identity and direction, display talents and abilities to communicate and provide a strong source of revenue as well.[155]

The National Academy of Recording Arts and Sciences (NARAS) began giving a "Grammy" award to religious recordings in 1961.[156] The award for that first year was won by Mahalia Jackson for *Everytime I Feel the Spirit*. In 1967 two awards were given for religious recordings. In 1968, NARAS added a third category, "Soul Gospel." Interestingly, the Soul Gospel award for that year went to Dottie Rambo, a white singer, who was accompanied by an Afro-American choir. This was for the album, *The Soul of Me*. The titles of the three NARAS categories for religious music have varied slightly in subsequent years. The current categories and their winners are:

Best Soul Gospel Performance: Mahalia Jackson, "How I Got Over" (Columbia);

Best Inspirational Performance (non-classical): Gary Paxton, "The Astonishing, Outrageous, Amazing, Incredible, Unbelievable World of Gary S. Paxton" (New Pax);

Best Gospel Performance (other than Soul Gospel): Oak Ridge Boys, "Where The Soul Never Dies" (Columbia).[157]

In 1976, for the first time, the Gospel Music Association presented Dove Awards for recordings other than in the southern gospel tradition. The present Dove Award categories for recordings are: Contemporary, Southern Gospel, Inspirational, and Best Gospel Record Album by a Non-Gospel Artist.[158]

The important part that recordings play in the ability of a gospel performing group to remain self-supporting dramatizes the need for a history of white gospel music recordings. To the writer's knowledge there is none.[159]

Television

Gospel music has been a part of television in the South since its inception. The Homeland Harmony quartet performed on the first television broadcast in Atlanta over WAGA-TV on March 8, 1949;[160] and the Blackwood Brothers performed over KMTV in Omaha, Nebraska, even before that, on December 25, 1948.[161]

The first complete gospel music television show was probably "Gospel Music Caravan" starring the LeFevre Family, the Blue Ridge Boys, the Prophets, and the Johnson Sisters.[162] Other prominent television shows in the past have been "Singing Time in Dixie" which was begun in 1964, the "LeFevre Family Show," "Gospel Roundup," and "TV Gospel Concert."[163]

The Lewis Family, a "Bluegrass Gospel" group in Augusta, Georgia, has probably been featured on television longer than any other group. They began their career in 1951, and have been performing regularly over WJBF-TV in Augusta since 1954.[164]

The *Gospel Music 1977 Directory & Yearbook* does not have a listing of television stations with gospel music programming; however, the syndicated television program "Gospel [Singing] Jubilee" has received the Dove Award as the "Best Gospel Television Program" every year that the awards have been given.[165] This program is a variety show of gospel performing groups hosted by Les Beasley, lead singer with the Florida Boys. The show is taped in Nashville, Tennessee, for syndication over fifty-seven television stations at the time of this writing.[166]

Performance Rights Organizations

The broadcasting of copyrighted music over television and radio, and the concert performance of copyrighted music for profit, carry the moral and legal obligation of providing compensation to the copyright holder for the use of such materials. Performance rights organizations came into being because of intentional and unintentional failures of some broadcast companies and performing organizations to fulfill this obligation, and the difficulty of individuals in maintaining records of users of their copyrighted materials.

The first American performance rights organization was the American Society of Composers, Authors, and Publishers [ASCAP] formed in 1919.[167] The second was SESAC,[168]founded in 1931. The third performance rights organization was Broadcast Music, Incorporated [BMI] which was founded in the early 1940s.[169] An attempt to organize a fourth performing rights organization in 1953, for gospel music only, prompted the only major court case involving gospel music known to the writer.[170] In this case, Affiliated Music Enterprises, Inc., *versus* SESAC, Inc.,[171] the latter organization was charged with having a monopoly on music published in shaped notes. Whereas SESAC, at that time, did represent almost all of the shaped note music publishers, it represented only approximately one-third of all gospel music published. This fascinating case was ultimately dismissed on the grounds that music performed from shaped notes is indistinguishable from music performed from round notes, and therefore "irrelevant to performing rights."[172] The judge also recognized that the plaintiff, Affiliated Music Enterprises, Inc., "desired to engage in similar monopolistic practices. . . ."[173] This court case apparently terminated attempts to form a fourth organization. The current list of gospel music publishers shown in Appendix C indicates a fairly even distribution of representation among the three existing performance rights organizations.

Gospel Sings and Their Promotion

The transition from the Gospel Singing Convention, where the majority of those attending join in the sight-singing of new songs, and where ensemble singing is a rarity; to the Gospel Sing, where the majority of those attending come as an audience to be entertained by gospel music singing ensembles, was shown in Chapter 4.

Beginning of Trend

Although, it is probably that ensemble singing as a brief respite, entertainment, and inspiration for the group singers was a part of the scheduled activities for singing conventions from their beginnings,[174] the trend toward full concert performance began to appear in approximately the 1920s. It was pointed out previously that this was at the time when radio broadcasting was gaining momentum and many gospel quartets began singing over the air. Listeners soon wanted to hear their favorite groups in person and in more than just an occasional performance—as would be the case at a singing convention. This, in turn, led to the Saturday night concerts before the all-day singings on Sunday. Aspiring professional groups, many of whom were trying to perform gospel music on a full-time basis, would announce over the radio that they would be at a certain sing on a certain date, thereby hoping to attract a large crowd. At these concerts the singers would charge a nominal admission or take up a "free-will offering," sell songbooks or sheet music, and sell their custom-made recordings.

Need for Larger Auditoriums

At the early stages, most gospel music concerts, generally called "sings," would take place in churches. In fact, many sings still do take place in churches. This is especially true when amateur and semi-professional singing groups provide the music. Sometimes even the most highly paid professional groups will schedule a Sunday concert at a church in order to build up good will and to maintain a contact with their grassroots support.[175] But it was in the smaller churches where the singing of gospel music was the most welcome, and where it continues to thrive.

It was not too long, however, before crowds larger than a church could hold were attracted to the concerts. Although documentation from secondary sources is almost non-existent, it is certain that individuals, later termed Promoters, would schedule several of the better-known groups and rent large auditoriums for this purpose. Often the concerts would be in conjunction with a fund-raising campaign for a charitable organization, or with an event such as a county fair. Negotiations for payment would be for a fixed fee or for a percentage of the gate receipts.

In the 1940s and early 1950s, gospel singing conventions were still a favorite activity, drawing very large crowds. Aspiring professional groups were often the featured performers. Edwards, who attended as many of these singing conventions as possible, kept a scrapbook between 1945 and 1955.[176] In 1955 he published a book which included photographs of "113 of the nation's finest gospel quartets."[177] This is undoubtedly the most complete list of ensembles which were active during that time. This list, as presented, by Edwards, is shown as Figure 8.

As previously stated, the All-Night Gospel Sing was originated by V.O. Stamps in 1938. This was in conjunction with the annual closing services of the Stamps-Baxter School of Music.[178] No admission was charged. The first "paid" all-night sing is said to have taken place in Atlanta, Georgia, in 1946.[179] Wally Fowler gained an even wider commercial audience for gospel music when he began promoting "All-Night Gospel Singings" at the Ryman Auditorium, home of the Grand Ol' Opry, in Nashville, Tennessee. The first was held on November 8, 1948.[180] Labreeska Hemphill describes the impact of this novelty:

In Nashville, Tennessee, a man named Wally Fowler had a brand new idea. Why not shift the Sunday all-day singings to Friday and Saturday nights and have all-night singings. After ironing out the wrinkles, he presented his plan to the public, and the all-night singing was born.[181]

Wally Fowler moved the singings from the churches, and rented huge auditoriums. Instead of asking one special group to perform, he invited many. The order of the proceedings was reversed. Now there were few congregational songs and many by the special groups. . . .

Soon all the Southland was astir with this unheard of innovation. A singing that lasted all night! Were they really going to sing all night? People came by the hundreds to see, purchasing their tickets at the door. Never had gospel singing experienced such a revolution, and never had it attracted the public on such a large scale.[182]

141

INDEX OF QUARTETS

Figure 8. Edward's 1955 list of gospel ensembles.

142

Long Distance Travel

Soon all-night sings began to be scheduled throughout the country, and popular quartets would be required to travel greater and greater distances. This was a grueling experience. Blackwood describes some of the discomfort of a quartet and an accompanist on a extended trip:

> There is simply no way for five men to ride comfortably for that long in a car.
> I tried sleeping sitting up. Then I'd get down on the floor and put my head on the seat. I'd try to lie down. Every position there was, we tried.
> There is simply no way to ride comfortably and try to sleep in a car. Not with five full-grown men.[183]

Some quartets began using airplanes for their traveling but that proved impractical. Complications included weather, lack of transportation to and from isolated airports, and "down time" necessitated by routine engine inspections and overhauls. The crash of one of the Blackwood Brothers' airplanes in 1954, which caused the death of R.W. Blackwood and Bill Lyles, served to conclude subsequent experiments with air travel.[184]

J.D. Sumner, who began singing bass with the Blackwood Brothers after the death of Bill Lyles, is credited with originating the idea of travel by bus. Considering the fact that now almost all gospel groups, and many performers of other styles of music, travel by bus, it is surprising to learn that this innovation was initially resisted.[185] After experimentation with used buses in 1955, the first new buses, custom-designed for gospel performers, were purchased in 1962 by the Blackwood Brothers and the Statesmen quartets.[186]

National Quartet Convention

J.D. Sumner is also credited with the idea of a National Quartet Convention, where all of the professional groups could

143

meet at one itme to share ideas and plans. Sumner describes the idea:

> This idea was fostered many years ago. . . . [I had] the notion that we have one time a year when we could get all gospel musicians together for two or three days in the same town. . . .
>
> The idea stemmed originally from the camp meetings we used to attend in Florida. Camp meetings were based on preaching, of course, but I couldn't understand why we couldn't do the same thing with singing.
>
> . . . In 1956 we held the first National Quartet Convention in Memphis. . . .
>
> Our first convention was a three-day affair. Thursday night fell flat, but Friday and Saturday were successful. The next year I picked out four of the top groups of the day—the Blackwood Brothers, Statesmen, Speer Family and LeFevres—and let them sing in a special Thursday night concert. Attendance picked up.[187]

The National Quartet Convention has continued to grow and is held annually during the same week as the Gospel Music Association Dove Awards.[188] The Twentieth Annual Session was held October 5 through 10, 1976 in Nashville, Tennessee. The performers chosen to sing on this program are generally considered to be the very best in the southern gospel tradition.[189]

Other Large Promotions

Another gospel promotion with a twenty-year history is the annual "Sun-down to Sun-up Gospel Singing" in Waycross, Georgia. This sing, traditionally held the last Saturday night in August, is sponsored by the Waycross Shrine Club as a benefit for crippled children.[190] For many years this singing and the one held in Bonifay, Florida, were the only true "all-night" singings.[191] The remainder of singings using the "all-night" appellation would generally conclude sometime between approximately midnight and two o'clock in the morning.

The gospel promotion advertised as the "World's Biggest" is held annually in Bonifay, Florida, on the Saturday before the Fourth of July. According to J.G. Whitfield, the promoter, its

144

peak attendance, verified by gate receipts, was 14,000 in 1974.[192] This number differs drastically from "estimated" attendance at many other gospel concerts appearing in advertisements and in fan magazines.

Other large promotions, but far from a complete listing, include: "Singing on the Mountain" in Bryson City, North Carolina; "Shenandoah Valley Sing" in Berryville, Virginia; "Blackwood Brothers Homecoming" in Memphis, Tennessee; "Dutchland Sun-down to Sun-up Festival" in Cripple Creek, Pennsylvania; "New England Sun-down to Sun-up Festival" in Spring Hill, Maine; "Albert E. Brumley Sundown to Sunup Singing" in Springdale, Arkansas; "All-Night Singing" in Watermelon Park, Indiana; and the "Singing News Fan Festival" (formerly the "International Gospel Song Festival") held in various locations.[193]

Gospel Talent Agencies

For many years gospel groups acted as their own managers and booking agents. One member of the ensemble would be assigned the managerial tasks in addition to his performance duties. A common practice was for the groups to operate without a written contract, often leading to misunderstandings of varying kinds. To satisfy the need for a more business-like manner of dealing with the increased demand for engagements by popular groups, Don Light established the first all-gospel talent agency in 1965. Light recalls:

> Most of the groups were managed and booked by a member of the group. I felt it was virtually impossible to sing and be a performer, spend 30 to 100 hours a week on a bus going to and from appearances, devote the amount of time on the phone required to do justice to the task of booking, and keep up on the latest happenings in the music business world.[194]

Light also initiated the consistent usage of written contracts, stating that "the gospel music business needed to be run as a business."[195]

145

The success of Light's agency soon led to the establishment of similar enterprises. At the time of this writing there are at least twenty-three talent agencies booking gospel music groups. Most of these agencies handle gospel music talent exclusively.[196]

Listings of Professional Gospel Singers

The list of gospel quartets [ensembles] compiled by Edwards from 1944 to 1955 was shown on page 142. Another list appeared as part of Gentry's *History and Encyclopedia of Country, Western, and Gospel Music* in 1961.[197] The forty-five "Gospel Singers," including soloists,[198] which he tabulated are shown as Figure 9 below.

Lee Roy Abernathy; Buford Abner and Swanee River boys; J.T. Adams; Barnette Brothers; James Blackwood and Blackwood Brothers Quartet; Blue Ridge Quartet; Cavaleers Quartet; Chuck Wagon Gang; John Daniel Quartet; Jimmy Davis; Don and Earl; Florida Boys Quartet; Foggy River Boys (Marksmen); Wally Fowler; Frank Stamps Quartet; Harmoneers Quartet; Harvesters Quartet; Homeland Harmony Quartet; Johnson Family Singers; Johnson Sisters; Jordanaires; Keller-York Quartet; LeFevre Quartet; Lewis Family; Masters Family; Marshall Pack; Plainsmen Quartet; Rangers Quartet; Rebels Quartet; Revelaires; Revelators Quartet; Ace Richman and Sunshine Boys Quartet; Senators Quartet; George Beverly Shea; Smith Sacred Singers; Sons of Song; Southern Gospel Singers; Speer Family; Spencer Family; Stamps-Baxter Quartet; Statesmen Quartet; Trace Family; Big Jim Waite; Weatherford Quartet; Wills Family Quartet; etc. [sic][199]

Figure 9. Gentry's 1961 list of gospel singers.

One group conspicuously absent from both Edwards's and Gentry's listings deserves mention both because of its longevity and for its contributions to gospel music. This is the Happy Goodman Family, formed in 1937 by Howard Goodman,[200] and winner in 1968 of the first NARAS Grammy award for a recording made by an exclusively southern gospel singing group.[201] The publish-

146

ing arm of this performing group, Journey Music Company, was the publisher of more songs chosen by the amateur performing groups of the Field Research than any other company.[202]

The current listing of "Artists/Musicians" affiliated with the Gospel Music Association is listed in Appendix C.[203]

Non-professional Gospel Sings

Gospel sings have become a ubiquitous phenomenon, especially in the South. During the two summers of the Field Research the writer noted that gospel sings were held on Friday and Saturday nights in almost every county surveyed. Many times sings would also be held on Thursday nights and during the day on Sunday. Although the writer did not solicit the information, it was volunteered that gospel sings were a part of almost every county's Bicentennial festivities.

Fan and Trade Periodicals

Interest in the performing activities of favorite gospel singing groups led to the publication of periodicals devoted to items of interest to the fans of these groups. These periodicals, in general, are supported by advertising and subscription sales. Many are promotional magazines for certain favorite groups and, consequently, their scope is limited. Often these periodicals have extremely short publishing histories.

The *Gospel Music 1977 Directory & Yearbook* lists a total of thirty-seven periodicals which cater to a gospel music constituency.[204] For several of these, such as *Billboard* and *Variety,* gospel music forms only a small portion of their coverage. At present, the two leading gospel-music-only periodicals are *The Singing News* and *Concert Life.*

Concert Life is published in a forty-eight to sixty-page, four-color magazine format. It began publication in 1974 and presently has a circulation of approximately 50,000.[205] *The Singing News* is published in a newspaper format and 1976 marked its eighth year of publication. *The Singing News* has the largest circulation of present periodicals devoted exclusively to gospel music. In 1976 this circulation was advertised as being over 250,000.[206]

Gospel Music Association

Activity and interest in gospel music concerts, sales of gospel music recordings, and sales of gospel sheet music continued to grow at a steady rate due to the commercial activities previously mentioned as beginning in the late 1940s. This growth, however, was on a sporadic basis and was prompted by aggressive groups and individuals who were intent in building their own loyal following. There was little coordination or communication between even the leading groups. The annual National Quartet Convention, mentioned previously, was the only semblance of unification in the gospel music industry; and this was a promotion where the performers were paid and the sponsor hoped to make a profit from the gate receipts. There was a growing need for a non-profit organization to serve as a central agency and as a coordinator of the myriad activities that were flourishing under the aegis of gospel music.

Charter and Beginning

Significantly, the very first article on the subject of gospel music which appeared in *Billboard* magazine concerned a proposed meeting of those interested in the forming of a Gospel Music Association. This meeting was held on June 3, 1964.[207] Of course the concept and planning of this organization had taken place months and even years before. On May 19, 1964, James Blackwood, J.D. Sumner, Cecil Blackwood, Dorothy Pate, and Don Butler applied for and received a Charter of Incorporation as a non-profit organization for the Gospel Music Association, Inc., from the State of Tennessee.[208] This Charter was made available to the fledgling organization in late 1964 and a tempo-

148

rary Board of Directors was appointed during the National Quartet Convention of that year.[209] Members of this first interim Board of Directors were:

Don Baldwin, John T. Benson, [Jr.], James Blackwood, Bill Hefner, Charlie Lamb, [Meurice] Maurice LeFevre, Urias LeFevre, Don Light, [Chairman], Hovie Lister, [W. F.] Jim Myers, W.B. Nowlin, Frances Preston, Warren Roberts, Larry Scott, Brock Speer, J.D. Sumner, [James S.] Jim Weatherington, and J.G. Whitfield.[210]

In 1965, at the National Quartet Convention, the first duly elected Board of Directors was installed. The officers and members of this Board of Directors were:

Honorary President: Tennessee Ernie Ford
First Vice-president: James Blackwood
Second Vice-president: Urias LeFevre
Secretary: Marvin Norcross
Treasurer: Don Light
Other members: Don Baldwin, Robert Benson, [Earl] Smitty Gatlin, Wes Gilmer, Jerry Goff, Rusty Goodman, Juanita Jones, Meurice LeFevre, [Hershel Lester] Hovie Lister, W.F. Myers, W.B. Nowlin, Harold Penn, Darol Rice, Brock Speer, [Chairman of the Board], J.D. Sumner, James Weatherington, Elon Whisenhunt, [C.W.] Buzz Wilburn, and Pat Zondervan.[211]

The 1977 listing of Officers and Directors of the Gospel Music Association is shown in Appendix C.

According to the Constitution of the Gospel Music Association, its purpose is simply "to foster interest among the general public and to further the spreading of the Gospel of Jesus Christ on earth."[212]

Milestones of Progress

Within a relatively short period of time the Gospel Music As-

149

sociation made significant progress in improving communications among the various facets of the burgeoning industry, and also in providing a focus for future development. In 1967, a full-time Executive Secretary, LaWayne Satterfield, was hired[213] and in 1968, Norma L. Boyd took over this position.[214]

In 1968, a monthly periodical in a newspaper format, *Good News,* was instituted by the Gospel Music Association. By 1975 fifteen other regular publications printing gospel music news exclusively had been established. It was decided, therefore, that the publication of *Good News* should not be in competition with the other periodicals, and the format was changed in that year to a newsletter for Association members only.[215]

In 1969, the Gospel Music Association instituted a "Dove Award" program, patterned after the National Academy of Recording Arts and Sciences' "Grammy Award." Presently the Dove Award is given in a total of seventeen categories, including an "Associate Award" voted upon exclusively by Associate Members for the most significant contribution to gospel music within the past year.[216] A list of Dove Award winners from 1969 through 1976 appears in Appendix C.

The Gospel Music Association also prepares an annual recording of the Top Ten Songs nominated for Dove Awards. The first of these recordings was released in 1970. These recordings should be invaluable for future research in gospel music.[217]

In 1971, a Gospel Music Hall of Fame was created to honor both living and deceased contributors to the promulgation of the Gospel through music. The criteria used in selecting members of the Hall of Fame and a list of the current members are included in Appendix C. The ground-breaking for an actual Hall of Fame edifice was conducted on October 9, 1976.[218] The building is to be located across from the Country Music Hall of Fame in Nashville, Tennessee.

In 1971, the first annual *Gospel Music Directory & Yearbook* was published. This was the first attempt to pull together the various facets of the gospel music industry into a central repository of information. Aside from brief editorials and advertising, the publication lists names and addresses of Artists/Musicians, Talent Agencies, Periodicals, Radio Stations, Record Companies,

Recording Studios, Performing Rights Organizations, and Publishers. The current listings in each of these categories are included in Appendix C.

Inroads of Racial Integration

The Gospel Music Association Hall of Fame members, and most recipients of the Dove Award, reflect the all-white and all-southern bias of the southern gospel tradition. Several inroads have been made toward a broadening of horizons, however, and although the movement is slight it is perhaps important that some of these manifestations be pointed out.

In 1969, in an overt effort to promote racial harmony, the Gospel Music Association chose an all-black group, Spirit of Memphis, to provide the total entertainment for the first Dove Awards program.[219] In 1971, another all-black group, Andrae Crouch and the Disciples, was the featured group for the Dove Awards banquet of that year.

In 1972, the first integrated southern gospel group was formed when Sherman Andrus joined the Imperials quartet.[220] In both 1975 and 1976 this quartet received the Best Male Gospel Group Dove Award, and in 1976 their album, *No Shortage,* received the Dove Award as Best Album in the Contemporary category.[221]

Mahalia Jackson has been nominated for the Hall of Fame (deceased category) for several years[222] and in 1976 Clevant Derricks and Thomas A. Dorsey were each nominated for the Hall of Fame (living category).

In 1976, Charlie Pride, Negro Country/Western singer, received a Dove Award for Best Gospel Record Album by a Non-Gospel Artist.

The broadening of Dove Award categories in 1976 to include Contemporary, Inspirational, and By A Non-Gospel Artist, for Albums-of-the-Year is also a significant milestone in the expansion of the theretofore southern-gospel-only guild.

Executive Director Appointed

In 1976, Don Butler was appointed the first Executive Director of the Gospel Music Association.[223] The present permanent staff of the Gospel Music Association, that is, aside from the Officers and Directors, is comprised of Don Butler, Executive Director; Norma L. Boyd, Executive Secretary; and a full-time secretary, Cindy London.

Future Plans

The completion of the Gospel Music Hall of Fame edifice is the primary goal of the organization at this time. Future plans, however, include additional overt attempts at racial integration, establishment of a grant for research in gospel music and perhaps, someday, the establishment of a Chair of Gospel Music at a college or university.[224]

Summary

The commercialization of gospel music has expanded from being limited solely to the stipends of the early music teachers and profits from the sale of songbooks, to include concert performances, phonograph recordings, full-time gospel radio stations, a proliferation of publishers, television programs; and a varied host of support personnel, many of whom are able to earn their full means of support from some aspect of gospel music.

The establishment of the Gospel Music Association in 1964, and its subsequent growth and leadership, can be seen as a strong factor in the beginning professionalization of gospel music.

Notes

1. Arthur Linwood Stevenson, *The Story of Southern Hymnology* (1931; rpt. New York: AMS Press, 1975), Chapter IX, "Is the Gospel Hymn Commercialized?," pp. 81–83, is only one example.
2. Robert W. John, "The American Singing School Movement, 1720–1780," *Journal of the American Musicological Society, VII* (Summer, 1954), 165.
3. Allen P. Britton, "The Singing School Movement In The United States," *Report of the Eighth Congress of the International Musicological Society* (New York: Barenreiter Kassel, 1961), p. 95.
4. Adoption of the term "gospel music" for Afro-American religious music is relatively recent. Most secondary sources viewed by the writer cite Thomas A. Dorsey's conversion and first gospel song in 1921 as its beginning; cf. Anna Bontemps, "Gospel—Rock, Church, Rock," *The Negro in Music and Art* (1967; 2nd ed.; New York: Publishers Company, Inc., 1968), p. 78. A scholarly history of the Afro-American gospel music tradition appears as Chapter 1 in Irene Viola Jackson, "Afro-American Gospel Music And Its Social Setting With Special Attention To Roberta Martin" (unpublished Doctoral dissertation, Wesleyan University, 1974). See also Eileen Southern, *The Music of Black Americans: A History* (New York: W.W. Norton & Co., Inc., 1971), pp. 402–404, 497–498.
5. Rhythm and blues.
6. Daniel Goldberg, "1969—Gospel Makes Great Industry Strides," *Billboard,* LXXXI (August 16, 1969), S-16.
7. Douglas B. Green, *Country Roots: The Origins of Country Music* (New York: Hawthorn Books, Inc., 1976), p. 147.
8. Joel Francis Reed, "Anthony J. Showalter (1858–1924): Southern Educator, Publisher, Composer" (unpublished Doctoral dissertation, New Orleans Baptist Theological Seminary, 1975), pp. 9–10; Showalter's genealogy is traced on p. 10.
9. Anthony J. Showalter and Aldine S. Kieffer, eds., *The Singing School Tribute.* A Collection of Music for Singing-Schools, Conventions, Choirs, and Musical Societies: with Rudiments of Music (Dayton, Virginia: Ruebush, Kieffer & Co., 1880), cited in Reed, ibid., p. 25, title page shown on his p. 26.
10. Anthony J. Showalter, "Brief Sketch of The Editor," *The Best Gospel Songs and Their Composers* [hereinafter referred to as *Best*] (Dalton, Georgia: The A.J. Showalter Company, 1904), n.p.
11. The National School Of Music, Roanoke, Alabama.
12. Reed, op. cit., pp. 34–35.
13. Christopher C. Stafford, "A.J. Showalter," *Vaughan's Family Visitor,* LXXI (August, 1971), 11.
14. Showalter, *Best,* loc. cit.; according to the same source, Showalter was also treasurer of the Perry Brothers Music Company of Chattanooga, Tennessee; vice-president of Cherokee Lumber and Manufacturing Company of Dalton, Georgia; and owner of an orchard of nearly 20,000 trees.
15. A.J. Showalter, *Class, Choir and Congregation;* For Singing Schools, Conventions, Normal Schools, Sunday Schools, Chorus Choirs [sic] and

153

Congregations (Dalton, Georgia: A.J. Showalter & Co., 1888); the cover of this collection is shown in Reed, op. cit., p. 64.

16. George P. Jackson, *White Spirituals in the Southern Uplands* (1933; New York: Dover Publications, Inc., 1965), p. 364.

17. A. J. Showalter and J. H. Tenney, *Work and Worship;* A Large and Varied Collection of Hymns and Tunes [etc.] (Dalton, Georgia: The A.J. Showalter Co., 1886).

18. Jackson, loc., cit.

19. Began December, 1884 as *Our Musical Visitor;* changed after three numbers to *The Music Teacher;* changed in January, 1900 to *The Music Teacher And Home Magazine;* ceased publication circa 1924; see Reed, op. cit., pp. 47–59.

20. Showalter, *Best,* loc. cit.

21. Reed, op. cit., p. 114; "later changed to the Southern Normal Conservatory," (no date cited).

22. Cf. ibid., pp. 114–118.

23. Stella Benton Vaughan, "History Of The James D. Vaughan Publishing Company," Installment IV, *Vaughan's Family Visitor,* LX? (1960?), p. 4; the "Installments IV-XI" made available to the writer had been separated from the publication.

24. R.A. Glenn and Aldine S. Kieffer, eds., *New Melodies of Praise:* A Collection of New Tunes and Hymns, for the Sabbath School and Praise Meeting (Singer's Glen, Virginia: Ruebush, Kieffer & Co., 1877); listed in Grace I. Showalter, *The Music Books of Ruebush & Kieffer 1866–1942: A Bibliography* (Richmond: Virginia State Library, 1975), p. 4.

25. Grace I. Showalter, ibid.

26. *Gospel Chimes* (1900), cited by Mrs. J.R. (Ma) Baxter and Videt Polk, *Gospel Song Writers Biography* (Dallas: Stamps-Baxter Music & Printing Company, 1971), p. 15; and several other references, none of which include further bibliographic information.

27. Jo Lee Fleming, "James D. Vaughan, Music Publisher, Lawrenceburg, Tennessee. 1912–1964" (unpublished Doctoral dissertation, Union Theological Seminary, 1972), p. 51; Fleming does not indicate where Vaughan's earlier publications were printed.

28. C.C. Stafford, "Composers of the Past: James D. Vaughan (1864–1941)" *Vaughan's Family Visitor,* LXXI (February, 1972), 5, 14.

29. Stella B. Vaughan, "History of The James D. Vaughan, Music Publisher," *Vaughan's Family Visitor* (1964); reprinted *Vaughan's Family Visitor,* LXXV (August, 1975), n.p. Cf. Fleming op. cit., p. 134, who says "beginning 1912."

30. Fleming, op. cit., p. 54, 114ff, 159; the original title was *The Musical Visitor,* changed to the present title "in the early 1920s." Although the company changed hands once since it was sold in 1964, the publication of the periodical has been continuous; the company is presently located in Cleveland, Tennessee.

31. Ibid., p. 49.

32. Ibid., p. 55.

33. Information in brackets from ibid.

34. Stella Benton Vaughan, "History" (1964), rpt. *Vaughan's Family Visitor,* LXXV (August, 1975), n.p.

154

35. Stella Benton Vaughan, "History" (1960?), op. cit., Installment V, p. 5 (second of 2 page 5's).
36. Vaughan, "History" (1964), loc. cit.
37. W.L. Muncy, Jr., *A History Of Evangelism in the United States* (Kansas City, Kansas: Central Seminary Press, 1945), pp. 166–167, states that the First Baptist Church of Shreveport, Louisiana, was the first local church in the U.S. to own and operate a broadcasting station; it began broadcasting a regular program in 1921; this may have included gospel music; also, Martin J. Neeb, Jr., "An Historical Study of American Non-Commercial AM Broadcast Stations Owned And Operated By Religious Groups, 1920–1966" (unpublished Doctoral dissertation, Northwestern University, 1967), pp. 627–635, lists eighteen stations which had begun broadcasting by 1922.
38. Vaughan, "History" (1964) rpt. *Vaughan's Family Visitor,* LXXV (September , 1975), p. 4.
39. Fleming, op. cit., p. 59; Fleming's statement that WOAN operated on a frequency of 600 kilocycles [kilohertz], however, is incorrect; the correct frequency was 650kHz; later this frequency was shared with and finally purchased by WSM in Nashville, Tennessee; cf. Vaughan, "History" (1964) rpt. *Vaughan's Family Visitor, LXXV* (October, 1975), p. 4.
40. Vaughan, loc. cit.
41. Ibid.
42. Ibid.
43. Members of this quartet were: J.E. Wheeler, M.D. McWhorter, Adlai Lowry and Herman Walker; apparently one of them was the accompanist.
44. Vaughan, "History" (1960?), Installment IV, p. 6.
45. Ibid., Installment V, p. 5 (second of 2 p. 5's).
46. Clarice (Mrs. J.R. "Ma") Baxter and Videt Polk, *Gospel Song Writers Biography* (Dallas: Stamps-Baxter Music & Printing Company, 1971), p. 227; the title was *Winsett's Favorite Songs.*
47. Ibid.; also, the Winsett Company was the first to publish one of John W. Peterson's songs. Cf. John W. Peterson with Richard Engquist, *The Miracle Goes On* (Grand Rapids: Zondervan Publishing House, 1976), p. 77; Peterson's first song, "Yet There Is Room" (1940), coincidentally, had the same title as Sankey's first song; cf. p. 22, above.
48. Ibid.
49. Eugene M. Bartlett, Jr., Director of Church Music, Oklahoma Baptist General Convention of the Southern Baptist Convention, personal interview, Nashville, Tennessee, December 7, 1976.
50. Baxter and Polk, op. cit., p. 83.
51. Jackson, op. cit., p. 389.
52. Letter from Bob Brumley, co-owner of Albert E. Brumley and Sons, January 19, 1977.
53. Ibid.
54. "I'll Fly Away" has also been recorded twice by Arthur Fiedler and the Boston Pops. These recordings are: RCA Victor LSC-2870, and RCA Victor ARLI-0274. Information courtesy of W.F. Myers, SESAC, Inc., New York.
55. Baxter and Polk, op. cit., p. 23.

56. Brumley, loc. cit.
57. The 1977 book was not available in time for the company to be represented at the 1976 National Gospel Singing Convention in New Mexico.
58. Brumley, loc. cit.
59. Ibid.
60. Baxter and Polk, op. cit., p. 44.
61. Ibid.
62. Ibid., pp. 44–45.
63. Don Butler, Executive Director, Gospel Music Association, telephone interview, December 15, 1976.
64. Not only southern rurals.
65. Bartlett, loc. cit., speaking of statements he had heard.
66. "Biographical Sketch," *Precious Memories of Virgil O. Stamps* (Dallas: Stamps-Baxter Music and Printing Company, 1941), p. VI.
67. *Harbor Bells;* Our 1925 Book—For Sunday-Schools, Singing Schools, Revivals, Conventions, and General Use in All Religious Gatherings, (Jacksonville, Texas: The V.O. Stamps Music Co., 1925).
68. "Biographical Sketch," loc. cit.
69. John Daniel (J.D.) Sumner, prominent gospel singer, personal interview, Nashville, Tennessee, October 9, 1976.
70. Ibid.
71. Baxter and Polk, op. cit., p. 2.
72. Ibid., p. 3.
73. Don Butler, Executive Director, Gospel Music Association, personal interview, Nashville, Tennessee, December 9, 1976.
74. Ibid.
75. Stamps' office was initially in Jacksonville, Texas.
76. "Biographical Sketch," loc. cit.
77. Butler, loc. cit.
78. In 1939, when this arrangement was made, the "Stamps" company had not been formed. Blackwood later became owner of the Stamps Quartet Company and, therefore, was in competition with Stamps-Baxter when the above was written. Apparently he did not wish to use their name.
79. Kree Jack Racine, *Above All: The Life Story of the Blackwood Brothers Quartet* (Memphis: Jarodoce Publications, 1967), pp. 81–82.
80. James Blackwood with Dan Martin, *The James Blackwood Story* (Monroeville, Pennsylvania: Whitaker House, 1975), p. 64.
81. Ibid., p. 63.
82. Dorothy Horstman, *Sing Your Heart Out, Country Boy* (New York: E.P. Dutton & Co., Inc., 1975), p. 35; this number is more than twice that given by any other source, oral or written, known to the writer; yet according to Butler, loc. cit., even this number is not completely unrealistic.
83. This was to cause deliberate confusion when his brother, Frank, formed a competing company, the Stamps Quartet Company, in 1945.
84. Jan Cain, "First All Night Singing Was Held 38 Years Ago [W.B. Nowlin Remembers]," *The Singing News,* VIII (June, 1976), 2A, 19A.
85. This may have been as much as 100,000 watts.
86. Blackwood and Martin, op. cit., p. 62–63.
87. Cain, loc. cit.
88. Ibid.

89. Letter from Shirley Beary, Doctoral candidate with disserta-tion-in-progress on Stamps-Baxter Music and Printing Company, January 30, 1977; also, Beary, telephone interview, February 6, 1977.
90. Racine, op. cit., pp. 84–85.
91. "Biographical Sketch," op. cit., p. IX.
92. "Brief History Of A Wonderful Man [J.R. Baxter] Who Has Gone To A Better World," *Gospel Music News,* XXVI (February, 1960), p. 4.
93. Butler, loc. cit.
94. Shirley Beary, "The Stamps-Baxter Music And Printing Company: A Continuing American Tradition; 1926–1976" (Doctoral disserta-tion-in-progress, Southwestern Baptist Theological Seminary), pp. 159–164 [page numbers cited may be slightly different in final docu-ment]; the periodical was begun in 1927 as the *Stamps-Baxter News;* changed in June 1934 to *The Southern Music News;* changed in March 1940 to *Gospel Music News;* changed to the [Stamps-Baxter] *Newsletter* in January 1975; discontinued November 1975.
95. Ibid., p. 69.
96. Began 1924 as the V.O. Stamps School of Music; changed to Stamps-Baxter School of Music "sometime after" Baxter joined the com-pany in 1926, according to ibid., p. 94.
97. "Brief History Of A Wonderful Man . . . ," loc. cit.
98. Began February 3, 1947; closed July 1953, according to Beary, op. cit., p. 102.
99. Ibid., p. 100.
100. Otis J. Knippers, *Who's Who Among Southern Singers and Composers* (Lawrenceburg, Tennessee: James D. Vaughan Music Publisher, 1937), p. 132.
101. Ibid.; this may not have been a true first, however. Additional informa-tion concerning the Stamps' Quartet recordings appears on p. 133 above.
102. C.C. Stafford, "Composers of the Past: Frank H. Stamps (1896–1965)," *Vaughan's Family Visitor,* LXXIII (April, 1974), 6; see also *Memories and Modern Songs* (Dallas: Stamps Quartet Music Company, Inc., 1955), p. 7.
103. Beary, op. cit., p. 41.
104. Lou Hildreth, gospel music entrepreneur and television personality who attended both schools, personal interview, Nashville, Tennessee, Decem-ber 6, 1976.
105. Mrs. Frank Stamps, "In Loving Memory Frank H. Stamps (1896–1965)," *Gospel Singing Journal* (Branson, Missouri), II (Winter, 1972), n.p.
106. This ambiguity was fostered to a great extent by the Stamps Quartet Mu-sic Company. In many cases it is difficult to separate the two companies in references made by both primary and secondary sources. The Stamps-Baxter Company maintained a dignified silence concerning the operations of the competing organization.
107. Baxter and Polk, op. cit., p. 9.
108. Letter from Dwight Brock, January 4, 1977.
109. Sumner, op. cit.; date may be inaccurate.
110. Ibid.
111. Jesse Burt and Duane Allen, *The History of Gospel Music* (Nashville: K & S Press Inc., 1971), p. 46; wording is vague.
112. Ibid.; in addition, Abernathy, loc. cit., writes: "I had a group traveling at

that time called "The Four Tones" we werre [sic] on W. D. O. D. Chattanooga . . . [sic] when war was declared. I printed my first sheet songs
(three of them) with their picture on it. Titles were, "I Thank My Savior
For It All" . . . ["] Back Home In U.S.A. ["] (gospel) and . . . [sic] our theme
song was also on it. [sic] "Won't It Be Glory There."

113. *Gospel Music 1977 Directory & Yearbook;* An Annual Publication of the
Gospel Music Association (Nashville: Gospel Music Association, 1976),
pp. 120–122; this list appears in Appendix C.

114. Cf. p. 163 above; these two are Tennessee Music and Printing Company
and Stamps-Baxter/Zondervan; the remaining publishers of convention
books apparently have not identified with the Gospel Music Association;
neither have Afro-American gospel music publishers; the name of the Sacred Harp Publishing Company, however, does appear. See list in Appendix C.

115. Marvin Norcross, Vice-president, Secretary, and Treasurer of Word, Inc.,
telephone interview, January 18, 1977.

116. Ibid.

117. This company was purchased by Word, Inc., on January 4, 1977 [after
Field Research had been completed]; according to Norcross, loc. cit.

118. See p. 119 above.

119. See pp. 64 above.

120. See p. 61 above.

121. Martin J. Neeb, Jr., "An Historical Study Of American Non-Commercial
AM Broadcast Stations Owned And Operated By Religious Groups,
1920–1966" (unpublished Doctoral dissertation, Northwestern University, 1967), pp. 627–635, lists eighteen non-commercial, religious sponsored radio stations which had begun broadcast operations by 1922. It is
likely that many of these stations broadcast religious music.

122. Blackwood and Martin, op. cit., pp. 55, 57.

123. Ibid., pp. 104–105.

124. I.e., no block religious programming or paid religious shows.

125. "San Diego Station Goes Gospel," *Billboard,* LXXXVII (January 18,
1975), 57.

126. Jim Black, Director Of Gospel Music, SESAC, Inc., personal interview,
December 9, 1976.

127. Marion Easterling, radio announcer, personal interview, Nashville, Tennessee, October 8, 1976.

128. Letter from SESAC, Inc., Nashville, Tennessee, to Guinness Superlatives, London, England, September 29, 1976.

129. J.G. Whitfield, gospel music concert promoter and publisher of *The
Singing News,* personal interview, Pensacola, Florida, September 7,
1976.

130. Dove Award winners, 1969–1976 are listed in Appendix C.

131. See p. 119 above.

132. Members of this quartet were Frank Stamps, Odis Echols, Palmer
Wheeler, Roy Wheeler, and Dwight Brock, accompanist; see Beary, op.
cit., p. 75.

133. Charles Novell, "Gospel Roots; Tapping America's Heritage," *Billboard,*
LXXXVIII (July 4, 1976), MR-78; this is the most recent published citation viewed by the writer.

134. Ibid.
135. Burt and Allen, op. cit., p. 44. In a personal letter to the writer, dated February 11, 1977, Abernathy states that he was twelve years old and the year 1925. He writes: "The lable [sic] was 'Columbia' (I have no record or no.) The song titles were 'Don't Be Knocking' written by my father Dee Abernathy . . . [and] 'The Rich Young Ruler' . . . also written by my father. . . ."
136. Blackwood and Martin, op. cit., p. 102.
137. Retaining a vestige of original personnel.
138. Harold Timmons, enthusiast requested by the Country Music Hall Of Fame to compile a discography of the Chuck Wagon Gang, telephone interview, December 13, 1976; their first gospel song, "The Son Hath Made Me Free," recorded by Columbia November 25, 1936, was released on Vocalion (#03472; March 10, 1937) and on as many as six other labels. This same song was released in June 1947 on Columbia 37670.
139. Bill Williams, "Chuck Wagon Gang," Billboard, LXXIX (October 14, 1967 sup.), 22.
140. Harlan Daniel, "From Shape Notes to Bank Notes: Milestones in the Evolution of White Gospel Music" (unpublished chronology presented at the Sixth Annual Meeting of the Popular Culture Association, session on white gospel music and the country tradition, Chicago, April 24, 1976), n.p. (Mimeographed.)
141. Timmons, loc. cit.; the present group is comprised of Anna (Davis), Rose (Karnes), Roy and Eddie Carter, brothers and sisters; their latest album is The Sweetest Songs We Know, Columbia KC 34044, February 23, 1976.
142. Williams, "Chuck Wagon Gang," loc. cit.
143. Timmons, loc. cit.
144. Burt and Allen, op. cit., p. 54. Their total number of recordings sold may have been eclipsed in recent years by improved promotion of other gospel recordings artists.
145. The International Music-Record-Tape Newsweekly; Main Office; 9000 Sunset Boulevard, Los Angeles, California 90069.
146. The final chart for 1976 is included in Appendix D.
147. The final chart for 1976 is also included in Appendix D.
148. An interesting study, in itself, would be to trace the transition from white to black in the Billboard charts.
149. Gerry Wood, Southern Editor, Billboard, personal interview, Nashville, Tennessee, December 10, 1976; although the above may still be true in toto, Norcross, loc. cit., states that this does not now apply to established groups who record for established companies with improved distribution methods.
150. "Word, Inc. Celebrates 25 Years," The Singing News, VIII (December 1, 1976), 1B-2B; cf. p. 129 above; also, Norcross telephone interview, loc. cit. Word, Inc., became a subsidiary of the American Broadcasting Companies (ABC) in November, 1974.
151. Ibid.; see also Don Light, "Jarrell McCracken Spreads The Word," Billboard, LXXVII (October 23, 1965 sup.), 38–40.
152. Ibid.
153. Norcross, loc. cit.; not only does Word, Inc., record more gospel music

than any other record company, its southern gospel label, Canaan, is its most profitable enterprise.

154. *GMA Directory,* op. cit., pp. 116–119. This list appears in Appendix C.
155. Bob Benson, Sr., "Records—An Asset To An Artist's Career," *GMA Directory,* op. cit., p. 7.
156. Grammy Award winners 1961–1976 are listed in Appendix E.
157. "Grammy Winners Presented; Gospel Segment Impressive," *Good News* (March, 1977), 4.
158. Dove Award Winners 1969–1976 are listed in Appendix C.
159. Cedric J. Hayes, *A Discography of Gospel Records,* 1937–1971 (København: Knudsen, 1973), is a 116-page discography of Afro-American gospel performances only.
160. "TV All-Star Revue," [WAGA-TV, Atlanta, Georgia], March 8, 1949 (Mimeographed); script of program retained as souvenir by Connor B. Hall, Cleveland, Tennessee.
161. Blackwood and Martin, op. cit., p. 107.
162. "Gospel As Seen Through The Video Tube," *Billboard,* LXXVIII (October 22, 1966 sup.), 58.; no dates given.
163. Ibid.
164. Steven D. Price, *Old As the Hills; The Story of Bluegrass Music* (New York: The Viking Press, 1975), p. 60.; Price incorrectly gives the location of WJBF-TV as Atlanta.
165. Dove Award winners 1969–1976 are listed in Appendix C.
166. J.G. Whitfield, loc. cit.; Whitfield was originator of "Gospel Singing Jubilee;" however, "Video Tube," *Billboard* (1966), op. cit., states "in some 90 markets."
167. Sal Candilora, "On Performing Rights Organizations—Why Three?" *Record World,* (March 4, 1972 and March 11, 1972), reprinted as a four-page public relations brochure of SESAC, Inc.
168. Originally, Society of European Stage Authors and Composers; due to increased Americanization the name was changed in approximately 1940 to the trade name SESAC, Inc., according to ibid.
169. Ibid.
170. "This is the only court case containing the words "gospel music" listed in *Words And Phrases,* a standard legal reference.
171. *Decisions of the United States Courts Involving Copyright, 1957–1958* [Copyright Office *Bulletin* No. 31] (Washington, D.C.: Library of Congress, 1959), pp. 6–25.
172. Ibid., p. 7.
173. Ibid., p. 6.
174. Excluding Sacred Harp Singings, where large group singing only is the rule.
175. "Music Is Outgrowth Of The Church," *Billboard,* LXXVIII (October 22, 1966 sup.), 34.
176. Ernest N. Edwards, *The Edwards Album* (Bessemer, Alabama: The Ernest N. Edwards Music Company, 1955), p. 2.
177. Ibid., p. 255; the total is not exactly 113, however; at least one is a duplicate and three are cartoons.
178. Cf. p. 126 above.
179. Novell, loc. cit.; no further details given.

160

180. Burt and Allen, op. cit., p. 35.
181. Fowler should not be credited with the origination of the all-night sing; see pp. 125 and 126 above.
182. La Breeska Rogers Hemphill, La Breeska; An Autobiography (Nashville: Hemphill Music Company, 1976), p. 69.
183. Blackwood and Martin, op. cit., p. 76.
184. Racine, op. cit., pp. 133–134.
185. Bob Terrell, J.D. Sumner; Gospel Music Is My Life (Nashville: Impact Books, 1971), p. 99.
186. "Gospel Quartets Take To The Road," Billboard, LXXVII (October 23, 1965 sup.), 12–13.
187. Terrell, op. cit., pp. 186–187.
188. The Convention, however, is a promotion and is not sponsored by the Gospel Music Association.
189. A list of performers at the 1976 National Quartet Convention is included as part of Appendix E.
190. The writer attended the Twentieth Annual Singing on August 21, 1976; a schedule conflict prevented its being held on the traditional date.
191. Elton Whisenhunt, "Billboard Goes To An All Night Sing," Billboard, (LXXVII (October 23, 1965 sup.), 20.
192. Whitfield, loc. cit.
193. Compiled from word-of-mouth and recent advertisements in The Singing News and Concert Life.
194. "Talent Agency For Gospel Artists," Billboard, LXXVIII (October 22, 1966 sup.), 26.
195. Ibid.
196. GMA Directory, op. cit., p. 108; a listing of these talent agencies appears in Appendix C.
197. Linnell Gentry, ed., A History and Encyclopedia Of Country, Western, and Gospel Music (Nashville: McQuiddy Press, 1961), p. 379; the 1969 "completely revised" edition of this work does not contain such a listing.
198. Richard Jackson, United States Music; Sources of Bibliography and Collective Biography (Brooklyn: Institute for Studies in American Music, 1973), p. 33, criticizes Gentry for not including Afro-American gospel singers.
199. Gentry, loc. cit.
200. Jamie Buckingham, O Happy Day: The Happy Goodman Story (Waco: Word Books, Publisher, 1973), pp. 136–137; originally named the Goodman Trio.
201. Ibid., p. 222.
202. Cf. pp. 129, 130 above; Journey Music Company was purchased by Word, Inc., on January 4, 1977; after Field Research had been completed.
203. Of these more than 300, less than ten, judging from their names, are of Afro-American or other ethnic minority constituency.
204. This list of periodicals is shown in Appendix C.
205. Concert Life [Mechanicsburg, Pennsylvania], IV (November/December, 1976), 5, 13.
206. The Singing News [Pensacola, Florida], VIII (November 1, 1976), 1A.
207. "Gospel Music Association Organization Set June 3," Billboard, LXXVI (May 2, 1964), 1.

208. State of Tennessee, Charter of Incorporation, May 19, 1964, recorded Book 145, pp. 224–227.
209. Racine, op. cit., p. 183.
210. Gospel Music Association Minutes, October 10, 1964; also a photograph of these officers and board members appeared in *Billboard,* LXXVII (October 23, 1965 sup.), 66, *sans* Baldwin, Lamb, Myers, Preston, and Roberts; [Preston's name was omitted]; information in brackets is from the latter source; also, Burt and Allen, op. cit., pp. 70–71 state that Myers was president; Speer, first vice-president; Sumner, second vice-president; Bob MacKenzie [sic] secretary; and Bob Benson [sic], treasurer; several internal contradictions appear in this last source.
211. Gospel Music Association Minutes, October 16, 1965; also, a photograph of these officers and board members appeared in *Billboard,* LXXVII (October 30, 1965), 18, *sans* Baldwin, Ford, Jones, Meurice LeFevre, Lester, Rice, Whisenhunt, and Zondervan; information in brackets is from the latter source.
212. Constitution of the Gospel Music Association, Article I, Section 2, (November 21, 1976), n.p.
213. "GMA Gains In Stature," *Billboard,* LXXIX (October 14, 1967 sup.), 7.
214. "Mrs. Boyd Is Good News For GMA," *Billboard,* LXXXI (October 11, 1969), 44, 46.
215. [Norma L. Boyd], "The Gospel Music Association," (Nashville: The Gospel Music Association, [1976]), (Mimeographed.), n.p.
216. Ibid.
217. According to "GMA Gains In Stature," op. cit., a GMA produced album containing the most popular song from each of fourteen top groups was issued in 1967.
218. Jan Cain, "Gospel Music Hall Of Fame Ground-breaking," *The Singing News,* VIII (November 1, 1976), 17A 9A.
219. Bill Williams, "Racial Harmony GMA Theme," *Billboard,* LXXXI (October 11, 1969), 1, 43.
220. Bill Williams, "1st Integrated Gospel Act," *Billboard,* LXXXIV (February 26, 1972), 3ff.
221. This album also received a NARAS Grammy Award in the Best Gospel Performance (Other Than Soul Gospel) category for 1975. Andrus is no longer with the Imperials, however, cf. Jan Cain, "Sherman Andrus Becomes Shalom Vice Pres.," *The Singing News,* VIII (November 1, 1976), 1B, 15B.
222. According to Norma Boyd, personal interview, Nashville, Tennessee, December 13, 1976, Jackson has been nominated ever since her death in 1972. Her name did not appear on the nominating ballot, however, until 1975, and not on the final ballot until 1976; see Gospel Music Hall of Fame selection process in Appendix C.
223. "Butler Elected To Directorship Of Music Assn.," *Billboard,* LXXXVIII (November 13, 1976), 61.
224. Butler, loc. cit.

6

Methodology of Field Research

The methodology of the field research for this book consisted of the selection of a geographical area for investigation, identification of amateur family gospel music singing groups [hereinafter called groups] within the area, selection of one group per selected county, interview and tape recording of each selected group, analysis of the words and music of one song selected by each group, and comparison of each group's performance of its selected song with the printed music.

Selection of Geographical Area

The state of Georgia, and more specifically, the area of south Georgia, was chosen as the site of this investigation for a number of reasons. The primary reason for its selection was the writer's familiarity with the area and his awareness of some of the nature of the musical and religious life that could be expected to exist.

Georgia is located in an area where gospel music activity has historically been very strong. In George Pullen Jackson's map showing the areas where "American Religious Folksongs (White Spirituals) Were And/or Are Still Sung,"[1] Georgia is included from 1810 until the present. The previously mentioned Southern Musical Convention, the first singing society in the South,[2] was begun in Upson county, one of the selected counties for this study. Hamilton, Georgia, where B.F. White and Joel King compiled *The Sacred Harp,*[3] is located in this area of south Georgia. The South Georgia Singing Convention, mentioned in Chapter 4 as one of the earliest seven-shape singing conventions to adopt a state name, was begun by William Royal in 1875 in Irwin County, another of the selected counties. The Royal [Family] Singing Convention, also founded by William Royal, has been held annually in Irwin County since 1893.[4] The Annual Sundown to Sunup Gospel Sing in Waycross (Ware County)[5] held its twentieth session in 1976; and the Bonifay, Florida, Gospel Sing, advertised as the "Biggest All Night Singing In The World,"[6] is forty-five miles southwest of the Georgia state line in Seminole County.

The manner in which Georgia is divided into counties made it particularly suitable for a research study of this nature. Georgia, the largest state east of the Mississippi River, is divided into 159 counties, more counties than any other state in the Union except Texas. The large number of relatively small counties afforded convenient discrete units, each of which could be investigated separately.

In order to further define the population of the study, only the counties in the four southernmost of the ten Congressional Districts in Georgia were chosen. These four southernmost Congressional Districts encompass an area larger than the combined area of the remaining six Districts. Counties in these four Districts are predominantly rural, with the largest metropolitan centers being Savannah (Chatham County), Columbus (Muscogee County), and Macon (Bibb County). These four selected Congressional Districts contain a total of ninety counties, with each county approximately 365 square miles in area, and with the county seats approximately twenty to twenty-five miles apart.[7]

A further subdivision of area was accomplished by choosing at random twenty-five of these south Georgia counties. The shaded portions of the Georgia map, shown as Figure 10, indicate the locations of the counties which were selected. A listing of the twenty-five selected counties, with their population figures according to the 1970 Census,[8] is presented as Figure 11. Also shown in Figure 11 are the numbers of groups the researcher was able to identify in each county.

It should be pointed out that the twenty-five randomly selected counties listed below include the largest county (in population) of the south Georgia area under consideration. Chatham County is also the fourth largest county in the state. Also in-

Figure 10. Congressional Districts, reapportioned in 1972. Figures in each county indicate 1970 population. Shaded areas indicate those counties selected for study.

165

cluded was the seventh largest county in the state (Bibb). At the other extreme, the second smallest county (Quitman), and the smallest county in the state (Echols) were also chosen.

The geographical dispersion of the random sample appeared satisfactory; with three sea-coast, two southernmost, and four counties located along the western border. Only one county (Upson) bordered the northern limits of the area, and one county (Crawford) had mutual borders with three other selected counties.

Since Goldstein suggests that the field researcher not be a resident of the area,[9] it was fortunate that the county in which the researcher had previously resided was not among those chosen by the random selection process.

County	County Population	County Seat	County Seat Population	Groups Identified
Bibb	143,418	Macon	122,423	9
Brantley	5,940	Nahunta	974	20
Bulloch	31,585	Statesboro	14,616	7
Charlton	5,680	Folston	2,112	10
Chatham	187,816	Savannah	118,349	9
Chattahoochee	25,813	Cusseta	1,251	None
Cook	12,129	Adel	4,972	10
Crawford	5,748	Knoxville	Courthouse Only	6
Dooly	10,404	Vienna	2,341	4
Early	12,682	Blakely	5,267	7
Echols	1,924	Statenville	Courthouse Only	2
Effingham	13,632	Springfield	1,001	7
Irwin	8,036	Ocilla	3,185	9
Jenkins	8,332	Millen	3,713	5
McIntosh	7,371	Darien	1,826	3
Miller	6,424	Colquitt	2,026	14
Montgomery	6,099	Mt. Vernon	1,579	1
Peach	15,990	Ft. Valley	9,251	5
Pulaski	8,066	Hawkinsville	4,077	2
Quitman	2,180	Georgetown	578	None
Upson	23,505	Thomaston	10,024	16
Wayne	17,858	Jesup	9,091	14
Wheeler	4,596	Alamo	833	4
Wilcox	6,998	Abbeville	781	4
Worth	14,770	Sylvester	4,226	9
			TOTAL:	177

Figure 11. Population of selected counties and county seats, and number of groups identified.

Identification of Singing Groups

In each of the twenty-five selected counties an attempt was made to identify groups which had become reasonably well known throughout the county. In the less populous counties the researcher attempted to identify *all* such groups, although complete success would be difficult to substantiate. In the more populous counties identification of groups was much more difficult. Persons residing near a church located in a rural area, for example, could reasonably be expected to know someone who attended the church. The same expectation did not hold true with persons residing near churches in the larger towns and cities. Telephone surveys, in general, were also of little value.[10] It was the writer's experience that gospel singing groups would more likely be found in churches that did not have a telephone or in churches having a telephone but with no person present to answer it when church was not in session. Information was obtained almost invariably by word-of-mouth. Some of the procedures used to obtain this information will be detailed subsequently. Many instances could be cited of the researcher's being able to locate a group only through the most complicated and serendipitous of circumstances. No claim is made, therefore, for having identified the total population in even the geographical limitations that were imposed. Nevertheless, the writer was able to identify a total of 177 groups which met the criteria for inclusion in this study.[11]

The reader is cautioned against interpreting the number of family singing groups that the writer was able to find as being completely indicative of the total amount of gospel music activity in the area in question. The delimitations of the study automatically excluded almost all duets[12] and soloists, and excluded the two most popular types of performing groups in gospel music—female or mixed trios, and male or mixed quartets—unless more than two of the members were related. Geographical considerations also served to exclude some groups, particularly those with homes close to a county line, where some members of a group lived in a non-selected county. In all cases where any of the delimitations of the study were in question, it was reasoned better to err on the side of caution and to exclude the group from the study.

The very best means of locating the family singing groups was by contacting a member of each church in the county, preferably the pastor or person in charge of music. For this an invaluable aid was a county map published by the Georgia Department Of Transportation and available at each courthouse or forest ranger station free or for a nominal charge. These county maps show by symbol most of the churches in the rural areas and often identify them by name.

Another valuable source of information was interaction with persons who worked at local restaurants and crossroads stores. The information obtained in these places was surprisingly accurate, sometimes much more so than that of the pastors or music directors previously mentioned. Less valuable sources, although not completely devoid of information, were local Chambers of Commerce (if any), local newspapers, and local radio stations. These latter sources were of much greater value in the more populous counties where it was impractical to contact every church or crossroads store.

Associational offices of the area Protestant churches were located only in the larger metropolitan areas and these were unable to provide any specific information on local performing groups.

The procedure that the researcher followed upon initially entering a community was to ask if the person contacted could direct him to *anyone* who was interested in gospel music. Upon finding such persons, more specific questions regarding *family* singing groups were asked. Gradually a list of names would emerge, each of which was notated on a 3x5 card. In as far as possible, each family group mentioned to the researcher was contacted, and all information verified by at least one active member of the group or by an immediate relative. After an indefinite period of time, from as little as one day of intensive canvassing in the smallest county to as many as six days in the larger counties, the investigator would reach a point where each new contact would mention only names that had been previously elicited. When this point was reached the researcher assumed that

168

the area had been canvassed thoroughly. It was a point of satisfaction to the writer that in conversations with gospel musicians in other counties, when names were mentioned concerning groups in a county which had been under investigation, only once was a group mentioned that had been overlooked. In this case a young couple and their children had moved to Chatham County, previously cited as the most populous in the study, within the previous two weeks.

Selection of Performing Groups

After compiling a list of names from as many readily available sources as possible, one family from each county was chosen by random sample for an interview, which included the making of a cassette tape recording of their performance. Only two groups, when re-contacted, were unwilling to be interviewed and recorded. In these cases another group was substituted at random from the remaining list of names of the appropriate county. Random selection was used to obviate any bias upon the part of the researcher. It should be emphasized that because of the random selection process the performing group chosen from any specific county should not be considered the "best" or most representative for that particular county. The reader is referred to the Summary of Performing Groups in Chapter 7 for details concerning the variety of groups interviewed.

Interview and Tape Recording of Each Randomly Selected Performing Group

Interview

The interview consisted of eliciting information utilizing a list of standard items as an Interview Guide. This Interview Guide is shown as Figure 12.

1. Names of family members
2. Church affiliation
3. Voice parts
4. Instruments played
5. Family relationships
6. Years performing together
7. Availability of family historical records and photographs
8. Changes which had occurred throughout the years
9. Publications used
10. Favorite songs
11. Favorite recordings
12. Favorite radio and television stations and programs
13. Performance agenda past and present
14. Future plans

Figure 12. Interview guide.

Approximately mid-point in the field research, the investigator began asking the occupations of those members of the family group who worked. Although this additional information was interesting, it was not considered significant enough to re-contact each of the previous groups. Another afterthought, also not considered significant enough for re-contact, was the taking of photographs. This taking of photographs was begun late in the first summer of field research.

In addition to the standard items sought, members of each group were encouraged to discuss gospel music in general and to express their opinion of what was important. A question pertaining to the handling of money received for performance[13] was not asked although in many instances the information was volunteered.

Tape Recording

The tape recording of the selected groups was accomplished by using a Panasonic Model RQ-320S monaural cassette tape recorder which has a hand-held microphone attached to the unit by

170

a coiled cable. The recorder has provisions for the use of chromium-dioxide tape and for automatic recording level, but these features were not utilized. The ten groups interviewed during the summer of 1975 were recorded using TDK SD[14] tape. Those interviewed during the summer and fall of 1976 were recorded using Scotch Highlander/Low Noise[15] tape.

The researcher informed each group that only one song was needed, but that they should not feel restricted to the performance of only one song. Facility for performance ranged from one group which had difficulty performing even the one song without an obvious error, to another group which completely filled both sides of a C-60 cassette with ease.

Except when requested to let the tape run continuously, the researcher followed a procedure of starting the recording device then motioning to the leader of the group to begin his or her introduction. At the conclusion of each song the recorder volume control was turned down completely before the machine was stopped. Although this procedure resulted in a certain amount of artificiality and made some of the groups feel ill-at-ease, it seemed to be preferred. With this procedure it was possible for the group to talk between the recording of different songs without having to be conscious of the tape recorder monitoring conversation.

Song Selection

When the group had recorded all of the songs they wished to sing, the researcher asked them to choose one song for his investigation. In many cases this choosing process became the most time-consuming portion of the interview and taping procedure. Much discussion and many requests for playbacks would ensue. Almost invariably the researcher would be asked his opinion of which was the best song. In each of these cases it was necessary to explain that in order for the researcher's personal bias to be kept out of the study it was imperative for the group to make the decision.

Once the decision was made regarding the song chosen for

171

analysis, the title and publication information was copied, a copy of the music was secured, and the copyright holder was written a letter requesting permission to quote both words and music. Several of the letters to publishers were returned due to change in address. This necessitated further research in locating the present addresses of these companies. No copyright holder who was contacted refused permission or charged a fee for the use of the published materials.

Two of the selected performing groups had composed several of their own songs. Unfortunately these songs had not been reduced to notation, therefore the group was asked to choose only a song from its repertory that could be compared with published music. In one other instance, a group chose a song which had been learned by ear from a tape recording made of a radio broadcast. Upon investigation it was learned that the original group had also performed by ear. In this case an alternative song, previously chosen by the group as a precaution against such an eventuality, was substituted.

Analysis of Words and Music

Analysis of Text

The text of each song chosen by a performing group was analyzed for the essence of its religious content and its general character or mood. Value judgments regarding the religious philosophy presented, the grammatical accuracy, or the inherent truth of the statements made were avoided. The meaning of the text was reduced to as concise a form as possible. For example, the song, "Heaven Came Down And Glory Filled My Soul," by John W. Peterson, was reduced to: First stanza: "Joy of Conversion;" Second stanza omitted; Third stanza: "Hope of Heaven." Stanzas omitted by a performing group were also omitted from the analysis. In addition, each song was tabulated as being Personal or Impersonal. Due to the fact that almost every song was considered Personal because of frequent usage of personal pro-

172

nouns, a subjective evaluation of the intensity of the personal references was made. No attempt was made to count the specific number of personal pronouns in any song.

The data obtained from the analysis of the text were tabulated and summarized in narrative form. This summary appears in Chapter 7.

Analysis of Music

The printed music for each song chosen by a performing group was analyzed for its Melody, Range of the melody, presence or absence of an Anacrusis, Harmony, Tonality, Meter, Rhythm, Texture, Form, Dynamic Markings, and Tempo Indications. This was done by examining each song from each of the musical standpoints and itemizing the findings. These findings were tabulated and a summary of the results expressed in narrative form. This narrative summary appears in Chapter 7.

Comparison of Performance with Printed Music

The tape-recorded performance of each song selected by each group was compared with the printed music of the same song. The objective of such comparison was not to look for mistakes or to identify a "right" or "wrong" interpretation. The objective was to identify performance practice which could be considered general characteristics of the *genre*. A check-sheet was devised which served to focus the writer's attention on various aspects of the performance. A condensed form of the check-sheet used is shown as Figure 13. The actual check-sheets utilized provided more space in which to write descriptive comments.

A check-sheet was used for each song in the study. Brief descriptions of significant deviations from the printed page, if any, were verbalized in narrative form. Recurrent patterns of performance were summarized in narrative form. This summary appears in Chapter 7. A description of each amateur family gospel

	Same	Changed	More Complex	Simplified	Brief Description
Melody					
Harmony					
Rhythm					
Texture					
Form					
Dynamics					
Tempo					
Text					
Accompaniment					
Amplification					
Change of Key					
Introduction					
Other					

Figure 13. Check-sheet for comparison of recorded performance with printed music.

music singing group, along with a copy of the song selected as their most representative performance, is included in Appendix A. Appendix A also includes photographs of many of the performing groups.

Notes

1. George Pullen Jackson, *Another Sheaf of White Spirituals* (Gainesville: University of Florida Press, 1952), p. xiii.
2. Curtis Leo Cheek, "The Singing School And Shaped-note Tradition: Residuals In Twentieth-Century American Hymnody" (unpublished Doctoral dissertation, University of Southern California, 1968), pp. 145, 161.
3. See p. 76 ff. above.
4. Karen Luke Jackson, "The Royal Singing Convention, 1893–1931: Shape Note Singing Tradition in Irwin County, Georgia," *The Georgia Historical Quarterly* (Winter, 1972), pp. 498–499.
5. Not one of the selected counties, but within the south Georgia area.
6. "Bonifay Sing Date July 2," *The Singing News,* February 1, 1977, 1A.
7. Derived from figures in *Governmental Guide* (Georgia edition; Madison, Tennessee: n.n. 1975), pp. 39, 87.
8. Ibid, pp. 28–32.
9. Kenneth S. Goldstein, *A Guide For Field Workers in Folklore* (Hatboro, Pennsylvania: Folklore Associates, Inc., 1964), p. 9 footnote.
10. The Macon, Georgia (Bibb County), telephone directory, for example, lists five pages of churches in the Yellow Pages. A telephone survey of these churches yielded very meager results.
11. These criteria, mentioned previously in Chapter 1, were: 1. At least three members related by blood or marriage; 2. Amateur in the sense of receiving less than fifty percent of total income from gospel music activities; 3. Have performed away from home church at least once within the previous year.
12. Only one duet was chosen in the random sample. In this case a mother and daughter sang, accompanied at the piano by another relative.
13. The acceptance of a nominal fee or a "love offering" for performance did not exclude a group from being considered "amateur." See Definitions on p. 2 above.
14. TDK Electronics Corporation, 755 Eastgate Boulevard, Garden City, New York 11530.
15. Minnesota Mining & Manufacturing Company, Saint Paul, Minnesota 55101.

7
Review of Field Research

As previously stated, the field research for this study took place in south Georgia during the summer of 1975 and the summer and fall of 1976. During the course of the research, a total of 177 amateur family gospel music singing groups [hereinafter called groups] which met the criteria for inclusion in this study[1] were identified. From these 177 groups, twenty-three were chosen by random selection for an in-depth interview. The interview included the tape recording of the group performing at least one song. Details of the methodology of the field research appear in Chapter 6.

Each group chosen for interview was assured that its performance would not be judged against any arbitrary standard nor compared with other groups in the survey. Some collation of information, however, is essential for the preservation of an accurate summary of present-day amateur performance practice of white gospel music in the South. In addition, the reader may wish to compare his interpretations with those of the writer. For these reasons, when necessary, performing groups or their songs are identified by a number within parentheses. This number refers to the number of the respective county as listed in alphabetical order in Appendix A. Also included in Appendix A are transcripts of the interviews of each group, along with a copy of the music of the song selected by each group as being their most representative performance.

Characteristics of Performing Groups

Family Relationships

The twenty-three randomly selected groups included a wide range of family relationships. No groups were exactly alike. Predictably, the majority of family groups were comprised of parents and children. The several exceptions to this rule were:

Husband and wife, and husband's brother and sister (2);
Brother and sister, the sister's brother-in-law, and two distant cousins (4);
Six cousins and a non-related friend (12);
Three sisters (13);
Two brothers, their sister, and their uncle (16);
Husband and wife, and husband's sister (19).

Groups comprised of one parent and children included:

Mother, four sons, one daughter (5);
Mother, daughter, niece as accompanist (14);
Father, three sons, non-related accompanist (22);
Mother, two sons, non-related accompanist (23);
Mother, two daughters, son-in-law (24).

Combinations of two parents and their children formed the largest number of groups:

Father and son, instrumentalists; mother and two non-related female vocalists; non-related instrumentalist (1);
Father, mother, daughter (3) (10) (18);
Father, mother, daughter, vocalists; son, instrumentalist (25);
Father, mother, daughter, son (17);
Father, mother, daughter, son; non-related accompanist (21).

177

Several groups contained more than one family:

Father, mother, two sons; father's brother and his wife (7);
Mother, two daughters; additional two sisters, their sister-in-law and their cousin; one non-related vocalist (8);
Father, mother, vocalists; their two sons, instrumentalists; additional husband and wife, vocalists; two non-related instrumentalists (9);
Husband and wife, vocalists; their daughter, accompanist; wife's sister and her husband, vocalists (11);
Husband and wife, their two daughters; additional husband and wife (15).

The three most similar groups (father, mother, and daughter) listed above were not identical, although in each of these cases the father sang lead and the mother sang alto. In one case (18) the daughter simply doubled the lead, in another (3) the daughter doubled the lead but also played piano, and in the third (10) the daughter sang a high harmony part (tenor).

Church Affiliation

The overwhelming majority of the members of the groups belonged to Baptist denominations. Forty-seven persons belonged to Southern Baptist or Missionary Baptist churches. In general, these two designations of Baptists were considered synonymous by members of the groups. Nine belonged to Free Will Baptist churches; eight to Holiness Baptist; and three to Pentecostal Baptist congregations. It is significant that none of the selected groups belonged to a "First Baptist Church," the designation usually adopted by the largest Baptist congregation in southern communities.[2]

The next most represented denomination was the Church of God, with fifteen; followed by Evangelistic, with eight; Christian, with six; [United] Methodist, with six; "Gospel Assembly" (no official denominational name), with four; Assembly of God, three; and Four-Square Gospel, one.[3]

Occupations

As stated in Chapter 6, the interviewer did not begin asking the occupations of the members of the groups who were employed until approximately the mid-point of the first summer of the field research. Groups from counties (1) (8) (17) (19) were not asked their occupational status. Information from counties (9) (13) (15) (23) (24) should be considered incomplete in that all members of these groups were not asked their occupations. No group was re-contacted in order to elicit employment information. Group (14), which consisted of three females, did not have any members who were employed. The occupations of the members of the groups who were asked fell into a predominantly working-class category. Several persons were owners of small businesses or held lower management positions with larger corporations. The total list of occupations cited is presented as Figure 14.

Accountant
Auto Battery salesman/deliveryman; pastor of mission
Auto repair; body and paint specialist
Bank employee
Bank teller
Beauty parlor owner
Church organist
Clothing store owner; Tax and bookkeeping service
Construction company purchasing agent
Department of Family and Children's Services employee
Farm Bureau employee
Farm supply company store operations manager
Georgia Forestry Commission employee
Grocery store owner
Heating and air-conditioning company employee
Hospital stock clerk

Insurance company secretary
Insurance salesman
Lunchroom aide for elementary school
Machine works employee
Minister of Music for Baptist Church
Paper company electrician
Paper company shift worker
Pastor of church
Plumber and pipefitter
Professional trombonist
Railroad company clerk
Railroad company section foreman
Restaurant waitress
Service station attendant (part-time)
Sheet glass company owner
Study hall aide for high school; organist for church
Supermarket clerk
Teacher of Bible at church-sponsored day-school; secretary
    to Minister of Music
Telephone company operator
Tire company employee (named twice)
Tire and Appliance company employee
Truck driver (deliver mobile homes), owner of truck
USAF retired, grocery store manager

Figure 14. Occupations.

Voice Parts

Only one group (14) performed as a duet. In this case the daughter sang lead, the mother sang alto, and her niece played the piano accompaniment.

Two groups performed as female trios. One of these groups (13) performed *a cappella* with one of the women singing the tenor part higher than the soprano and alto parts. In the other female trio (1), which performed with accompaniment, one of the women sang the tenor part lower than the soprano and alto parts. Other trios included:

180

Male lead, child doubling lead, alto (3) (17) (18);
Male lead, alto, female high tenor (10);
Male lead, female doubling lead on chorus, alto (19);
Male lead, alto, male tenor (23);
Female lead, child doubling lead, male tenor (25).

Only one group (22) performed as a male quartet. This group, however, sang in unison rather than in four-part harmony. Other quartets included:

Male lead on verse, female lead on chorus (these vocalists sang mid-range harmony part when not singing lead); alto, bass (2);
Soprano, alto, tenor, bass (2);
Male lead, alto, male tenor, bass (16);
Male lead, alto, female high tenor, bass (9) (21);
Male and female lead (in octaves), male and female doubling alto/tenor part (two-part harmony) (11); soprano, alto doubled, male tenor (24).

Groups containing more than four vocalists included:

Female lead, alto, two male tenors, two basses (5);
Five sopranos, two altos (8);
Two sopranos, two altos, one male tenor doubling same part as altos, bass (12);
Male lead, two children doubling lead, alto, bass (15).

In several instances the designation of a harmony part as alto, tenor, or bass was arbitrary upon the part of the researcher. In other cases the designation given by the performer (e.g. the melody sung an octave low designated as "bass") was used. It should be noted that the traditional four-part groupings of soprano, alto, tenor, and bass was utilized by only two groups. The number of instances of male lead should also be noted. Of the twenty-three groups, over half utilized a male lead or the lead was shared by both male and female.

181

Instrumentation

Most of the groups (2) (4) (8) (10) (11) (12) (14) (16) (17) (18) (21) (22) (23) (24) performed with piano alone as accompaniment. One group (5) performed with amplified guitar alone as accompaniment. Another group (15) performed with acoustic guitar alone as accompaniment. Combinations of instruments included:

Acoustic guitar and piano (3);
Piano, electric bass, drums (1);
Electric guitar, electric bass, drums (7);
Two acoustic guitars, tambourine (19);
Piano, electric lead guitar, electric rhythm guitar, electric
     bass (9);
Two acoustic guitars, electric bass (25).

Only one group (13) performed with no accompaniment.

Years Performing Together

The number of years that groups had been performing together varied by a wide margin. Three groups (4) (8) (15) measured their time together in months. Six groups (1) (5) (7) (17) (19) (22) had been together from six to ten years. Three groups (2) (16) (21) had been together from eleven to fifteen years. One group (23) had been together for nineteen years; another group (3) had been together for twenty-three years; another (24) for twenty-four years. The group with the most longevity (13) had been singing together for a total of thirty-two years. This group, the previously mentioned female trio which sang *a cappella*, had been performing in public since the youngest member was five years old.

Family Historical Records

Despite the number of years that some groups had been performing together, no group had preserved memorabilia of past performance in any systematic manner. Specifically, there were no diaries, scrapbooks, family Bible entries, or preserved letters detailing performance activities. Some groups were able to give oral histories of past musical activities however, and several groups came from families with long histories of interest in music, especially religious music. Only one group (10) had a family background in the Sacred Harp tradition and only four groups (9) (13) (18) (23) had roots in the singing school and singing convention tradition. Eight groups (9) (10) (13) (14) (18) (19) (21) (23) had adult members who had earlier sung with parents, relatives, or siblings, but none of the groups considered themselves to be perpetuating a tradition of family singing group activity. For the most part, the concept of performing as a family singing group was original with each group.

Changes throughout the Years

For many of the groups (4) (7) (8) (11) (16) (17) (19) (22) no changes had occurred throughout the years. With two significant exceptions, (16) (22), most of these groups with no changes had been performing together for a relatively short period of time. Other groups (1) (3) (5) (10) (18) had added children as they grew old enough to participate. Still other groups (13) (25) had lost members as siblings or children lost interest or moved away. Other groups (2) (12) (14) (15) (21) (24) had both gained and lost members through the years, for various reasons. In still other groups (9) (23) the family members had remained constant, but other members of the group had changed.

Publications Used

Sources of music for the different groups also varied widely. In general, most groups felt free to utilize appropriate songs from any available source. The basic sources were hymnbooks, sheet music, song collections, singing convention books, original compositions, and songs learned by ear from recordings, radio,

183

television and from other performers. The chart shown as Figure 15 gives the basic source of music as cited by the various groups.

County	Hymn books	Sheet Music	By Ear	Other Performers	Convention Books	Song Collections	Original Compositions
(1)		x	x	x			
(2)	x	x					
(3)	x	x	x	x ("best way")	x	x	
(4)		x			x	x	
(5)	x	x					x(use music for all except original compositions)
(6)	No Groups						
(7)	x	x	x				
(8)		x					
(9)	x	x		x	x		
(10)	x	x	x			x	
(10)	x	x	x			x	
(11)		x (all)					
(12)		x	x (one song)		x		
(13)	x	x			x		
(14)	x	x			x (nothing by ear)		
(15)		x			x		
(16)		x			x		(nothing by ear)
(17)	x	x	x (most)		x		
(18)		x				x	
(19)	x	x	x (most)			x	
(20)	No Groups						
(21)			x (all)				
(22)		x (all)					
(23)		x			x	x	
(24)		x			x	x	
(25)			x (all)				

Figure 15. Basic sources of music.

It should be noted that all groups used sheet music, except the two groups which learned their songs exclusively by ear. For two groups the only music used was that published in sheet music form. Two groups volunteered that none of their music was

184

learned by ear and another group volunteered that only their original songs were learned by ear but that printed music was used in all other instances. These statements contrast with those of the two groups who stated that all of their music was learned by ear, and two additional groups who volunteered that most of their music was learned by ear.

Favorite Songs

Members of each group were asked to identify their favorite songs. These songs were not necessarily those included in the group's performing repertory. Some groups named more favorites than others, and several groups (17) (23) (25) did not select any songs as their favorite. In several instances the songs named were unfamiliar to the researcher. In other cases the title may have been familiar but the actual song, if performed, was different from that expected. All of the songs named as favorites are listed in Figure 16. Those songs which were named by more than one group are so indicated. For the most part, members of the groups did not cite composers of the songs. It is quite possible that in some cases members of a group intended songs by composers other than those supplied by the researcher.[4] The asterisk indicates those songs that were also selected by one of the groups as their most representative performance. In these cases a copy of the song appears in Appendix A.

Amazing Grace (John Newton; anonymous tune)
Because He Lives (William and Gloria Gaither) (named three times)
Because I Love You (original (5))
The Best Is Yet to Come (Jack Campbell)
Between the Cross and Heaven (William and Gloria Gaither)
The Blood Will Never Lose Its Power (Andrae Crouch)
Broken Pieces (Ruby Kitchen and James Martin, Jr.)
Build My Mansion Next Door to Jesus (Dottie Rambo)
City of Gold (Shirley Cohron)

185

Day by Day (*Godspell*) (Stephen Schwartz)
Didn't He Shine (Allen Reynolds and Bob McDill)
Faith Will Move Mountains
A Glimpse of Jesus (Cornelia Mears)
Glory Road (C. Cook) (named twice)
Going Home (William and Gloria Gaither)
Hallelujah Meeting (Ron Hinson)
Hallelujah Square (Ray Overholt) (named three times)
He (Richard Mullan and Jack Richards) (named twice)
Heaven Will Be Worth It All (R. Stufflebeam)
He Is Mine and I Am His (G. T. Speer)
He Put a Little Sunshine
He Touched Me (William Gaither) (named twice)
Here They Come (Beth Glass and Jim Wood)
He's My Friend (Henry Slaughter)
How Great Thou Art (Carl Boberg; trans. By Stuart K. Hine;
    anonymous tune)
I Asked the Lord (Johnny Lange and Jimmy Duncan)
I Believe (Ervin Drake, Irving Graham, Jimmy Shirl and Al
    Stillman)
I Believe It (William Gaither)
I Can Feel the Touch of His Hand (J.D. Sumner)
I'm His and He's Mine (Troy Lumpkin)
I Should Have Been Crucified (Gordon Jensen)
I've a Precious Friend (Henry Slaughter)
Jesus, I Love You (Original (5))
Jesus Is Coming Soon (R.E. Winsett) (named three times)
Jesus Is Mine (Wally Fowler and Virginia Stout Cook)
Jesus Opened Up the Way (E.M. Bartlett and Allen Webb)
Joshua (G.A. Thacker)
Let's Just Praise the Lord (William and Gloria Gaither)
The Lights of Home (J. Davis and R. Heady)
Living on Higher Ground (B. Thornhill)
Long, Long Ago
*Love Is Why (W.F. Bill Lakey, V.B. Vep Ellis, David Ellis)
One Day at a Time (Marijohn Wilkins and Kris
    Kristofferson) (named four times)
One Day too Late (Lanny Wolfe)

186

The Prettiest Flowers [Will Be Blooming] (Albert E.
    Brumley)
Put Your Hand in the Hand (Gene MacLellan)
Remind Me, Dear Lord (Dottie Rambo)
Satisfied (Martha Carson)
Sheltered in His Arms [Sheltered In The Arms Of God (?)
    (Dottie Rambo)]
Something Beautiful (William and Gloria Gaither)
Stroll over Heaven
Sunset Trail
Sweetest Words Ever Said
*Sweet, Sweet Spirit (Doris Akers)
*Ten Thousand Years (Elmer Cole)
That I Could Still Go Free [That I May Go Free (?) (R.
    Hinson)]
The King Is Coming (William Gaither)
There's a Rainbow (There's a Rainbow in the Sky (?) (Marcy
    Tigner)]
This Is the Day (N. Harmon)
Touching Jesus (John Stallings)
*Touring That City (Harold Lane) (named twice)
Victory in Jesus (E.M. Bartlett)
*What a Beautiful Day (Aaron Wilburn and Eddie Crook)
Why Me (Kris Kristofferson) (named three times)
Will the Circle Be Unbroken (A.P. Carter)
Without Him (Mylon R. LeFevre)

Figure 16. Favorite songs.

It is interesting to note that none of the songs which had
been listed as "America's Favorite Hymns" in 1953[5] were cited by
any members of any of the groups. This may simply indicate that
active performing groups are more strongly influenced by songs
of current popularity. The song cited more often than any other,
"One Day At A Time," (named four times) received the Gospel
Music Association Dove Award as "Best Gospel Song Of The
Year" in 1975.[6] The fact that only eight songs were named more
than once reflects the intense individuality of each group. For
some unexplained reason most of the groups did not cite as favor-

187

ites those songs which they later chose as their most representative performance example.

Favorite Recordings

Members of the groups were also asked to identify their favorite recordings. In most cases, instead of naming specific single selections or phonograph albums, members of the groups would name favorite recording artists. Occasionally these favorite recording artists were popular local groups. The complete list of responses is shown as Figure 17. Four groups (13) (16) (22) (25) did not identify a favorite recording or recording artist.

Anderson Family (local?)
Wendy Bagwell and the Sunlighters
Blackwood Brothers (named twice)
[Old] Blackwood Brothers
Blue Ridge Quartet
Chuck Wagon Gang (named twice)
Couriers, *Across The Country* (album?)
Dixie Echoes
Downings, *This Is How It Is* (album?)
Florida Boys, *Make Happy Tracks* (tape)
[Old] Florida Boys
Bill Gaither Trio (named four times)
Gospel Carriers (local)
Gospel Lads
Gospel Three (local)
Peggy Grimsley, *God Walks These Hills* (album) (local)
Happy Goodman Family (named three times)
Hinson Family (named three times)
Hinson Family, "From Out of the West They Came" (single
    selection?)
Hudson Family (local) (named twice)
Hymnsmen (local) (differentiated from professional group
    with same name)
Impact Brass and Sound (Ozark Bible College) (album)

188

Jackson Brothers
Wendy Johnson and the Messengers
Kingsmen
LeFevres (named five times)
LeFevres, "Stepping on the Clouds" (single selection)
Lewis Family
Melody Makers (local)
[Old] Osmond Brothers (hymns)
The Peacemakers (local?)
Elvis Presley (gospel albums)
Purpose (folk musical) (album)
Dottie Rambo
Second Chapter Of Acts (group)
Sego Brothers and Naomi (named twice)
Marilyn Sellers (local?)
Speer Family (named three times)
Speer Family, "Between the Cross and Heaven" (title song
    of album)
Statler Brothers
Ray Stevens, "Turn Your Radio on" (single selection)
Jimmy Swaggart
Sounds Of Gospel (local)
Statesmen Quartet (named three times)
Thrasher Brothers
Will the Circle Be Unbroken (album; various artists)

Figure 17. Favorite recordings.

The wide range of responses precludes any conclusion that
the amateur practitioners of gospel music are overly influenced
by any one source. Only eleven recording artists were the mutual
favorites of more than one group. The recording ensemble cited
as favorite by more groups than any other was the LeFevres.
This ensemble was cited five times as a favorite recording group
and once for a specific recording. Inasmuch as the LeFevres are
an Atlanta-based group with considerable longevity, it is reasonable that they would be favorites among the gospel singers of
south Georgia. However, the six responses from the possible
twenty-three respondents indicates that even this ensemble can

189

hardly be considered a major influence affecting performance practice among the population of this study.

Favorite Radio Programs

Members of each group were asked to identify their favorite radio programs. For the most part responses to this item consisted of the naming of a radio station and a description of the programming of the station. Often different members of a group would name different radio stations. The complete listing of all radio stations and radio programs cited is shown as Figure 18. The number in parentheses is an indication of stations named by more than one group, not by different members of a single group. Members of four groups (3) (9) (14) (18) stated that they listened to very little radio programming.

WBIT (Adel) ("Only to gospel singing part")
WBHB (Fitzgerald) General Programming (some gospel)
WCEH (Hawkinsville) Country/Western (some gospel) (named twice)
WCRY (Macon) Classical
WCUP (Tifton) Classical
WDEN (Macon) Country/Western
WFAV-FM (Cordele) General Programming (some gospel)
WKTZ (Jacksonville, Fla.) Classical and Semi-classical
WLOR (Thomasville) gospel all Sunday afternoon
WMAZ (Macon) Top 40 (named twice)
WMGR (Bainbridge) gospel 10:15–11:00 daily; Sunday 7–12.
WMJM (Cordele)
WMTM AM-FM (Moultrie) Full-time Gospel
WSIZ (Ocilla) Country/Western and Gospel
WSOJ (Jesup) Full-time Gospel (named four times)
WGTA (Thomaston) some gospel programming
WTJH (East Point) Full-time Gospel
WUFF (Eastman)
WVOH (Hazlehurst)

190

WVOP (Vidalia)
WYNR (Brunswick) "Singing Gospel Time" (6–12 Sundays)
(named twice)
WZAT (Savannah) "Breakfast with Burl [Womack]" (gospel)
(named twice)
[no call sign given] (Waynesboro) Full-time Gospel
"Rock Music Stations" (named twice)
"Mull Singing Convention" (no further identification)[7]

Figure 18. Favorite radio stations and radio programs.

Favorite Television Programs

Members of each group were also requested to identify their favorite religious music television programs, if any. Three groups (9) (17) (24) indicated that television was watched very rarely. Two families (2) (24) did not have a television set in the home. On the other hand, one group (23) volunteered that watching television was preferred to listening to the radio, and another group (4) indicated that television was watched but that gospel programs were rarely selected. The listing of favorite television programs and favorite television stations cited is shown in Figure 19.

It should be noted that "Gospel Jubilee," often called "Gospel Singing Jubilee," was cited as a favorite program by more than one-half of all the groups in the survey. As such, this program may be said to exert more influence on gospel music performance practice than any other single source identified during the course of the field research. As stated in Chapter 5, this program is a gospel variety show, produced in Nashville, Tennessee and hosted by Les Beasley, lead singer of the Florida Boys quartet. "Gospel Jubilee" has received a Dove Award for "Best Gospel Television Program" every year the award has been presented by the Gospel Music Association.[8]

"America Sings"
Billy Graham (named twice)
Gospel Hour (Columbus, WTVM) (named twice)

191

"Gospel Jubilee" (named thirteen times)
Lewis Family (Augusta)
Oral Roberts (named six times)
PTL ["Praise the Lord"] Club (named twice)
Rex Humbard (named four times)
Sego Brothers and Naomi
"Spring Street" (former Southern Baptist Convention program)
"The Trebles" (Macon) [This group was one of the selected amateur groups (1) in the Field Research)
"Warren Roberts Presents"
Wendy Johnson and the Messengers (named twice)
WMAZ-TV (Macon) some gospel programming
WTOC-TV (Savannah) some gospel programming

Figure 19. Favorite television programs and television stations.

Before an undue amount of influence is attributed to this program, however, it should be mentioned that two groups (3) (18) stated that the program hours conflicted with "church time." The only time they were able to watch the program was while absent from church services. A similar conflict of interest may have been experienced, but not verbalized, by other groups.

Performance Agenda Past and Present

Each group was asked to cite anecdotes from significant past performances or present activities. The anecdotes are included with the interview information of the various groups as detailed in Appendix A. Often instead of anecdotes, the members of the groups would simply cite events in which they had participated. The most frequently occurring similar response was made by groups (1) (4) (13) (16) (18) (21) (24) citing occasions where they had performed with other, more prominent groups, and been well received. The next most frequently occurring similar response was made by groups (1) (2) (5) (9) (13) (18) citing occasions when their audience had made a deeply emotional or spiritual response to their music. The third most often cited response was

192

made by groups (2) (5) (7) (11) (21) relating humorous or embarrassing moments which had occurred in connection with earlier performances. Two groups (5) (11) related instances where individual members or the entire group had been moved by personally touching experiences during the course of a performance.

The most often cited performing events were revivals (12) (14) (15) (19) (23), followed by benefit concerts (3) (9) (10), camp meetings (12) (19) (24), and radio programs (16) (17) (25). Performing for nursing homes, homecomings, and funerals received two responses each from various groups. It is probable that several of the other groups had also participated in such activities but did not choose to cite them. One group (25) had performed regularly over television in the past and another group (1) was making its television debut the very evening in which the group was interviewed by the researcher. At the other extreme, two groups (8) (15) had only recently made their debut in a performance other than in their home church.

Two groups (1) (10) stated that they had previously entered the amateur talent contest at the Bonifay, Florida, gospel sing. A member of one of these groups stated that she was glad for the experience but it was one of those things she would never do again.

Remuneration for Performers

As stated in Chapter 6, groups were not asked questions pertaining to their handling of finances as long as the researcher was assured of their amateur status as defined in Chapter 1. It was also stated in Chapter 6 that several of the groups volunteered information concerning their handling of funds. A total of nine groups volunteered such information. In general, these were the more active groups and, apparently, each had evolved its policy of money management in some proportion relative to the group's ideals versus expenses.

Three groups (2) (3) (11) stated they never accepted money for singing. One group (4) stated they had never been offered money, but probably would not accept unless they became so

193

good that they would have to give up their jobs. Another group (13) had previously accepted "love offering" but no longer did so. "Love offering" is the term used to refer to the collection from the audience of donations to be distributed among the performers.

The only group which was not an exclusively gospel singing group (19) accepted payment for entertainment functions but refused to accept payment from churches for religious performances.

Of the three remaining groups mentioning the subject, all accepted fees or donations, but each handled the money in slightly differing ways. One of them (1) placed all offerings into a special bank account from which were paid all food and gasoline expenses for engagement trips. Their clothing was purchased from out-of-pocket, and they had had to borrow money in order to make recordings and to buy a van. Another group (9) used money collected in order to buy clothes, or divided the money equally among the members of the group. Occasionally donations were returned to the sponsoring church. All equipment (and the group had a considerable amount) had been purchased from out-of-pocket. The third group (10) charged a set fee ($150), or a percentage of the profits, for an all-night sing. No set fee was charged for church performances but "love offerings" were accepted. Separate records were kept of all money earned for gospel performances and this money was used to defray expenses. Clothes, with one exception, had been purchased from out-of-pocket.

Future Plans

The final interview item posed to each group concerned future plans. In many cases this item seemed to take the members of the group by surprise. Often a spokesman would utter a cliche such as, "Keep on keeping on," or sing a phrase from the previously mentioned popular gospel song, "One Day At A Time." For the most part, responses to this item came as afterthoughts rather than as carefully laid plans for the future. Consequently, the largest number of similar responses came from groups (2) (12) (15) (16) (21) (22) who had no definite plans or who stated that their future was very unpredictable. Equally divided were groups (5) (11) (12) (13) (23) who predicted difficulty remaining together (for a variety of reasons); and groups (2) (3) (8) (14) (18) who foresaw major improvement in the near future.

Several responses were couched negatively. Two groups (1) (9) had no plans to become professional and four groups (2) (3) (11) (24) had no plans to make a recording. By way of contrast, two groups (16) (19) stated that they would like to make a recording, and four groups (or members of the groups) (10) (14) (19) (25) stated that they would like to become professional performers, although not necessarily of exclusively gospel music.

Although the phraseology was couched in a variety of ways, many of the groups stated that they wished to improve in order to reach more people, or more simply, to continue to be of service for the Lord.

Characteristics of the Selected Songs

Upon completion of the aforementioned interview, each group was requested to sing at least one song. As groups were not limited to the singing of only one song, in several cases quite a large number of songs were performed. The performance of each group was recorded by the researcher, using a portable monophonic cassette tape recorder. Details of the methodology of the tape recording appear in Chapter 6. Upon completion of the tape-recording session, each group was asked to select one song (if several had been performed) for comparison with published music. With only two exceptions, the song selected by each group as its first choice was used for the comparison of printed music with performance practice. One exception was the group (21), mentioned in Chapter 6, whose first choice had been a song learned from a tape recording of a radio broadcast. Subsequent investigation revealed that this song had been composed and harmonized orally by the radio performers themselves. The other exception was a group (3) whose first choice had been a song learned by ear from another amateur performing group many years previously. The researcher was unable to find a published song with the same title. In both of the above instances an-

195

other song, selected in advance by each group as a precaution against such an eventuality, was substituted.

Songs and Composers

No duplicates appeared among the songs selected by the amateur groups. This again is a reflection of the individuality of the amateur performers, and also a reflection of the availability of a great quantity of gospel music from which they were able to choose. The complete list of selected gospel songs is shown alphabetically by title in Figure 20. Subsequent references to these songs will be cited numerically by county as they appear in Appendix A.

County	Title	Author/Composer
(22)	"At the Crossing"	Mosie Lister
(19)	"Daddy Sang Bass"	Carl Perkins
(11)	"Had It Not Been"	Rusty Goodman
(13)	"Heaven Came Down and Glory Filled My Soul"	John W. Peterson
(4)	"Help Me Lord, to Stand"	Byron Faust
(21)	"I Won't Walk without Jesus"	Ronny [sic] Hinson
(9)	"I'll Soon Be Gone"	Joel Hemphill
(25)	"Jesus Found Me"	
(10)	"Jesus, Savior, Pilot Me"	Edward Hopper (author) J. E. Gould (composer)
(5)	"Lord, I Want to Be a Christian"	Negro Spiritual
(23)	"Love Is Why"	W. F. (Bill) Lakey and V. B. (Vep) Ellis (authors), David Ellis and V.B. (Vep) Ellis (composers)
(16)	"Love, Like the Love of God"	David Ingles
(1)	"Oh What a Love"	David Reece
(14)	"Reach Out to Jesus"	Ralph Carmichael
(12)	"Sweet, Sweet Spirit"	Doris Akers
(18)	"Ten Thousand Years"	Elmer Cole
(2)	"The Lighthouse"	Ronnie [sic] Hinson
(24)	"The Unseen Hand"	A. J. Sims
(8)	Through Faith, I Still Believe"	James McFall
(15)	"Touring That City"	Harold Lane
(7)	"Walking the Sea"	Ernest Rippetoe
(17)	"What a Beautiful Day (For The Lord to Come Again)"	Aaron Wilburn (author); Eddie Crook (composer)
(3)	"Where We'll Never Grow Old"	James C. Moore

Figure 20. Selected songs.

196

Not only were there no duplicate songs chosen; only one composer, Ronny Hinson,[9] was the writer of more than one song (2) (21). It is significant, as a reinforcement of one of the differences between gospel songs and traditional English hymnody, that of the twenty-three songs, nineteen were conceived as a complete entity, words and music, by one person. One of the songs (5), a Negro spiritual, is of unknown authorship. Only three songs (10) (17) (23) had separate authors for the words and composers for the music. Even in one of these songs (23) a joint-author was also listed as a joint-composer.

Publishers

The diversity of the gospel music chosen is also shown in the number and location of the publishing companies represented. As stated previously, three of the songs (3) (5) (10) were in the Public Domain. The largest number of songs from one publisher were those (2) (11) (17) published by Journey Music, a company recently purchased by Word, Incorporated of Waco, Texas. Publishers represented by two selections each were Benson Publishing, Nashville, Tennessee (18) (24); Hemphill Music, Nashville, Tennessee (8) (9); and Lillenas Music Company, Kansas City, Missouri (22) (23). Companies represented by only one song were:

Cedarwood Publishing Company, Nashville, Tennessee (19);
LeFevre-Sing Publishing Company, Atlanta, Georgia (16);
Lexicon Music, Woodland Hills, California (14);
Lynn Music Company, Brewster, New York (1);
Manna Music, Burbank, California (12);
Singspiration, Incorporated, Grand Rapids, Michigan (13);
Songs of Calvary, Fresno, California (21);
Ben Speer Music Company, Nashville, Tennessee (15);
Stamps-Baxter Music, Dallas, Texas (7);
Tennessee Music Company, Cleveland, Tennessee (25);
James D. Vaughan, Music Publisher, Cleveland, TN (4).[10]

Melody

The melodies of the songs were analyzed for their scale structure, range, and presence or absence of chromaticism. In addition, each song was examined for the presence or absence of an anacrusis, that is, the use of one or more preliminary notes prior to the first strong rhythmic pulse.

Scale structure. The largest number of melodies, twelve, were based on the seven-tone major scale. Six melodies were based on a hexatonic or six-tone scale, and five were based on a pentatonic or five-tone scale. The six-tone and five-tone scales upon which these latter melodies were based could be considered gapped major scales; that is, they were oriented within a predominantly major scale structure with the omission of the fourth or seventh degree, or both. None of the melodies were oriented within a minor or modal pattern.

Range. The range of the majority of the melodies, fifteen, was exactly one octave. Only one song had a range of a minor seventh. Three songs encompassed an octave-and-second, and one song spanned an octave-and-third. Surprisingly, three songs (2) (12) (17) had the extended range of an octave-and-fourth.

Chromaticism. In contrast to Hitchcock's description of the earlier gospel hymns as being "chromatically engorged,"[11] only a limited number of the current songs employed chromaticism to any great extent. A total of only nine songs utilized any chromatic tone in the melody. In five of these nine songs the chromaticism was limited to a single tone, generally employed in conjunction with harmony of the secondary dominant. Only four of the songs (3) (7) (14) (23) may be said to possess an abundance of chromaticism in either their melody or in their harmony.

Anacrusis. Apparently the amateur performers of gospel music have a predilection for songs containing an anacrusis. A total of seventeen songs began with a upbeat. Of these, the largest number, twelve, began with two notes before the first strong pulse. Three began with three notes, and two began with one note. Only six songs began on a downbeat.

Tonality and Key

As previously stated, each melody was examined for its scale structure. In addition, each song was examined for its overall tonality and key. Without any exceptions, all songs were written in a major tonality. This exclusive use of major tonality is consistent with most previous descriptions of gospel songs appearing in related literature. The key most often selected was that of E-flat major. A total of eight songs were composed in this key. The remaining most popular keys, listed in descending numerical order of preference, were: F, with five; B-flat and G, with three each; A-flat, with two; and D-flat and C, with one each.

Meter and Rhythm

Meter. Consistent with traditional hymnody, simple meter was most often utilized for the selected songs. It is interesting that triple meter (3/4-time) was chosen more frequently than quadruple meter (4/4-time). A total of ten songs were written in 3/4-time and nine were written in 4/4-time. *Alla Breve* (¢) was used for one song. The compound meters of 6/8, 12/8, and 6/4 were also utilized for one song each.

Rhythm. Realistically, none of the selected gospel songs may be said to be very difficult rhythmically. This is not to say that several of the songs do not appear complex on the printed page. In general, this visual complexity is a result of an endeavor to show changes between or among verses due to different syllabification. Another reason both for visual and vocal complexity is an endeavor to represent the rhythms of songs which were apparently conceived orally. Songs considered moderately complex by the writer include (4) (8) (11) (21) (23). Songs considered relatively simple rhythmically include (1) (7) (16) (19) (24). The remainder of the songs fall somewhere between these two rather nebulous extremes. Rhythmic patterns employed most frequently were: dotted quarter note followed by an eighth note (♩· ♪), found in twelve of the songs; and a mild syncopation

199

(generally ($\flat$ $\sharp$ $\flat$) or ($\flat$ $\sharp$)), also found in twelve songs. The frequent use of syncopation contrasts with Pierce's description of the earlier gospel hymns as ([having] a strongly defined rhythm and no syncopation. . . ."[12] Only four songs (10) (12) (13) (14) employed the rhythm pattern of a dotted eighth note followed by a sixteenth note ($\sharp$). This also contrasts with Downey's description of earlier gospel songs as "often employing the dotted-eighth and sixteenth-note pattern of a marching tune."[13]

Texture

The texture of the largest number of songs, twelve, was completely homophonic. That is, each note of the melody was accompanied by harmony notes within an identical rhythmic structure. An additional seven songs were written in a predominantly homophonic style, but with some movement of the inner voices while the melody part held an occasional sustained tone. Two songs (5) (9) employed brief usage of a call-and-response pattern, but again, within a predominantly homophonic structure. Only one song (4) was written in a mildly contrapuntal style with the melody migrating through the voice parts. Even here the contrapuntal style was employed only within the chorus. The verse was written in strict homophony. One song (12) was published as a solo with keyboard accompaniment.

The selection by the amateur performers of songs composed in predominantly homophonic style contrasts markedly with Tallmadge's statement that ". . . responsorial and antiphonal practice . . . may well be the most important structural characteristic of the [gospel song] genre.[14]

Harmony

In general, the harmony of the songs could also be considered relatively simple. Most songs consisted of predominantly tonic (I), subdominant (IV), and dominant (V) [or dominant seventh (V^7)] harmony; with occasional use of the submediant (vi) or brief modulation to the secondary dominant (II). It should be noted, however, that only one of the songs (21) used exclusively tonic, subdominant, and dominant [seventh] harmony with no embellishment whatever. Each of the other songs made occasional usage of more complex harmony. This was generally attributable to the addition of a seventh, or to the use of passing tones. Songs (1) (12) (14) (23) contained harmonies substantially more complex than those in the other songs. In general, this complexity consisted of the use of minor chords other than the submediant; additions of sixths, sevenths, and ninths; the use of a major mediant (III or III^7), and the occasional use of diminished or augmented chords.

Form

As anticipated, the overwhelming majority of the songs were written in verse-and-chorus form. Twenty-one songs were identified in the printed music as being in this form. An additional song (14), although not so designated, was also in verse-and-chorus form. Only one song (10) was in ABA form.

The songs written in verse-and-chorus form were not exactly alike, however. The majority, fifteen, were written in AB form, with the "B" section serving as the beginning of the chorus. An additional five songs, including the aforementioned song not labeled in the music as being in verse-and-chorus form, were written in A (A) B (A) or A (A) BA form. In these cases the capitalized letter within parentheses indicates a phrase similar to but not identical to the phrase represented by the capitalized letter not so enclosed. Also in these cases, the capital letter "B" represents a dissimilar phrase which forms the beginning of the chorus, An additional two songs (1) (15) were composed in A (A) form. In these cases, both the verse and the chorus were very similar musically.

In the great majority of songs the verse was sixteen measures long, and the chorus was also of sixteen measures duration. In four of the songs (4) (15) (19) (25) the chorus was twice as long as the verse. Only three songs (1) (8) (13) included a coda.

Shaped Notes

As previously stated, the publication of music in shaped notes has nothing to do with the sound of the music once it is performed. Nevertheless, a great deal of gospel music is published in shaped notes. Of the twenty-three songs included in Appendix A only four (5) (12) (13) (14) are not printed in shaped notes. Of these, at least three (5) (12) (13) are available for purchase in shaped notes. As it is reasonable to assume that these three were not *originally* published in shaped notes, no attempt was made by the writer to procure copies in that form.

Texts

The text of each of the selected songs was examined for the essence of its religious content. If possible, the complete song was summarized into one sentence. In several cases, however, a song would require more than one description in order to be summarized accurately. The basic religious content of all of the songs is shown as Figure 21. Songs from which the basic religious content was derived are identified by a number as they appear in Appendix A.

Anticipation of Heaven (3) (9) (13) (15) (18) (19) (22) (23) (25);
Anticipation of Christ's Second Coming (17);
Peace, Love, Joy, from Conversion (1) (13) (23) (25);
Awe of, and desire for, the Love of God (16);
Rejection of past life (21);
Desire to improve personal virtues, become more like Christ (5);
Christ's walking upon the sea (7);
Peter and John healing of lame man (21);

202

Faith in Biblical account of Christ's miracles, death and resurrection (8);
Jesus symbolized as a lighthouse (2);
Jesus symbolized as a nautical pilot (10);
Prayer for help (4);
Assurance of Jesus' constant availability to help (14);
Comfort of knowing Jesus (1);
Dependence on Jesus (21);
Jesus' guiding hand (24);
Almost tangible presence of the Holy Spirit (12);
Exhortation of second person to have faith in Christ (7);
Exhortation of second person to believe in Jesus (12);
Exhortation of second person to accept Jesus' help (14);
Christ's sacrifice due to His love (23);
Speculation of personal fate if Christ had not sacrificed Himself (11);
Memory of hard times and family togetherness (19).

Figure 21. Basic textual content of songs.

The most frequently recurring theme, stated in nine of the songs, was that of anticipation of Heaven. The next most frequent theme, but occurring in only four songs, concerned the joys and rewards of conversion. The mood of the songs, in general, could be considered to be optimistic. Expressions of self-abasement were very rare.

All of the songs were personal in some manner. The least personal song (7), a re-telling of the story of Christ's walking upon the sea, contained a second person reference in its third verse. Over one-half of the songs, (1) (4) (5) (8) (9) (10) (13) (18) (19) (23) (24) (25) were considered intensely personal in the subjective evaluation of the researcher. Three songs (11) (16) (22), not including the aforementioned song considered least personal, were adjudged less personal than the remainder.

Most of the songs were written in the first person. Five songs (7) (9) (10) (12) (14) contained at least one verse with a second person reference. Three songs (7) (22) (23) had at least one verse couched in the third person or contained a third person reference.

Characteristics of Performance Practice

The tape recorded performance of each selected song was analyzed and compared with the published music in order to identify significant traits which could be considered characteristic of the amateur performance of gospel music. As an aid in this analysis, each selected song was transferred from its individual cassette tape to a one-quarter-inch reel-to-reel tape, recorded at seven-and-one-half inches per second (7-1/2 IPS). This reel-to-reel tape[15] became the master tape for an additional cassette tape[16] containing each of the twenty-three selected songs in numerical order as listed alphabetically by county in Appendix A.

As stated previously, each group was assured that its performance would not be compared critically against any arbitrary standard nor compared with any other group in the survey. Identification of groups, therefore, is intended for purposes of illustration only.

Melody

For the most part, the sung melody was the same as that written. No group sang the melody with complete accuracy regarding its pitch and rhythm. Nevertheless, the greatest number of groups (1) (4) (5) (8) (10) (12) (13) (14) (15) (23) performed their song without significant deviation from the written melody. Almost an equal number, however, (2) (3) (9) (11) (16) (18) (19) (22) (24) made slight but distinct alterations to the melody. Only four groups (7) (17) (21) (25) may be said to have altered the melody significantly, each in the direction of increased complexity. This alteration consisted chiefly of the embellishment of the existing melody, rather than vocal improvisation using the written melody as a point of departure. This relatively faithful adherence to the written melody may be considered a fundamental difference between white gospel music performance and Afro-American gospel music performance.

Harmony

The singing of harmony by ear appears to be another characteristic of white southern gospel music singing. In a total of twelve groups (3) (7) (8) (9) (10) (11) (14) (15) (17) (19) (21) (24) the sung harmony was similar to but not exactly the same as that written. In general, the modified harmonies were sung as a composite of the written alto and tenor parts. An additional three groups (5) (12) (25) altered the harmony in the direction of increased complexity. Conversely, one group (22) sang in unison, and three groups (2) (13) (18) modified the harmony slightly in the direction of simplicity. Only four groups (1) (4) (16) (23) adhered faithfully to the published harmony. For the most part, the instrumental harmony, while performed in an improvisatory style, adhered closely to the published harmonic structure.

Rhythm

No group performed the rhythm of its song with complete accuracy to the published rhythmic patterns. In fact, the aforementioned lack of accuracy regarding the singing of the melody was more often due to rhythmic inaccuracies than to pitch deviations. Nevertheless, the great majority of songs, sixteen, were performed with only minor alterations to the rhythm. Two additional songs (13) (14) were performed in a basically correct fashion but with the occasional addition or subtraction of a beat or portion of a beat. In two songs (10) (24) the meter was changed from 3/4-time to 4/4-time. In both of these cases the recurrent pattern (♩. ♪) was changed to (♩ ♪ ♪) provide the additional beat. Only one song (21) was considered to be altered in the direction of increased rhythmic complexity, and two songs (17) (25) were considered rhythmically simplified.

Texture

As previously stated, the texture of most of the songs was

that of homophonic style with only occasional use of moving parts in the inner voices or with relief responsorial and antiphonal effects. Most groups (3) (4) (8) (11) (14) (16) (18) (23) (24) retained the textures indicated, although in some cases the song was performed in only two-part or three-part harmony. Three additional groups (9) (13) (19) retained the basic texture but with slight modifications. The most significant deviation in texture was in the use of a soloist for the verse with the full group joining in on the chorus. Most groups utilizing this texture (7) (10) (15) (17) (21) (22) had the soloist sing alone on the verse. Two additional groups (1) (2) accompanied the soloist with a sung vowel background. One of the aforementioned groups (7) utilized a soloist for the chorus also, with the remainder of the group singing in responsorial style.

It should be noted that one group (5) changed its song from a written call-and-response style to a homophonic style with moving inner parts. By way of contrast, another group (25) changed its song from homophonic style to antiphonal and responsorial style.

One group (12) changed its song, written as a single vocal line with piano accompaniment, to that of a three-part homophonic style with moving inner voice parts. Conversely, another group (22) changed its song, originally written as four-part homophonic, to that of a soloist for the verse, and unison for the chorus.

Form

The form of all but one (10) of the songs, as previously stated, was that of verse-and-chorus. Eight of the groups (1) (2) (3) (11) (12) (16) (18) (24) followed the written form without any modifications other than the addition of a brief instrumental introduction. Modifications by other groups generally consisted of omitting a stanza, omitting a chorus between stanzas, adding an interlude between stanzas, repeating the chorus, and adding a coda. Several of these modifications were often utilized in the same song.

Four groups (3) (4) (16) (23) omitted one stanza, and one group (13) omitted the chorus between stanzas two and three. Six groups (7) (9) (10) (14) (17) (25) added an interlude between the chorus and the last stanza sung. One group (21) began with the chorus, and six groups (7) (9) (15) (17) (21) (22) repeated the chorus at least once.

As previously stated, three of the songs (1) (8) (13) had a coda written into the music. In each of these cases the written coda was utilized. An additional nine groups (5) (7) (8) (9) (10) (15) (17) (19) (21) devised their own coda, which generally consisted of the repetition of the last several measures of the song. In several cases (7) (15) (22) the repetition of the complete chorus served as the coda.

Dynamics

Only one of the songs (1) had any dynamic markings indicated on the printed music. In performance, these dynamic markings were not followed.

In the subjective evaluation of the researcher, the largest number of groups, eleven, (5) (8) (10) (11) (12) (13) (14) (15) (16) (19) (21) sang *mezzo-forte* (*mf*) throughout their performance. That is, the members of the group sang with full voice, yet without an apparent effort to achieve dynamic contrasts or to push their voices to a volume beyond their limitations. An almost equal number, ten, (3) (4) (7) (9) (17) (18) (22) (23) (24) (25) were subjectively considered to have sung at a dynamic level of *forte* (*f*) throughout their performance. This may have been due to the presence of naturally louder voices or due to a mental image retained by the researcher of the apparent expenditure of energy exhibited by the performers during the recording session. No attempt was made to use electro-mechanical equipment to determine volume levels. The use of amplification equipment by many of the groups would have invalidated such measurement.

Two groups (1) (2) achieved dynamic contrast through variety in texture. In both of these cases the verses which were sung by a soloist while the other members of the group sang a vowel accompaniment were noticeably less loud than the respective choruses which were sung full-voiced by all members of the group.

Tempo

Metronomic tempi were clocked by listening to the tape recording of the respective performances. Only one song (11) had any indication of tempo printed with the music. In this case "very slow" was suggested. The group performed this song at an approximate metronome marking of ♩=92.

Tempi chosen for the remainder of the songs ranged from a low of one-pulse=60 to a rate of one-pulse=150, with very little evidence of grouping into identifiable patterns. The entire spectrum of metronome markings is shown as Figure 22. Metronomic tempi, however, do not accurately represent the subjective impression of "fast" or "slow" which characterize the performances. For example, the subjective impression of the performance of the song, "Jesus, Savior, Pilot Me" (10) is not as slow as its metronomic rate of (♩=60) would suggest. This is due in part to the piano accompaniment which supplies an impression of a faster movement. Conversely, the song "Touring That City" (15) does not appear to be sung as rapidly as its tempo of ♩=150 would suggest.

Metronome Marking	Song (s)	Metronome Marking	Song (s)
60	(7) (10)	88	(4) (22)
63	(24)	92	(11)
66	(13)	96	(5) (25)
69	(2)	100	(9) (19)
72	(1)	108	(8) (17)
76	(16) (23)	112	(18)
80	(3)	120	(12) (21)
84	(14)	150	(15)

Figure 22. Metronomic tempi of performed songs.

Songs that subjectively appear to be performed "fast" are (9)

208

(12) (13). Songs appearing to be performed "slow" are (3) (14) (24). The remainder of the songs are performed creating the impression of a moderate tempo.

Text

The texts of the songs were sung accurately by the majority of the groups. Fifteen groups made no alteration of the words whatever. Three of these fifteen groups (4) (16) (23), however, omitted one stanza from their song. Eight groups (1) (2) (3) (5) (7) (19) (21) (25) made slight alterations to the printed text. One of these groups (3) also omitted a stanza from its song. None of the deviations from the text could be considered substantative alterations.

Introduction

Each group, except the one which performed *a cappella* (13), used some form of instrumental introduction prior to the sung portion of the performance. In the majority of cases piano alone was used for this introduction. For ten groups the piano introduction was approximately four measures in length and was generally derived from the final measures of the respective song. One group (21) used a piano arpeggio as introduction, and another group (10) used a two-measure introduction. Longer piano introductions included groups (17) (12) (23) who used approximately five, six, and eight measures respectively. One group (9) utilized piano and electric bass for a four-measure introduction.

Several guitar introductions were in the form of an arpeggio or a single-chord strum. Groups (3) (15) (25) began in this fashion. Two groups (5) (19) utilized a complete introduction performed on the guitar, and one group (7) used guitar, electric bass, and drums for a complete introduction.

Amplification

The use of amplified instruments in accompaniment was mentioned previously in reference to instrumentation. In addition, eight groups (1) (5) (7) (9) (10) (11) (21) (22) performed using amplification for the voices. This was generally accomplished by the use of individual hand-held microphones connected to a control unit (Mixer) at which adjustments for balance could be made. The use of amplification by slightly over one-third of the randomly selected family groups is considered significant by the researcher.

Change of Key

Apparently another significant aspect of the performance of gospel music is the changing of the key from that appearing in the published music. A total of eleven groups changed the original key. Of these, ten were in the direction of lowered pitch. One group changed the key in the direction of raised pitch. Key changes and directions are itemized as Figure 23.

It should be noted, however, that several of the instruments used for accompaniment were not tuned to standard pitch. Five groups (4) (5) (11) (19) (25) performed with instruments tuned approximately one-half step low. Of these five groups, three were accompanied by guitar and two by piano. One additional group (7) utilized a guitar tuned approximately one-half step high.

Changed From	To	Direction and Distance	Group
Eb	D	Down /2-step	(3)
Eb	C	Down minor third	(5) (15) (16)
Bb	G	Down minor third	(10) (19)
Ab	Eb	Down Perfect Fourth	(1)
G	D	Down Perfect Fourth	(7)
F	C	Down Perfect Fourth	(17)
Bb	Eb	Down Perfect Fifth	(24)
F	G	Up Major Second	(25)

Figure 23. Change of key by performers.

210

Instrumental Improvisation

As previously stated in reference to the accuracy of the melody, the use of vocal improvisation other than the occasional embellishment of the melody is apparently not a characteristic of the performance of white southern gospel music. The use of some form of improvisation, however, does seem to be a characteristic of the accompaniment. Of the twenty-three groups, only one accompanist (4) performed the music without significant deviation from the printed page. One additional group (13) performed *a cappella.* In the remaining groups the accompaniment was performed with at least some stylistic elements that could be considered improvisation. In the majority of cases the improvisation was considered "chordal" for want of a better term. By this, it is meant that the improvisation was not melodic, but consisted of the playing of additional chordal tones in a rhythm pattern consistent with the rhythm of the song. The range of skills displayed in the use of this chordal improvisation varied widely. Several instrumentalists, however, exhibited a great deal of skill and expertise in providing improvisatory accompaniments. Instrumentalists for groups (1) (9) (12) (21) (22) demonstrated highly developed skills. Accompaniments for these groups included melodic as well as chordal improvisations.

Summary

The amateur practitioners of gospel music, as revealed by the field research were, in general, intensely individualistic, showing little evidence of musical influence from any single source. Most belonged to small, fundamentalist, church congregations and limited their performances to gospel music only. Many of the groups had been performing gospel music for a considerable number of years.

Sex of the performers was fairly evenly divided between male and female. Over one-half of the groups utilized a male lead, or the vocal lead was shared by both male and female.

Occupations of the performers tended to fall into a predomi-

211

nantly working-class category, yet few of the groups accepted any remuneration for their performances. Very few groups had made any definite plans for the future. Apparently most were content simply to perform whenever requested.

Songs selected by the amateur performers reflected both the individuality and the unsophistication of the musicians. Most of the songs were published in shaped notes and were generally composed with limited technical demands. All were written in major keys. The words to approximately one-third of the songs concerned the anticipation of Heaven, although the remainder of the songs were more diverse in subject matter. All of the songs were personal in some respect and over one-half were considered intensely personal.

The performance of the music was generally characterized by the close, but not exact, following of the published intent of the composer. Vocal improvisation, when performed, was generally limited to brief embellishments of the existing melodic line. Vocal harmony was generally characterized by singing by ear rather than by adherence to the published part. The texture of the music was generally homophonic with occasional use of moving inner voices, or even more infrequent use of a simple contrapuntal style.

The form of almost all of the songs was that of verse-and-chorus. In approximately one-third of the cases, the verse was performed by a soloist, with the complete group joining in on the chorus. In performance, the omission of a stanza or the repetition of the chorus were the most frequent deviations from the published form. Codas were often fashioned from the repetition of the chorus or from the repetition of the final measures of a song.

Most groups sang full-voiced throughout their performance. Little apparent effort was made to achieve dynamic contrast. Slightly more than one-third of the groups performed with amplification of the voices.

All groups but one performed with accompaniment. Piano was the instrument most often utilized for accompaniment. Other accompanying instruments included guitar, electric bass, drums, and tambourine.

Almost one-half of all the groups changed the key from that published in the music. With only one exception, the change of key was in the direction of lowered pitch. Some form of improvisation in the instrumental accompaniment was also a characteristic of the performance of all but two of the songs. In several cases the instrumental improvisation was considered highly skillful.

Notes

1. These criteria, mentioned previously in Chapter 1, were: 1. At least three members related by blood or marriage; 2. Amateur in the sense of receiving less than fifty percent of total income from gospel music activities; 3. Have performed away from home church at least once within previous year.
2. First Baptist Churches were represented in the 177 total groups, however. No Presbyterian or Episcopal churches were so represented.
3. Denominational names are as cited by the groups.
4. The assistance of Norma L. Boyd, Executive Secretary of the Gospel Music Association, in the compilation of composer information is gratefully acknowledged.
5. "What Are America's Favorite Hymns," The Christian *Century,* LXX (September 16, 1953), n.p., reprinted in Linnell Gentry, *A History and Encyclopedia of Country, Western, and Gospel Music* (Nashville: McQuiddy Press, 1961), p. 126. These hymns, listed in order are: The Old Rugged Cross, The Love Of God; In The Garden; What A Friend We Have In Jesus; Beyond The Sunset; Precious Lord, Take My Hand; Rock Of Ages; It Is No Secret; Abide With Me; No One Ever Cared For Me Like Jesus.
6. Dove Award Winners 1969–1976 are listed in Appendix C.
7. Programs, station call signs, and locations are as cited by interviewees, and compared with the list of gospel radio stations shown in Appendix C.
8. Dove Award Winners 1969–1976 are listed in Appendix C.
9. Sometimes spelled Ronnie.
10. The names of all publishers, with the exception of James D. Vaughan, are cited as they appear in the *Gospel Music 1977 Directory & Yearbook* (Nashville: Gospel Music Association, 1976), pp. 120–122. [The complete *Directory* listing appears in Appendix C.] The Vaughan company is not listed in this source. The Vaughan company is presently owned by the Tennessee Music Company. Also, Singspiration, Incorporated and Stamps-Baxter Music are both owned by the Zondervan Corporation of Grand Rapids, Michigan. Several of the above names and addresses vary slightly from letterhead information obtained from correspondence with the companies. The variant information appears with the music in Appendix A.
11. Hugh Wiley Hitchcock, *Music In The United States: A Historical Intro-*

duction (2nd ed.; Englewood Cliffs, New Jersey: Prentice-Hall, 1974), p. 104.

12. Edwin H. Pierce, " "Gospel Hymns' and Their Tunes," *The Musical Quarterly,* XXVI (July, 1940), 356.
13. James C. Downey, "Revivalism, the Gospel Songs and Social Reform," *Ethnomusicology,* IX (May, 1964), 120.
14. William H. Tallmadge, "The Responsorial and Antiphonal Practice in Gospel Song," *Ethnomusicology,* XII (May, 1967), 219.
15. BASF [Badische Anilin-& Soda-Fabrik AG] 67 Ludwigshafen, Germany.
16. Duplicate copies of this cassette tape are available from the writer, at cost, upon request. Please address inquiries to Stanley H. Brobston, TDK SA-C90, Baxley, GA 31513.

8

Summary, Conclusions, and Implications for Future Research

Summary

The historical precedent for a religious hymnody designed to appeal to unsophisticated musical tastes is well established. It is perhaps symbolic that the soloist and choir of angels who announced the "gospel" of the birth of Christ chose as an audience a group of shepherds, or plain folk. Present-day gospel music also seems to find its greatest number of adherents among plain folk.

Music has been important in religious life in America from its beginning. The first book published in the English-speaking colonies of North America was the *Bay Psalm Book* (1640), a translation of the Psalms into singable English meter. The ninth edition of this *Bay Psalm Book* (1698) was the first book containing music notation published in the English-speaking colonies.

American musical institutions, such as the singing schools and singing societies, began as a means of improving religious music performance. Some of these institutions later became the foundation of much more highly sophisticated schools of musical performance. Yet the same institutions also formed a vehicle for the perpetuation of the concept and practice of a simple, unsophisticated, intrinsically American, religious hymnody.

Evangelism, the attempt to convert non-believers to Christianity, often brought with it a use of a popular religious hymnody, designed to attract and sway large audiences. In some cases these audiences, in their enthusiasm, were able to create their own appropriate music. Widespread religious upheavals, in America were the "Great Awakening" (approximately

215

1725–1750) and the "Great Revival" (approximately 1800–1805). Both of these spontaneous intensifications of religious fervor were accompanied by the creation and use of a popular and unsophisticated religious hymnody.

The title of the songbook series, *Gospel Hymns* (1875–1885), used in the evangelistic campaigns of Moody and Sankey (1871–1899) brought about the widespread use of the term "gospel music" to identify popular religious hymnody. Neither the use of the term nor the style of the music was original with Moody and Sankey, however. The title had been used several times previously and the style of the music had been antedated by the Sunday School songs. It was the enormous popularity of the *Gospel Hymn* series which made "gospel" a generic term for the style concept. The *Gospel Hymns* were the product of urban composers and lyricists, but they were intentionally designed to appeal to unpretentious tastes.

The term "gospel music" came also to be applied as an identification of the southern style of popular religious hymnody. This hymnody had evolved from the singing school and singing convention traditions. Southern publishers of gospel music were strong advocates of music reading and often conducted or sponsored singing schools and singing conventions. A unique aspect of southern religious music publication was the continuation of the use of shaped note-heads. The shaped note-heads, originally intended as an aid in sight-singing (Little and Smith, 1798), had been discarded by urban proponents of better music. Southern publishers did not agree. With only slight modification (Aikin, 1846), these shaped note-heads became a distinguishing characteristic of the southern style of gospel music.

The most prominent and influential publisher of southern religious hymnody was the Ruebush-Kieffer Company of Dayton, Virginia (1866–1942). Other influential publishers were: A.J. Showalter of Dalton, Georgia (1880–1926); James D. Vaughan, Music Publisher, of Lawrenceburg, Tennessee (1900-present); and Stamps-Baxter Music & Printing Company of Dallas, Texas (1925-present). Present-day corporations which are influential in gospel music are: The Benson Company of

216

Nashville, Tennessee; Word, Incorporated, of Waco, Texas; and The Zondervan Corporation of Grand Rapids, Michigan.

Southern gospel music began to attract a wider audience as commercial radio (1920) enabled the music to be heard by those who did not usually attend the singing conventions. Popular radio performing groups, many of whom were also featured singers at large group-singing conventions (first State Convention 1932; National Convention 1937), began to concertize. The making of disc recordings by gospel musicians also tended to increase audience exposure to gospel music. By approximately 1940, gospel music began to evolve into an entertainment industry, but without any unified sense of direction. It was not until the gospel concert promotion entitled the National Quartet Convention (1956) that any semblance of unity appeared among the highly individualistic coterie of gospel professionals.

The Gospel Music Association (1964), a non-profit organization, was instituted in order to provide focus and leadership for the burgeoning industry. This organization has apparently been highly successful, and its plans for the future appear to be well framed.

In addition to the professional gospel music industry, there exists a large population of semi-professional and amateur gospel music performers. The present study also undertook to ascertain the extent of this population and to identify the style of music by some objective means. Twenty-three amateur family gospel music performing groups from twenty-five counties in south Georgia were chosen at random for an examination of the characteristics which comprise the gospel music genre. As stated previously, to the writer's knowledge this is the first study of gospel music in which an objective method was used in the selection of representative performers or in the selection of music for analysis. A summary of the field research is presented in Chapter 7.

A composite family gospel singing group, derived from the summary of the Field Research, would consist of a mother, father, one or two children, and a non-related friend. The non-related member would probably be an instrumentalist. The family usually would be members of a Baptist church, but not the largest Baptist church in the county. Both the father and mother

217

would be employed in working-class occupations. They would not be farmers, although their residence would be in a rural community.

The family nucleus would have been accustomed to performing as a unit for approximately eight years and the mother and father would have performed together as a unit prior to the children being old enough to participate with the group. A piano would be the accompanying instrument. The father would sing lead, the mother would sing alto, and the children and non-related member would double the same parts or sing one additional part. If an additional instrument were used it would probably be an electric bass.

Few books or other reading material would be in the home and it is unlikely that the group would have preserved any written material pertaining to their performing activities. Members of the group would be able to recount many previous performance experiences, however. The performances would have been conducted generally within a fifty-mile radius of their home. The majority of the group's performances, other than for their own church, would have been for revival meetings of neighboring churches, or for amateur gospel sings. The group would not have accepted any remuneration for performing. The group would sing gospel music exclusively.

Music chosen for performance would be taken from a variety of sources but would include several pieces of sheet music of recent popularity. Most songs would have been learned by using a copy of the music as a guide, but occasionally a song would have been learned by ear. The harmony parts would have been learned by ear, using the contour of the printed music as a guide.

The group would pride itself upon being unique. No attempt to imitate other performing groups, whether professional or local, would be admitted. Favorite songs, favorite recordings, and favorite radio stations would be different from those of other similar groups, and preferences would probably differ within the group. The group would enjoy watching the television program "Gospel Jubilee," however, and would spontaneously sing a fragment of the theme song as soon as the name of the program was mentioned.

The songs performed by the group would be written within the range of one octave for the melody, and would present few technical demands. The songs would begin with an anacrusis and have little or no chromaticism. The songs would all be written in major keys, but the group would transpose the key several steps lower. The transportation would present few difficulties as the songs would contain only tonic, subdominant, and dominant harmonies with perhaps the occasional use of the submediant. A brief modulation to the secondary dominant would occur in the chorus. The songs would be written in verse-and-chorus form and when performed, the verse would be sung by a soloist. Few of the songs in the group's repertoire would contain more than two stanzas. If the written song contained more than two stanzas, only two of the stanzas would be performed.

The songs would be written in simple meter. An equal number of songs in 3/4-time and 4/4-time would be included in the repertory of the group. The rhythm of the songs would not be difficult, although some syncopation would be present. Adherence to the published rhythm would not be exact.

The words of the songs would be unequivocally religious and would include some reference to Heaven, and the anticipation of going there. The words to the songs would not be altered during performance. The songs would be sung full-voiced. The singing would be accompanied by slight bodily movements intended to lend emphasis to certain words, or to unconsciously keep time to the music. No attempts at dynamic contrast would be made. It would not be unusual for the group to sing with amplification, using individual hand-held microphones. Songs would be performed at a moderate tempo.

The singing of the songs would be preceded by a brief instrumental introduction. At the conclusion of the song the chorus would be repeated and the final four measures repeated again as a coda.

The songs would be published in shaped notes, but the group would be unaware of the purpose for the note shapes.

The group would have made no definite plans for the future although some member of the group might possess aspirations for a career in music.

Conclusions

Gospel music, throughout its hundred-year history of being identified by the term, has been deprecated or comparatively neglected by the majority of music historians. This deprecation or neglect is especially true regarding the writings of church music historians. Nevertheless, the music of popular hymnody has held considerable attraction for a large number of adherents. These adherents have, in general, been comprised of those with relatively unsophisticated musical tastes. Apparently the many adherents of gospel music are unaware of or unconcerned about the opinions of self-proclaimed arbiters of taste.

The music has been almost exclusively the product of American composers, although some texts, notably those by Isaac Watts, may have been taken from European sources. Although it is not folk music in the sense of being anonymously composed, the genre could be considered folk music in a sense, due to the large number of relatively unknown contributors who create the words and the music.

Gospel music, for the most part, has been, and is, created for use in a worship service where the music is simply an adjunct to the preaching. In the south, however, a tradition of performing and enjoying the music for its intrinsic value has been perpetuated since the days of the early eighteenth century singing schools. The most recent modification of this tradition is manifested in the proliferation of gospel music concerts, called "gospel sings."

Based upon the writer's study, it appears that popular religious hymnody in America is thriving and shows no indication of diminishing.

Implications for Future Research

Gospel music, as a subject for scholarly research, is replete with areas deserving additional investigation. The following suggestions should be considered only a partial listing. Although many of the areas overlap, these suggestions are presented as groupings of similar studies. The groupings are: Biographical studies: Institutional studies; Comparative studies; Related disciplines; Firsts; Discographies; and Studies using methodology similar to the field research of the present study.

Biographical Studies

One of the most obvious needs is for detailed biographical studies to be conducted of many of the persons cited in the above text. The recent studies of publishers such as A.J. Showalter[1] and James D. Vaughan[2] are welcome contributions. Also, current dissertations-in-progress on the lives and contributions of Philip P. Bliss[3] and Daniel B. Towner[4] should prove invaluable in defining the roles of these leaders in the history of popular religious hymnody. Many other research needs exist.

The contributions of many of the composers and compilers of Sunday School songs, such as William Batchelder Bradbury (1816–1868); William James Kirkpatrick (1839–1921); John R. Sweney (1837–1899); George Frederick Root (1829–1895); and the compilers of the *Gospel Hymns* series, such as Ira David Sankey (1840–1908); James McGranahan (1840-1907); and George Coles Stebbins (1846–1945), await in-depth documentation. The contributions of Philip Phillips (1834–1895), comparatively neglected in related literature, should prove interesting. A republication of Phillips' *Song Pilgrimage Around the World*[5] could promote additional interest in his contributions to gospel music.

An earlier composer and compiler, whose accomplishments as an individual have also been neglected, is Charles Wesley (1707–1788). In general, writings about Wesley have been combined with those concerning his brother, John, and his grandson, Samuel S. Wesley. Charles Wesley's contribution of an estimated 6,500 hymns should provide justification for an individual biography.

Although Ruffin has recently completed an excellent biography of Fanny Crosby,[6] drawing upon new material and primary sources, a need still exists for someone to undertake the overwhelming task of compiling her complete works. From the complete works could be published a selected anthology of her published and unpublished poems.

Homer Alvan Rodeheaver (1880–1955), whose contributions include not only song leading and music publishing, but also pioneering efforts in radio broadcasts and disc recording, is also deserving of an in-depth biography. A republication of his *Twenty Years with Billy Sunday*[7] would again make available fascinating insights into Rodeheaver's techniques of mass audience song leading.

Charles Alexander (1867–1920), a predecessor of Rodeheaver, also was a master of mass audience song leading. As the prototype for many revivalist song leaders, including Rodeheaver, he, too, should prove to be an interesting biographical study. A republication of Davis' *Twice Around the World with Alexander, Prince of Gospel Singers*[8] should bring to light heretofore difficult-to-find information about Alexander.

The contributions of Isham Emmanuel Reynolds (1879–1949), first chairman of a music department in a Southern Baptist theological seminary (1915), should also be documented in scholarly fashion. His years in this position and the number of lives he must have influenced could possibly be reflected in the number of amateur singers in the Field Research who were members of Baptist churches.

William Hauser (1812–?), a North Carolinian who eventually made Georgia his home, could be the subject of several investigations. Jackson's description of Hauser and his publications should whet the mental appetites of any number of scholars in several different disciplines. To quote Jackson, "He was a doctor, preacher, editor, teacher, composer, and singer."[9] He published one songbook in four-shaped notation and, thirty years later, a second book in seven-shaped notation. The first book, the *Hesperian Harp* (1848), according to Jackson, "had the name of being the largest and most comprehensive song collection that had, up to that time, appeared in America."[10] His later book, the *Olive Leaf* (1878), was the last of the big oblong songbooks compiled by southerners and published in the North.[11]

The personality of Benjamin C. Unseld (1843–1923) is also

222

fascinating. This well-trained, well-established musician, the first secretary of the New England Conservatory,[12] had to be coerced by Aldine Kieffer to teach shaped note music reading. Yet he devoted much of the latter part of his life to the teaching of shaped note music to southerners. How far-reaching was his influence? What were his educational objectives? What was his teaching methodology? An anthology of his writings and of his own music is almost a *sine qua non* for future scholarship of southern gospel hymnody.

The publishing history of the Stamps-Baxter Music and Printing Company has been the subject of a recent investigation by Beary.[13] Due to the substantial influence of this company, the individual biographies of Virgil Oliver Stamps (1892–1940), Jesse Randolph Baxter (1887–1960), and his wife, Clarice Howard Baxter (?–1972), would undoubtedly reveal additional information of merit.

Members of the Gospel Music Hall of Fame,[14] other than those previously mentioned, could well be the subjects of scholarly biographical studies. Although several of these names are well known to gospel music aficionados, they remain obscure to the lay public. Information concerning the lives and contributions of these leaders should be a welcome addition to public knowledge.

Recent popular biographies of well-known gospel music personalities, such as the Speer Family,[15] J. D. Sumner,[16] the Happy Goodman Family,[17] the Blackwood Brothers,[18] La Breeska Hemphill,[19] and John W. Peterson,[20] provide some insights into the musical and cultural milieu of gospel music. Scholarly investigations of the lives and contributions of these, and other, personalities, combined with bibliographies of their music and discographies of their recordings, would yield even greater insights.

Other gospel music leaders, such as the Benson family, William and Gloria Gaither, the LeFevres, and the Chuck Wagon Gang, should be interviewed and their history documented while they are still active. Due to the apparent disinclination of many gospel musicians to retain written documentation about their activities, oral history techniques would perhaps be highly beneficial in such information gathering. Oral history data could possibly prevent a futile search for written materials after the participants have deceased.

Institutional Studies

In addition to studies of individuals, a need exists for accurate documentation of the contributions to gospel music by various institutions. The history of Moody Bible Institute, for example, has been documented by Getz,[21] and the role of the institution in relation to gospel music has been touched upon by Hustad.[22] However, no full-scale documentation of the Moody Bible Institute's considerable contributions to gospel music has yet been attempted.

The Joseph Funk, Ephraim Ruebush, and Aldine S. Kieffer complex of family, acquaintances, publications, teachings, writings, and influences has not been the subject of a complete investigation. Eskew's examination of the early music,[23] Hall's study of the *Musical Million* periodical,[24] and Grace Showalter's detailed bibliography of the musical publications of the Ruebush-Kieffer company[25] could provide points for departure.

The publishing company of Biglow and Main and that of the John Church company, both mentioned in the text as the co-publishers of the *Gospel Hymns* series, were highly influential in the early propagation of gospel music. The histories of these companies should be documented in scholarly fashion. Included in such studies should be some record of what percentage of their publication was printed in shaped notes.

The camp-meeting revivalism of the early 1800s has been the subject of quite a number of studies. That the camp-meeting tradition has continued to the present is often neglected in many of these writings. An investigation of the hymnody used in contemporary camp meetings could be the subject of an interesting monograph.

The southern gospel music singing convention tradition could also be the subject of several investigations. Significant local singing conventions, national holiday singing conventions,[26]

New Year's Eve singing conventions, state singing conventions, and the National Gospel Singing Convention could well be the recipients of separate scholarly endeavors. Although many similarities would exist among the various types of singing conventions listed, each should provide enough individual distinctions to become the subject of a worthwhile study. An example of an excellent individual study is Karen Jackson's history of the Royal Singing Convention in Irwin County, Georgia.[27]

The National Quartet Convention, previously mentioned as being highly significant in the recent history of gospel music, could be the subject of a fascinating study. Although this "convention" is a gospel concert promotion, the fact that those chosen to perform are often considered the best among the professional groups should be justification for documentation of those chosen to perform over the span of its twenty-year history.

Other attempts need to be made to identify the best, or most active, performing groups of the past. This should include finding the names of the groups who were authorized to represent the Vaughan publishing company, and those quartets who were given automobiles as part of their remuneration for representing the Stamps-Baxter music company.

Other gospel music publishing companies have yet to be made the subject of individual studies. Among these companies could be the R. E. Winsett Music Company (Dayton, Tennessee); the Hartford Music Company/Albert E. Brumley and Sons (Powell, Missouri); and the Parham/Morris, Morris/Henson, J.M. Henson Music Company (Atlanta, Georgia).

The shaped note music schools could provide several areas for investigation. Individual schools such as the Virginia Normal Music School (Dayton, Virginia); the A.J. Showalter Southern Music Normal Institute (Dalton, Georgia); the Vaughan School of Music (Lawrenceburg, Tennessee); the Stamps-Baxter School of Music (Dallas, Texas), could be studied for their historical value. Present-day shaped note music schools[28] could also provide interesting subject matter for documentation.

Although the Vaughan music company has been the subject of a recent study,[29] this investigation was concerned primarily with the company publications. The role of the Vaughan music

225

company in the spread of southern gospel music via radio, recordings, and concertizing has yet to be documented.

Comparative Studies

A number of comparative studies also come to mind. Sankey's *Sacred Songs and Solos* (1874), published in England, compared with Bliss and Sankey's *Gospel Hymns and Sacred Songs* (1875), published in America, could yield some fascinating similarities and differences. A comparison of the Sunday School songs appearing in the first issue of *Gospel Hymns,* with those included in later editions, should be an intriguing investigation. The songs included in Bliss' *Gospel Songs* (1874), compared with those chosen for inclusion in the *Gospel Hymns and Sacred Songs* should also be interesting.

Comparative studies need not be restricted to musical materials. A critical examination of the crowd psychology techniques used by Sankey, Alexander, Rodeheaver, and Barrows, could yield many rewards to an imaginative scholar.

Previously suggested in the text was the possibility of comparing the effectiveness of teaching sight-singing via the use of shaped notes, with the effectiveness of teaching sight-singing via the use of the English Tonic Sol-Fa system of notation. It is doubtful that even dramatically superior results by either of the systems would convince the alternate proponents to discard their favored system. However, it is possible that a reinforcement of the Kyme study,[30] showing superior skills and enthusiastic participation by those students taught via shaped notes, could convince some American music publishers of the value of printing public school music in the shaped note format.

Another comparison previously suggested in the text was the tracing of the transition of all-white to all-black of the gospel music recordings listed in the "Best-Selling" charts of *Billboard* magazine. As it is probable that this transition was simply the result of an editorial policy change, a more significant comparison would be that of the differences in performance practice between white southern gospel music performers, and

Afro-American gospel music performers. The field research of the present study should provide some point of departure for such a comparison.

A comparison of the music and social customs of Sacred Harp singing conventions, with that of the music and social customs of gospel music singing conventions, should yield interesting results. Along a similar line, a comparison of the music and social customs of white southern gospel singing concerts, with the music and social customs of country and western music concerts should also prove intriguing.

Related Disciples

It has been previously mentioned that research in gospel music need not be restricted to musical materials. Implications abound for research in related disciplines.

The religious aspect of the singing conventions, both four-shape and seven-shape, needs to be examined. Many singers attend singings away from their homes almost every Sunday. In what is a predominantly fundamentalist religious society, the music *is* their religion. It would seem that this feature of the singing conventions could provide several hypotheses for theological scholars to investigate.

The musical education of the Sunday School song and gospel hymn composers could be the subject of an interesting study. Several of these composers studied with well-known pedagogues in Europe and America, yet they were effective in composing for a mass audience comprised mainly of those with unpretentious musical tastes.

The musical education of present-day gospel song composers could prove to be another interesting study. It is certain that the range would include those with little or no formal education in music,[31] through those with Masters degrees,[32] to those upon whom honorary Doctorates have been conferred.[33]

Apparently the majority of the composers of gospel music have had very little formal training. Yet their writing has considerable variety within the limitations of its *genre*. Aside from the

227

aspect of research, much of this music could be adapted for instrumental use. The variety in the part-writing, combined with limited technical demands, would make excellent instructional material for string quartets or other instrumental combinations where independence among the performers of the inner parts is being encouraged. Arrangements of the songs into extended instrumental concert pieces could prove attractive to a wide audience.

The subject of musical taste may be difficult for an objective study. It does seem, however, that an investigation could be devised that would define in terms of timbre and vocal production what a southern rural vocalist considers "good." There is no question but that this definition would be somewhat different from that of a conservatory-trained voice pedagogue. The rural method of vocal production apparently does not harm the voice. Singers of advanced age are the rule more often than the exception at singing conventions, and in many cases the elderly singers can perform with the vigor of youth.

The informational communication of shaped note singing activities is an anachronism. Information concerning singings is transmitted by word-of-mouth, by announcements made at concluding moments of conventions themselves, and by postcard or letter. Rarely are Sacred Harp singings or gospel singing conventions announced in newspapers or over radio and television. Although *Vaughan's Family Visitor* publishes a schedule of singing conventions, this list is far from complete. The editor of this publication estimates the listing to represent only ten percent of the actual singings held, if that many.[34] The similar limitation of the Sacred Harp *Directory and Minutes* was alluded to in the above text. An implication for future research here is that information concerning these activities is not easily accessible. Researchers of the subject must develop skills in word-of-mouth information seeking. It would seem that the subject of the communication itself could be formulated into an acceptable research proposal.

Firsts

The historical significance usually attached to first occurrences should justify a closer examination of several items which have implications for the history of gospel music. For example, the first singing school, cited by Cheek as occurring in Boston in 1720,[35] may not have occurred in the North at all. Reference has previously been made to the citation by Britton of the diary entries of William Byrd, of Virginia, in 1710 and 1711. These entries concerned Byrd's attendance at a singing school.[36] An accurate date and place for the first singing school in the North American colonies has yet to be established.

The earliest edition of John Tufts's *An Introduction To The Singing of Psalm-Tunes,* presumably published in 1721, has not been located. As this is considered by most authorities to be the first music textbook published in what is now the United States, the discovery of a genuine first edition would be a highly significant achievement.

Also shrouded in mystery is the location of the first singing society in the south. All sources viewed by the writer agree that this was the Southern Musical Convention, begun in Upson County, Georgia in 1845. Sources that state that the specific location was Huntersville, Georgia,[37] however, are incorrect. According to the writer's research in Upson County, Georgia a community named Huntersville has never existed. Local historians agree that the community in question may have been Hootonville, yet this is entirely conjecture. The town of Hootonville no longer exists. Accurate information concerning the beginning of the Southern Musical Convention has yet to be compiled. The subsequent history of the Southern Musical Convention could also prove to be a research topic of merit.

The history of seven-shape singing conventions is also extremely vague. The first state convention has been cited by the writer as the Alabama State Convention in 1932. The lack of documentation to support such a statement was also mentioned.[38] Individual studies of significant state gospel music singing conventions need to be undertaken before a substantiated "first" convention can be named.

229

The first all night gospel sing was cited as the closing cere-
mony of the Stamps-Baxter School of Music in 1938. Accurate information concerning this highly significant event is also
difficult to obtain. Scholarly documentation of this event would
help dispel many of the myths that have been created, and also
provide a basis for further studies of gospel music concert activities. In the same fashion, accurate information concerning the
first "paid" all night sing (Atlanta, 1946) and the first Carnegie
Hall concert (New York, 1962)[39] needs to be obtained. Who were
the sponsors? Who were the performers? What songs were sung?
What was the attendance? What was the audience reaction?
These, and other questions remain to be answered.

Other first occurrences, such as the first gospel group to perform over the radio; the first gospel group to make a disc recording for a major recording company; the first publication of gospel
sheet music; the first gospel group to perform over television;
and the first complete gospel music television show; all need to
be verified by scholarly investigation.

Discographies

The history of gospel music should not be limited to words
written about the music. The compilation of discographies and
the accumulation of significant recordings into an easily accessible location would prove highly beneficial to future gospel music
research. Discographies considered essential by the writer include the Rodeheaver "Rainbow Records," the Vaughan publishing company recordings, and the recordings made by Frank
Stamps and the All-Stars. Discographies of other individual
groups should also be compiled. Recordings cited in existing listings, such as the Grammy Award Winners (from 1961) and the
Dove Award Winners (from 1969), should be made available in a
central repository. The Gospel Music Hall of Fame edifice, when
completed, should be such a location.

Methodology Similar to the Field Research

Implications for future research would not be complete without the suggestion that the concept of the writer's Field Research procedures be replicated with studies of other gospel music performing groups. A modified replication of the study, delimited to Afro-American gospel groups, should provide an interesting comparison of genres. A similar study limited to quartets, without reference to family relationships, should also provide some musical differences from the present study. Also, a similar study, but using a population of only professional performing groups, should yield interesting data regarding what song each group considers its most representative performance.

Gilbert Chase had issued a challenge to researchers of the music of the South to become liberated from "restrictive categories, unilateral approaches, narrow aesthetic attitudes, archaic academic concepts, and unilinear historical methods."[40] In accepting this challenge, the implications for future research become unlimited.

Notes

1. Joel Francis Reed, "Anthony J. Showalter (1858–1924): Southern Educator, Publisher, Composer" (unpublished Doctoral dissertation, New Orleans Baptist Theological Seminary, 1975).
2. Jo Lee Fleming, "James D. Vaughan, Music Publisher, Lawrenceburg, Tennessee. 1912–1964" (unpublished Doctoral dissertation, Union Theological Seminary, 1972).
3. Bob J. Neil, "Philip P. Bliss (1838–1876): Gospel Hymn Composer and Compiler" (dissertation-in-progress, New Orleans Baptist Theological Seminary).
4. Edward Perry Carroll, "Daniel Brink Towner: Educator, Church Musician, Composer, and Church Music Editor" (dissertation-in-progress, New Orleans Baptist Theological Seminary).
5. Philip Phillips, *Song Pilgrimage Around the World (Chicago, 1880)*; the writer has been unable to locate a copy of this publication.
6. Bernard Ruffin, *Fanny Crosby* (Philadelphia: A Pilgrim Press Book from United Church Press, 1976).
7. Homer Alvan Rodeheaver, *Twenty Years with Billy Sunday* (Winona Lake, Indiana: The Rodeheaver Hall-Mack Co., 1936).
8. George Thompson Brown Davis, *Twice Around the World with Alexan-*

der, *Prince of Gospel Singers* (New York: The Christian Herald, 1907); the writer has been unable to locate a copy of this publication.

9. George Pullen Jackson, *White Spirituals in the Southern Uplands* (1933; New York: Dover Publications, Inc., 1965), p. 70.
10. Ibid., p. 72.
11. Ibid., p. 323.
12. Christopher C. Stafford, "B. C. Unseld," *Vaughan's Family Visitor,* LXX (January , 1971), 6.
13. Shirley Beary, "The Stamps-Baxter Music And Printing Company: A Continuing American Tradition, 1926–1976" (unpublished Doctoral dissertation-in-progress, Southwestern Baptist Theological Seminary).
14. Members of the Gospel Music Hall of Fame are listed in Appendix C.
15. Paula Becker, *Let the Song Go On (Fifty Years of Gospel Singing with the Speer Family)* (Nashville: Impact Books, 1971).
16. Bob Terrell, *J. D. Sumner; Gospel Music Is My Life* (Nashville: Impact Books, 1971).
17. Jamie Buckingham, *O Happy Day; The Happy Goodman Story* (Waco: Word Books, Publisher, 1973).
18. Kree Jack Racine, *Above All; The Life Story of the Blackwood Brothers Quartet* (Memphis: Jarodoce Publications, 1967); and James Blackwood with Dan Martin, *The James Blackwood Story* (Monroeville, Pennsylvania: Whitaker House, 1975).
19. La Breeska Rogers Hemphill, *La Breeska* (Nashville: Hemphill Music Co., 1976).
20. John W. Peterson and Richard Engquist, *The Miracle Goes On (Grand Rapids:* Zondervan Publishing House, 1976).
21. Gene A. Getz, *MBI, The Story of Moody Bible Institute* (Chicago: Moody Press, 1969).
22. Donald Hustad; "Moody Bible Institute's Contribution To Gospel Music" (Moody Bible Institute *Founder's Week Messages,* 1968 (?), pp. 281–294; copy provided the writer by MBI does not contain bibliographic information.
23. Harry Lee Eskew, "Shape-note Hymnody in the Shenandoah Valley, 1816–1860" (unpublished Doctoral dissertation, Tulane University, 1966).
24. Paul M. Hall, "The *Musical Million:* A Study and Analysis of the Periodical Promoting Music Reading through Shape-notes in North America from 1870 to 1914" (unpublished Doctoral dissertation, Catholic University, 1970).
25. Grace I. Showalter, *The Music Books of Ruebush & Kieffer, 1866–1942: A Bibliography* (Richmond: Virginia State Library, 1975).
26. Fourth-of-July, Memorial Day, and others.
27. Karen Luke Jackson, "The Royal Singing Convention, 1893–1931: Shape Note Singing Tradition in Irwin County, Georgia," *The Georgia Historical Quarterly* (Winter, 1972), 495–509.
28. Listed on p. 101 above.
29. Fleming, loc. cit.
30. George H. Kyme, "An Experiment in Teaching Children to Read Music with Shape Notes," *Journal of Research in Music Education,* VIII (Spring, 1960), 3–8.

31. Joel Hemphill, telephone interview, December 19, 1976.
32. Jesse Burt and Duane Allen, "Harold Lane," *The History of Gospel Music* (Nashville: K & S Press Inc., 1971), p. 160.
33. Peterson and Engquist, op. cit., p. 80.
34. Connor B. Hall, editor, *Vaughan's Family Visitor*, personal interview, Cleveland, Tennessee, November 15, 1976.
35. Curtis Leo Cheek, "The Singing School and Shaped-note Tradition: Residuals in Twentieth-century American Hymnody" (unpublished Doctoral dissertation, University of Southern California, 1968), p. 99.
36. Allen P. Britton, "The Singing School Movement in the United States," *Report of the Eighth Congress of the International Musicological Society* (New York: Barenreiter Kassel, 1961), p. 91.
37. George Pullen Jackson, "The Story of the Sacred Harp 1844–1944," reprinted in B. F. White and E. J. King, *The Sacred Harp* (1844; 3d ed., 1859); Nashville: Broadman Press, 1968), p. x; for example.
38. See p. 97 above.
39. The Carnegie Hall concert was not mentioned in the text because of lack of documentation; oral sources indicate that it was very poorly attended.
40. Gilbert Chase, "The Significance of the South in America's Musical History," William Carey College *Faculty Bulletin,* I (May 1970), p. 4.

Bibliography

A. Books

Adorno, Theodor W. *Introduction to the Sociology of Music.* New York: The Seabury Press, 1976.

Alford, Delton L. *Music in the Pentecostal Church.* Cleveland, Tennessee: Pathway Press, 1967.

Allen, Cecil J. *Hymns and the Christian Faith.* London: Pickering & Inglis Ltd., 1966.

American Music Before 1865 in Print and on Records; A Biblio-Discography. Brooklyn: Institute for Studies in American Music, 1976.

Apel, Willi. *Harvard Dictionary of Music.* 2d ed. Cambridge, Massachusetts: The Belknap Press of Harvard University Press, 1969.

Appel, Richard G. *The Music of the Bay Psalm Book: 9th Ed. (1698).* Brooklyn: Institute for Studies in American Music, 1975.

Averitt, Jack N. *Georgia's Coastal Plains.* 3 vols. New York: Lewis Historical Publishing Co., Inc., 1964.

Bailey, Albert E. *The Gospel in Hymns: Backgrounds and Interpretations.* New York: Charles Scribner's Sons, 1950.

Barfield, Louise C. *History of Harris County, Georgia 1827–1961.* Columbus, Georgia: Louise Calhoun Barfield, printed by the Columbus Office Supply Company, 1961.

Barzun, Jacque. *Music in American Life.* Garden City, New York: Doubleday & Co., Inc., 1956.

Baxter, Mrs. J.R. (Ma), and Videt Polk. *Gospel Song Writers Biography.* Dallas: Stamps-Baxter Music & Printing Co., 1971.

Beattie, David J. *The Romance of Sacred Song.* London: Marshall, Morgan & Scott, Ltd., 1935.

Becker, Paula. *Let the Song Go On: Fifty Years of Gospel Singing with the Speer Family.* Nashville: Impact Books, 1971.

Benson, Louis F. *The English Hymn: Its Development and Use in Worship.* 1915; Richmond, Virginia: John Knox Press, 1962.

————. *The Hymnody of the Christian Church.* 1927; Richmond, Virginia: John Knox Press, 1956.

Birge, Edward B. *History of Public School Music in the United States.* 1928; Washington, D.C.: Music Educators National Conference, 1966.

Bishop, Selma L. *Isaac Watts' Hymns and Spiritual Songs (1707) A Publishing History and a Bibliography.* Ann Arbor: The Pierian Press, 1974.

Blackwood, James, with Dan Martin. *The James Blackwood Story.* Monroeville, Pennsylvania: Whitaker House, 1975.

Blume, Friedrich, ed. *Protestant Church Music. A History.* 1964; New York: W.W. Norton & Co., 1974.

Boles, John B. *The Great Revival 1787–1805; The Origins of the Southern Evangelical Mind.* Lexington: The University of Kentucky, 1972.

Bradford, Gamaliel. *D.L. Moody, A Worker in Souls.* New York: George H. Doran Co., 1927.

Breed, David R. *The History and Use of Hymns and Hymn Tunes.* New York: Fleming H. Revell Co., 1903.

Brook, Barry S., Edward O. D. Downes, and Sherman Van Solkema, eds. *Perspective in Musicology.* New York: W.W. Norton & Co., Inc., 1972.

Bruce, Dickson Davies, Jr. *And They All Sang Hallelujah: Plain-Folk Camp-Meeting Religion, 1800–1845.* Knoxville: University of Tennessee Press, 1974.

Buckingham, Jamie. *O Happy Day: The Happy Goodman Story.* Waco: Word Books, Publisher, 1973.

Burrage Henry S. *Baptist Hymn Writers and Their Hymns.* Portland, Maine: Brown Thurston & Co., 1888.

Burt, Jesse, and Duane Allen. *The History of Gospel Music.* Nashville: K. & S. Press Inc., 1971.

Campbell, William Giles, and Stephen Vaughan Ballou. *Form and Style.* 4th ed. Boston: Houghton Mifflin Company, 1974.

Chase, Gilbert. *America's Music from the Pilgrims to the Present.* 1955; Rev. 2nd ed. New York: McGraw-Hill Book Company, 1966.

————. *Two Lectures in the Form of a Pair.* Brooklyn: Institute for Studies in American Music, 1973.

Cleall, Charles. *The Selection and Training of Mixed Choirs in Churches.* London: Independent Press, 1960.

Conn, Charles W. *Like a Mighty Army, Moves the Church of God, 1886–1955.* Cleveland, Tennessee: Church of God Publishing House, 1955.

Cook, Harold E. *Shaker Music: A Manifestation of American Folk Culture.* Lewisburg, Pennsylvania: Bucknell University Press, 1973.

Crawford, Richard. *American Studies and American Musicology.* Brooklyn: Institute for Studies in American Music, 1975.

Crawford, Richard Arthur. *Andrew Law, American Psalmodist.* Evanston, Illinois: Northwestern University Press, 1968.

Crouch, Andrae, with Nina Ball. *Through It All.* Waco: Word Books, Publisher, 1974.

Dahlback, Karl. *New Methods in Vocal Folk Music Research.* Norway; Oslo: Oslo University Press, 1958.

Davenport, Frederick Morgan. *Primitive Traits in Religious Revivals.* 1905; rpt. New York: Negro Universities Press, 1968.

Davis, George Thompson Brown. *Twice Around the World with Alexander, Prince of Gospel Singers.* New York: The Christian Herald, 1907.

Dett, R. Nathaniel. *Religious Folk-Songs of the Negro,* 1927; rpt. New York: AMS Press, Inc., 1972.

Directory and Minutes of Annual Sacred Harp Singings 1975–1976). n.n., n.d.

Edwards, Arthur C., and W. Thomas Marrocco. *Music in the United States.* Dubuque, Iowa: Wm. C. Brown Co., 1968.

Edwards, Ernest N. *The Edwards Album.* Bessemer, Alabama: The Ernest N. Edwards Music Co., 1955.

Ellinwood, Leonard. *The History of American Church Music.* 1953; rev. ed. New York: Da Capo Press, 1970.

Elson, Louis C. *The History of American Music.* New York: The Macmillan Co., 1904.

Etherington, Charles L. *Protestant Worship Music Its History and Practice.* New York: Holt, Rinehart and Winston, 1962.

Evans, Charles. *American Bibliography: A Chronological Dictionary of All Books, Pamphlets and Periodical Publications Printed in the United States of America 1639 to 1820.* 1903; New York: Peter Smith, 1941.

Ewen, David. *Music Comes to America.* New York: Allen, Towne & Heath, Inc., 1947.

———. *Panorama of American Popular Music.* Englewood Cliffs, N.J.: Prentice-Hall, Inc., 1957.

Findlay, James F., Jr. *Dwight L. Moody American Evangelist, 1837–1899.* 1969; rpt. Grand Rapids: Baker Book House, 1973.

Fisher, Miles Mark. *Negro Slave Songs in the United States.* 1953; rpt. New York: Russell & Russell, 1968.

Foote, Henry Wilder. *Three Centuries of American Hymnody.* 1940; rpt. Hamden, Connecticut: Archon Books, 1968.

Fountain, David G. *Isaac Watts Remembered.* Worthington, England: Henry E. Walter, Ltd., 1974.

Gabriel, Charles Hutchinson. *The Singers and Their Songs; Sketches of Living Gospel Hymn Writers.* Chicago: The Rodeheaver Co., 1916.

Gaddis, Vincent, H., and Jasper A. Huffman. *The Story of Winona Lake: A Memory and a Vision.* Winona Lake, Indiana: The Rodeheaver Company, 1960.

Getz, Gene A. *MBI, The Story of Moody Bible Institute.* Chicago: Moody Press, 1969.

Gillis, Frank, and Alan P. Merriam, comp. and eds. *Ethnomusicology and Folk Music; An International Bibliography of Dissertations and Theses.* Middletown, Connecticut: Wesleyan University Press, 1966.

Goldstein, Kenneth S. *A Guide for Field Workers in Folklore.* Hatboro, Pennsylvania: Folklore Associates, Inc., 1964.

Goodspeed, E. J. *A Full History of the Wonderful Career of Woody and Sankey, in Great Britain and America . . . and Everything of Interest Connected with the Work.* 1876; rpt. New York: AMS Press, Inc., 1973.

Goreau, Laurraine R. *Just Mahalia, Baby.* Waco: Word Books, 1975.

Gorham, B.W. *Camp Meeting Manual; A Practical Book for the Camp Ground.* Boston: H.V. Degen, 1854.

Gould, Nathaniel Duren. *Church Music in America.* Boston: A. N. Johnson, 1853.

Governmental Guide. Georgia edition; Madison, Tennessee: n.n., 1975.

Graves, Allen Willis, and B.B. McKinney. *Let Us Sing.* Nashville: Broadman Press, 1942.

Green, Douglas B. *Country Roots: The Origins of Country Music.* New York: Hawthorne Books, Inc., 1976.

Grubbs, John W., ed. *Current Thought in Musicology.* Austin: University of Texas Press, 1976.

Grubbs, Lillie Martin. *History of Worth County, Georgia for the First Eighty Years 1854–1934.* Macon: The J.W. Burke Co., 1934.

Hall, Jacob Henry. *Biography of Gospel Song And Hymn Writers.* 1914; rpt. New York: AMS Press, 1971.

Hartley, Kenneth R. *Bibliography of Theses and Dissertations in Sacred Music.* No. 9 in Detroit Studies in Music Bibliography, 1967.

Hayes, Cedric J. *A Discography of Gospel Records, 1937–1971.* Kobenhavn: Karl Emil Knudsen, 1973.

Haywood, Charles. *A Bibliography of North American Folklore and Folksong.* 2d rev. ed. New York: Dover Publications, 1961.

Heilbut, Tony. *The Gospel Sound: Good News & Bad Times.* New York: Simon and Schuster, 1971.

Hemenway, F. D., and Charles M. Stuart. *Gospel Singers and Their Songs.* New York: Hunt and Eaton, 1891.

Hemphill, La Breeska Rogers. *La Breeska.* Nashville: Hemphill Music Co., 1976.

Hines, Jerome. *This Is My Story, This Is My Song.* Westwood, New Jersey: F.H. Revell Co., 1968.

Hitchcock, Hugh Wiley. *Music in the United States: A Historical Introduction.* 2nd ed. Englewood Cliffs, New Jersey: Prentice-Hall, Inc., 1974.

Hixon, Donald L. *Music in Early America: A Bibliography of Music In Evans.* Metuchen, New Jersey: The Scarecrow Press, 1970.

Homes, Nathaniel. *Gospel Musick.* London: Printed for Henry Overton in Popes-Head Alley, 1644.

Hooper, William Loyd. *Church Music in Transition.* Nashville: Broadman Press, 1963.

Horn, Dorothy Duerson. *Sing To Me of Heaven; A Study of Folk and Early American Materials in Three Old Harp Books.* Gainesville: University of Florida Press, 1970.

Horstman, Dorothy. *Sing Your Heart Out, Country Boy.* New York: E.P. Dutton & Co., Inc., 1975.

Howard, John Tasker. *Our American Music.* New York: Thomas Y. Crowell Co., 1965.

————, and George Kent Bellows. *A Short History of Music in America.* 1957; New York: Thomas Y. Crowell, 1967.

Humbard, Rex. *To Tell the World.* Englewood Cliffs, New Jersey: Prentice-Hall, Inc. 1975.

Huxford, Folks. *Pioneers of Wiregrass Georgia; A Biographical Account of . . . The Original Counties of Irwin, Appling, Wayne, Camden and Glynn.* 6 vols. Adel, Georgia: Patten Publishing Co., 1951–1971.

Jackson, George Pullen. *Another Sheaf of White Spirituals.* Gainesville: University of Florida Press, 1952.

————. *Down East Spirituals and Others.* 1943; rpt. New York: Da Capo Press, 1975.

————. *Spiritual Folk-Songs of Early America.* 1937; rpt. New York: Dover Publications Inc., 1964.

————. *The Story of the Sacred Harp 1844–1944.* Nashville: Vanderbilt University Press, 1944.

————. *White and Negro Spirituals, Their Life Span And Kinship.* 1943; rpt. New York: Da Capo Press, 1975.

————. *White Spirituals in the Southern Uplands.* 1933; rpt. Hatboro, Pennsylvania: Folklore Associates, Inc., 1964. Also rpt. New York: Dover Publications, Inc., 1965.

Jackson, Richard. *United States Music; Sources of Bibliography and Collective Biography.* Brooklyn: Institute for Studies in American Music, 1973.

James, Joseph Summerlin. *A Brief History of the Sacred Harp.* Douglasville, Georgia: New South Book and Job Print, 1904.

Johnson, Charles. *The Frontier Camp Meeting; Religion's Harvest Time.* Dallas: Southern Methodist University Press, 1955.

Jones, Charles Edwin. *Perfectionist Persuasion: The Holiness Movement and American Methodism, 1867–1936. Methuchen, New Jersey: The Scarecrow Press, Inc., 1974.*

Julian, John, ed. *A Dictionary of Hymnology.* Rev. ed. London: John Murray, 1907.

Kaufmann, Helen. *From Jehovah to Jazz; Music in America from Psalmody to the Present Day.* New York: Dodd, Mead & Co., 1937.

Keith, Edmond D. *Christian Hymnody.* Nashville: Convention Press, 1956.

Kerr, Phillip Stanley. *Music in Evangelism and Stories of Famous Christian Songs.* Glendale, California: Gospel Music Publishers, 1939.

Knippers, Ottis J. *Who's Who Among Southern Singers and Composers.* Lawrenceburg, Tennessee: James D. Vaughan Music Publisher, 1937.

Krehbiel, Henry Edward. *Afro-American Folksongs: A Study in Racial and National Music.* New York: G. Schirmer, 1914.

Lewis, Bessie. *McIntosh County, Georgia.* Darien: Ashantilly Press, 1966.

Lillenas, Haldor. *Modern Gospel Song Stories.* Kansas City, Missouri: Lillenas Publishing Co., 1952.

Lomax, John A., and Alan Lomax. *Folk Song U.S.A.* New York: New American Library, 1975.

Lorenz, Edmund S. *Church Music; What a Minister Should Know About It.* New York: Fleming H. Revell Co., 1923.

————. *Practical Church Music.* New York: Fleming H. Revell Company, 1909.

————. *The Singing Church; The Hymns It Wrote and Sang.* Nashville: Cokesbury Press, 1938.

Lovelace, Austin Cole, and William C. Rice. *Music and Worship in the Church.* New York: Abingdon Press, 1960.

Lowens, Irving. *Music and Musicians in Early America.* New York: W.W. Norton & Co., Inc., 1964.

McCutchen, Robert Guy. *Our Hymnody: A Manual of the Methodist Hymnal.* New York: The Methodist Book Concern, 1937.

McLoughlin, William Gerald, Jr. *Billy Sunday Was His Real Name.* Chicago: University of Chicago Press, 1955.

————. *Modern Revivalism: Charles Grandison Finney To Billy Graham.* New York: Ronald Press Co., 1959.

Mahan, Katherine Hines. *Showboats To Soft Shoes: A Century Of Musical Development in Columbus, Georgia. 1828–1928.* Columbus: Columbus Office and Supply Company, 1968.

Malone, Bill C. *Country Music, USA: A 50-Year History.* Austin: University of Texas of Texas Press, 1968.

Marks, Harvey B. *The Rise and Growth of English Hymnody.* Rev. 2nd ed. New York: Fleming H. Revell Co., 1938.

Marrocco, William Thomas, and Harold Gleason, comps. and eds. *Music in America: An Anthology from the Landing of the Pilgrims to the Close of the Civil War, 1620–1865.* New York: W.W. Norton, 1964.

Mathews, W.S.B. *A Hundred Years of Music in America.* Chicago: G.L. Howe, 1889.

Mead, Rita H. *Doctoral Dissertations in American Music: A Classified Bibliography.* Brooklyn: Institute for Studies in American Music, 1974.

Memories and Modern Songs. Dallas: Stamps Quartet Music Co., Inc., 1955.

Metcalf, Frank Johnson. *American Writers and Compilers of Sacred Music.* 1925; rpt. New York: Russell & Russell, 1967.

————. *American Psalmody: Or, Titles of Books Containing Tunes Printed in America from 1721 to 1820.* 1917; rpt. New York: Da Capo Press, 1968.

Moody, William Revell. *D.L. Moody.* New York: The Macmillan Company, 1930.

————. *The Life of Dwight L. Moody by His Son.* New York: Fleming H. Revell Company, 1900.

Morris, James. *The Preachers.* New York, St. Martin's Press, 1973.

Muncy, W.L., Jr. *A History of Evangelism in the United States.* Kansas City, Kansas: Central Seminary Press, 1945.

NARAS 18. New York: Pilgrim Press Copr., [1976].

Nason, Elias. *The American Evangelists, Dwight L. Moody and Ira D.*

Sankey . . . And a Sketch of the Lives of P.P. Bliss and Dr. Eben Tourjee. Boston: D. Lothrop & Co., Publishers, 1877.

Nettl, Bruno. *Folk Music in the United States; An Introduction.* Detroit: Wayne State University Press, 1976.

Ninde, Edward Summerfield. *The Story of the American Hymn.* New York: The Abingdon Press, 1921.

Nottingham, Carolyn Walker and Evelyn Hannah. *History of Upson County, Georgia.* 1930; rpt. Vidalia: Georgia Genealogical Reprints, 1969.

Oldham, Doug, and Fred Bauer. *Doug Oldham: I Don't Live There Anymore.* Nashville: Impact Books, 1973.

Peterson, John W., with Richard Engquist. *The Miracle Goes On.* Grand Rapids: Zondervan Publishing House, 1976.

Phillips, Philip. *Song Pilgrimage Around the World.* Chicago: n.n., 1880.

Poling, David. *Songs of Faith—Signs of Hope.* Waco: Word Books, Publisher, 1976.

Pratt, Waldo Seldon. *Musical Ministries in the Church.* 1901; 6th issue, enl. New York: G. Schirmer, 1923.

Price, Steven D. *Old as the Hills: The Story of Bluegrass Music.* New York: Viking Press, 1975.

1975 Proceedings of the Fifty-Sixth Annual Session of the South Georgia Sacred Harp Singing Convention. n.n., n.d.

Racine, Kree Jack. *Above All: the Life Story of the Blackwood Brothers Quartet.* Memphis: Jarodoce Publication, 1967.

Revitt, Paul Joseph. *The George Pullen Jackson Collection of Southern Hymnody: A Bibliography.* Los Angeles: University of California Library, 1964.

Reynolds, William Jensen. *A Survey of Christian Hymnody.* New York: Holt, Rinehart and Winston, Inc., 1963.

Ritter, Frederic Louis. *Music in America.* New York: Charles Scribner's Sons, 1883. Also, 1890; rpt. New York: Johnson Reprint Corporation, 1970.

Rodeheaver, Homer Alvan. *Hymnal Handbook for Standard Hymns and Gospel Songs.* Chicago: The Rodeheaver Company, 1931.

———. *Twenty Years with Billy Sunday.* Winona Lake, Indiana: The Rodeheaver Hall-Mack Co., 1936.

Rogers, John, ed. *The Biography of Eld. Barton Warren Stone, Written by Himself.* Cincinnati: Published for the Author by J.A. & U.P. James, 1847.

Routley, Erik. *The Church and Music.* 1950; rev. ed. London: Duckworth & Co., Ltd., 1967.

242

————. *Church Music and Theology.* 1959; 2nd impression. Philadelphia: Muhlenberg Press, 1960.

————. *Hymns and Human Life.* 1952; 2nd ed. Grand Rapids: Wm. B. Erdmans Publishing Co., 1959.

————. *The Music of Christian Hymnody.* London: Independent Press, 1957.

Twentieth Century Church Music. New York: Oxford University Press, 1964. Also London: Herbert Jenkins, Ltd., 1964.

Ruffin, Bernard. *Fanny Crosby.* Philadelphia: A Pilgrim Press Book from United Church Press, 1976.

Sablosky, Irvin. *American Music.* Chicago: University of Chicago Press, 1969.

Sankey, Ira David. *My Life and the Story of the Gospel Hymns and of Sacred Songs and Solos.* 1907; New York: AMS Press, 1974.

————. *Sankey's Story of the Gospel Hymns and of Sacred Songs and Solos.* Philadelphia: The Sunday School Times Company, 1906.

Scholes, Percy A. *The Puritan and Music in England and New England.* New York: Russell & Russell, 1962.

Sharp, Cecil James, and Maud Karpeles. *English Folk Songs from the Southern Appalachians.* 2 vols. London: Oxford University Press, Humphrey Milford, 1917–1932.

Shaw, Ralph Robert, and Richard H. Shoemaker. *American Bibliography:* A Preliminary Checklist. 22 vols. New York: Scarecrow Press, 1958–1966.

Shea, George Beverly, with Fred Bauer. *Songs That Lift the Heart.* Old Tappan, New Jersey: Fleming H. Revell Co., 1972.

————. *Then Sings My Soul.* 1968; Old Tappan, New Jersey: Spire Books, Fleming H. Revell Company, 1971.

Showalter, Anthony Johnson. *The Best Gospel Songs and Their Composers.* Dalton, Georgia: The A.J. Showalter Co., 1904.

Showalter, Grace I. *The Music Books of Ruebush & Kieffer, 1866–1942: A Bibliography.* Richmond: Virginia State Library, 1975.

Smith, Timothy L. *Revivalism and Social Reform in Mid-Nineteenth-Century America.* New York: Abingdon, Press, 1957.

————. *Called Unto Holiness: The Story of the Nazarenes: The Formative Years.* Kansas City, Missouri: Nazarene Publishing House, 1962.

Southern, Eileen. *The Music of Black Americans: A History.* New York: W.W. Norton & Co., Inc., 1971.

Spaeth, Sigmund. *A History of Popular Music in America.* New York: Random House, 1948.

————, ed. *Music and Dance in the Southeastern States.* New York: Bureau of Musical Research, 1952.

Steere, Dwight. *Music in Protestant Worship.* Richmond: John Knox Press, 1960.

Stebbins, George C. *Reminiscences and Gospel Hymn Stories.* New York: George H. Doran Co., 1924.

Stevenson, Arthur Linwood. *The Story of Southern Hymnology.* 1931; rpt. New York: AMS Press, 1975.

Stevenson, Robert Murrell. *Patterns of Protestant Church Music.* Durham, North Carolina: Duke University Press, 1953.

————. *Protestant Church Music in America.* New York: W.W. Norton & Co., Inc., 1966.

Stoutamine, Albert. *Music of the Old South; Colony to Confederacy.* Rutherford, New Jersey: Fairleigh Dickinson University Press, 1972.

Sweet, William Warren. *Revivalism in America; Its Origin, Growth and Decline.* 1944; Gloucester, Massachusetts: Peter Smith, 1965.

Sydnor, James Rawlings. *The Hymn and Congregational Singing.* Richmond: John Knox Press, 1960.

Terrell, Bob. *J.D. Sumner; Gospel Music Is My Life.* Nashville: Impact Books, 1971.

Terry, Lindsay. *How to Build an Evangelistic Church Music Program.* Nashville: Thomas Nelson Inc., 1974.

Waters, Ethel. *To Me It's Wonderful.* New York: Harper & Row, Publishers, 1972.

Wayland, John Walter. *Joseph Funk. Father of Song in Northern Virginia.* Dayton, Virginia: The Ruebush-Kieffer Co., [1911?]

Weisberger, Bernard A. *They Gathered at the River: The Story of the Great Revivalists and Their Impact upon Religion in America.* Boston: Little, Brown and Co., 1958.

Whittle, Daniel Webster. *Memoirs of Philip P. Bliss.* New York: A.S. Barnes & Co., 1877.

Wilgus, D.K. *Anglo-American Folksong Scholarship since 1898.* New Brunswick, New Jersey: Rutgers University Press, 1959.

Wohlgemuth, Paul W. *Rethinking Church Music.* Chicago: Moody Press, 1973.

B. Tunebooks and Hymnals

Aikin, Jesse B. *The Christian Minstrel: A New System of Musical Notation.* 1846; 104th ed. Philadelphia: T.K. Collins, Jr., 1858.

Barrows, Cliff. *Billy Graham Song Book.* Minneapolis: The Billy Graham Evangelistic Association, 1969.

Bliss, Philip P., and Ira D. Sankey. *Gospel Hymns and Sacred Songs.* New York: Biglow & Main; Cincinnati: John Church & Co., 1875.

————, and Ira D. Sankey. *Gospel Hymns No. 2.* New York: Biglow & Main; Cincinnati: John Church & Co., 1876.

————. *Gospel Songs.* Cincinnati: John Church & Co., 1874.

Bradbury, William B. *Oriola: A New and Complete Hymn and Tune Book. For Sabbath Schools.* 1859; 30th ed. enl. Cincinnati: Wilstach, Baldwin & Co., 1871.

————. *Bradbury's Golden Chain of Sabbath School Melodies.* New York: Ivison, Phinney & Company, 1861.

Brooks, James H. *Gospel Hymns.* St. Louis: Published by the Old School Presbyterian, 1871.

Funk Joseph. *Die Allgemein Nutzliche Choral-Music.* Harrisonburg, Virginia: Laurentz Wartmann, 1816.

————. *Genuine Church Music.* Winchester, Virginia: J. W. Hollis, Printer, 1832.

————, and Sons. *The Harmonica Sacra, A Compilation of Genuine Church Music.* 1851; 13th ed. Singer's Glen, Virginia: Joseph Funk's Sons, 1869.

Glenn, R.A., and Aldine S. Kieffer. *New Melodies of Praise.* Singer's Glen, Virginia: Ruebush, Kieffer & Co., 1877.

Gospel Melodies. Petersburg, Virginia: Printed and Published by Stith E. Burton, Intelligencer Press, 1821.

Hauser, William. *The Hesperian Harp: A Collection of Psalm and Hymn Tunes, Odes and Anthems.* Philadelphia: T.K. Collins, Jr., 1853.

————, and Benjamin Turner. *The Olive Leaf: A Collection of Beautiful Tunes, New and Old.* Wadley, Georgia: Wm. Hauser, M.D., and Benjamin Turner, 1878.

Hopkinson, Francis. *A Collection of Psalm Tunes.* Philadephia: n.n., 1753.

Kent, John. *Gospel Hymns.* 1803?; Boston: Reprinted and published by Lincoln & Edmands, 1811.

Law, Andrew. *The Art of Singing.* 4th ed., 1803; Cambridge, Massachusetts: W. Hilliard, 1805.

245

Little, William, and William Smith. *The Easy Instructor.* 1798; Philadelphia: n.n., 1801.

Lowery, Robert, and W. Howard Doane. *Pure Gold for the Sunday School.* New York: Biglow & Main, (Successors to William B. Bradbury), 1871.

McCurry, John Gordon. *The Social Harp.* 1855; facsimile ed. Athens: University of Georgia Press, 1973.

Mather, Richard, Thomas Welde, and John Eliot. *The Whole Booke of Psalms Faithfully Translated into English Metre.* Cambridge, Massachusetts: The Press of Stephen Day[e], 1640.

Mote, Edward. *Hymns of Praise, A New Selection of Gospel Hymns.* London: n.n., 1836.

Phillips, Philip. *The Gospel Singer, for Sabbath Schools.* Philadelphia: Lee and Walker, 1874.

―――. *Hallowed Songs.* 1865; rev. ed. Cincinnati: Hitchcock & Walden, 1871. Also, New York: Harper Brothers, 1871.

―――. *The Singing Pilgrim.* New York: Philip Phillips & Co., 1866.

Salwey, Thomas. *Gospel Hymns.* London: J. Hatchard and Son, 1847.

Sankey, Ira David, James McGrananhan, and George C. Stebbins. *Gospel Hymns No. 3.* New York: Biglow & Main; Cincinnati: John Church & Co., 1878.

―――, et al. *Gospel Hymns Combined.* New York: Biglow & Main; Cincinnati: John Church & Co., 1879.

―――, et al. *Gospel Hymns No. 4.* New York: Biglow & Main, Cincinnati: John Church & Co., 1881.

―――, et al. *Gospel Hymns Consolidated.* New York: Biglow & Main; Cincinnati: John Church & Co., 1883.

―――, et al. *Gospel Hymns No. 5 With Standard Selections.* New York: Biglow & Main; Cincinnati: John Church & Co., 1887.

―――, et al. *Gospel Hymns No. 6.* New York: Biglow & Main; Cincinnati: John Church & Co., 1891.

―――, et al. *Gospel Hymns 5 and 6 Combined.* New York: Biglow & Main; Cincinnati: John Church & Co., 1892.

―――, et al. *Gospel Hymns Nos. 1 to 6.* New York: Biglow & Main; Cincinnati: John Church & Co., 1894.

―――, James McGranahan, George C. Stebbins, Philip P. Bliss. *Gospel Hymns Nos. 1 to 6 Complete.* 1894; 1895 "Excelsior Edition" rpt. New York: Da Capo Press, 1972.

―――. *Sacred Songs and Solos.* London: Morgan And Scott, n.d.

Showalter, Anthony Johnson. *Class, Choir and Congregation.* Dalton, Georgia: A.J. Showalter & Co., 1888.

————, and Aldine S. Kieffer. *The Singing School Tribute*. Dayton, Virginia: Ruebush, Kieffer & Co., 1880.

————, and J.H. Tenney. *Work and Worship*. Dalton, Georgia: The A.J. Showalter Co., 1886.

Showalter, Noah D., ed. *New Harmonia Sacra*. 20th ed. Dayton, Virginia: Ruebush-Kieffer Company, 1942.

Stamps, Virgil Oliver. *Harbor Bells*. Jacksonville, Texas: The V. O. Stamps Music Co., 1925.

Tufts, John. *An Introduction to the Singing of Psalm-Tunes*. 1721?; 5th ed. 1726; rpt. Philadelphia: For Musical Americana by Albert Saifer, Publisher, 1954.

Walker, William. *The Christian Harmony*. 1866; rev. ed., 1873; Philadelphia: E.W. Miller, 1901.

————. *Southern Harmony, and Musical Companion*. 1835; 1854 new ed. rpt. Los Angeles: Pro Musicameriana, 1966.

Waters, Horace. *The Sabbath-School Bell*. New York: Published by Horace Waters, 1859.

Watts, Isaac. *Hymns and Spiritual Songs. In Three Books*. 1707; London: Printed by J.H. for M. Lawrence at the Angel in the Poultry, 1716.

White, Benjamin Franklin. *Original Sacred Harp; Denson Revision*. 1844; Kingsport, Tennessee: Kingsport Press for the Sacred Harp Publishing Company, 1971.

————, and E.J. King. *The Sacred Harp*. 1844; 3d ed., 1859; rpt. Nashville: Broadman Press, 1968.

C. Articles and Periodicals

Adams, James Truslow, ed. *Dictionary of American History*. 2nd ed. rev. New York: Charles Scribner's Sons, 1946.

Alabama State Gospel Singing Convention [Program]. Montgomery, Alabama: n.n., 1976.

Apel, Willi, ed. *Harvard Dictionary of Music*. 2nd ed. Cambridge, Massachusetts: Harvard University Press, 1969.

Billboard, LXXVII (October 23, 1965 sup.), 66.

Billboard, LXXVII (October 30, 1965), 18.

"Biographical Sketch," *Precious Memories of Virgil O. Stamps*. Dallas: Stamps-Baxter Music and Printing Co., 1941.

Blom, Eric, ed. *Grove's Dictionary of Music and Musicians*. 5th ed. New York: St. Martins Press, Inc., 1966.

"Bonifay Gears For Largest Crowd Ever," *The Singing News,* VIII (June 1976), 1A.

"Bonifay Sing Date July 2," *The Singing News,* IX (February 1, 1977), 1A.

Bontemps, Anna. "Gospel—Rock, Church, Rock," *The Negro in Music and Art.* 1967; 2nd ed. New York: Publishers Company, Inc., 1968, pp. 77–81.

"Brief History of a Wonderful Man [J.R. Baxter] Who Has Gone to a Better World," *Gospel Music News,* XXVI (February 1960), 3–4.

British Books in Print, 1976. London: Whitaker & Sons Ltd., 1976.

Britton, Allen P. "The Singing School Movement in the United States," *Report of the Eighth Congress of the International Musicological Society.* New York: Barenreiter Kassel, 1961.

"Butler Elected to Directorship of Music Assn.," *Billboard,* LXXXVIII (November 13, 1976), 61.

Cain, Jan. "First All Night Singing Was Held 38 Years Ago," *The Singing News,* VIII (June 1976), 2A, 19A.

―――. "Gospel Music Hall of Fame Groundbreaking," *The Singing News,* VIII (November 1, 1976), 17A, 9A.

―――. "Sherman Andrus Becomes Shalom Vice Pres.," *The Singing News,* VIII (November 1, 1976), 1B, 15B.

"Camps," *The Herald,* LXXXVII (July 1975), 22–23.

Candilora, Sal. "On Performing Rights Organizations—Why Three," *Record World,* (March 4, 1972 and March 11, 1972). Reprinted as a four-page public relations brochure of SESAC, Incorporated.

Chase, Gilbert. "The Significance of the South in America's Musical History," William Carey College *Faculty Bulletin,* I (May 1970), 1–5.

Compton's Encyclopedia. 1922; Chicago: F.E. Compton Co., Division of Encyclopaedia Britannica, Inc., William Benton, Publisher, 1971.

Concert Life [Mechanicsburg, Pennsylvania], IV (November/December 1976), 5, 13.

Davidson, James Robert. *A Dictionary of Protestant Church Music.* Metuchen, New Jersey: Scarecrow Press, 1975.

Decisions of the United States Courts Involving Copyright, 1957–1958. Copyright Office *Bulletin* No. 31. Washington, D. C.: Library of Congress, 1959.

Dorsey, Thomas A. "Precious Lord, Take My Hand," *Moody Monthly,* LXXVI (April 1976), 44–46.

Dorson, Richard M. "Is There a Folk in the City?" *Journal of American Folklore,* LXXXII (1970), 187.

248

Downey, James C. "Revivalism, the Gospel Songs, and Social Reform," *Ethnomusicology,* IX (May 1964), 115–125.

Encyclopaedia Britannica. Chicago: Encyclopaedia Britannica, Inc., William Benton, Publisher, 1971.

Foote, Henry Wilder. "An Account of the Bay Psalm Book," *The Papers of the Hymn Society,* VII. New York: The Hymn Society of America, 1940.

Gehman, Henry Snyder, ed. *The New Westminster Dictionary of the Bible.* Philadelphia: The Westminster Press, 1970.

Gentry, Linnell, ed. *A History and Encyclopedia of Country, Western, and Gospel Music.* Nashville: McQuiddy Press, 1961. Also, 2nd ed., completely revised. Nashville: Clairmont Corp., 1969.

Goldberg, Daniel. "1969—Gospel Makes Great Industry Strides," *Billboard,* LXXXI (August 16, 1969), S-16.

"GMA Gains in Stature," *Billboard,* LXXIX (October 14, 1967 sup.), 7.

"Gospel as Seen Through the Video Tube," *Billboard,* LXXVIII (October 22, 1966 sup.), 58.

"Gospel Music and Friends," *Music Cataloging Bulletin* [Music Library Association], V (March 1974), 4.

"Gospel Music Association Organization Set June 3," *Billboard,* LXXVI (May 2, 1964), 1.

Gospel Music 1977 Directory & Yearbook. Nashville: Gospel Music Association, 1976.

"Gospel Quartets Take to the Road," *Billboard,* LXXVII (October 23, 1965 sup.), 12–13.

Graham, John R. "Early Twentieth Century Singing Schools in Kentucky Appalachia," *Journal of Research in Music Education,* XIX (Spring 1971), 77–84.

Hustad, Donald P. "Moody Bible Institute's Contribution to Gospel Music," *Founder's Week Messages.* Chicago: Moody Bible Institute, 1968, pp. 281–294.

———. "Music and the Church's Outreach," *Review and Expositor,* LXIX (Spring 1972), 177–185.

"In Memoriam J.R. 'Pap' Baxter, Jr.," *Gospel Music News,* XXVI (February 1960).

Jackson, George Pullen. "Buckwheat Notes," *The Muscial Quarterly,* XIX (October 1933), 393–400.

Jackson, Karen Luke. "The Royal Singing Convention, 1893–1931: Shape Note Singing Tradition in Irwin County, Georgia," *The Georgia Historical Quarterly* (Winter 1972), 495–509.

John, Robert W. "The American Singing School Movement, 1720–1780,"

Journal of the American Musicological Society, VII (Summer 1954), 165–166.

Keith, Edmond D. "Baptist Church Music in Georgia," *Viewpoints Georgia Baptist History,* I (1967), 9–22.

"Kieffer Memorial Number," *Musical Million,* XXXIX (August 1908).

Kyme, George H. "An Experiment in Teaching Children to Read Music With Shape Notes," *Journal of Research in Music Education,* VIII (Spring 1960), 3–8.

Lang, Paul Henry, ed. *One Hundred Years of Music in America.* New York: G. Schirmer, 1961.

Light, Don. "Jarrell McCracken Spreads the Word," *Billboard,* LXXVII (October 23, 1965 sup.), 38–40.

Lowens, Irving, and Allen P. Britton. "*The Easy Instructor* (1798–1831): A History and Bibliography of the first Shape Note Tune Book," *Journal of Research in Music Education,* I (Spring 1953), 30–55.

McDonald, William J., ed. *New Catholic Encyclopedia.* New York: McGraw-Hill Book Co., 1967.

McKissick, Marvin. "The Function of Music in American Revivals since 1875," *The Hymn,* IX (October 1958), 107–117.

Morton, O.F. "The Ruebush-Kieffer Company. A Record of Seventy Years in the Publishing of Music," *Musical Million,* XLII (August 1911), 83–87.

"Mrs. Boyd Is Good News for GMA," *Billboard,* LXXXI (October 11, 1969), 44, 46.

The Musical Advocate and Singer's Friend, I (July 1859).

"Music Is Outgrowth of the Church," *Billboard,* LXXVIII (October 22, 1966 sup.), 34.

Myers, Weldon T. "Aldine S. Kieffer, the Valley Poet, and His Work," *Musical Million,* XXXIX (August 1908), 229–236.

1976 National Gospel Singing Convention [Program]. Roswell, New Mexico: n.n., 1976. Also, *1969 [Program].* Cleveland, Tennessee: n.n., 1969.

New English Bible, with the Apocrypha. Cambridge: Oxford University Press, 1970.

Novell, Charles. "Gospel Roots; Tapping America's Heritage," *Billboard,* LXXXVII (July 4, 1976), MR-78.

Noyes, Morgan P. "Louis F. Benson, Hymnologist," *The Papers of the Hymn Society,* XIX. New York: The Hymn Society of America, 1955.

Pierce, Edwin H. " 'Gospel Hymns' and Their Tunes," *The Musical Quarterly,* XXVI (July 1940), 355–364.

Reynolds, William Jensen. *Companion to Baptist Hymnal.* Nashville: Broadman Press, 1976.

————. *Hymns of Our Faith.* Nashville: Broadman Press, 1964.

"San Diego Station Goes Gospel," *Billboard,* LXXXVII (January 18, 1975), 57.

Savelle, Max. *Seeds of Library; The Genesis of the American Mind.* 1948; Seattle: University of Washington Press, 1965.

Scholes, Percy A. *The Oxford Companion To Music.* 10th ed. rev. London: Oxford University Press, 1970.

Seeger, Charles. "Contrapuntal Style in the Three-voiced Shaped-note Hymns," *The Musical Quarterly,* XXVI (October 1940), 483–493

The Singing News [Pensacola, Florida], VIII (November 1, 1976), 1A.

Stafford, Christopher C. "A.J. Showalter," *Vaughan's Family Visitor,* LXXI (August 1971), 11.

————. "B.C. Unseld (1843–1923)," *Vaughan's Family Visitor,* LXX (January 1971), 6, 10.

————. "Composers of the Past: Frank H. Stamps (1896–1965)," *Vaughan's Family Visitor,* LXXIII (April 1974), 6.

————. "Composers of the Past: James D. Vaughan (1864–1941)," *Vaughan's Family Visitor,* LXXI (February 1972), 5, 14.

Stamps, Mrs. Frank. "In Loving Memory Frank H. Stamps (1896–1965)," *Gospel Singing Journal* [Branson, Missouri], II (Winter 1972), n.p.

"Talent Agency for Gospel Artists," *Billboard,* LXXVIII (October 22, 1966 sup.), 26.

Tallmadge, William H. "The Responsorial and Antiphonal Practice in Gospel Song," *Ethmomusicology,* XII (May 1967), 219–238.

The Thomaston Herald [Georgia], July 6, 1872; July 10, 1875; July 7, 1877.

Thompson, Oscar, ed. *The International Cyclopedia of Music and Musicians,* 9th ed. New York: Dodd, Mead & Co., 1964.

Vaughan, Stella Bentor. "History of the James D. Vaughan Publishing Company," *Vaughan's Family Visitor,* LX? (1960?), 4; and subsequent installments.

————. "History of the James D. Vaughan, Music Publisher," (1964); rpt. *Vaughan's Family Visitor,* LXXV (August, 1975), n.p.; and subsequent installments.

————. Rupert Cravens, and Oliver S. Jennings. "A Brief History of the National Singing Convention 1936–1968," *Souvenir Book* of the 32nd Annual Session of the National Singing Convention. Plainview, Texas: n.n., 1968.

Webster's New Twentieth Century Dictionary of the English Language.

251

Unabridged 2nd ed. Printed in the United States of America: Collins World, 1975.

Whisenhunt, Elton. "Billboard Goes to an All Night Sing," *Billboard,* LXXVII (October 23, 1965 sup.), 20.

————. "Chuck Wagon Gang," *Billboard,* LXXIX (October 14, 1967 sup.), 22.

Williams, Bill. "Distribution Is Major Problem for Gospel-Specializing Labels," *Billboard,* LXXXVII (January 18, 1975), 61.

————. "1st Integrated Gospel Act," *Billboard,* LXXXIV (February 26, 1972), 3 ff.

————. "Racial Harmony GMA Theme," *Billboard,* LXXXI (October 11, 1969), 1, 43.

"Word, Inc. Celebrates 25 Years," *The Singing News,* VIII (December 1, 1976), 1B-2B.

World Book Encyclopedia. Chicago: Field Enterprises Educational Corporation, 1969.

D. Unpublished Materials

Abernathy, Lee Roy. Member, Gospel Music Hall of Fame, Living Category. Personal correspondence with the writer, February 11, 1977.

Beary, Shirley. "The Stamps-Baxter Music and Printing Company: A Continuing American Tradition, 1926–1976." Unpublished Doctoral dissertation-in-progress, Southwestern Baptist Theological Seminary.

————. Southwestern Union College, Keene, Texas. Personal correspondence with the writer, December 23, 1976 and subsequent.

Boyd, Norma L. Executive Secretary, Gospel Music Association, Nashville, Tennessee. Personal correspondence with the writer, August 30, 1976 and subsequent.

[————.] "The Gospel Music Association." Nashville: The Gospel Music Association, [1976]. (Mimeographed.)

Brock, Dwight. Former President of Stamps-Baxter Music and Printing Company, Dallas, Texas. Personal correspondence with the writer, January 4, 1977.

Brumley, Bob. Co-owner, Albert E. Brumley and Sons, Music Publishers, Powell, Missouri, Personal correspondence with the writer, January 19, 1977 and subsequent.

Carroll, Edward Perry. "Daniel Brink Towner: Educator, Church Musician, Composer, and Church Music Editor." Unpublished Doctoral dissertation-in-progress, New Orleans Baptist Theological Seminary.

Cheek, Curtis Leo. "The Singing School and Shaped-note Tradition: Residuals in Twentieth-century American Hymnody." Unpublished Doctoral dissertation, University of Southern California, 1968.

Clements, William Manning. "The American Folk Church: A Characterization of American Folk Religion based on Field Research among White Protestants in a Community in the South Central United States." Unpublished Doctoral dissertaton, Indiana University, 1974.

Daniel, Harlan. "From Shape Notes to Bank Notes: Milestones in the Evolution of White Gospel Music." Unpublished chronology presented at the Sixth Annual Meeting of the Popular Culture Association, Chicago, April 24, 1976. (Mimeographed.)

Doughty, Gavin Lloyd. "The History and Development of Music in the United Presbyterian Church in the United States of America." Unpublished Doctoral dissertation, University of Iowa, 1966.

Downey, James Cecil. "The Music of American Revivalism." Unpublished Doctoral dissertation, Tulane University, 1968.

Ellerbe, Marion Fred. "The Music Missionary of the Southern Baptist Convention: His Preparation and His Work." Unpublished Doctoral dissertation, The Catholic University of America, 1970.

Ellington, Charles Linwood. "The Sacred Harp Tradition of the South: Its Origin and Evolution." Unpublished Doctoral dissertation, Florida State University, 1970.

Eskew, Harry Lee. "Shape-note Hymnody in the Shenandoah Valley 1816–1860." Unpublished Doctoral dissertation, Tulane University, 1966.

———. New Orleans Baptist Theological Seminary. Personal correspondence with the writer, December 6, 1976 and subsequent.

Fleming, Jo Lee. "James D. Vaughan, Music Publisher, Lawrenceburg, Tennessee. 1912–1964." Unpublished Doctoral dissertation, Union Theological Seminary, 1972.

Georgia State Singing Convention By-Laws, dated October 12, 1959.

Gospel Music Association Constitution, dated November 21, 1976. (Mimeographed.)

Gospel Music Association Minutes. October 10, 1964 and October 16, 1965.

Hall, Paul M. "The *Musical Million:* A Study and Analysis of the Periodical Promoting Music Reading Through Shape-notes in North

America from 1870 to 1914." Unpublished Doctoral dissertation, Catholic University of America, 1970.

Jackson, Irene Viola. "Afro-American Gospel Music and its Social Setting with Special Attention to Roberta Martin." Unpublished Doctoral dissertation, Wesleyan University, 1974.

———— -Brown. Yale University. Personal correspondence with the writer, January 15, 1975 and subsequent.

Johnson, Talmadge. President, National Gospel Singing Convention. Personal correspondence with the writer, December 22, 1976.

Kaufman, Lee Jack. "A Historical Study of Seven Character Shaped Note Music Notation." Unpublished Doctoral dissertation, University of Virginia, 1970.

Loessel, Earl Oliver. "The Use of Character Notes and Other Unorthodox Notations in Teaching the Reading of Music in Northern United States During the Nineteenth Century." Unpublished Doctoral dissertation, Michigan, 1959.

McCall, Bevoda C. "Georgia Town and Cracker Culture: A Sociological Study." Unpublished Doctoral dissertation, University of Chicago, 1954.

McCommon, Paul Cinton. "The Influence of Charles Wesley's Hymns on Baptist Theology." Unpublished Doctoral dissertation, Southern Baptist Theological Seminary, 1948.

McCulloh, Judith. University of Illinois Press. Personal correspondence with the writer, December 20, 1976 and subsequent.

Neeb, Martin J., Jr. "An Historical Study of American Non-commercial AM Broadcast Stations Owned and Operated by Religious Groups, 1920–1966." Unpublished Doctoral dissertation, Northwestern University, 1967.

Neil, Bob J. "Philip P. Bliss (1838–1876): Gospel Hymn Composer and Compiler." Unpublished Doctoral dissertation-in-progress, New Orleans Baptist Theological Seminary.

Observations and Notes taken by the writer during 1975 and 1976 Georgia singing conventions.

Peterson, Robert Douglas. "The Folk Idiom in the Music of Contemporary Protestant Worship in America." Unpublished Doctoral dissertation, Columbia University, 1972.

Reed, Joel F. "Anthony J. Showalter (1858–1924): Southern Educator, Publisher, Composer." Unpublished Doctoral dissertation, New Orleans Baptist Theological Seminary, 1975.

Ricks, George Robinson. "Some Aspects of the Religious Music of the United States Negro: An Ethnomusicological Study with Special

Emphasis on the Gospel Tradition." Unpublished Doctoral dissertation, Northwestern University, 1960.

SESAC, Incorporated, Nashville, Tennessee. Letter to Guiness Superlatives, London, England, dated September 29, 1976.

Sims, John N. "The Hymnody of the Camp Meeting Tradition." Unpublished Doctoral dissertation, Union Theological Seminary, 1960.

Stansbury, George William. "The Music of the Billy Graham Crusades, 1947–1970: An Analysis and Evaluation." Unpublished Doctoral dissertation, Southern Baptist Theological Seminary, 1971.

Tennessee Charter of Incorporation. [Gospel Music Association, Incorporated.] Book 145, pp. 224–227, May 19, 1964.

"TV All-Star Revue." [WAGA-TV, Atlanta, Georgia.] Script of television program, March 8, 1949. (Mimeographed.)

E. Interviews

Alford, Delton L. Lee College. Cleveland, Tennessee, November 15, 1976.

Bartlett, Eugene M., Jr., Director of Church Music, Oklahoma Baptist General Convention of the Southern Baptist Convention. Nashville, Tennessee, December 7, 1976.

Black, Jim. Director of Gospel Music, SESAC, Incorporated. Nashville, Tennessee, December 9, 1976.

Blackwood, James. Member, Gospel Music Hall of Fame, Living Category. Nashville, Tennessee, October 5, 1976.

Boyd, Norma L. Executive Secretary, Gospel Music Association. Nashville, Tennessee, October 5, 1976 and subsequent communications.

Brown, Hyman. Shaped note singing school teacher and composer. Commerce, Georgia, June 27, 1975.

Butler, Don. Executive Director, Gospel Music Association. Nashville, Tennessee, December 9, 1976 and subsequent communications.

Easterling, Marion. Gospel music radio announcer. Nashville, Tennessee, October 8, 1976.

Hall, Connor B. Editor, Tennessee Music and Printing Company and James D. Vaughan, Music Publisher, publishing companies. Nashville, Tennessee, October 6, 1976; and Cleveland, Tennessee, November 15, 1976, and subsequent communications.

Hamrick, Raymond. Sacred Harp aficionado and collector of rare tunebooks. Macon, Georgia, September 8, 1976.

Hemphill, Joel. Professional gospel singer and composer. Telephone interview, December 10, 1976.

Hildreth, Lou. Gospel music entrepreneur and television personality. Nashville, Tennessee, December 6, 1976.

Housewright, Wiley. Florida State University. Telephone interview, September 6, 1976.

Hustad, Don Paul. Southern Baptist Theological Seminary. Louisville, Kentucky, November 12, 1976.

Huxford, John. Valdosta State College. Valdosta, Georgia, August 10, 1976 and September 6, 1976.

Jennings, Oliver S. Former President, Tennessee State Gospel Singing Convention. Telephone interview, December 16, 1976.

John, Robert W. University of Georgia. Athens, Georgia, October 12, 1976.

Lister, Mosie. Member, Gospel Music Hall of Fame, Living Category. Nashville, Tennessee, October 6, 1976.

Mahan, Katherine. Columbus College. Columbus, Georgia, July 21, 1976.

Myers, W.F., "Jim." Vice-President, SESAC, Incorporated. New York, New York, January 21, 1977 and subsequent communications.

Norcross, Marvin. Vice-President, Word, Incorporated. Telephone interview, January 18, 1977.

Nowlin, W.B. Gospel music concert promoter. Atlanta, Georgia, September 18, 1976.

Odlum, Norman. Vice-President, SESAC, Incorporated. Nashville, Tennessee, October 7, 1976 and New York, New York, November 4, 1976, and subsequent communications.

Orell, Lloyd. Gospel music concert promoter. Nashville, Tennessee, October 7, 1976.

Reynolds, William J. Chairman, Church Music Department of the Baptist Sunday School Board of the Southern Baptist Convention. Nashville, Tennessee, October 5, 1976 and subsequent communications.

Speer, Brock. Member, Gospel Music Hall of Fame, Living Category. Nashville, Tennessee, October 8, 1976 and subsequent communications.

Stafford, Christopher C. Shaped note singing school teacher and gospel music composer. Roanoke, Alabama, July 20, 1976.

Sumner, J.D. Professional gospel music singer and composer. Nashville, Tennessee, October 8, 1976.

Timmons, Harold. "Chuck Wagon Gang" enthusiast and discographer. Telephone interview, December 13, 1976.

Tremaine, John. Asbury Theological Seminary. Wilmore, Kentucky, November 11, 1976.

Whitfield, J.G. Gospel music concert promoter and publisher of *The Singing News*. Pensacola, Florida, September 7, 1976.

Wood, Gerry. Southern Editor, *Billboard*. Nashville, Tennessee, December 10, 1976.

Yarbrough, Dorsey. National School of Music. Roanoke, Alabama, July 20, 1976.

Appendix A

The Twenty-three Groups and
Their Songs

Appendix A contains the transcriptions of the interviews of the randomly selected amateur family gospel music singing groups of the field research. The methodology used in conducting this field research was detailed in Chapter 6. A review of the field research was presented in Chapter 7.

Twenty-five south Georgia counties were chosen at random for investigation. In two of these counties the researcher was unable to find any groups that met the criteria for inclusion in the study. Although data were available for only twenty-three counties, the original number of twenty-five counties was retained for clarity of presentation. The two counties (6) (20) in which no groups were identified are listed as "No Data Available."

The reproduction of the song chosen by each group as its most representative performance is not included with the interview data. The songs are presented as a collection following the cumulative interview information. Each song is identified by the number and the corresponding county name of the group by whom it was selected.

Interviews

(1) Bibb County (August 5, 1975)

"The Trebles"

Paul Jones (husband)—piano
Bonnie Jones (wife)—lead/high tenor
Kerry Jones (son, age 14)—electric bass
Delores "D" Mitchell—alto/low tenor
Theresa Walker—alto
Mike Holmes—drums

The Joneses and all other members of the group reside in Macon, the county seat. The Joneses and "D" Mitchell attend West Highland Baptist Church; Theresa Walker attends the Four-Square-Gospel Church; and Mike Holmes is Minister of Music at Eastside Baptist Church.

The group was originally begun in 1962 and performed until 1965. After a hiatus, the group was reorganized in 1972. The basic group has not changed. Kerry and Mike were simply added.

Only Bonnie has a prior history of performing in a family group. She, her sister, and another girl performed as a trio for approximately three years.

The present group uses sheet music; learns from hearing other groups at sings; and copies recordings, converting the songs into their own arrangements. They do not use hymnbooks or convention books. All songs performed are their personalized arrangements.

The favorite song of the group is "Without Him," chosen because of its message. Favorite recordings include those by the Speer Family; Bill Gaither Trio; Hinson Family; Kingsmen; LeFevres; and the Statesmen Quartet. Collectively the members of the group own approximately sixty to seventy records.

Their favorite radio station is WCRY in Macon, stated to have classical programming. There is no gospel radio station in Macon. Kerry listens to rock music but doesn't perform with any rock groups.

Their favorite television program, broadcast over WSB-TV (Atlanta), is "Gospel Singing Jubilee." They also watch the WTVM (Columbus) "Gospel Hour."

Highlights of past performances include a concert at Sinclair Baptist, approximately a year ago, where a girl with tears in her eyes told them she hadn't wanted to come to the program but her mother had insisted. The girl said she had been touched by their music, and intended to meet with her pastor for counseling. Also, approximately six to eight months ago in Shurlington, a friend was undergoing serious surgery. When the group made an altar call for concerted prayer, the entire congregation came forward.

Other significant past performances included a December, 1974 gospel sing at the Macon Opera House. Other groups present were the Hinson Family and the Sunny South Quartet. The Trebles felt that they had been as well received as the professional groups.

In June, 1973 the group entered the Amateur Talent Contest at the Bonifay, Florida all-night sing. According to one member of the group, that was "one of those things you'll never do again." Among other inconveniences, the public address system was faulty and the temperature was 110 degrees.

The group was interviewed the evening of their television debut over WMAZ-TV, Macon. Future plans for the group include the improving of their television presentation. At the time of the interview the group had no plans to become professional.

All offerings received by the group go into a special bank account. The group had borrowed money in order to make a recording and to purchase a van. They would like to buy a bus. They also want to "grow and to reach more people." Members of the groups pay for food, gasoline, and clothing from out-of-pocket.

As previously stated, the interview was conducted on the evening of the group's television debut. Songs performed on this debut, and recorded by the researcher, were "I Came To Praise the Lord," "Don't Ever Let Go," "O What a Love," "I'm Looking for Jesus," "Hallelujah Square," "One Day at a Time," "Jesus, I Believe What You Said," "I'll Go," and "God Is God" [sic]. The song selected as their most representative performance was "O What a Love."

Additional observations by Paul Jones included an opinion that gospel music has changed considerably within the last twenty years. There is more variety now. Some of it employs the sounds of classical music, or rock music. Previously, gospel music only sounded like singing convention music. The piano style has changed also. More emphasis is placed upon improvisation. With the addition of electric bass and drums, the left hand doesn't have to carry the rhythm, as Paul had been taught.

Cutting a recording cost the group $2,100 for 1000 records and 250 eight-track tapes. Their recording was produced by Mission Records in Nashville, Tennessee. The fee included $80 per studio musician for a six-hour recording session. A color photograph of the group for the album cover added $75 to the price. Delivery took approximately eight weeks from the time the master tape was recorded until the records were received.

(2) Brantley County (September 11, 1976)

Eugene Velie Family

Gary Velie (husband)—solo lead on verse/harmony on chorus
Edna Velie (wife)—piano/lead on chorus
Bradley Velie (brother, age 18)—bass
Cindy Velie (sister, age 17)—alto

Members of the group are able to perform on instruments and sing voice parts other than those listed. Gary can play trombone and can sing any harmony part. Edna can play accordion. Bradley can play piano, trumpet, and trombone, and can sing any harmony part. Cindy can play piano, saxophone, and clarinet, and can sing any voice part. In addition, their father, Eugene Velie, often sings with the group. He sings lead and plays guitar, piano, or organ. Voicing and instrumentation listed above is that used in the song selected by the group as its most representative performance.

Eugene Velie, Bradley and Cindy reside in the community of Atkinson, approximately ten miles from Nahunta, the county seat. Gary and Edna Velie reside in Jacksonville, Florida, approximately seventy-five miles from Atkinson. All attend church in Jacksonville, Florida. The church they attend is the non-denominational Jacksonville Assembly. This Assembly is loosely affiliated with other non-denominational churches that are often designated as Gospel Assembly.

Eugene Velie is a plumber, pipefitter, and salesman of Shakely home care products. Gary is also a plumber and

Left to right: Adeline Velie holding Aaron, Eugene, Cindy, Bradley, Gary, and Edna. (Edna was pianist for song selected as most representative.)

Eugene outside

Bradley, Edna, and Gary with Cindy playing piano

Cindy

pipefitter. The female members of the group are not employed. Bradley is a sophomore at Valdosta State College, where he is majoring in accounting.

The group was begun fifteen years ago, when Cindy was two years old. The group at that time was comprised of a daughter, La Ree; and sons, Greg, Gary, and Jeff. The older children have since moved away.

Eugene was the oldest of twelve children, all of whom were musical. He had sung with his parents as a performing group. Eugene first sang with his mother over the radio.[1] Eugene's grandfather on his father's side was a fiddler. This grandfather had four sons, all of whom had children who became accomplished musicians. Eugene has lived in Wisconsin most of his life, only recently settling in Georgia.

Favorite songs of the group are those by William Gaither, such as "Something Beautiful" and "Because He Lives." Many additional favorite songs are strictly from their church. These are "dispensational songs" that deal with the doctrine and Plan of Salvation as their church views it. Other favorite songs are "Remind Me, Dear Lord" by Dottie Rambo, and "A Glimpse of Jesus" by Cornelia Mears.

Favorite recordings include those by the Gaithers, the Goodmans, the "old" Blackwood Brothers, and the "old" Florida Boys. The adjective "old" apparently signifies a musical style change. Their favorite radio station is WKTZ in Jacksonville, Florida which is said to program classical and semi-classical music. Mrs. Velie, a non-singer but enthusiastic supporter of the group, prefers listening to WSOJ, full-time gospel radio, in Jesup, Georgia.

The group does not watch television and there is no television set in the home. Their church suggests but does not mandate the non-watching of television.

The group related few experiences of past performances. Gary mentioned an embarrassing moment six or seven years ago when he came in ahead of the others during an *a cappella* selection. Mrs. Velie mentioned that the group's best performance was when all six children sang "The King Is Coming" for a church service. They had included instruments with their singing.

Members of the group agreed that the song had not sounded as well in subsequent performances.

Eugene stated that his mind had been made up not to become a professional performer of gospel music. He stated that the professionals are too hypocritical and too commercial. Approximately five years ago a talent promoter wanted to promote the children but Eugene refused. The group does not charge for performances.

Future plans are unpredictable, although members of the group foresee a major improvement. Gary is beginning to take music more seriously. There are no plans to make a recording. The group does not feel this would be appropriate or consistent with their Christian testimony.

Songs performed for the researcher were "The Lighthouse," "Sweet, Sweet Spirit," "Learning To Lean," and "I Won't Turn Back." The song selected as their most representative performance was "The Lighthouse."

(3) Bulloch County (October 2, 1976)

"The County Echoes"

Johnny Motes (husband)—acoustic guitar/lead
Geraldine Motes (wife)—alto
Tronda Motes (daughter, age 10)—piano/lead

The Motes reside near the community of Portal which is approximately fifteen miles from Statesboro, the county seat. They attend a Pentecostal Baptist Church, located approximately five miles from Portal. According to the Motes this is the only Pentecostal Baptist church in Georgia.

Johnny is self-employed as a truck driver. He owns his truck, which is presently leased to National Trailer Convoy. He hauls mobile homes. Geraldine works in the Willow Hill school lunchroom.

"The County Echoes" were begun approximately three years ago. The original group consisted of Johnny, Geraldine, and Ty-

Left to right: Geraldine, Tronda, Johnny,
and Johnny's mother, Mrs. Motes

Pentecostal Baptist Church

Geraldine, Tronda, and Johnny

Geraldine and Johnny with Tronda playing piano

ler "Shorty" Finch, Jr. Finch left the group about six months ago and Stronda has been training to take his place.

Johnny and Geraldine have been singing together ever since they were married, twenty-three years ago. Both were in the same class in school. Both Johnny's and Geraldine's mothers were pianists for separate Methodist churches. Geraldine sang with her three sisters in church choir. She was also song leader for the Youth Choir of her church as a teenager. Johnny sang only congregationally with his parents. Neither has kept any records or souvenirs of previous performances.

The group uses sheet music, hymn books, and song books. Sometimes they buy phonograph albums and learn songs from them by ear. Often they learn songs from other groups. They consider this the "best way." Johnny has written about twelve songs. He has written out the words to these songs, but sings the music by ear. He has intended to send away tape recordings of the songs in order for them to be notated, but has never done so. Geraldine has written one song. Neither Johnny nor Geraldine can read music. Both, however, follow the shape of the printed musical line as an aid in learning new songs. Tronda is beginning her second year of piano lessons and her parents are pleased with her progress.

Favorite songs are "One Day at a Time," "Hallelujah Square," "Build My Mansion Next Door to Jesus," "Jesus Is Coming Soon," and "Touring That City."

Favorite recordings are those by the Chuck Wagon Gang, Happy Goodman Family, Sego Brothers and Naomi, Hymnsmen (local Cobbtown group), Blackwood Brothers, and the Hudson Family (local Swainsboro group).

Although Johnny listens to radio occasionally while driving his truck, he states that few good programs are available. Concerning television, the group enjoys watching the Lewis Family program, broadcast from Augusta. They also enjoy "Gospel Singing Jubilee," but it is presently scheduled during church time. The Florida Boys (host of "Gospel Singing Jubilee") were Johnny's favorite group when he was a schoolboy.

Past performances include an Easter Seal benefit sing in Sylvania, and a performance at the sports arena in Statesboro.

They have sung in many of the area churches. Johnny states that the best place to perform is the Bethany old folks home in Statesboro. They enjoy singing in churches. Members of the group feel they can sing "from the heart" more so in churches than in recreational buildings. They sing regularly at their own church. All of their singing is "from the heart." This is one of the reasons they have written many of their own songs.

Future plans are simply to sing when requested. The group does not sing for money. At one time they had contacted a man in Columbia, South Carolina, about the possibility of making a recording. When Finch left the group these plans were abandoned. They hope Tronda will blossom as a pianist.

Their dream is that their older married sons will move nearby so they can sing together as a family group. The Motes could possibly join with other local groups but do not feel that they have much in common with them.

Songs performed for the researcher were "All That I Am," "Come Go with Me" (original), "Pay Day," "You Will Always Find Him There," "God Is My Co-Pilot" (original), and "Where We'll Never Grow Old." The song selected as their most representative performance was "Pay Day." This song had been learned by ear from another amateur group several years previously. "Where We'll Never Grow Old" was chosen as an alternate selection in the event a copy of the music to their first choice could not be found. As the researcher was unable to find music for "Pay Day," the song "Where We'll Never Grow Old" was used as the group's representative selection.

(4) Charlton County (September 2, 1976)

John Hilton (brother)—tenor
Alice Hilton Murray (sister)—soprano
Jesse Turner (brother-in-law)—bass
Euthra Tice (second cousin)—alto
Ginger Carter (third cousin)—piano

Much of the area of Charlton County is occupied by the

272

Left to right: Euthra Tice, Jesse Turner, Ginger Carter, Alice Murray, and John Hilton

Sand Hill Baptist Church

273

Okefenokee Swamp and the Okefenokee National Wildlife Refuge. The members of the group reside in a sparsely populated area approximately sixteen miles from Folkston, the county seat. All members of the group attend Sand Hill Baptist Church, although Ginger is technically a member of Calvary Baptist Church in Folkston.

All members of the group are employed. John is a section foreman for the Seaboard Coastline Railroad. Alice works for the First National Bank in Folkston. Jesse is employed by the Georgia Forestry Commission. Euthra is a clerk for the Seaboard Coastline Railroad. Ginger is employed by the Department of Family and Children's Services in Folkston.

The group has been performing together for approximately six months. There have been no changes since starting. None of the members has a history of performing with a family group before. John and Alice attended singing school when they were approximately age ten or younger. Their father was a well-known song leader and sponsored convention sings until he died in 1965. Their mother continued sponsoring singing conventions for approximately two additional years.

Members of the quartet do not consider themselves to be music readers although all follow the line of the notes as they sing. Ginger took piano lessons for three years, when she was in the third, fourth, and fifth grades in school. She can sing alto but does not sing with the group.

Publications used by the group include sheet music, convention books and convention-style hymnbooks. Favorite songs are "The Prettiest Flowers," "Jesus Opened Up the Way," "He's My Friend," "I've a Precious Friend," "Heaven Will Be Worth It All," "I Believe It," and "He Put a Little Sunshine."

Favorite recordings are those by the Chuck Wagon Gang. A favorite radio program is "Singing Gospel Time" heard on Sunday mornings from 6:00 to 12:00 over WYNR in Brunswick. Members of the group do not regularly watch gospel music programs on television.

A significant past performance was when the group was well received at a Philadelphia, Pennsylvania, Free Will Baptist conference as they sang "Jesus Opened Up The Way."

When asked about future plans, John stated they were going to, "Let our hair grow, put on dark glasses, and head for Nashville." More seriously, the group stated that they would probably have to remain local due to their work schedules. They have considered buying a public address system, but none is needed at Sand Hill. The church has very live acoustics. The group has never been offered money for singing and probably would not accept if such were offered, that is, as John said, ". . . unless we got real good and had to give up our jobs."

Songs performed for the researcher were "I've a Precious Friend," "Jesus Opened Up the Way," "They're Having a Big Revival," "Help Me, Lord, to Stand," "I Just Began to Live," "I Should Have Been Crucified," "How Long Has it Been," "Because He Lives," and "The Lord Is My Shepherd." The song selected as the group's most representative was "Help Me, Lord, To Stand."

(5) Chatham County (September 22, 1976)

"The Wesley Arnold Family"

Wesley Arnold (husband)—manager and sound technician
Martha Arnold (wife)—soprano
Wesley Arnold, Jr. (son, age 20)—amplified acoustic guitar/lead and harmony
Lee Arnold (son, age 18)—bass
Andrea Arnold (daughter, age 17)—alto
Steven Arnold (son, age 15)—bass
Kenney Arnold (son, age 13)—tenor

Lee and Kenney are learning to play electric bass, although electric bass was not used during the group's performance for the researcher. Steve is also evolving into the sound technician for the group.

Chatham is the most populous county of the Field Research area. The Arnold's reside within the city limits of Savannah, the county seat. Members of the group attend the suburban Quacco

Left to right: Lee, Martha, Steven, Wesley, Sr., Wesley, Jr., Andrea, and Kenney

Quacco Road Mission

Lee, Steven, Andrea, and Martha

Kenney and Wesley, Jr.

277

Road Mission, sponsored by Calvary Baptist Temple (Southern Baptist Convention) in Savannah.

Wesley is pastor of the Quacco Road Mission. He also works full-time as a salesman/truck driver for Diamond Batteries, a division of an automobile parts store. He has been with the battery company for three years. Formerly, for eighteen years, he had been a full-time pastor. Martha teaches Bible at the Calvary Baptist Temple Day School and is also secretary to the Minister of Music. Wesley, Jr., works as a stock clerk for the Georgia Regional Hospital in Savannah. Lee works for Deen Heating and Air Conditioning.

The group has been performing together for approximately three years. They began by spontaneously singing in the car on trips. In earlier stages the children sang with other young people. The group has evolved to its present make-up. Steven joined the group later than the other children due to voice change problems. All of the other children have been in the group from the beginning.

Neither Wesley nor Martha sang with their parents. Martha sang solos before marriage. Wesley was a dancer. He taught dancing before his conversion. The group may have retained some early church bulletins indicating their performances, but basically they have no historical records.

The group utilizes sheet music, hymnbooks, and original compositions by Wesley, Jr. The latter songs have not been notated. Members of the group can read music and they always use music except for the original songs. For these, Wesley, Jr., teaches the music part by part. Sometimes the group re-arranges songs to fit their needs.

Favorite songs are "Because I Love You" (original), "Jesus, I Love You" (original), "Victory in Jesus," "Let's Just Praise the Lord," and a medley from the religious musical *Alleluia*. Favorite recordings include the debut album of a group named Second Chapter of Acts. Albums by the Gaither's and by the Speer Family are also favorites. One member of the group stated he liked "Gaither's music and the Speer's performance of it."

Only Andrea mentioned a favorite radio program. She enjoys the Burl Womack gospel program heard over WZAT in Savannah. Favorite television programs include "Gospel Singing Jubilee," Oral Roberts—for the music, and a former program of the Southern Baptist Convention entitled "Spring Street."

The group recalled a humorous incident in a previous performance when Wesley, Jr., had difficulty with his guitar strap. Lee teased Wesley, Jr., in front of the audience—then had difficulty with his own bass guitar strap. The group enjoy singing songs where Martha, Andrea, and Steven take different leads. On one occasion the group thought they could leave Andrea home, but it didn't work. According to Wesley, Sr., leaving one child out changes the "Arnold Sound."

Without further elaboration, Wesley, Jr., stated that in July, 1975 he felt God had used the group in a special way. The music was used as a means to minister. Martha added that their music is not intended as a concert but as a means to minister. She says that music is an effective ministry with youth and adults. Lee stated that initially he enjoyed the concerts but not the practicing. Wesley, Sr., stated that the group has become more disciplined recently. They do not perform so often that it becomes tiresome. They enjoy their concerts. The group agreed that singing has brought the family closer together. All of the children feel they have a part in the ministry.

When asked about future plans, Kenney began to sing the chorus of the currently popular gospel song "One Day at a Time." Wesley, Sr., stated that with two boys of college age it was going to be harder to stay together. Lee wants to obtain more education. Andrea said that she feels the family will always be together. The family is very close. Wesley, Jr., stated that music will always be a part of his life.

Wesley, Sr., said he had left the pastorate to become an evangelist. He was to do the preaching and the children were to do the singing. It didn't work. They are re-grouping now. He still feels that the family as a continuing unit might work, if it is God's will. He would like to use the Quacco Road Mission as a home base for an outreach ministry.

Songs performed for the researcher were "Jesus Came to My Assistance" (original), "Lord, I Want to Be A Christian," "Jesus Loves Me" (original), "Jesus Is The Only Hope" (original), "Noah" (original),"Rollercoaster Christian Blues" (original), "I've Been Redeemed," a medley of choruses, and "Sweet, Sweet Spirit." The song selected as most representative of the group was "Lord, I Want To Be A Christian."

(6) Chattahoochee County

No Data Available

Much of the area of Chattahoochee county, and most of the population are assigned to the large Army Base, Fort Benning. This area and population were excluded from the survey. In the remaining area of the county and in the county seat, Cusseta, the researcher was unable to identify any groups meeting the criteria for inclusion in the study.

(7) Cook County (August 13, 1976)

"The McGee Family"

Robert McGee (husband)—bass
Carolyn McGee (wife)—lead
Morris McGee (son, age 15)—drums
Allen McGee (son, age 11)—electric bass
L.C. McGee (brother)—electric guitar/tenor
Brenda McGee (wife of L.C.)—alto

The McGee children also sing as a group, "The McGee Children." This group includes the daughters of L.C. and Brenda:

Angie McGee (age 12)—lead or harmony
Abby McGee (age 10)—alto
Marianne McGee (age 8)—lead or harmony

Although Allen does not sing with the adults, he sings as

280

Left to right: Allen, Robert, Carolyn, Brenda, and L.C. McGee

Morris McGee

281

well as plays electric bass when with the children. He sings the bass part an octave high.

The McGee families reside within the city limits of Adel, the county seat. They attend the Friendship Church of God in Valdosta, approximately twenty-three miles from Adel.

Robert owns a sheet glass installation company. L.C. works for an automobile repair company as a body and paint specialist.

The group has been performing together for approximately one-and-one-half years. Carolyn had always wanted to sing in a gospel group. She talked Brenda into singing with her, and L.C. began playing the guitar for them. He talked Robert into making the group a quartet.

Brenda and Carolyn had both sung with their sisters when younger. When Carolyn was small she often rode the bus with her aunt to attend gospel sings. She did not sing for a period of approximately ten years. She began singing with Brenda in church approximately two years ago.

Neither Robert nor L.C. had sung with their parents or siblings. L.C. played guitar as a teenager. He was in a Future Farmers of America string band that went to a competition in Kansas City. Later, he often played for square dances—until he was "shot at." According to L.C., "That wound it up." He stopped playing guitar when he got married, fifteen years ago. He did not start again until he began playing for Carolyn and Brenda.

Robert is the only "unsaved," or non-Christian adult of the group. He is becoming more interested and concerned about his spiritual and moral life. In a private conversation with the researcher, Robert told of a recent fire which destroyed much of his business. He had had three premonitions about the fire. Robert attributed the fire to his breaking of a vow he had made to God.

The group uses sheet music and hymnbooks. They often learn songs by ear from tape recordings. They sing and play only by ear.

Favorite songs include "Jesus Is Mine" (new), "Hallelujah Meeting," "Glory Road," "The Best Is Yet to Come," "Sweetest Words Ever Said," and "Satisfied" (old). The (new) and (old) designations apparently were intended to distinguish these songs from other gospel songs having the same title.

Favorite recordings are those by the Inspirations and by Wendy Johnson and the Messengers. The Inspirations are their favorite group.

The group listens only to the gospel music programs of WBIT radio. Their favorite television program is "Gospel Jubilee," viewed on Sunday mornings.

Past performances include those at Ochlochnee Baptist Church, where they enjoyed the spiritual atmosphere. Once, on a trip to a Jennings, Florida Baptist church, the group forgot their microphone cords and had to return thirty miles in order to get them.

For concerts, the group makes up a list of songs in advance, although they sometimes depart from the list. They do not plan their spoken testimonies in advance. L.C. and Carolyn serve as announcers. The children enjoy concertizing. They do not feel as though they are being pushed into performing.

Future plans include wanting to make a recording. The parents want their children to become good performers of gospel music. L.C. stated that he wants to "get closer to the Lord."

Both the children and the adult groups performed for the researcher. The "McGee Children" sang "Hallelujah Meeting," "He'll Call My Name," "Jesus Is a Soul Man," "When I Walk on the Streets of Gold," "John the Revelator," "Me and Jesus," and "Love Will Roll the Clouds Away." The adult group sang "Living in Canaan Land," "Satisfied," "Walking the Sea," "Sweetest Words He Ever Said," "Jesus Is Mine," "I Never Shall Forget the Day," "O What a Happy Day," "Joshua," "We're Not Home Yet, Children," "When God Passes Judgment on That Day," "Old Moses Prayed," "The Best Is Yet to Come," "Ananias," and "Just Say the Word." Both groups performed all songs from memory. The song chosen as the group's most representative selection was "Walking the Sea."

(8) Crawford County (August 8, 1975)

"Fellowettes"

Dorothy Genthner (mother)—piano
Donna Genthner (daughter, age 22)—soprano

Left to right: Loretta Walker, Brenda Peacock, Dorothy Genthner, Robin Genthner, Donna Genthner, and Joanne Hamlin

Robin Genthner (daughter, age 16)—soprano
Joanne Hamlin (non-related)—soprano
Brenda Peacock (Joanne's sister-in-law)—alto
Loretta Walker (non-related)—alto

Two additional members of the group were unable to attend the interview session due to personal reasons:

Linda Wood (Joanne's sister)—soprano
Wanda Dixon (Joanne's cousin)—alto

Members of the group reside in a sparsely populated area of the county. They attend Fellowship Evangelistic Church, located approximately nine miles from Knoxville, the county seat.

The "Fellowettes" were originally begun in 1972. This group included thirteen singers, a pianist, and Mrs. Genthner as director. This organization disbanded in 1974, due to some personal reasons of Mrs. Genthner (having nothing to do with music). The group have reorganized only within the past three months. All of the present members, except Loretta, were in the previous group. In the present organization Mrs. Genthner serves as accompanist and no one directs.

No one in the group has a family history of gospel music singing.

Music for the group is obtained from many sources. These sources include sheet music written by Dottie Rambo, Bill Gaither, and Joel Hemphill. Mrs. Genthner purchases all of the music. She has many song collections, but does not use convention songbooks.

Favorite songs are "Sheltered In His Arms," "He Touched Me," "He," "Didn't He Shine," and "Faith Will Move The Mountains." Favorite recordings include gospel songs as performed by Elvis Presley, the Statler Brothers, the Statesmen Quartet, and Marilyn Sellers.

Favorite radio stations are WDEN, Macon, stated to have country and western programing; and WMAZ, Macon. Members of the group enjoy the music of the television presentation of Oral Roberts and Billy Graham.

The debut of the group was two weeks ago, July 29, 1975, at the Roberta Nursing Home. They also performed last Sunday, August 3, 1975, at their church.

Future plans are "to get better." They were scheduled to sing for at least two evenings for their church's revival, during the week of August 10, 1975. They had also been invited to perform at a Fifth Sunday Sing at New Elam Church on August 31st. Acceptance of this invitation depended upon final approval by their pastor.

Songs performed for the researcher were "Through Faith, I Still Believe," "Where Goes The Wind?" "Lord, Take The Hand Of This Child," "Didn't He Shine?" and "Just Put Your Faith In Jesus." The song chosen as the group's representative selection was "Through Faith, I Still Believe."

(9) Dooly County (July 31, 1975)

"The Happy Singers"

Buford A. Calhoun (husband)—lead
Thelma Calhoun (wife)—alto
Ricky Calhoun (son, age 20)—lead guitar
Tony Calhoun (son, age 18)—electric bass
Vernon Kirksey (non-related, age 18)—piano
Jeffrey Sumners (non-related, age 17)—rhythm guitar
Wilbur Carroll (non-related)—bass
Edna Carroll (wife of Wilbur)—tenor (an octave high)

The group rehearses at the Calhoun residence, which is located approximately four miles south of Vienna, the county seat. The Calhoun's attend Sharon Baptist Church, located in Crisp County. Vernon Kirksey attends Byronville Baptist in Dooly County. The Carroll's attend Turner Chapel (Free Will Baptist) in Taylor County. Jeffrey Sumners, who arrived late, was not asked his church of attendance.

Buford Calhoun is employed by Glover's Machine Works in Cordele.

"The Happy Singers" have been performing together for six years. The only personnel changes have been in the tenor and bass singers. Their first record album was made with Bobby Pope, tenor, and Mike Duckworth, bass. Their second album was made with Dennis Folks, tenor, and Mike Duckworth, bass. The Carroll's have been with the group approximately six months. (Buford is not pleased with the Carroll's sound.)

The group has a great deal of music. They use sheet music, old hymnbooks, convention songbooks, and various collections of gospel music. Among the latter are *Songs of Praise and Hope* (Pensacola, Florida: collected by J.G. Whitfield, 1974), *Songs of Zion* (Stamps-Baxter's 2nd 1973 book), *Banner Hymns* (Cleveland, Tennessee: White Wing Publishing House, n.d.), and *Favorite Songs and Hymns* (Stamps-Baxter, 1939). For performance, the group utilize a large looseleaf notebook with clear plastic pages. Songs to be performed are placed into the pages behind the plastic leaves. The notebook is placed upon a large wooden music stand for use by the vocalists. The instrumentalists do not use music. The pianist has a list of songs and their appropriate keys. All of the instruments, with the exception of the piano, are amplified. All four vocalists use individual hand-held microphones.

Both Buford and Thelma have a history of singing as a family group. Buford, with his four brothers and four sisters, sang with his father. His father was a singing-school teacher. Buford's father and three uncles also performed as a male quartet. Thelma and her sister formerly sang with a gospel group.

Buford's favorite song is "Living On Higher Ground," which is recorded on their second album. Thelma's favorite is "Stroll Over Heaven." They have few records and "no time to listen to them." Their favorite record is of the Melody Makers, a local group from Abbeville.

The group listens to the radio while traveling to concert performances. They generally listen to a Cordele or an Eastman station. Buford stated that he watches very little television—"maybe one Western a week."

Much of the group's spare time is spent practicing. The quartet practices on Tuesday nights, and the entire group practices on Thursday nights. During the taping session, the instrumentalists appeared very eager to perform. Often they would start a song before the members of the quartet were ready. All of the instrumentalists were quite proficient.

A significant past performance was in Tampa, Florida, in 1973, at a Free Will Baptist church. The group sang a song the congregation had not heard before and "the altar just filled up" [with people praying].

The group has sung for various building funds, the March of Dimes, the Heart Fund, and for a variety of churches within ten surrounding counties. They try to limit their bookings to three per weekend, although they have sung as many as five. Often the group must turn down requests to perform.

Money collected is divided equally among the members of the group, or used to buy clothes. Sometimes donations are returned to the host church. Buford bought all of the equipment for the group out of his own pocket. He considers this his mission. He states, "They'll listen to singing when they won't listen to preaching."

Buford has not tried to promote his group. Their first album was made simply because they wanted to make one. The second album was made in order to improve upon the first. All members of the group agreed that there was an obvious difference between the two albums.

Future plans are to keep singing and to try to improve. Buford has no plans to turn professional. If he did it would be "just for the love of it."

Songs performed for the researcher were "I'm Getting Ready to Leave This World," "He'll Go with You," "Just a Little Talk with Jesus," "Keep Singing," "Look for Me at Jesus' Feet," "I'll Soon Be Gone," "I'll Fly Away," "Stepping on the Clouds," "When I Walk on the Streets of Gold," "Ready to Leave," "I Won't Have to Worry," and "I Never Shall Forget the Day." The song selected as most representative of the group was "I'll Soon Be Gone."

(10) Early County (August 1, 1976)

Harold Weems Family

Harold Weems (husband)—piano/lead
Joan Weems (wife)—alto
Pam Weems (daughter, age 16)—tenor (an octave high)

Both Harold and Joan are able to sing lead or harmony. Another daughter, Karen (age 10), does not sing with the group. In addition to their family group, Harold and Joan sing with Harry White in a gospel trio called "The Countrymen."

The Weems family attend the Sowhatchee Missionary Baptist Church. This church is located approximately seven miles from Blakely, the county seat.

Harold sells insurance. He has done so "for years and years." He also promotes gospel concerts. He has promoted an annual all-night sing in Blakely for the previous two years.

The Weems Family

Joan, Pam, and Harold

289

Sowhatchee Missionary Baptist Church

Welcome to all

The Weems family trio has no definite beginning date. Pam is not too interested in singing, although she usually performs with the group when requested. Occasionally she has refused. The parents have not pushed to form a family group. Joan states, "You can't take away childhood from your children."

Harold and Joan have always sung. Harold's mother and father had an organ in their home. His mother played by ear and his father played by shaped notes. Harold had eight siblings in his family. All of the brothers and sisters could sing and interchange various parts. Harold's father was a leader of Sacred Harp sings, but Harold never cared for that kind of music. He often sang with his family for church specials. Joan's mother plays piano by ear. Her father also sings, but does not read music. Joan, with her mother, sister, and brother, sang in church ensembles. Her brother is currently the choir director of a church in Phenix City, Alabama. Joan often sang solos in church and for high school occasions.

Harold considers himself a "fiend" about music. He had to learn music by himself because his parents could not afford to give him lessons. He learned to play guitar from a book. It bothers him that his children are not interested in lessons. Harold played and sang country music for twenty years. He doesn't do it any more except for his own pleasure. The reason for stopping is because he "got saved" by accepting Christ. The places, or "joints," where country music is played precludes his participation as a performer now. He still loves to listen to it. Harold stated that he had often performed gospel music before he accepted Christ. He cared only for the music. Joan began pointing out the meaning of the words of the songs he sang. According to Joan, "He sung himself to conviction." Harold has been active as an exclusively gospel music singer for approximately five years.

The group uses sheet music, old hymnals, and song books. They sometimes copy songs from records and tapes. Often songs are changed in order to "put self into it." They do not try to imitate anyone else.

Joan's favorite song is "I Can Feel the Touch of His Hand," as sung by the Stamps Quartet. Harold prefers "He Is Mine and I Am His" by "Dad" Speer. The group formerly closed concerts with the latter song. They do not often sing the song now because of a special memory attached to it. The group had sung this song at Spring Creek Baptist Church on Lake Seminole only two weeks before the mass murder of six members of the Allday family. "Shugie" Allday, a close friend of the Weems's, had been in attendance at the sing. His widow requested the group to sing the song at the funeral. She said that "Shugie" had been singing the song all of the day before he was killed. Harold and Joan stated that they have many other favorite songs. According to Joan, "We don't do a song unless we feel the Spirit of God in it." She further stated, "You've got to feel the Spirit within yourself or it comes out void." Their favorite recording is the Florida Boys' tape, *Make Happy Tracks.*

The only gospel television program the group is able to receive regularly is "Gospel Singing Jubilee." Occasionally they are able to get Wendy Johnson and the Messengers.

Past performances include a sing in Phenix City, Alabama, with Higher Ground, a professional group. On October 31, 1975 the Weems, with three other groups, sponsored a benefit sing for Bryan Sellers. Sellers had fallen while engaged in water sports and had become paralyzed. He is better now. Joan said, "It did us more good to take money and give it to someone in need." The group also finds it touching to sing for the Nursing Home in Blakely.

The group charges a set price, generally $150, or a percentage of the gate receipts, to perform at an all-night sing. They do not set a fixed fee for a church performance. They do accept "love offerings" if the church chooses to take up a donation for their sake. The group maintains separate records of money earned for performance. They try to use this money to pay for their expenses. Clothes, with one exception, have been paid for out-of-pocket. The group owns a 1949 Fitzjohn (Army Surplus) bus. They have made two "old" (1970, 1972) record albums.

Regarding future plans, Harold said, "I can't speak for Joan or Pam, but Harry White and I would go full-time if offered the chance." Joan states that she does not know how full-time groups with families in school are able to do it. Pam wants to become a veterinarian. She states that she is not very much interested in gospel music. Her goals lie in another direction. Karen plans to begin piano lessons in September.

The group performed five songs in succession (no pause between songs) for the researcher. These were "Jesus, Savior, Pilot Me," "He Touched Me," "Glory Road," "The Eastern Gate," and "I'll See You In The Rapture." The song chosen to represent the group was "Jesus, Savior, Pilot Me."

(11) Echols County (August 11 and 16, 1976)

"The Relatives"

Bob Wise (husband)—lead
Mildred (Millie) Wise (wife)—lead
Margaret Collier (sister of Mildred)—alto
Willie Rae Collier (husband)—tenor (double alto part)
Beverly Collier (daughter, age 17)—piano

The interview of the adult members of the group took place on August 11, 1976. Beverly was out of town. The tape recording of songs, and interview of Beverly, was conducted on August 16, 1976.

Echols County is the least populous county in Georgia. Technically, the county seat, Statenville, is limited to the area of the courthouse only. The surrounding community, however, is also popularly called Statenville. Members of the group reside next-door to one another within the community of Statenville. They attend the Statenville Baptist Church.

Both Bob and Willie Rae work for the Owens-Illinois Papermill in Clyatville. Bob is an electrician and Willie Rae is a shift-worker.

The group have been singing together "off-and-on" for approximately four to six years. No adult member of the group had sung with their parents. A member of the group stated that square dances had brought them together. Singing in the church came after marriage. The idea of singing as a family group more

293

or less evolved. They attribute Beverly's piano playing as having brought the group together.

Beverly has been playing piano since she was in the second grade, ten years ago. She quit lessons in the eighth grade. She would like to resume lessons while in college. She is a freshman at Valdosta State College, where she is majoring in sociology. She plans to minor in music. The group tries to work their singing around Beverly's plans. This cooperation with Beverly has kept the group together as long as it has. Beverly was pianist for the church, and she felt confined by the responsibility. She is not as interested in religious music now. She wants to enjoy being a teenager.

The group uses sheet music almost exclusively. When a song is heard that they like, the group "put out a searcher for it." One copy of the music is purchased for Beverly. What they call a "cheat sheet" (words only) is copied for the quartet. Beverly teaches the harmony by note. She often re-arranges the songs to fit their needs. They indicate on the "cheat sheet" when members of the quartet are to come in.

Margaret's favorite song is "One Day at a Time." Willie Rae considers the most meaningful song to be "I Should Have Been Crucified." Millie prefers "The Lights of Home." Bob's favorite is "Jesus Is Coming Soon." Other favorites are "He Touched Me" and "Hallelujah Square." Beverly's favorite music is not gospel music. She prefers soul music, (not rock)—music with a Rhythm and Blues sound. Beverly likes the faster gospel songs such as "Just a Little Talk with Jesus." She also enjoys "Why Me, Lord?" and "I Find No Fault in Him."

Favorite groups include the Inspirations, the Dixie Echoes, and the Hinson Family. Favorite local groups are the Gospel Three, from Stockton (a group they consider similar to theirs), and the Sounds of Gospel, from Valdosta. Beverly's favorite groups are Marvin Gaye, the Osmond Brothers and other teenage groups. She has no gospel favorites.

Members of the group watch "Gospel Jubilee" on television every Sunday morning. When camping in Florida, they are able to watch Wendy Johnson and the Messengers.

They enjoy listening to a gospel radio program called the

294

Willie Rae and Margaret Collier with "Millie" and Bob Wise

Beverly Collier

"Mull Singing Convention." The programming consists mainly of songs recorded by the Chuck Wagon Gang.

Significant past performances include a concert, about four years ago, when the group sang on a program with two professional groups, the Georgians, and Higher Ground. They were "very scared." Bob was so nervous he introduced his wife as "Willie" instead of "Millie." The group was pleased that the Georgians had had to borrow their sound equipment, however. Bob stated that the most touching concert he remembers was when his mother and father were in the audience hearing the group sing for the first time. His parents were crying and Millie was crying. Another touching performance was their first appearance before kinfolk in Cecil. They were all crying. Bob also remembered a performance when he was singing a solo. He forgot the second verse. He couldn't remember a word. The pianist played the song all the way through, and Bob was able to sing the third verse correctly.

Members of the group stated that their first experience singing in front of the holiness church audience was initially frightening. There was much hand-clapping and speaking in unknown tongues. The group enjoyed the response after they became accustomed to it. Millie said that in holiness churches "you feel like you're touching more people." Millie also stated that it was harder to sing for their own church than for anyone else. Willie Rae said that the reason for this is "because you know they can see through you. They will say something to you."

Future plans include trying to talk the wife of the school principal into playing piano for them. Beverly's going to college has slowed their performance activity. They have no desire to cut a record. The group has tapes of when they first began. Often the group use a tape recorder while practicing.

The group has "never charged a penny." They give donations back to the host church. The group donated piano lights to two churches in which they performed because of the obvious need. According to Bob, they have "never been booked as a first-line group." The group choose songs they do not have to put a lot into because they do not have time to work on them.

Additional comments include a statement by Beverly that

she did not think playing the piano for the family group either helped or hindered her during the teenage growing-up years. In another context, Margaret stated, "When I go to a gospel sing I don't want to hear a lot of preaching. I don't mind a little testifying."

Songs performed for the researcher were "Sheltered In The Arms of God," "I've Been Changed," "I Should Have Been Crucified," and "Had It Not Been." The song chosen to represent the group was "Had It Not Been."

(12) Effingham County (September 25, 1976)

"Parker Cousins"

Debbie Parker (sister, age 21)—piano
Steve Parker (brother, age 16)—bass
Peggy Parker (sister, age 14)—lead
Pam Parker (cousin, age 16)—alto
Joe Parker (brother of Pam, age 11)—alto/tenor
Susie Parker (cousin, age 13)—lead
Donny Yarbrough (no relation, age 17)—tenor (double alto part)

An additional member of the group, Randy Parker (age 18), brother of Pam and Joe, is away at college. All members of the group, except Joe, consider themselves to be music readers. Three are members of their high school band, five sing in their high school chorus, and four take private piano lessons.

Members of the group reside in a sparsely populated area of the southern portion of the county. All members of the group, except Donny, attend the First Christian Church in Rincon, approximately thirteen miles distant. Rincon is located approximately eight miles south of Springfield, the county seat. Donny attends the Marlow Methodist Church. The community of Marlow lies approximately ten miles southwest of Springfield.

Debbie is employed by the Southern Bell Telephone Company as a switchboard operator. Steve works part-time as a gaso-

Left to right: Peggy Parker, Donny
Yarbrough, Joe, Pam, Steve, and Susie
Parker

An additional photo of the group

298

line service station attendant. Pam is employed as a waitress by Woody's restaurant in Rincon. Donny considers himself to be a professional trombonist. He did not detail the exact nature of his employment.

The group has been performing together for seven years. The initial group consisted of Debbie, Peggy, Pam, and Susie. Steve and Randy joined soon thereafter. Joe joined the group when Randy left for college. Donny, not a regular member of the group, is more or less a substitute for Randy.

The group has retained few historical records. Approximately four years ago a local newspaper featured a story about the group. No one kept a copy of the write-up. The group did keep a handbill with their picture on it as a souvenir of participation in a recent church homecoming in Mississippi.

For musical materials the group uses chorus books primarily. They also use sheet music and camp songs. One song has been learned by ear.

Favorite songs include "Joshua," "Sweet, Sweet Spirit," "There's a Rainbow," and "Why Me, Lord?" Favorite groups are the Gospel Lads, the Blackwood Brothers, Impact Brass and Sound (of Ozark Bible College), and the Jackson Brothers.

Members of the group enjoy listening to the gospel music program "Breakfast with Burl," over radio station WZAT in Savannah. They also enjoy watching the television program "Gospel Singing Jubilee."

Significant past performances include the previously mentioned homecoming program in Mississippi. For the past two years they have led the singing for the full week of camp at the Christian Church camp in Sylvania. The group performed for an area-wide Sweetheart Banquet sponsored by the Christian Church. They also sang at the church's New Year's Eve service. They have participated in several local revival meetings.

The group has no definite future plans. It is anticipated that as the older children leave for college the group will only be able to perform during the summer.

The group performed one song for the researcher. The chosen song was "Sweet, Sweet Spirit." The song utilized by the group was published as a single vocal score with piano accompa-

299

niment. Donny wrote out a bass part for Steve, and arranged an alto/tenor part (unison except for several chords) for the other members of the group who sing harmony.

(13) Irwin County (July 26, 1975)

"The Dover Sisters"

Mattie Lou (Dover) Wilson (sister)—lead
Jessie Dean (Dover) Bishop (sister)—tenor (an octave high)
Wynell (Dover) Hickey (sister)—alto

Although the song chosen by the group was performed a cappella, other songs were performed with accompaniment. Jessie Dean, called Dean, played the piano for these songs. She can also play the organ. Wynell, too, can play piano.

Irwin County is the site of the Royal [Family] Singing Convention. The interview and taping session was conducted at the Mystic Baptist Church, which is located next-door to the Royal [Singing Convention] Tabernacle. Mystic is located approximately six miles from Ocilla, the county seat. Members of the group reside in various locations within the county.

Mattie Lou attends Prospect Baptist Church. Jesse Dean is a member of Pine Level Methodist Church. Wynell is a member of the previously mentioned Mystic Baptist Church.

Mattie Lou is employed by the Farm Bureau in Ocilla.

The group has been performing in public for thirty-two years, since Mattie Lou was five years old. At one time, twenty-two years ago, four sisters were in the group. The group originated in singing school. In this school each of the four sisters was seated with a different group of friends. The singing master started the full class singing a familiar song. While the song was in progress, he went through the group and selected those he considered as having the best voices. He asked four singers thus chosen to form a quartet. Without knowing who they were, he had chosen the Dover sisters.

Members of the group have sung in concert with both par-

300

ents. They have also sung in a group comprised of their parents, themselves, and their children. The three sisters have a total of fourteen children.

The parents of the Dover sisters are still alive. They were in a string band and played for dances "long ago." The father played guitar and the mother played mandolin. Insofar as known, neither of the parents played or sang with *their* parents.

Publications used by the group include hymnbooks, convention songbooks, and sheet music. Favorite songs include "One Day at a Time," "Love Is Why," and "Sunset Trail." The latter song is the group's most favorite selection.

Musical tastes vary within the group. Dean prefers classical music. She owns three or four classical recordings, and generally listens to WCUP radio in Tifton. This radio station is said to program classical music. Mattie Lou does not own a record player. She listens to WBHB radio in Fitzgerald. This station is said to have general programming. She enjoys its daily gospel music broadcasts. Wynell prefers country/western and gospel music. She listens to WSIZ radio in Ocilla.

Both Dean and Mattie regularly watch the Billy Graham and Oral Roberts television presentations.

The group is not as active now as in the past. They currently sing mostly for revivals and funerals. Significant past performances include a revival in Tifton where an old man requested them to sing "Wasted Years." Although the group hardly knew the song, they were able to sing it perfectly. The old man told how he had wasted his years. He died a few weeks later. Also, the group sang regularly for a diabetic who later stated that their singing had won him to Christ.

In the 1950s, the sisters appeared on a program with the Statesmen Quartet in Atlanta. In the late 1940s [sic], the group sang three or four times at the Waycross Festival [sic] with the LeFevres and the Statesmen. One summer the group was gone every day, singing all over the South. They only came home in order to leave laundry.

The group formerly accepted "love offerings," or donations collected at church concerts. They no longer do so. Future plans

301

are to stay together as much as possible. Twice a year the three sisters go out to dinner together.

Songs performed for the researcher were "Love Is Why," "Heaven Came Down and Glory Filled My Soul," "Sunset Trail," and "Rainbow In The Clouds." The song chosen as most representative of the group was "Heaven Came Down and Glory Filled My Soul."

(14) Jenkins County (October 10, 1976)

Mary Johnson (mother)—alto
Cindy (Johnson) Kersey (daughter)—soprano
Patty Bennett (niece, age 14)—piano

Although the group performs as constituted above, Cindy is more active as a soloist. Patty can also sing soprano, but she does not sing with the group.

Members of the group reside in a sparsely populated area near the western border of the county. They attend the Deep Creek Free Will Baptist Church, located approximately seventeen miles from Millen, the county seat. No member of the group is employed.

Mrs. Johnson and Cindy have been performing together for approximately seven years. Patty has been their accompanist for about one and one-half years. The church pianist was used as an accompanist before Patty joined the group.

Mrs. Johnson has been singing since approximately age three. She sang duets with her twin sister, and also sang duets with her brother. When singing with her brother, a guitar was used for accompaniment. No historical or souvenir information has been retained.

While in high school, Cindy was lead singer for a rock group, Masters of Time. They went "all over Georgia." The group consisted of five boys and Cindy. After marriage, her husband said that such activity was not appropriate for a married woman. Cindy thinks the group "could have gone somewhere." When she left, the rock group disbanded.

Debbie Parker

Cindy Kersey and Mary Johnson

Patty Bennett

Deep Creek Free Will Baptist Church

304

Publications used by the gospel group include "lots of sheet music," song collections, and hymnbooks. None of their music is learned by ear. Mrs. Johnson reads music by the contour of the musical line. Cindy learned some music while in public school. She played flute for a while, and also took several guitar lessons. Patty has been taking piano lessons for one year and two months. She reads music and does not play by ear. She does improvise part of her accompaniment, however, using the published music as a point of departure.

Mrs. Johnson has written one song, "Up On The Mountain." She sent the song away to be notated [by George Liberace] and had a demonstration recording made. According to Mrs. Johnson, the group making the recording did not sound good, and it discouraged her. She has not written any songs since.

A favorite song of all members of the group is "One Day Too Late." Mrs. Johnson enjoys songs such as "He" and "I Believe." Patty's favorite song is "Broken Pieces."

Favorite recordings include those by Wendy Bagwel and the Sunliters, the Bill Gaither Trio, and the Hudson Family (a local group from Swainsboro). Mrs. Johnson also enjoys recordings made by amateur groups from Greenville, South Carolina, and from Jacksonville, Florida. (She was unable to recall the names of these groups.)

Mrs. Johnson rarely listens to the radio. Cindy stated that "not much is available." Patty regularly listens to the full-time gospel format radio station in Waynesboro.

Members of the group seldom watch televised gospel music programs, except on Sundays. They occasionally watch the Oral Roberts presentation, or the service televised from Charleston Heights Baptist Church in South Carolina. They also watch the Rex Humbard television presentation. Mrs. Johnson states that the music of the latter show is "fantastic." "They run the gamut from old-time religion to rock-and-roll religion."

The group did not cite any significant past performances. They sing approximately once every three or four months outside their own church. The performances are usually for local revival services.

Mrs. Johnson thinks that Patty is going to become a great pianist. She thinks that Cindy "has potential as a singer, but probably won't use it." Cindy would like to sing full-time with a group, but not necessarily a gospel music performing group. Patty's dream is to be a classical or a gospel pianist. Mrs. Johnson stated that she wants to raise hogs.

The song performed by the group for the researcher was "Reach Out To Jesus."

(15) McIntosh County (July 18, 1975)

"Singing Servants"

C.A. "Shorty" Wallace (husband)—acoustic guitar/bass vocalist
Sandra Wallace (wife)—alto
Sonya Wallace (daughter, age 7)—lead
Georgia Wallace (daughter, age 5)—lead
David Riddle (no relation)—lead
Shirley Riddle (wife of David)—piano

The interview and taping session took place in the Riddle home, located within the city limits of Darien, the county seat. The Wallace's reside in the northern area of the country, near the community of South Newport, approximately sixteen miles distant. The Wallaces attend the South Newport Baptist Church. The Riddles attend the Townsend Baptist Church, located approximately thirteen miles from Darien. David Riddle is employed by the Darien Bank.

The group has been performing together for two months. Even this brief period of performance activity was interrupted by illness. "Shorty" is presently recovering from a mild heart attack.

Neither family has a history of singing as a family group. David formerly sang with a semi-professional group called the Gospel Carriers and Jeannine. This group is located in Pembroke, Georgia. David left the group when he and his family moved to Darien.

When the "Singing Servants" were initially formed, Pearl

306

Douglas, "Shorty's" aunt, played organ. Judy Wallace, another of "Shorty's" aunts, played piano. Brian Gardner, David's brother-in-law, sang tenor.

The present group generally uses sheet music acquired from a variety of sources. They sometimes use song collections such as *Gospel Caravan of TV Favorites,* and the *Country and Western Hymnal.* Some of the group's favorite songs are "Hallelujah Square," "I Am His and He Is Mine," "This Is the Day," "Touring That City," "Why Me?" and "One Day at a Time." Sonya likes "Put Your Hand in the Hand," and Georgia likes "Long, Long Ago."

Gospel recordings make up approximately one-third of the Riddle's record collection, "but they are the only ones listened to." The Riddle's favorite recordings are those by the LeFevres, the previously mentioned Gospel Carriers (their one recording), the Anderson Family, the Blue Ridge Quartet, and an "old" Osmond Brothers album of their singing of hymns. The Wallaces cite as favorite recording artists the Thrasher Brothers, the Hinson Family (their most favorite), Eva Mae and the LeFevres [sic], and Johnny Cook and the Happy Goodman Family [sic].

The Riddles listen to WNYR radio in Brunswick, which programs some gospel music. They also listen to WSOJ, full-time gospel format radio in Jesup. They must hook their radio antenna to their television antenna in order to receive the latter station. The Wallaces listen to WSOJ almost exclusively. According to "Shorty," "If it ain't gospel music, it's not worth listening to."

Both families watch television channel 11 (CBS in Savannah) for the programs, "America Sings," and "Oral Roberts." They watch channel 22 (Savannah) for "Singing Jubilee" and "Rex Humbard." Another favorite television program is "PTL" [Praise The Lord]. This is stated to be two hours of religious broadcasting from 10:00 to 12:00 every morning.

The group has sung in each of their home churches. They have also sung for the Morgan Hill Methodist Church, for a revival and for a barbecue supper. Another performance by the group was at the South Newport Assembly of God Church.

Future plans depend to a great extent upon "Shorty's"

307

health. He recently experienced the previously mentioned heart attack. He also suffers from back problems. If his health improves an attempt will be made to regain former members of the group and expand their performance schedule.

Songs performed for the researcher were "I Am His and He Is Mine," "Touring That City," "Thank God I'm Free," and "One Day at a Time." The song chosen as the group's most representative performance was "Touring That City."

(16) Miller County (July 25, 1976)

"The Clenney Family"

Randy Clenney (brother)—lead
Rudy Clenney (brother)—tenor
Shirley (Clenney) Kimbrel (sister)—piano/alto
John Clenney (uncle)—bass

Members of the group reside in various locations in the county. All are members of the Bellview Freewill Baptist Church, which is located approximately nineteen miles from Colquitt, the county seat.

Randy is employed as an accountant by the George Daniels CPA firm. Rudy is a purchasing agent for the Daniels Construction Company. Shirley is not employed, John owns and operates a grocery store.

The group has been performing for approximately ten to twelve years. There have been no changes in the personnel of the group.

John attended singing schools held in churches "a long time ago." John's brother, since deceased, was the father of the other members of the group. He was a minister and, according to John, taught his children "praise to God through music." Shirley said he taught that "singing is expressing the soul's adoration to God." Randy stated that his father had children around the piano almost every night. Each of the eight children in the family learned how to play the piano to some extent. The family regu-

Left to right: John, Randy Clenney, Shirley Kimbrel, and Rudy Clenney

Bruce Kimbrel

Inside of Bellview Freewill Baptist
Church

The exterior of Bellview Freewill Baptist
Church

310

larly sang together for church specials during Christmas and Homecoming Week.

One of John's sisters, Susie Shiver, has written several songs. John wrote the words to one of her songs.

At one time, Shirley sang with John's two daughters and a distant relative. These four girls were featured on a regular radio program.

Shirley has been playing piano by ear since she was five years old. She took piano lessons while attending public school. Her high school piano teacher also coached her in singing, but she has had no formal voice training. According to John, "If it wasn't for Shirley, our group couldn't sing." Shirley has two children, Bruce (age 9) and Leigh Ann (age 5). She and her children have also performed as a group. Bruce recently entered as a vocal soloist in the Freewill Baptist youth competition. He won first place in the state and was second runner-up at the National Youth Conference in Tulsa, Oklahoma. He sang "I Will Serve Thee," by William Gaither.

Other Clenney Family children have sung together in various groupings.

For musical materials the adult group uses sheet music or convention songbooks. They do not use hymnbooks nor sing by ear.

Randy's favorite songs are "Because He Lives," and "The King Is Coming." John prefers "Going Home." Shirley cited as favorites "Redemption Draweth Nigh," and "My Tribute." She also likes "Bill Gaither songs." Shirley has "really enjoyed his music."

No member of the group owns any recordings. They listen to WMGR radio in Bainbridge, which programs gospel music from 10:15 to 11:00 A.M. daily and on Sunday from 7:00 to 12:00 noon. They also listen to WLOR in Thomasville, which programs gospel music "all Sunday afternoon."

Members of the group are able to receive "Gospel Singing Jubilee" over three television stations: Tallahassee, Florida; Dothan, Alabama; and Albany, Georgia. They enjoy watching and listening to the Inspirations and the Hinson Family, ensembles featured regularly on the program.

Speaking of past performances, Shirley stated that one of

311

the best times was when the group went to Columbus to sing in a concert with several other groups. Members of the group also enjoy performing for church homecomings. The group once had a regular radio program for three or four months.

Future plans are uncertain. Shirley would like to make a recording of their group but Randy and Rudy have been too busy with their jobs.

Additional comments by members of the group include a statement that "some gospel music today doesn't have a true message in it. We have been picky." Randy stated that the group often modified their songs. He said, "You can't sing some of this music like it's written—unless you can really read music." Shirley added that, "You have to sing it like you feel it."

Songs performed for the researcher included "You Have Given Life To Me," sung as a solo by Bruce. Ensemble numbers included "Love, Like The Love of God," "Going Home," "Because He Lives," one verse of "The Sweetest Song I know," "All Because of God's Amazing Grace," "Redemption Draweth Nigh," and "Homecoming Week." The song chosen as most representative of the group was "Love, Like The Love of God."

(17) Montgomery County (July 19, 1975)

Hugh Nesmith Family

Hugh Nesmith (husband)—lead
Vivian Nesmith (wife)—alto
Rhonda Nesmith (daughter, age 13)—piano
David Nesmith (son, age 11)—lead

Rhonda also sings alto on certain selections.

The Nesmith family lives in the southern portion of the county, near the community of Uvalda. They are members of the Uvalda Church of God. Uvalda is located approximately eleven miles from Mount Vernon, the county seat.

The adult members of the group have no previous history of singing as a family group. This group has been singing together

312

for approximately one year. They will sing any time they are requested. They have had about ten bookings outside their home church, and they have also sung over the radio. It should be stated that the group, especially Rhonda, appeared very eager to perform. The writer was treated with an impromptu concert the afternoon of initial contact.

The group does not use too much printed music, although they have a hymnbook, some sheet music, and a Dottie Rambo song collection. Generally they hear a song over the radio and learn it by ear.

Members of the group regularly listen to WVOH radio in Hazlehurst. They do not watch very much television. All of the group's collection of recordings (approximately forty to forty-five albums) are of gospel music. Favorite professional groups are the Sego Brothers and Naomi, Dottie Rambo, the Lewis Family, the LeFevre family, and the Inspirations.

Rhonda learned to play the piano by ear and by watching the pianist at church. She can play in the keys of C, F, and Bb. Rhonda took piano lessons for two months but has since stopped. Her father stated that the piano lessons "were ruining" her ability to play gospel music.

Songs performed for the researcher included "Joshua," "What A Beautiful Day," "I've Come Too Far," "Ready To Leave," "When I Wake Up To Sleep No More," "Stepping On The Clouds," "Something I Can Feel," "The Best Is Yet To Come," and "Living In Canaan Land." All songs were performed from memory. The song selected as most representative of the group was "What A Beautiful Day (For The Lord To Come Again)."

(18) Peach County (September 28, 1976)

Steve Rowland Family

Steve Rowland (husband)—lead
Mary Jo Rowland (wife)—piano/alto
Andrea Rowland (daughter, age 10)—lead

313

The Rowlands: Steve holding Kelly,
Andrea, and Mary Jo

Steve and Andrea Rowland with Mary Jo
playing piano

314

Steve, Andrea, and Mary Jo Rowland

The Rowlands also have a son, Kelly (age 3). Andrea can play some piano. She took lessons for almost a year.

The Rowlands reside in a rural area of the county near the community of Centerville. Their home is located approximately eighteen miles from Fort Valley, the county seat. They attend the First Assembly of God Church in Fort Valley.

Steve is employed by Goldkist Farm Supply in Perry as a store operations manager. Mary Jo works as a secretary for Jefferson Standard Insurance in Macon.

The Rowlands have been singing together for more than ten years. They met through music. Mary Jo often played the piano in the girls' dormitory while attending Southern Business University in Atlanta. Steve, who was attending Marse Business College in Atlanta, often "hung around." They sang together a few times before their marriage, generally as a trio including Mary Jo's sister. Andrea has been singing with the group for approximately two years.

Mary Jo is the daughter of a Baptist preacher. She began singing in a trio at the age of ten. Her father taught shaped note

315

singing school and Mary Jo attended singing schools. Her music reading, however, is "strictly lines and spaces." She took two years of piano lessons and played saxophone in her high school band. Mary Jo's sister, Janice Ridley, sings with a semi-professional gospel group, The Peacemakers, from Calhoun, Georgia. This sister has had one song published, and The Peacemakers have made three phonograph albums. They are working on a fourth recording. Mary Jo's family included seven children, and all are musical. She had retained some souvenirs of their singing together.

Steve came from an Assembly of God religious background. He previously sang with his sister. While in high school, Steve won first place in Boy's Solo in the District Meet. He went to the state competition but did not place. He was also running track at the time. (His high school graduating class had only ten members. He was involved—"overworked," as Mary Jo put it—in a wide variety of scholastic and extra-curricular activities).

For musical materials the group uses sheet music, generally songs written by Dottie Rambo or William Gaither. They also utilize songs from the *Country Western Hymnal* and the *New Songs of Inspirations* (series) song collections.

Favorite songs include "City of Gold," "Touching Jesus," "I Asked The Lord," "Because He Lives," and "Ten Thousand Years." The Rowlands own about twenty-five recordings. One of the recordings is stated to be of classical music; the remainder are of gospel music. Steve's favorite recording is a tape made from an album owned by his mother, where Larry Joe Wright sang as a soloist using a recorded soundtrack. Mary Jo's favorite singer is Jimmy Swaggert. The Rowlands also enjoy the three albums made by the previously mentioned Peacemakers. Their favorite of these three albums is entitled *I've Been on the Mountain*. They have "practically worn it out." Steve considers this first album the group's best—because it is "basic."

The Rowlands state that a gospel music radio station is located in Warner-Robins. Mary Jo listens to it while driving to work. Occasionally she listens to a radio station in Cochran. Steve states that he is "not much of a radio listener." The members of the group sometimes watch the Oral Roberts television presentations. They also watch the Rex Humbard church services. Occasionally they are able to watch "Gospel Singing Jubilee," but it is usually scheduled during their church time.

Significant past performances include times when the group has performed special music at their church. On several occasions their pastor has not preached but has given an "invitation" immediately following the group's performance. The group has also performed at gospel sings with other groups. They sing regularly at an unnamed nursing home. At this nursing home, often an old Negro man's eyes will well with tears when the group sings. There, also, Mary Jo is impressed by an elderly woman, confined to a wheelchair, who plays piano for the home's religious services.

Steve has always wanted to sing bass in a gospel quartet. This dream has not materialized. He would like to have a singing family, and hopes that Kelly will grow up to become a good singer or a good instrumentalist. Mary Jo would also like to form a family group. Children "get to" her. She enjoys the closeness of her family. Steve hopes that one of the children will develop a strong lead voice so he can sing bass. This would fit his voice better.

Additional comments include remarks by Steve that he is sometimes disheartened with the trend toward "mod" music. He states that gospel music, "should not sound like secular music." It should be separate. Mary Jo, too, doesn't care for a lot of instruments, "such as drums." She states, "In our faith we hold gospel music to be pretty sacred." The Rowlands "can't stand to see gospel singers who look like a bunch of hippies, with sequins all over their clothes or with clothes skintight." "You can't concentrate on the songs for watching the show." They prefer gospel concerts to be inspiring, without so much entertainment. They have attended three or four professional gospel sings, but generally enjoy church sings better.

The song performed for the researcher was "Ten Thousand Years."

(19) Pulaski County (July 28, 1975)

"Cedar Creek"

Freddy Hogg (husband)—acoustic guitar/lead
Lynn Hogg (wife)—tambourine/alto
Jeannie Hogg (Freddy's sister)—acoustic guitar/soprano

Lynn can also play the autoharp. The group is not an exclusively gospel music performing group. In addition to gospel, they perform a mixture of folk, Pop, country, and Bluegrass music.

The members of "Cedar Creek" reside within the city limits of Hawkinsville, the county seat. They are members of the Broad Street Baptist Church (Southern Baptist Convention) in Hawkinsville.

The members of the group have been performing together for approximately three years. There have been no personnel changes.

The Hoggs have an extensive family history of musical activity. Jeannie sang previously with her father. The Hoggs' grandmother, who is still alive, and her three sisters were the Hall Family Female Quartet in the 1930s. Before that, their grandmother's uncle Warren [Hall?], his wife and daughter, were the College Trio in the 1920s. They sang for a "long" time. Their grandmother's grandmother, Winnie Hall, was the "leading singer" on the Primitive Baptist circuit of five churches at the turn-of-the-century. Some historical information has been retained, although it is not readily accessible. The Hoggs' grand-uncle (grandfather's brother), James Hogg, is a Professor [of music?] at Florida State University. He played guitar over the radio during the 1920s.

Lynn's father [unnamed] is a disc jockey for WCEH radio in Hawkinsville. The programming of this station is stated to be country/western.

Publications used by the group include the vocal score from *Godspell,* sheet music, and several hymnbooks. They generally learn their songs by ear from records or radio. Some of their songs are learned by ear from the Sego Brothers and Naomi, seen on television.

Favorite songs include "Amazing Grace," "Jesus Is Coming Soon," "Will The Circle Be Unbroken?" (Freddy's favorite), and "Day By Day" (favorite of the two girls). Favorite recordings include the album *Will the Circle Be Unbroken,* a collection by various artists. Another favorite album is *God Walks These Hills,* recorded by a friend, Peggy Grimsley. The group also enjoy the recording of the folk musical *Purpose,* the music of which they are in the process of learning.

Favorite radio stations include the previously mentioned WCEH, and WMAZ (Macon). The programming of the latter station is said to be "Top Forty." Favorite television programs are the "Sego Brothers and Naomi" and "Gospel Jubilee."

The group get paid for performing at parties. They refuse to accept payment from churches. Significant past performances include those for the Methodist Mens' Club; a Methodist Camp Meeting; a Youth Revival at Mars Hill Baptist Church; and an Eastern Star meeting. A favorite memory is of a Baptist Sunday School party where they were particularly well-received.

Future plans are ambitious. The group already has a tentative contract to perform regularly at a Stuckey's supper club. They would like to make a recording. Freddy would like to become a professional musician, preferably playing Bluegrass music.

Songs performed for the researcher were "Jesus Is Coming Soon," "Daddy Sang Bass," "Day By Day," "Will The Circle Be Unbroken?" "Amazing Grace," and "Brother Love's Traveling Salvation Show." The song selected as the group's most representative performance was "Daddy Sang Bass."

(20) Quitman County

No Data Available

In population Quitman county is the second smallest county in Georgia. Although some gospel music activity does exist in the

319

county, no groups meeting the criteria for inclusion in the study could be found.

(21) Upson County (October 14, 1976)

Billy Reeves Family

Billy Reeves (husband)—bass
Carleen (Bransford) Reeves (wife)—alto
Mike Reeves (son, age 23)—lead
Jenny Reeves (daughter, age 18)—tenor an octave high
Tina Reeves (daughter, age 13)—tenor an octave high
Marvin Helms (no relation)—piano

Carleen can also play piano and sing any part. She is organist for the church. Mike can also sing bass and play piano. Two additional members of the group were not present for the interview and recording session. Randy (son, age 22) plays trumpet and electric bass. Hank Phillips (no relation) plays electric bass.

Members of the group reside within the city limits of Thomaston, the county seat. They are members of Clark's Chapel Baptist Church in Thomaston.

Billy, retired from the U.S. Air Force, is manager of the Sing Foods grocery store in Thomaston. Carleen is employed as a study hall aide at Robert E. Lee High School in Thomaston. Mike works for Tire Master.

The basic family group has been performing together for eleven years. They began training, but not singing in public, while stationed in Germany in 1963. The group at that time consisted of the parents, their sons, and Jenny. They did not own a piano so they purchased a stereo record player and several gospel recordings. Songs were learned by ear from the recordings.

Billy had previously sung with his brother's quartet, the Harmony Boys. He also sang with a semi-professional group, the Sunnyland Quartet in Tampa, Florida. This group often sang with the professional group, the Florida Boys, in concerts. Billy's

320

Left to right: Jenny, Mike, Carleen, Billy,
and Tina Reeves

Marvin Helms

Mike Reeves

Tina, Carleen, and Bill Reeves

father, a non-singer, had provided for Billy to take voice lessons and piano lessons.

Carleen had previously sung with her sisters in a trio. Her mother loved music, but for a hobby, not as a performer.

Billy and Carleen met through music. When Billy's family moved from the county into the town of Thomaston, Billy wanted to form a quartet. He asked a friend to recommend a good pianist. Carleen was the pianist for Zion's Chapel. For the first practice Carleen came with her hair in pigtails and "looking like Judy Canova." A group was formed including Carleen's aunt and other non-related members. Billy and Carleen were married two years later, when Carleen turned eighteen.

Marvin Helms, pianist for the group, "plays for everyone in Upson county." He is much in demand for weddings, funerals, and other occasions where a pianist is needed. He states that his parents were not particularly musical. He began playing the piano by observing his sister during her piano lessons and picking up what she learned. He began piano lessons himself at the age of eight. Marvin has been a neighbor and friend of the Reeves and the Bransfords all of his life. He stated that he was around Carleen's family more than his own.

The Reeves family "used to sing all the time." Lately, they have been working with the church Youth Choir, which takes up a lot of their time. A vocal ensemble from the Youth Choir, called the Chapel-Heirs, and a quartet, of which Mike is the leader, are direct results of the Reeves's work with the youth of their church. Jenny was formerly president of the Robert E. Lee High School Singers, and received the 'Singers' Cup" for musicianship.

The group generally learn new material by hearing a recording and liking a certain song. They then buy the record and a copy of the sheet music of the song. All songs are rearranged to fit the group. Most of their repertory is of "up-to-date" music. Many of the songs they have sung have "wound up to be in the Top Ten."

Favorite songs include "Between The Cross And Heaven," "Because He Lives," "That I Could Still Go Free," "Glory Road," "Here They Come," and "The Blood Will Never Lose Its Power."

Billy owns forty-eight gospel recordings, including an early pressing by "Mom" and "Dad" Speer. Marvin also has a large collection of gospel records. Marvin's favorite recording is the Couriers' *Across the Country* album. Carleen prefers the Downings' album, *Live This Is How It Is.* Mike enjoys Ray Stevens' "Turn Your Radio On." Billy's favorite is the Speers' version of "Between the Cross And Heaven." Jenny likes the Hinsons' singing "From Out Of The West They Came," and Tina prefers the LeFevres's performance of "Stepping On The Clouds."

Radio stations listened to include WTGA (local), which has some gospel programming. They also listen to the full-time gospel format station, WTJH, in East Point.

Favorite television programs include "Gospel Singing Jubilee," "Rex Humbard," "The Trebles" [this group is also one of the groups (1) interviewed during the Field Research], "Warren Roberts Presents," "Oral Roberts," and "PTL [Praise The Lord] Club."

Billy related a humorous experience in a previous performance while he was with the Sunnyland Quartet. The group was scheduled to perform at a church homecoming. They found a church, set up their equipment, and completed almost an entire program before finding out they were at the wrong church! Marvin stated that he enjoys the followship of the Fourth Saturday Sings at the Courthouse in Eufaula, Alabama. A fond memory of Carleen's is of singing gospel music *a cappella* for her German friends overseas. A significant event for Billy and Carleen was "meeting Bill Gaither, about ten years ago."

Future plans are not specific. Billy wants his children to enjoy gospel singing and to carry on the tradition. Mike plans to stay with gospel music "but branch out into different ways."

Marvin expressed an opinion that "gospel music, in Georgia, is dying." He did not elaborate.

Songs performed for the researcher were "When I Wake Up That Morning," "Jesus Is Still The Answer" performed as a piano solo by Marvin, and "I Won't Walk Without Jesus."

The song selected as the group's most representative performance was "When I Wake Up That Morning." The group had learned this song from a tape recording of a radio broadcast. Subsequent investigation revealed that the song had been composed and harmonized by ear. The song "I Won't Walk Without Jesus," previously selected as a substitute performance, was utilized for the analysis of the group's performance practice.

(22) Wayne County (July 15, 1975)

J.T. Simmons and Sons

J.T. Simmons (father)—lead
Marshall Simmons (son, age 18)—lead
Freddy Simmons (son, age 14)—solo lead
Gary Simmons (son, age 10)—lead
Mrs. Jackie Daniels (no relation)—piano

The Simmons reside within the city limits of Jesup, the county seat. They attend the Jesup Church of God, sometimes referred to as the Downtown Church of God. Mrs. Daniels is the pianist for the church.

Mr. Simmons is employed by the H & H Tire and Appliance Company in Jesup.

The group has been performing together for approximately four years. There have been no personnel changes. Mr. Simmons does not have a history of singing gospel music with his parents.

The group uses sheet music purchased at a local Christian bookstore or at gospel sings. They own thirty or forty songs printed as sheet music. The Simmons also own approximately fifty recordings. All of their recordings are of gospel music. Only gospel music is allowed in their home. Their favorite song is "What A Beautiful Day (For The Lord To Come Again)."

The radio station most often listened to is WSOJ. This local station has a full-time gospel format. Occasionally members of the group listen to other radio stations. Their favorite television program is stated to be "Rex Humbard," seen on Sunday mornings at 8:30.

Almost all of the group's performances have been for their home church. When asked, they will perform for other audiences. Performances outside of their home church have usually been for homecomings at other churches.

Members of the group have no specific future plans.

Members of this group were courteous but not talkative. Twice the researcher was asked by Mr. Simmons, "Are you sure this is not going to cost me anything?" The researcher reassured him that it would not cost anything, but that the group would not be remunerated for their services either.

The song performed for the researcher was "At The Crossing."

(23) Wheeler County (July 8, 1975)

The Clark Family

Annice Clark (mother)—alto
Larry Clark (son, age 27)—lead
Kim Clark (son, age 23)—tenor
Jean (Browning) Williams (no relation)—piano

Jennifer McNeal (no relation), not the usual pianist for the group, accompanied the Clarks for several songs performed during the taping session. Jean Williams, recently married and moved away, was remembered to be visiting with her parents. She was telephoned and asked to come over. The song chosen to represent the group had Jean as accompanist. Annice can also play piano to a limited extent.

The Clark family was the first group to be interviewed and recorded by the researcher.

Members of the Clark family reside in separate but nearby homes slightly beyond the city limits of the town of Glenwood. Glenwood lies approximately seven miles east of Alamo, the county seat. Members of the group belong to the United Methodist Church in Glenwood.

Annice owns and operates a beauty parlor in Glenwood.

The group has been performing together since Larry was eight years old. Annice also sings in a quartet with her father,

P.J. Towns, and other members, Henry Montford and Lee Montford. Annice's father sang with his father, George Towns, sometime around 1900. (George Towns was born approximately 1860.) There is no known family history of singing earlier than this. No documentation of family musical history exists except for a collection of convention songbooks. These books date back indefinitely and are not immediately accessible. They are packed away in boxes.

Both Larry and Kim attended Brewton Parker Junior College (Southern Baptist Convention), where they were active in musical organizations. Pianist Jean Williams is a recent graduate of Georgia Southern College, where she majored in music.

For musical materials the group use song collections, convention books, and sheet music.

Members of the group stated that they watch television more often they listen to radio. The radio station listened to most often is WVOP in Vidalia. Favorite television stations are WMAZ-TV in Macon, and WTOC-TV in Savannah. Both stations carry regular gospel programs.

Favorite recordings include albums by the Speer Family, the LeFevres, and Hovie Lister and the Statesmen Quartet.

The group has sung for funerals, church services, revivals, and homecomings. The quartet with whom Annice sings also performs special music for singing conventions. The trio has not done so.

Future plans are not specific. Annice would like to do more. The boys are indifferent. The group feels handicapped by the lack of a pianist.

Larry mentioned that his taste in gospel music differed from a lot of the gospel music performed over radio and television today. He prefers songs with piano accompaniment only, and much close harmony. He feels that the voices are the important thing and not extra instruments.

Annice and Kim appeared eager to sing. Larry had to be coaxed. He indicated that his voice was not responding well due to lack of practice. Kim stated that he was in good voice because he sang in the bathtub every night.

Songs performed for the researcher were "Heaven Will

327

Surely Be Worth It All," "Love Is Why," "Follow Me," "What A Day That Will Be," "I Thank My Savior For It All," "Do You Ever Think To Pray?" "Do You Know My Jesus?" "Love Is Why" with Jean playing the piano, and "In The House Of The Lord." The song chosen as the group's most representative selection was "Love Is Why" with Jean playing the piano.

(24) Wilcox County (August 9, 1975)

Celia Nutt Family

Celia Nutt (mother)—piano/alto
Mary (Nutt) Wood (daughter)—alto
Marlene (Nutt) Vaughan (daughter)—soprano
Joe Vaughan (Marlene's husband)—tenor

Celia can also play organ and sing any part. Both Mary and Marlene can exchange voice parts. Joe can play "some" guitar. Two occasional members of the group did not perform on the selection chosen to represent the group. Richard Nutt (son) can sing lead or bass. Stephan Wood (grandson) sometimes plays guitar or drums with the group.

Richard's children also perform as a family group.

This organization consists of:

Judy Nutt (mother)—piano
Sherri Nutt (daughter, age 11)-alto or soprano
Sondra Nutt (daughter, age 9)—soprano
Richie Nutt (son, age 6)—lead

Celia Nutt resides within the city limits of the community of Pitts. This town is located approximately fifteen miles west of Abbeville, the county seat. Other members of the group reside in various locations throughout the county. Celia attends the Pine City Holiness Baptist Church, located about two miles from Pitts. Mary's husband, Vaughan Wood, Jr., is pastor of this

Marlene and Joe Vaughan, Celia Nutt, and Mary Wood

Left to right: Sondra, Richie, Judy, and Sherri Nutt

church. Joe is pastor of the Bethany Holiness Baptist Church in Coffee County. Richard Nutt and family attend the Pleasant View Missionary Baptist Church, located near the northern border of Wilcox County.

The family group has been performing together since 1951. At that time Marlene was three, Margie (another daughter) was five, Mary was eight, and Richard was ten. Another family group was also begun at that time. This was the Pine City Junior Quartet, which included Richard, Mary, and two cousins, Jimmy and Benson Nutt. The latter group was regularly featured on a radio program. Marlene won a countywide talent contest at the age of three. She sang the gospel song "Satisfied."

Celia did not sing with her parents. Her mother had an uncle who taught singing school. This uncle taught Celia's mother. Celia did not begin playing the piano until after her husband was killed in an automobile accident. She went to one singing school at church, in 1951, then taught herself. Many nights when she couldn't sleep she would stay up and practice. Now she plays constantly. She is pianist for her church and is also pianist for the denominational camp meeting, held in Douglas, Georgia. Celia especially enjoys playing for camp meeting.

Publications used by the group include sheet music, convention songbooks published by Tennessee Music or Stamps-Baxter, and the *New Songs of Inspiration* series. Celia also subscribes to the gospel music periodical *The Singing News*.

Favorite songs include "How Great Thou Art" and "singing convention-type songs." The favorite recording of the group is one by the professional group the Inspirations. Very few recordings are owned but all of these are of gospel music. Celia does not have a record player now.

Several favorite radio stations were listed by members of the group. The "best" is said to be WCEH in Hawkinsville. This station is said to have general programming, including some gospel. Other favorite radio stations cited are WUFF in Eastman, WMTM in Cordele, and WFAV-FM in Cordele. Celia listens to the latter station while at work [occupation unstated]. Its programming is said to be general, with some gospel included.

Celia does not own a television set. She does not want one

because she feels it would hinder her practicing. She watches television when visiting in the homes of her children.

Celia recalled a past performance when the children were small. They had gone to a sing with another group, as their guests. The audience kept demanding that the Nutt family continue to perform.

Future plans are to continue "singing in the service of the Lord." Celia is proud that two of her sons-in-law are preachers. Sometimes the family goes to a church in Jacksonville, Florida where her sons-in-law alternate preaching and everyone in the family sings in a group to provide special music.

Songs performed for the researcher were "Just As Long As Eternity Rolls," "The Unseen Hand," "There Is A River" performed as a solo by Marlene, and "What A Lovely Name" performed as a duet by Sherri and Sondra. The song chosen as the group's most representative performance was "The Unseen Hand."

(25) Worth County (July 30, 1976)

"The Gene Johnson Gospel Singers"

Eugene Johnson (husband)—acoustic guitar/tenor
LaVerne Johnson (wife)—acoustic guitar/alto
Tony Johnson (son, age 19)—electric bass/lead
Lori Johnson (daughter, age 14)—lead

LaVerne most often sings lead. When LaVerne sings lead Eugene usually sings tenor, although Eugene can also sing lead. Tony usually sings a low harmony part. Lori can also sing tenor an octave high. Another son, Terry, formerly sang with the family. He left the group when he married, approximately a year ago.

The Johnsons reside within the city limits of Sylvester, the county seat. They attend the Riverside Holiness Baptist Church in Moultrie, approximately twenty-five miles distant.

Eugene works for Firestone Tire Company in Albany.

LaVerne and Lori Johnson

Lori and Eugene Johnson

Tony Johnson

LaVerne owns a clothing store in which she works three days a week. She also operates a tax and bookkeeping service from her home. Tony is employed by a local supermarket.

Eugene and LaVerne have similar family backgrounds. LaVerne, age forty-one, has been singing for thirty-five or more years. Her earliest memory is of singing. After supper her family would sit on the front porch and sing *a capella*. Of the ten children in the family, seven were girls. LaVerne's mother could read music but she taught the children to sing harmony by ear. All but three of the children learned to play guitar. LaVerne did not sing in public with her parents. However, when LaVerne was approximately twelve years old she and two sisters, aged fourteen and eight, formed a trio, the Hall Sisters. They sang in several churches. The older of these sisters, Vernelle Bates, is now with a ladies trio, the Evangelettes, in Moultrie. LaVerne's older brother, Denvill Hall, with his wife and three daughters, comprise the group Sounds of Victory, also in Moultrie. LaVerne's younger sister, with her three sons, are now the Thompson Family and perform Bluegrass gospel in Grand Ridge, Florida.

Eugene also comes from a family of ten children. Nine of these children were boys. All but two learned to play guitar. Eugene's father played guitar for dances. At the age of eight or ten Eugene began playing guitar with his father at these "frolics." Later, Eugene sang with his brothers in a group called the Johnson Brothers. One of Eugene's brothers, with his wife and daughters, now comprise the Fulton Johnson Gospel Singers in Albany. Another brother, Medford Johnson, sings in a trio with his wife and his church pastor, also in Albany. Medford's two oldest children play instrumental accompaniment for this trio.

Eugene and LaVerne met when he was seventeen and she was sixteen. Eugene soon began singing with the girls' group. This quartet often sang with Jim and Jesse and the Virginia Boys, performing the gospel music portion of the country group's Saturday night radio program.

Eugene and LaVerne were married when he was twenty and she was nineteen. Music brought them together after a lover's quarrel. While dating, they had had an argument and agreed to break-up. Unknowingly, a close friend asked the performing group to sing for her mother's funeral. They could not bring themselves to refuse their close friend, therefore the couple was forced to reunite. They were married shortly thereafter.

The quartet was reduced to a trio when one of LaVerne's sisters married and moved away. The Johnson's sons began singing with the group when Terry was eleven and Tony was nine. [Apparently the other sister also left the group at an unspecified time.] When Terry left the group, recently, Lori took his place.

The family group has sung "all over Georgia, quite a bit in Florida, and some in Texas and Alabama." They sang several times for a television program in Florida. They have also sung over the radio "off-and-on for twenty years." Until recently the group was scheduled some place almost every weekend. Tony's job at the supermarket now restricts their travel. Also, Eugene stated that the years of extensive travel "tells on you." Engagments now are usually limited to singing for church homecomings on Sundays. Other requests are turned down.

The Johnson family learn all of their songs by ear from listening to recordings. They do not own any printed music. They listen to the all-gospel format radio station in Moultrie. If a song is heard that they like, they try to find the recording in a store. If the record can not be found they call the radio station for information. The record is played several times and the group picks a key that suits their voices. They do not perform the song exactly as played on the recording. According to LaVerne, "We straighten out the curves to suit us." LaVerne considers herself "a nut for harmony."

The group has no real favorite song. "Gospel music is all we've ever sung." Favorite songs vary with personal mood. Various statements made include, "Music is sort of burning inside you—it has to come out—it comes out as feeling." "When I'm depressed I sing songs of encouragement. The words stick with me. When I'm happy I sing a different kind of song. A person could tell what kind of mood I'm in by what I'm singing."

The Johnsons watch the television program "Gospel Singing Jubilee" on Sunday mornings. Of the groups featured on this program they currently like the Hinson Family the best. Favorite groups "come and go." Another favorite group is the Inspirations. Tony enjoys watching and listening to the bass players. (The Thompson Family taught him how to play bass. He often practices in the bathroom for hours at a time.)

Future plans are indefinite. Eugene wants to continue singing but to cut down on traveling. Tony has begun playing bass for a gospel group, Sounds of Maranatha, in Albany. He would go with a professional group if requested—"but not for the money, for the enjoyment."

The Johnson family considers itself a "Country Gospel" performing group. Songs performed for the researcher were "Glory Road," "I Came on Business for the King," "I'll Be Alright When I Touch Calvary," "In The Beginning," "I Have Hope," and "I'm So Glad He Found Me" [title as stated by the group]. The song chosen as the group's most representative performance was "I'm So Glad He Found Me." The accurate title of this song is "Jesus Found Me."

(1) Bibb County

Oh What A Love

Words and Music by
DAVID REECE

1. Now that I know my new Mas-ter, (new Mas-ter,) Now that old things are be-hind;(things be-hind;) He has for-giv-en and blessed me, (He blessed me,) Now I have found peace of mind, (of mind.)
2. Giv-ing His life to re-deem me, (re-deem me,) Hold-ing my hand day by day; (day by day;) Giv-ing me hope for 'o-mor-row, (to-mor-row,) Hear-ing each time I pray, (I pray.)

CHORUS

Oh, what a love that He gave me, gave, He gave me,

(2) Brantley County
The Lighthouse

Words & Music
Ronnie Hinson

1. There's a light - house on the hill - side that o - ver -
2. Ev - 'ry - bod - y that lives a - bout us says, tear that

looks life's sea, When I'm tossed it sends out a
light - house down, The big ships don't sail this way an - y

light, - - - - that I might see; And the
more, there's no use of it stand - ing 'round; Then my

light that shines in dark - ness, now will safe - ly lead us o'er,
mind goes back to that storm - y night, when just in time I saw the light.

If it was - n't for the light - house, my ship would
Yes, the light from that old light - house that stands up

338

be no more. And I thank God for the light - house,
there on the hill.

I owe my life to Him, For Je - sus is the light - house,

and from the rocks of sin; He has shone a light a -

round me that I could clear - ly see, If it

was - n't for the light - house, tell me, where would this ship be?

The Lighthouse - - 2

Where We'll Never Grow Old

J. C. M.

Jas. C. Moore

1. I have heard of a land on the far a-way strand, 'Tis a beau-ti-ful
2. In that beau-ti-ful home where we'll never-more roam, We shall be in the
3. When our work here is done and the life-crown is won, And our troubles and

home of the soul; Built by Je-sus on high, there we nev-er shall die,
sweet by and by; Hap-py praise to the King thru e-ter-ni-ty sing,
tri-als are o'er; All our sor-rows will end and our voic-es will blend,

CHORUS

'Tis a land where we nev-er grow old. Nev-er grow old,
'Tis a land where we nev-er shall die.
With the loved ones who've gone on be-fore.

Where we'll

Nev-er grow old, In a land where we'll nev-er grow old; Nev-er grow

old, nev-er grow old, In a land where we'll nev-er grow old.

Where we'll

340

(4) Charlton County

Help Me Lord, to Stand

B. F.

Byron Faust

1. Help me oh, Lord, to do Thy will, hum-bly now I pray, Help me, to
2. Help me when I am prone to stray from Thy bless-ed fold, Help me to
3. Help me to walk the nar-row road, Lord, I hum-bly pray, Help me to

Thee, my serv-ice give, all a-long my way; That I, oh, Lord, may
walk in Thine own way, to the gates of gold; And when I'm bur-dened
bear some oth-ers load, struggling in the way; Help me to build up-

live for Thee, do Thy blest command, When try-ing moments come to me,
down with care, hold me by Thy hand, And when my load is hard to bear,
on the Rock, not up-on the sand, And when shall come the tempest shock,

CHORUS.

help me Lord to stand. Help me, oh, Lord, to stand each
Help me, oh, Lord, to stand each

shock, That comes a-long my way;
tem-pest shock, That comes a-long my way, a-long my way;

Help Me Lord, to Stand

Help me to stand up-on the rock,
Help me to stand up-on the sol-id Rock,

And live for Thee each day. Be Thou
And live for Thee each day, for Thee each day. Be Thou my

my guid-ing Star, my guid-ing Star, And hold me by Thy
guid - ing Star, And hold me by Thy

hand, yes, by Thy hand; And when I face the judg - ment
hand; And when I face the judgment,

bar, Help me, oh, Lord, to stand.
judgment bar, Help me, oh, Lord, to stand, to brave-ly stand.

Lord, I Want to Be a Christian

Words and tune I WANT TO BE A CHRISTIAN, Traditional Negro Spiritual; adapted, John W. Work, Jr., and Frederick J. Work, 1907.

(6) Chattahoochee County

No Data Available

Walking the Sea

Words & Music by
Ernest Rippetoe

1. Out up - on Gal - i - lee one night, An - gry waves dashed in
2. Vain - ly they strove to right the wrong There where the fu - ry
3. Trou - bles some times may round you roll While on your voy - age

mad - 'ning height, As the dis - ci - ples sailed in fright,
was so strong Hop - ing up - on the shore ere long
to the goal, Just as they did in days of old

O - ver the deep; Row - ing a - gainst con - tra - ry
Safe - ly to be; Je - sus they saw while there, dis-
On Gal - i - lee, Faith - ful - ly strive your bark to

wind, Know - ing not what might be the end, Je - sus came,
mayed, Him un - to whom they looked for aid, Say - ing: "'Tis
guide, Know - ing thru storm you'll safe - ly ride, Je - sus is

He their dear - est friend,
I, be not a - fraid," Walk - ing the sea!
ev - er at your side,

345

Walk - ing the sea,

Walk - ing the storm - y sea,

Walk - ing the sea,

Walk - ing the roll - ing sea,

Je - sus at night came un - to them Walk - ing the sea;

yes, walk - ing the sea;

Walk - ing the sea,

Walk - ing the storm - y sea,

Walk - ing the sea,

Walk - ing the roll - ing sea,

Je - sus at night came un - to them Walk - ing the sea.

yes, walk - ing the sea.

Walking The Sea - 2

346

Through Faith, I Still Believe

Words & Music
James McFall

347

hap - pened just like the Bi - ble said, That a low - ly man named

Je - sus healed the sick and raised the dead; Made the lame to

walk, the dumb to talk, and caused the blind

to see, I was - n't there, but through faith, I still be - lieve.

Through Faith, I Still Believe--2

I'll Soon Be Gone

Words & Music
Joel Hemphill

1. We're liv - ing in per - il - ous times, each day brings new dis - tress.
2. Well, soon the crum-bling works of man must all be count - ed loss,

But God has told us in His Word to pray and do our best;
And those who built up - on the sand must pay the aw - ful cost;

To keep our lamps all trimmed and bright, our wed - ding gar - ments on.
So why not kneel and pray to - day, the Spir - it leads you on.

And some - thing mov - ing in my soul says, "Child, you'll soon be gone."
Then, with the saved, you, too, can say, thank God, I'll soon be gone.

CHORUS

I'll soon be gone from this old world be-low,
I know I'll soon be gone
Yes, I know I'll be gone from this old world be-low,
I'll soon be

To heav - en's throne e - ter - nal joys to know;
Heav - en's throne, shin - ing throne, ev - er know;

So with - out fear, I'll wait to hear the an - gel's trum - pet's tone,

And on that day I'll soar a - way, Oh, yes I'll soon be gone.
Oh, yes, I'll soon be gone.
I'll soon be gone.

I'll Soon Be Gone - - 2

Jesus, Savior, Pilot Me

Edward Hopper

J. E. Gould

1. Je - sus, Sav - ior, pi - lot me O - ver life's tem - pes - tuous sea;
2. As a moth - er stills her child, Thou canst hush the o - cean wild;
3. When at last I near the shore, And the fear - ful break - ers roar

D.C.—Chart and com - pass came from Thee, Je - sus, Sav - ior, pi - lot me.
D.C.—Won-drous Sov-'reign of the sea, Je - sus, Sav - ior, pi - lot me.
D.C.—May I hear Thee say to me, "Fear not, I will pi - lot Thee."

Unknown waves be - fore me roll, Hid-ing rocks and treach'rous shoal;
Boist'rous waves o - bey Thy will When Thou say'st to them, "Be still"
'Twixt me and the peace-ful rest, Then, while lean-ing on Thy breast,

351

Had It Not Been

Words and Music
Rusty Goodman

1. – Just sup - pose God searched through Heav - en, He could - n't find one will - ing to be; The su - preme sac - ri - fice that was need - ed, That would buy e - ter - nal life

2. But, I'm so glad He was will - ing to drink His bit - ter cup, Al - though He prayed, "Fa - ther, let it pass from Me; Oh, I'm so glad He did - n't call Heav - en's an - gels, "From my hands pull the nails

352

CHORUS

G G9 G7 C

for you and me. Oh! HAD IT NOT BEEN for a place called Mount
that tor - ment me. Oh!

G

Cal - v'ry, HAD IT NOT BEEN for the old rug - ed

D G7 3 C

cross; HAD IT NOT BEEN for a Man called Je -

G D7 C G

sus, Then for - ev - er my soul would be lost .

Had It Not Been - 2   Harmony
Jimi Hall

Sweet, Sweet Spirit

Words and Music by
DORIS AKERS

1. There's a sweet, sweet Spir-it in this place, _____ and I
   know that it's the Spir-it of ____ the Lord. _____ There are
   sweet ex-press-ions on each face, _____ and I

(2. There are) bless - ings you can - not re - ceive _____ till you
   know Him in His full - ness, and ____ be - lieve. _____ You're the
   one to pro - fit when you say, _____ "I am

(3. If you) say He saved you from your sin, _____ now you're
   weak, you're bound, and can - not en - ter in, _____ you can
   make it right if you will yield; _____ you'll en -

Sweet, Sweet Spirit-2

355

Heaven Came Down and Glory Filled My Soul

J. W. P.

John W. Peterson

1. O what a won-der-ful, won-der-ful day— Day I will nev-er for-get;
2. Born of the Spir-it with life from a-bove In-to God's fam-'ly di-vine,
3. Now I've a hope that will sure-ly en-dure Aft-er the pass-ing of time;

Aft-er I'd wan-dered in dark-ness a-way, Je-sus my Sav-ior I met.
Jus-ti-fied ful-ly thru Cal-va-ry's love, O what a stand-ing is mine!
I have a fu-ture in heav-en for sure, There in those man-sions sub-lime.

O what a ten-der, com-pas-sion-ate friend— He met the need of my heart;
And the trans-ac-tion so quick-ly was made When as a sin-ner I came,
And it's be-cause of that won-der-ful day When at the cross I be-lieved;

Shad-ows dis-pel-ling, With joy I am tell-ing, He made all the dark-ness de-part!
Took of the of-fer Of grace He did prof-fer— He saved me, O praise His dear name!
Rich-es e-ter-nal And bless-ings su-per-nal From His pre-cious hand I re-ceived.

Used by Permission

356

Reach Out To Jesus

Words & Music by
Ralph Carmichael

1. Is your bur - den hea - vy as you bear it all a - lone?
2. Is the life you're liv - ing filled with sor - row and des - pair?

Does the road you trav - el har - bor dan - ger yet un - known?
Does the fu - ture press you with its wor - ry and its care?

Are you grow - ing wea - ry in the strug-gle of it all?
Are you tired and friend-less, Have you al - most lost your way?

Je - sus will help you when on His name you call.
Je - sus will help you just come to Him to - day.

TOURING THAT CITY

Words & Music by
Harold Lane

1. Man-y times I have won-dered 'bout the sights of that cit-y, and__ all that my
2. Here on earth we have trou-bles that to us seem so heav-y, but in Heav-en no

eyes shall be-hold;____ I will see all the won-ders when I
one will be sad;____ Mom and Dad will be sing-ing, Heav-en's

en-ter that cit-y there for-ev-er to be safe in His fold.____
praise will be ring-ing for the dear-est Friend I ev-er had.____

CHORUS

Some morn-ing you'll find me tour-ing that cit-y, where the Son of God is the

Light,_____ You'll find me there on the streets_ so pret-ty, made of gold_ so pure and so bright;_ With Je - sus, the One, Who gave me the vic - t'ry, Who_ led me a - cross the di - vide,_____ Some morn - ing you'll find me tour - ing that cit - y, where with Him I will ev - er a - bide._

Touring That City - 2

(16) Miller County

Love, Like The Love of God

Words and Music by
DAVID INGLES

1. Be there a man who would give his son to die on a cru-el tree? ____
2. I stand in awe each ____ break of morn to in His ____ pres-ence be,
3. When at the end you will need a friend to guide you ____ safe-ly o'er, ____

And be there a man who would reach down his hand to re-deem and watch
Can I a ____ mor-tal soul be filled with such love and com-
There's on-ly ____ one and He gave His own son and His love lasts for-

o- ver me. ____
pas-sion as He. ____ Oh for a love like the one up a-bove,
ev- er more. ____

CHORUS

Oh! ____ for the love ____ of God: ____ Search-ing, pray - ing,

long - ing for ____ a love ____ like the love ____ of God. ____

Published by LeFevre-Sing Publishing Company, Atlanta, Ga.

(17) Montgomery County

What A Beautiful Day
(FOR THE LORD TO COME AGAIN)

Words by Aaron Wilburn

Music by Eddie Crook

1. As I wake up with the morn - ing of each day that pass - es by,
2. All my earth - ly dis - ap - point - ments and my tri - als here be - low,

And I lis - ten to the sounds — up - on my ear;
Fade a - way when I re - mem - ber His last words;

I can't help but keep a watch to - ward the east - ern sky,
He said He'd re - turn and re - ceive His chil - dren un - to Him,

And I won - der if the trum - pet will be the next sound that I hear.
And I'm long - ing to look up - on the face of my Lord.

What A Beautiful Day (For The Lord To Come Again)—2

CHORUS

What a beau - ti - ful day for the Lord to come a -gain,

What a beau - ti - ful day for Him to take His chil - dren home;

Melody in alto . . . .

Oh, how I long to see His face and to touch His nail-scarred hand,

What a beau - ti - ful day for the Lord to come a - gain!

364

Ten Thousand Years

E. C.

Elmer Cole

1. Soon I'll come to the end of my jour-ney, And I'll meet the
2. We will just be-gin to sing love's sweet sto - ry, It's a song

one who gave His life for me: I will thank Him for the love
that the an-gels can-not sing: "I'm re-deemed by the blood

that He gave me, And ten thou-sand years or more I'll reign with
of the Sav-ior", And ten thou-sand years or more I'll praise His

CHORUS

Him. Ten thousand years we'll just be started, ten thou-sand
name.

years we've just be-gun: The bat-tle's o-ver and the

vic-t'ry's been won ten thou-sand years and we've just be - gun.

(19) Pulaski County

DADDY SANG BASS

Words and Music
Carl Perkins

1. I re - mem - ber when I was a lad, times were hard and things were bad;
2. I re - mem - ber af - ter work, ma - ma would call in all of us;

But there's a sil - ver lin - ing be - hind ev - 'ry cloud. Just poor
You could - hear us sing - in' for a coun - try mile. Now, lit - tle

peo - ple. that's all we were, try'n' to make a liv - in' out of black land dirt;
broth - er has done gone on, - but I'll re - join him in a song;

We'd get to - geth - er in a fam - 'ly cir - cle sing - in' loud.
We'll be to - geth - er a - gain up yon - der in a lit - tle while.

CHORUS

me and lit - tle broth - er would join right in there;
ma - ma sang ten - or
Dad - dy sang bass,

Daddy Sang Bass - 2

(20) Quitman County

No Data Available

(21) Upson County

I Won't Walk Without Jesus

Words and Music by
RONNY HINSON

1. Used to be when I was sin-nin', Satan stood off some-where grin-nin' as the pleas-ures that he brought just turned on me. Tear drops came like rain a fall-in' 'till I heard my Sav-ior cal-lin'. "If you can't go on an-y-more just lean on Me."

2. (A beg-gar) lame at the gate was sit-tin', And all his life he'd been re-gret-tin'. 'Cause he'd nev-er stood or took a stroll on down the street. Then Pe-ter and John hap-pened by his way. "Look up-on us." ole Pe-ter did say. "Rise up and walk in the name of the Lord," and he leaped to his feet.

CHORUS:

And I won't walk with-out Je-sus. I won't talk with-out Je-sus. And I re-fuse to live one day ___ as be-fore. ___ No, I won't go without Je-sus. It just ain't so with-out Je-sus. 'Cause ev-'ry-thing that I would do, it just won't do ___ without the Lord. ___ 2. A beg-gar Lord. ___

I WON'T WALK WITHOUT JESUS - 2

(22) Wayne County

At the Crossing

M. L.

Mosie Lister

1. There's a riv-er some-where that's called Jor-dan, And they say that it's deep and it's wide; And they say that the king and the beg-gar On that shore will stand side by side.

2. Though the riv-er is dark and stor-my, It will pass like a dream in the night; And my soul will a-wake in the morn-ing In re-gions of end-less de-light.

CHORUS

At the cross-ing of the Jor-dan, Why should I be a-fraid? There'll be Some-one there who loves me to guide me 'cross the riv-er To end-less joys a-bove.

(23) Wheeler County

Love Is Why

W. F. (Bill) Lakey
V. B. (Vep) Ellis

David Ellis
V. B. (Vep) Ellis

1. He nev-er said I'd have sil-ver or gold, Yet He has prom-ised me
2. I was a-stray full of sin with its shame, There was no peace with-in,
3. Tho' I have none of this world's precious goods, Yet I'm an heir to all

rich-es un-told; He nev-er suffered a life with-out care, Yet He re-
I was to blame; Tho' un-de-serv-ing, My life so de-filed, Now to my
Heav-en af-fords; Tho' I may nev-er a-chieve earth-ly fame, Yet all of

CHORUS

lieves ev'-ry bur-den I bear.
God I have been rec-on-ciled.   Sin stained the Cross with the blood of my Lord,
Heav-en can call me by name.

Yet He per-mit-ted it with-out a word; Why, tell me why He re-

Rit. . . . .

deemed you and me? Love is why you and I   are   free.

Used by Permission

372

The Unseen Hand

A. J. S.   Owned by Author   A. J. Sims

1. There is an un-seen hand to me, That leads thru ways I can-not see;
2. His hand has led thru shad-ows drear, And while it leads I have no fear;
3. I long to see my Sav-ior's face And sing the sto-ry "Saved by Grace"

While go-ing thru this world of woe, This hand still leads me as I go.
I know 'twill lead me to that home, Where sin nor sor-row e'er can come.
And there up-on that Gold-en Strand, I'll praise Him for His guid-ing hand.

Chorus

I'm trusting to the unseen hand, That guides me thru this weary land;
And some sweet day I'll reach that strand, Still guided by the (Omit) un-seen hand,

(25) Worth County
Jesus Found Me

Words and Music by
Adger M. Pace

1. I was on the moun - tain, wan - d'ring from the foun - tain,
2. I will love Him ev - er, part from Him, no, nev - er,

When I heard my Sav - ior speak to me;
He's the tru - est friend I ev - er knew;

Come to me re - lent - ing, of your sins re - pent - ing,
When I see Him yon - der, love will still grow fond - er

I will lead you out where you can see. .
In that hap - py land be - yond the blue.

CHORUS

And I'm so glad He found me, in love un - bound me,

Jesus Found Me—2

with arms a-round me, Led me to the

shel - ter, now I'm one of His fold;

And, O, the joy of know - ing, with heart o'er - flow - ing.

some - day I'm go - ing To my home in

glo - ry and walk on streets paved with gold.

Appendix B

Constitutions and By-laws

SOUTH GEORGIA SACRED HARP SINGING CONVENTION

1. The Officers of this Convention must consist of a President, Vice-President, and Secretary and Treasurer.
2. The duties of the President are to preside at all meetings and to require good order, appoint committees, and put all questions before the Convention which are properly moved and carried.
3. The duties of the Vice-President are to preside during the absence of the President.
4. The duties of the Secretary and Treasurer are to keep a record of all business transated by the Convention and receive all money collected and attend to the printing of the Minutes.
5. The duties of the various committees appointed by the President are to serve in the capacity appointed and to give their full attention and support.
6. The Officers of this Convention shall be elected annually.
7. This Convention will be opened at each session by a song, followed by prayer.
8. All leaders and singers of the Sacred Harp shall be priviledged to participate in this Convention under rules and regulations adopted by the Convention.
9. The text books of this Convention shall be none other than the Sacred Harp.
10. No distintion will be made in the various recent revisors of the original Sacred Harp.

RULES AND REGULATIONS OF THE CONVENTION

1. All motions made and seconded shall be put to the body unless withdrawn by the mover.
2. All persons wishing to speak on any subject shall arise and address the President.
3. No person shall speak more than once on any subject without first getting permission from the President.
4. The President shall not have the power to vote unless in case of a tie. Then he shall have the power to cast his vote.
5. The President, wishing to speak before the Convention on any subject. shall appoint some one temporary President, if the Vice-President is absent.

MONEY RECEIVED AND EXPENDITURES OF THE CONVENTION

Balance in Bank	$175.93
Public Collection for Minutes	137.00
Donation	50.00
Balance in Bank	412.93
Food for Convention	160.00
Balance	252.93
Paid Ham Printing C.., for printing Minutes	76.50
Georgia Sales Tax	2.30
Mailing Expense	25.00
Balance in Bank	149.13
Paid for 30 Denson Books	105.00
Balance in Bank	44.13

BY-LAWS

GEORGIA STATE SINGING CONVENTION

ARTICLE I. NAME

The name of this organization shall be the Georgia State Singing Convention.

ARTICLE II. OBJECTS

The objects of this organization shall be:

(a) To form a state convention, composed of all of the regular singing conventions or societies in the several counties of the State of Georgia.

(b) To bring together the members of the convention or socities once a year for the purpose of creating a closer relation of good fellowship, a better understanding among men, a greater love and interest in the study of music and gospel singing, and to inspire men and glorify God.

(c) To teach that organization, cooperation and reciprocity are better than rivalry, strife and destructive competition.

ARTICLE III. MEMBERSHIP

Sec. 1. Membership of this organization shall be composed of delegates elected or appointed by a regular county singing convention or society of Georgia.

Sec. 2. Each county in the State shall be entitled to a minimum of three delegates. A county having two separate singing conventions or societies shall be entitled to not more than five delegates from the entire county.

Sec. 3. All past Presidents of the State Convention shall be considered delegates-at-large and shall not reduce the number of regular delegates from his particular county.

Sec. 4. Registration fee of $5.00 per delegate shall be paid by each county convention or society before such delegate shall be seated in the business session.

Sec. 5. Registration fee of $5.00 shall be paid by each Past President before he shall be seated in the business session.

Sec. 6. All delegates so seated and officers, with the exception of members of Supreme Council, shall have equal vote on all matters.

ARTICLE IV. OFFICERS

Sec. 1. The officers shall be a President, a 1st Vice-President, a 2nd Vice-President, a Secretary, a Treasurer, a Chaplain, and a Supreme Council, composed of three Past Presidents of the State Convention.

Sec. 2. All officers shall be elected each year.

Sec. 3. No officer shall serve more than one term in succession in the same capacity. (Sec. 3, Article IV, deleted by unanimous vote of Convention 10-12-59.)

Sec. 4. The officers, preferably, shall be elected from the vicinity in which the next Convention will be held.

Sec. 5. Delegates shall elect the officers for the ensuing year at the regular annual business session, by a majority vote of those present, after recommendations have been presented by the Executive Committee, provided the location for the next Convention has been agreed upon. If such location has not been decided, the Executive Committee shall have the power to elect the officers when the location has been agreed upon.

Sec. 6. Duties of the President are to: (a) preside at the State Convention; (b) enforce impartially the by-laws of the Convention; (c) appoint an Executive Committee, with a minimum of seven members, and such other committees and aides as are necessary to carry on the ordinary functions of the Convention; (d) fill any vacancy occurring in any office; (e) call special meetings, with the consent of the Executive Committee; and (f) finance the Convention in any fair and reasonable manner.

Sec. 7. Duties of the 1st Vice-President are to: (a) preside in the absence of the President; and (b) assist the President in his other duties.

Sec. 8. Duties of the 2nd Vice-President are to: (a) preside in the absence of both the President and 1st Vice-President; and (b) assist the President in his other duties.

Sec. 9. Duties of the Secretary are to: (a) keep a fair and impartial record of the proceedings; (b) read the Minutes and other communications at the regular business session; (c) handle all correspondence; (d) forward the Minutes, a copy of the by-laws and other records to the newly elected Secretary within 60 days after the annual session; and (e) furnish a copy of the by-laws to any county convention requesting same upon payment of $1.00 to defray cost.

Sec. 10. Duties of the Treasurer are to: (a) Keep an accurate record of all funds received and disbursed; (b) collect all dues; (c) disburse funds upon proper authority; (d) make a financial report to the regular business session; and (e) forward a copy of the by-laws to the newly elected Treasurer within 60 days after the annual session.

Sec. 11. Duties of the Chaplain are to open and close the meetings with prayer.

Sec. 12. Duties of the Supreme Council are to: (a) serve as a Standing Committee on the interpretation of the by-laws; (b) settle any question as to the seating of a delegate or any other question presented by the delegates; (c) remove, after suitable warning, any officer or member of the Executive Committee who fails to execute his duties satisfactorily to the Supreme Council; and (d) locate the place for the next Convention, if no place is agreed upon by the Executive Committee and the majority of the delegates present.

Sec. 13. The Executive Committee, appointed by the President, shall: (a) make recommendations of new officers; (b) select the Supreme Council; (c) select delegates to the National Convention; (d) serve as Program Committee; (e) authorize disbursement of funds; and (f) select the location for the next Convention, with approval of majority of delegates present.

ARTICLE V. MEETINGS

Sec. 1. Regular annual session of the Convention shall meet on the second Sunday in October and on the Saturday before.

Sec. 2. Regular annual business session of the Convention shall meet immediately following Saturday afternoon session or immediately preceding Saturday evening session.

Sec. 3. The Convention shall not be held in any county twice consecutively, unless in an emergency or with the consent of the majority of delegates present.

Sec. 4. Special meetings may be called by the President, with the consent of the Executive Committee, at such times and places as may seem advisable.

Sec. 5. A majority of delegates present shall constitute a quorum.

Sec. 6. Any unoffensive manner may be used to express appreciation of singers and audience; no musical instrument is barred. Any "clowning," mock-shouting or other unchristianlike acts or manners of interpretation of gospel songs shall be caused to cease immediately by the President.

Sec. 7. This Convention shall not endorse the use of any particular song book in preference to another, nor discriminate against any gospel publication in any way.

Sec. 8. This Convention shall not endorse any political organization or action.

ARTICLE VI. MANUAL

The rules contained in Demeter's Manual or Parliamentary Law and Procedure shall govern in all cases to which they are applicable, and in which they are not inconsistent with the by-laws.

ARTICLE VII. AMENDMENTS

Sec. 1. These by-laws may be amended by a majority of those present at any regular session of the Convention.

Sec. 2. Amended by-laws go into effect immediately upon adoption.
Adopted this 12th day of October, 1959.

E. W. OVERSTREET, Secretary

Note: The above by-laws were formulated and adopted as of 10-12-59 by the Georgia State Singing Convention, after having been drawn up for approval and recommended by the following: 1958 Officers and Executive Committee.
Above by-laws were read to the Convention on October 12, 1958, by E. W. Overstreet, Secretary.

381

CONSTITUTION AND BYLAWS OF THE NATIONAL GOSPEL SINGING CONVENTION

Organized in 1936
From Revised Copy

Article 1. Name

The name of the organization shall be THE NATIONAL GOSPEL SINGING CONVENTION for the promotion of GOSPEL SINGING.

Article 2. Object

The object of this convention shall be to promote GOSPEL SINGING in a spiritual way throughout the USA and no other kind of songs and singing shall be permitted. All "clowning" mock-shouting, or any other un-christian acts and manners of interpretation of GOSPEL songs shall not be permitted; and should any singer or group of singers violate this rule it shall be the duty of the chair to interrupt such violation and enforce this rule then and there. All special singers shall also be expected to sing in the grand chorus.

Article 3. Members

Members of this convention shall be the publishers of GOSPEL songbooks in the USA, and one State Convention from each state in the USA. Each publisher of Gospel songbooks shall have a right to send one voting delegate or the equivalent thereof to this convention, and each state convention shall have a right to send three voting delegates which shall include the outgoing president of said state convention and two others appointed by him. Each past president of the National Singing Convention shall also be an honorary delegate for life and shall have one full vote at each regular business session. All these delegates shall be called directors and shall have full control of the affairs of the convention, including the election of its various officers, etc.

Article 4. Officers

The officers of this convention shall be a president, a vice-president, a secretary and a treasurer (the Secretary and treasurer may be one and the same if so desired by the directors) elected in any way the directors may desire at each annual meeting of the convention. The officers shall assume office at the first regular meeting following their election and shall serve for a period of one year or until their successors are elected and seated. A vacancy in any office may be filled at any regular meeting for the remainder of the term by the directors.

Article 5. Committees

There shall be but one standing committee, and this shall be the program committee, composed of the directors as stated before, one from each publisher. There shall be a committee of ushers, composed of as many as may be needed, and as many other committees as from time to time may seem necessary.

Article 6. Supreme Council

There shall be a supreme council composed of members, one each from the various publishers of Gospel songbooks in the USA, and all questions shall be subject to the approval or disapproval of this body, and their decision shall be final.

Article 7. Meetings

There shall be but one regular meeting each year, and this shall begin at 1:00 p.m. on Saturday before the third Sunday in November, and continue through Saturday night and Sunday of the third Sunday in November. Special meetings may be called by the president with the consent of the directors at such time and place as may seem advisable to the directors

Article 8. Dues

Each publisher represented in the convention shall be required to pay twenty-five dollars ($25.00) dues at each annual session of the convention, and each state convention represented shall be required to pay forty-five dollars ($45.00) dues at each annual session. These dues are to be paid to the treasurer of this convention on or before the date of the business session of the directors to be held on Saturday p.m. before the third Sunday in November. The change of the amount of dues was voted in at the Pass Convention in 1972.

Article 9. Amendments

Proposed amendments to this consitution must be presented in writing at a regular meeting, read by the secretary at such meeting and left on the table until the next regular meeting, when a vote on such amendment or amendments shall be taken. If two-thirds of the members present at the regular meeting vote in favor of such amendement or amendments, this constitution shall be amended.

No selling of books shall be allowed in the convention hall while the convention is in session. But publishers, if they so desire may sell books during the noon recess or prior to the opening of the sessions or the closing of the same.

ORDER OF BUSINESS

Prayer
Roll call of Publishers.
Reading of Minutes of preceding meeting.
Receipt of communications, bills, etc.
Report of committees.
Unfinished business.
New business.
Selection of next meeting place.
Election of officers for next year.
Adjournment.

Bylaws

Article 1. Quorum

Three directors present shall consitute a quorum. All directors shall be expected to be registered and present at the opening of the business session to be held not later than 3:00 p.m. Saturday before the third Sunday in November.

Article 2. Rights and Duties of Members

Each publisher member shall be accorded equal showing in the convention, but to be represented on the floor of the convention in order, he must have at least three different leaders or three different groups of singers. The same singer or singers shall not be permitted to occupy the floor twice in successive order. In other words, if only one representative of a publisher be present, he or she must take his or her third turn around and the number of encores each singer or singers shall have shall be determined by the audience, at the discretion of the directors. Each publisher must give to the secretary ahead of time the name of his singer or singers to appear in order on the floor so that the secretary may register them in proper order, thus enabling the president to eliminate all unnecessary loss of time in making introductions. The program committee shall at all times, as the program progresses, see that no two special singers or two groups of special singers shall immediately succeed each other without one or more intervening chorus numbers, unless such cannot be avoided. Personal introductions of special singers shall not be permitted by any one unless called for by the chair. Delegates to the NATIONAL GOSPEL SINGING CONVENTION from each state with invitations for the convention must have an organized State Convention or a convention where congregational singing predominates. (The last item voted in at the 1966 Convention.)

Each Publishing Company shall be furnished three hotel or motel rooms if needed. (It is customary for the host of the Convention to furnish lodging on Saturday night only for the delegates and wives, publishers, and past presidents and their wives.) Also the officers of the convention if not convenient for them to return to their homes.

Article 3. Books

Each publisher must have plenty of his books to supply each singer in the great chorus in order to be represented in the convention.

Article 4. Finance

A finance committee shall be appointed by the president to canvass the convention cities to secure money to be used to defray the expenses of the convention.

Article 5. Location

The convention shall not be held in any city or town twice consecutively unless in an emergency or with the unanimous consent of the directors.

Article 6. Powers and Duties of Officers

THE PRESIDENT: The president shall occupy the chair at all meetings, preserve order, decide all questions of order (unless an appeal is made to the directors), state and put all questions, announce the result of all votes, introduce all singers and groups of singers appearing on the program as given them by the secretary, thus eliminating loss of time for groups to make their own introductions.

THE VICE-PRESIDENT: The vice-president shall assist the president in his duties and occupy the chair in his absence.

THE SECRETARY-TREASURER: The secretary-treasurer shall keep a record of all business affairs of the convention, see that all publishers are properly registered, furnish the president with the name of the singer or singers, and also furnish him with the names of publishers as they come in alphabetical order. He shall have charge of all money belonging to the convention and keep a correct record of same, and pay it out only upon the proper authority of the directors. It shall be his duty also to write all publishers of sacred songbooks anywhere in the United State, inviting them to attend and cooperate with this convention in its aims and ideals.

It was voted at the 1966 convention to "Establish a permanent file and library for the National Singing Convention at Gospel Singers of America, Inc."

PRAYER
All Read

Our living, loving God in Heaven—
Keep us humble
Keep us thankful
Help us to serve
Thee and our
fellow man.
Amen.

Appendix C

Gospel Music Association

CONSTITUTION

OF

GOSPEL MUSIC ASSOCIATION

ARTICLE I

Name and Purpose

Section 1. The organization shall be called the Gospel Music Association, Inc.

Section 2. The purpose of the Gospel Music Association, which is a non-profit organization, shall be to foster interest among the general public in gospel music and to further the spreading of the Gospel of Jesus Christ on earth.

Section 3. The organization shall be incorporated under the laws of the State of Tennessee under the name and style of Gospel Music Association, Inc.

Section 4. The officers of the corporation shall be the same as the officers of the Association, and the Board of Directors of the Association shall be the Directors of the corporation. The By-Laws of the Association shall be the By-Laws of the corporation.

ARTICLE II

Officers and Board of Directors

Section 1. The officers shall be a President, and Executive Vice-President, and such other Vice-Presidents as the Board of Directors may, from time to time, elect, and a Secretary and a Treasurer.

Section 2. The Board shall consist of individuals, none of whom may be officers, and such Trustees as are from time to time elected by the Board of Directors, and who shall be elected as provided in the By-Laws.

ARTICLE III

Membership

The membership shall consist of persons interested in the field of gospel music.

ARTICLE IV

Meetings

There shall be not fewer than four (4) nor more than five (5) regular meetings each year of the Board of Directors, and one (1) annual meeting of the members of the Association, together with such special meetings as may be called from time to time by the President or Chairman of the Board, or which may be called by the Executive Secretary upon request of twenty-five percent (25%) of the Board membership, and with five (5) days written notice from the President, Chairman of the Board, or Executive Secretary. The regular Board meetings shall be set a year in advance from the first Board meeting, and confirmation of regular meetings shall be made by the Secretary at least ten (10) days in advance of each regular meeting.

11/21/76

ARTICLE V

Amendment

Section 1. To amend the Constitution, the proposed amendment must be subscribed by ten (10) members of the Association and presented in writing to the President and the Board of Directors at least thirty (30) days before the annual meeting at which it is to be considered.

Section 2. An amendment may also be proposed by two-thirds (2/3) vote of the Board of Directors and Officers and Trustees.

Section 3. An amendment to the Constitution may be adopted by two-thirds (2/3) vote of those present and voting at the annual meeting of the members of the Association.

11/21/7

BY-LAWS
OF

GOSPEL MUSIC ASSOCIATION

ARTICLE I

Location

The office and location of the Association shall be in Nashville, Davidson County, Tennessee.

ARTICLE II

Membership

Section 1. The membership shall be composed of those persons interested in the field of gospel music.

Section 2. Application for membership shall be made in writing to the Board of Directors in such form as the Board of Directors may, from time to time, establish and shall contain a statement as to the particular segment of the gospel music field in which the applicant is primarily interested, together with a subscribed statement that the applicant accepts and agrees to be bound by the Constitution and By-Laws of the Association. An affirmative vote of two-thirds (2/3) of the Directors is necessary for the approval of any applicant as a member and his classification to section. Such approval need not be made by the Board of Directors assembled in meeting but may be signified by individual written vote. However, in the event that any Director shall notify the Executive Secretary within thirty (30) days after submission of the applications to the Directors that he deems it to be the best interest of the Association for any specific application for membership to be considered by the Board in meeting assembled, then consideration of such application shall be deferred until the next regular meeting of the Board, at which time the affirmative vote of two-thirds (2/3) of the Directors shall be necessary for approval, as set forth hereinabove.

Section 3. A member may be expelled from the Association when, upon the presentation of written charges signed by two (2) or more members, fourteen (14) members of the Board of Directors shall find that his continued membership is not to the best interest of the Association. A copy of such written charges shall be furnished to the member accused not less than two (2) weeks prior to the meeting of the Board of Directors for the consideration of his case, and such accused member shall have the right to appear and present evidence on his own behalf. Each member of the Association agrees to be bound by the decision of the Board of Directors in these matters.

Section 4. Membership dues shall be as follows, or as established from time to time by the Board of Directors: Fifteen Dollars ($15.00) per year for trade category members, Twelve Dollars ($12.00) for Associate category members, and One Hundred Dollars ($100.00) for Organizational memberships to be paid annually; and One Hundred and Fifty Dollars ($150.00) for the life of a member.

Section 5. The membership shall be divided into sixteen (16) sections or categories, and the Board of Directors shall determine with which category each member shall be affiliated. These categories are as follows:

1. Artists-Musicians
2. Broadcast Media

11/21/75

389

3. Record Company
4. Promoters
5. Publishers
6. Trade Paper
7. Composer
8. Radio-TV
9. Performance Licensing Organizations
10. Associate
11. Directors-at-Large
12. Talent Agencies/Artist Management
13. Youth
14. Advertising Agencies/Public Relations
15. Merchandisers/Distributors
16. Regional Associations (as defined by Board Resolution)

ARTICLE III

Officers

Section 1. Officers of the Association shall consist of a President, an Executive Vice President, or such other number of Vice Presidents as the Board of Directors, from time to time, may elect by increasing or decreasing to one (1) the number of said Vice Presidents, a Secretary and a Treasurer, all of whom shall be elected by the Board of Directors for a term of one (1) year, but may be removed from office at any time by an affirmative vote of two-thirds (2/3) of the directors, in meeting assembled or by proper proxy filed prior to the elections.

Section 2. The officers of the Association shall be ex-officio members of the Board of Directors and shall attend all meetings of the Board of Directors and shall attend all meetings of the Board of Directors and shall have the right to vote at such meetings.

Section 3. The President shall be the chief executive officer of the Association, and shall preside at all meetings of the members and the Board of Directors. In his absence or at his request the Chairman of the Board shall preside. The President shall see that all orders and resolutions of the Board of Directors are carried into effect by committees or otherwise, subject, however, to the right of the Directors to delegate to any other officer, committee, or employee, any specific power, except such as by statute are exclusively conferred on the President. He shall be responsible to the Board of Directors for the proper performance of his duties as President of the Association.

Section 4. The President or Executive Vice President shall issue or cause to be issued all membership cards. He shall also issue or cause to be issued notice of all corporate meetings as required by these By-Laws.

The Executive Vice President and other Vice Presidents shall act in the stead of the President during his or their absences at his or their direction, respectively.

Section 5. The Secretary shall attend all meetings of the Board of Directors and of the membership and keep the minutes. He shall issue or cause to be issued notice of corporate meetings as required by the By-Laws and Constitution, and perform such other duties as may be prescribed from time to time by the Board of Directors.

11/21/75

2

390

Section 6. The Treasurer, subject to the supervision and direction of the Chairman of the Board of Directors, shall have the custody of the corporate funds and securities and shall keep full and accurate account of receipts and disbursements in books belonging to the Association and shall deposit all monies and other available effects in the name of and to the credit of the Association in such depositories as may be designated by the Board of Directors.

ARTICLE IV

Directors

Section 1. The Board of Directors shall consist of two (2) elected members per designated category, except the category of Regional Associates, which shall have one (1) director per region, except as may be otherwise herein provided.

Section 2. Each director shall hold office for a term of two (2) years, except as provided in Section 1 above; and provided, however, that ten (10) members of the first elected Board of Directors shall serve for a term of one (1) year. No Director shall be eligible for re-election for a successive term. Vacancies occurring from time to time on the Board of Directors shall be filled by a majority vote of the said Board at its first duly constituted meeting after the vacancy occurs.

Section 3. Meetings of the Board of Directors may be held at any time as designated by the President or Chairman of the Board upon written notice to each member, mailed to him at least ten (10) days in advance thereof at his address shown by the records of the Association.

Section 4. A quorum of Directors shall consist of one-half of all voting members of the Board of Directors and the officers and trustees of the Association, as then constituted. A majority of those present shall have the authority to take any authorized action except as otherwise provided herein.

Section 5. The general powers of the Board of Directors shall be to manage, conduct and control all business affairs and property of this Association, and to do all such lawful acts and things, with reference thereto, and exercise all powers of the Association as are not by statute to be exercised or done by the membership.

Section 6. Any Director who during his term misses two (2) regularly scheduled quarterly Board meetings shall have his right to continue to serve as a Gospel Music Association Board Director individually considered by the Board in session. Each Director is responsible to notify in writing the Executive Secretary of any absence. Such notification must give the reason(s) necessitating the absence; and with the exception of emergency situations, should be submitted at least one (1) week prior to a Board meeting. The Executive Secretary will maintain necessary files and refer to the Membership Committee the second absence of any director. The Membership Committee will review all circumstances and make recommendations to the Board. A Director may be removed from the Board by a majority vote of those directors, officers, and trustees present at the Board meeting, and during which each individual absenteeism case will be reviewed and considered. The Chairman of the Board will advise any Director so removed of such action and of his right to appear at the next Board meeting to appeal the action if he so desires. Vacancies then may be filled in accordance with Section 2 of this Article IV of the By-Laws of the Gospel Music Association.

11/21/75

3

ARTICLE V

Trustees

There shall be, as additional members of the Board of Directors, Trustees, which shall consist of past Presidents of the Gospel Music Association, elected by the Board of Directors, by majority vote, who shall serve for life in said capacity or until their resignation, and who shall have an equal one (1) vote in all voting matters of the Board of Directors and shall enjoy full rights and privileges as a member of the Board of Directors of the Gospel Music Association.

ARTICLE VI

Elections

Section 1. Each trade category of the Association shall elect one (1) director annually for a two year term to the Board of Directors from each said category, except as otherwise provided in Article IV, Section 1. The entire membership, irrespective of category of membership, shall elect one (1) Director-At-Large annually for a two (2) year term and one (1) Director annually for a two (2) year term to represent the Associate membership.

Voting members shall receive, by U.S. Mail, from the Gospel Music Association Election Committee, a ballot of nominees, selected by the Nominating Committee of the Gospel Music Association Board of Directors, with proper "write in" provisions, 60 days prior to the annual membership meeting, which ballot shall be returned to the Election Committee within twenty (20) days of the date of the original mailing and/or to a designated independent auditor for tabulation.

The name of the two nominees receiving the highest number of votes shall be presented to the Election Committee and/or the independent auditors who shall remail the same, in like manner, to the membership for final balloting, and that nominee receiving a majority of votes shall be elected a director and board member, in the nominated category, to be installed at the annual meeting of members, for the ensuing term or until his successor is elected and installed.

In the event that no majority is attained by either nominee, then, in that event only, shall the nominee receiving the highest number of total votes, in both ballots, be elected, as above.

ARTICLE VII

Amendment

These By-Laws may be amended from time to time by an affirmative vote of two-thirds (2/3) of the entire Board of Directors (including the officers of the Association).

ARTICLE VIII

Resolutions

There shall be kept by the Association, in the offices of the Executive Secretary, a book of Resolutions, which shall contain all Board of Directors actions not in the form of an amendment to these By-Laws and in the form of Board action by Resolution.

Board action by Resolution shall take a majority vote of the Directors, Officers and Trustees present, and in excess of quorum requirements, at any proper meeting.

11/21/75   4

GOSPEL MUSIC ASSOCIATION

1977

OFFICERS

PRESIDENT

John T. Benson, III
365 Great Circle Rd.
Nashville, TN 37228
Tel: ·

TREASURER

Aaron Brown
825 19th Ave. So.
Nashville, TN 37203
Tel: (615) 327-0022

VICE-PRESIDENT

Norman Odlum
10 Columbus Circle
New York, NY 10019
Tel: (212) 586-3450

VICE-PRESIDENT

Charlie Monk
2 Music Square West
Nashville, TN 37203
Tel: (615) 244-3936

TRUSTEE

Brock Speer
5318 Anchorage Dr.
Nashville, TN 37220
Tel: (615) 832-9472

EXECUTIVE DIRECTOR

Don Butler
P.O. Box 23201
Nashville, TN 37202
Tel: (615) 242-0303

EXECUTIVE VICE-PRESIDENT

Hal Spencer
2111 Kenmere Dr.
Burbank, CA 91504
Tel: (213) 843-8100

CHAIRMAN OF THE BOARD

Ed Shea
2 Music Square West
Nashville, TN 37203
Tel: (615) 244-3936

VICE-PRESIDENT

Wendy Bagwell
4155 Ridge Rd.
Smyrna, GA 30080
Tel: (404) 794-9106

VICE-PRESIDENT

Lou Hildreth
P.O. Box 50
Nashville, TN 37202
Tel: (615) 255-8751

TRUSTEE

Marvin Norcross
P.O. Box 1790
Waco, TX 76703
Tel: (817) 772-7650

LEGAL ADVISOR

R. David Ludwick
Barksdale, Whalley, Gilbert & Frank
7th Floor, Third National Bank Bldg.
Nashville, TN 37219
Tel: (615) 244-0020

SECRETARY

Helen Maxson
10 Music Square East
Nashville, TN 37203
Tel: (615) 259-3625

VICE-PRESIDENT

Joe Huffman
P.O. Box 7084
Greenville, SC 29610
Tel: (803) 269-3961

VICE-PRESIDENT

J. D. Sumner
P.O. Box 15532
Nashville, TN 37215
Tel: (615) 255-8595

TRUSTEE

W. F. Myers
10 Columbus Circle
New York, NY 10019
Tel: (212) 586-3450

TRUSTEE

Les Beasley
P.O. Box 12267
Pensacola, FL 32581
Tel: (904) 968-6052

393

394

TALENT AGENCY/ARTIST MGMT.

Bill Murray (1978)
365 Great Circle Rd.
Nashville, TN 37228
Tel: (615)

Bob Bray (1977)
P.O. Box 12514
Nashville, TN 37212
Tel: (615) 383-8883

DIRECTOR-AT-LARGE

Joe Moscheo (1978)
803 18th Ave. So.
Nashville, TN 37203
Tel: (615) 327-2835

Bob Benson, Sr. (1977)
365 Great Circle Rd.
Nashville, TN 37228
Tel: (615)

PUBLIC RELATIONS/ADVERTISING AGCY.

Wayne Buchanan (1978)
718 6th Ave. So.
Nashville, TN 37203
Tel: (615) 242-6508

Donna Hilley (1977)
8 Music Square West
Nashville, TN 37203
Tel: (615) 327-3162

REGIONAL DIRECTORS

Wayne Christian
121 W. Neal
Carthage, TX 75633
Tel: (713) 248-4751

GOSPEL MUSIC HALL OF FAME

Purpose

The Gospel Music Association has established the "Gospel Music Hall of Fame" as an institution devoted to recognizing and honoring noteworthy individuals for outstanding contributions to gospel music. The purpose of this document is to state details of the Hall of Fame selection process and criteria for evaluating candidates for the award.

The Selection Process

1. The process of selecting Hall of Fame winners will be divided into two phases:

   A. Nomination of candidates.
   B. Election of winners.

2. A Hall of Fame Committee of 12 shall be constituted and then vested with the responsibility for nominating a slate of Hall of Fame candidates; from this slate, winners will be chosen by a panel of approximately 100 Hall of Fame Electors.

The Hall of Fame Committee

1. This Committee shall consist of 12 voting members, each ultimately serving a three-year term.

2. The GMA President and Chairman of the Board shall serve as ex-officio non-voting members of the Hall of Fame Committee.

3. The Hall of Fame Committee shall elect its own chairman.

4. The initial Hall of Fame Committee, to be constituted under this provision, shall be created as follows:

   A. The Hall of Fame Committee in existence as of January, 1971, shall select a slate of 25 recommended candidates for the permanent Hall of Fame Committee, and names of willing incumbent committeemen shall be automatically included within the 25.

   B. This list of 25 shall be presented to the GMA Board of Directors at its first 1971 meeting for secret ballot election of 12.

   C. Of the 12, four shall serve a three-year term; four a two-year term; and four a one-year term. These terms shall be decided by lot within the committee.

5. Each year, before the expiration of the terms of four of its members, the Hall of Fame Committee shall itself elect four successor members to serve for three-year terms. These choices shall be presented to the GMA Board of Directors for validation. A member whose terms expire may again serve after the passage of one year.

6. Any and all membership of the Hall of Fame Committee shall be subject to the will of the GMA Board of Directors.

Electors

1. A panel of at least 100 Hall of Fame Electors shall be charged with the responsibility of selecting Hall of Fame winners.

2. Electors shall serve for three-year terms, with an indefinite number of separate or consecutive terms allowable at the discretion of the GMA Board of Directors.

3. The panel shall be constituted every third year at the annual fall meeting of the GMA Board. Vacancies may be filled or additions made at any quarterly meeting and may be subject to review at each annual meeting.

4. Election to the panel of Electors will be made by the GMA Board of Directors by a majority vote from a roster of recommended names prepared by a special temporary committee appointed by the Chairman of the Board. Any Board member may suggest additional names for consideration. Election of Electors will be on an individual basis, not as a panel.

5. The 12 members of the Hall of Fame Committee shall themselves also serve as Electors.

6. Officers and Directors of the GMA may themselves also serve as Electors, but this role is not automatic.

7. Electors must have participated actively in gospel music for at least ten years and must themselves merit respect and recognition for their accomplishments and/or knowledge in one or more aspects of gospel music. Electors shall be diverse in their activity categories and geographical locales. Electors shall be members of the Gospel Music Association; this provision may be waived by the GMA Board of Directors.

Nomination of Hall of Fame Candidates

1. Each year, between the fall Board of Directors Meeting and the spring Board of Directors meeting, the Hall of Fame Committee shall by majority vote nominate no less than ten nor more than twenty Hall of Fame candidates as official nominees.

2. Nominations will be guided by the Hall of Fame Criteria.

3. Nominees will be chosen "at large" by merit alone, irrespective of whether they are living or deceased, currently active or inactive, and irrespective of activity category. Two years after death must elapse to qualify a deceased candidate.

-2-

4. The aforementioned will be listed alphabetically on a ballot to be sent to Hall of Fame Electors no later than May 15, of each calendar year, together with a copy of the Hall of Fame Criteria and brief objective biographical sketches of each nominee not exceeding 100 words. Mailing will be executed by an important commercial auditing company.

5. Provision will be made on the ballot for an Elector to enter not more than one write-in nominee.

6. On the ballot Electors will be instructed to vote for no more than five most-preferred nominees, including any write-in vote. A reminder will be forwarded to all electors on June 15 to send in ballots.

7. Completed ballots must be returned to the independent commercial auditing company no later than July 15 of each calendar year, to be eligible for consideration.

8. Those electors not returning information as agreed shall be subject to removal by the Board of Directors.

Compilation of Nominations

1. The commercial auditing company will tally all votes received.

2. The five nominees receiving the greatest number of votes shall be considered finalists, and their names shall be entered alphabetically on a final ballot.

Final Balloting

1. Final ballots will be mailed by the auditing company to Electors no later than July 31 of each calanedar year.

2. Electors will be asked on the ballot to vote for no more than one of the finalist nominees.

3. Ballots must be received by the auditing company no later than September 1, of each calendar year to be eligible.

4. The nominee receiving the greatest number of votes shall be declared a Hall of Fame Winner. In case of tie, two winners would be declared.

Supplemental Slate of Deceased Candidates

It is recognized that the Hall of Fame process is relatively new, but gospel music itself has spanned many decades. Therefore, a supplemental selection process is evolved to assure deserved recognition to the historical heroes of gospel music. Whenever two consecutive years pass in which no deceased Hall of Fame winner is elected, then in the third year the following will occur:

-3-

398

1. In addition to the selection procedures heretofore described, the Hall of Fame Committee shall nominate an additional panel of deceased nominees only, in accordance with the procedures already described.

2. In such years, therefore, --no more frequently than every three years-- two instead of one, Hall of Fame winners will be elected, at least one of them a deceased honoree.

3. Execpt that for an indeterminate number of years after the inception of this honor, there shall be selected one living and one deceased winner, annually, and thereafter, by Board of Directors action, the preceeding provisions shall take full force and effect.

Announcement of Winners

Knowledge of Hall of Fame winners will be protected as secret information by the auditing company until the "Hall of Fame Event" is designated by the GMA Board of Directors, at which time the winners will be revealed and announced.

Review of the Selection Process

No less frequently than once every three years, the GMA Board of Directors shall review the Hall of Fame criteria and selection process and shall validate existing procedures or shall adopt those modifications deemed appropriate.

Criteria

The following section details specific criteria to guide the Electors of Hall of Fame winners.

1. Definitions

   A. Hall of Fame -- An institution sponsored and operated by the Gospel Music Association to recognize and honor noteworthy individuals for outstanding contributions to the advancement of gospel music.

   B. Hall of Fame Winners -- An individual honored by election to the Hall of Fame.

   C. Hall of Fame Award -- The physical trophy bestowed and presented to Hall of Fame winners.

   D. Hall of Fame Museum -- The Nashville, Tennessee, repository in which Hall of Fame winners are honored in special displays of portraits and tributes.

   E. Hall of Fame Event -- The occasion at which new Hall of Fame winners are first publicly announced and awards are presented.

   F. Hall of Fame Electors -- Those individuals designated by the Board of Directors of the Gospel Music Association to elect Hall of Fame winners.

-4-

G. Hall of Fame Criteria -- The guidelines by which the Hall of Fame Electors appraise and evaluate candidates and elect winners.

H. Hall of Fame Candidate -- Any individual associated with gospel music who qualifies for Hall of Fame consideration as defined in the Hall of Fame Criteria.

I. Hall of Fame Nominees -- Those outstanding individuals selected, among all candidates by the Electors, for final consideration in the selection process.

2. Hall of Fame Criteria

Candidates for the Hall of Fame shall be appraised by Electors in accordance with the criteria below:

A. Basic Standard -- A candidate basically is to be judged on the degree of his contribution to the advancement of gospel music and on the indelibility of his impact.

B. Individual Candidacy -- Only individuals may be elected to the Hall of Fame. Companies, publications, radio stations, and other groups -- many of which significantly foster gospel music -- are not eligible for Hall of Fame recognition.

C. Scope of Activity -- Flexible authority is vested in the Elector in identifying the scope of a candidate's activity in gospel music. He may have excelled in a narrow, specific sphere... such as, song writing, publishing, musician, recording artist, etc. He may have been active in several areas. In any event, a candidate must have achieved definitive leadership in his own field of gospel music activity. However, it is definitely not mandatory to honor the leaders in every activity related to gospel music. A candidate truly must compete with all candidates in all fields, as well as with all candidates in his own field.

D. Span of Influence -- The time factor of a candidate's impact on gospel music is completely flexible. It may cover an uninterrupted span of many years, or it may cover two of more distinct and separate time cycles. Conceivably, even, a candidate may earn Hall of Fame recognition by one transient act, momentary in time, providing the impact on gospel music is deemed significant enough. Longevity of involvement with gospel music, therefore, will not in itself warrant recognition in the Hall of Fame.

E. Influence on Others -- A most significant criterion in evaluating a candidate will be his inspirational effect on others... the degree to which he multiplies his influence through others to create impact on gospel music far beyond his own direct individual contribution.

F. Quanity vs. Quality -- A candidate's ability to expand the popularity of gospel music is a quantitative virtue. The professionalism of his activity is a "qualitative" one. Both qualitative and quantitative criteria are to be considered equally and separately important; conceivably, one may be present without the other.

-5-

G. <u>Devotion to Others</u> -- Furthering gospel music by selfless devotion to the interests of others may enhance the candidacy of an individual, but this is not essential to winning. The activities of a candidate may be completely self-devoted and still be considered significant enough to warrant recongition.

H. <u>Professional Conduct and Image</u> -- A candidate is expected to have practiced the highest calibre of professional conduct in order to enhance the public image of himself and of gospel music.

I. <u>Personal Morals and Behavior</u> -- The selection process is not a judgment of personal morals and behavior, providing the latter do not negatively affect the professional conduct of the candidate and the public image of gospel music.

GOSPEL MUSIC HALL OF FAME
CURRENT MEMBERS
(Year inducted)

Living

"Pappy" Jim Waites (1971)
　　　(Deceased Dec. 1973)
Albert E. Brumley, Sr. (1972)
Lee Roy Abernathy (1973)
James Blackwood, Sr. (1974)
Brock Speer (1975)
Mosie Lister (1976)

Deceased

G. T. "Dad" Speer (1971)
Lena Brock "Mom" Speer (1972)
James D. Vaughan (1972)
Denver Crumpler (1973)
[In 1973 a block of 10
individuals were inducted by
resolution of the Board of
Directors]
J. R. Baxter, Jr.
E. M. Bartlett
John Daniel
Adger M. Pace
Homer Rodeheaver
A. J. Showalter
V. O. Stamps
Frank Stamps
W. B. Walbert
R. E. Winsett
G. Kieffer Vaughan (1974)
Fanny Crosby (1975)
George Bennard (1976)

STATES PROCLAIMING GOSPEL MUSIC MONTH
1976

State	Month (Unless otherwise indicated)
ALABAMA	September
ARIZONA	March (Grand Canyon Quartet
ARKANSAS	September Convention)
CALIFORNIA	September
CONNECTICUT	September
DELAWARE	September
FLORIDA	November 1-7
GEORGIA	September
IDAHO	September
ILLINOIS	September
INDIANA	July 5-11
KENTUCKY	September
LOUISIANA	September
MICHIGAN	May 3-8
MINNESOTA	September
MISSISSIPPI	September
MISSOURI	September
NEVADA	September
NEW HAMPSHIRE	September
NEW JERSEY	September
NEW MEXICO	September
NEW YORK	September
OHIO	September 20-26
OKLAHOMA	September
OREGON	September
PENNSYLVANIA	September
RHODE ISLAND	September
SOUTH CAROLINA	September
SOUTH DAKOTA	September
TENNESSEE	September
TEXAS	June 13-20
VERMONT	September
VIRGINIA	May 2-9 (National Music Week--
WASHINGTON	September includes Gospel
WISCONSIN	October 1-7 Music)
WYOMING	September

List prepared by Norman Odlum, SESAC, New York, for the Gospel Music Association, November 4, 1976.

D O V E   A W A R D S

Selection Process

Purpose: To give public recognition, by the members of the Gospel Music Association and gospel music appreciators everywhere, of excellence and/or significant accomplishment in the quality and means of spreading the True Word through gospel music during the year preceding the presentation.

Electors: All persons who are active members of the Gospel Music Association in a trade category on the first day of the month prior to any one of the three balloting dates.

Balloting Process:

There shall be a total of three separate ballots mailed by an independent, commercial accounting firm to those trade members of the Gospel Music Association certified as current members. This certification of members will be conducted by the executive secretary of the Gospel Music Association in the presence of a member of the accounting firm.

First Ballot – Instructions and provision for nominating
Second Ballot – Listing of all persons, songs, albums, groups, etc.
 receiving 5 or more nominations on the first ballot.

Third Ballot – Respective categories listing the top five finalist in each category of balloting except for song of the year in which ten shall be listed.

Compilation of Ballots:

A commercial auditing firm will be hired to tabulate the ballots according to the following established procedure:

A. Voting

1. One nomination per category, per ballot.
2. Votes in second and third ballot limited to one vote per category, per ballot.
3. Vote in no more than 12 categories, per ballot
4. All nominations on second ballot and finalist on third ballot will be listed alphabetically.

B. In the event of a tie vote situation:

After compilation of the second ballot all names will be listed (i.e.) a tie for 5th place will result in six names on ballot in that particular category. Should there occur a tie in the compilation of the winner a duplicate award will be presented.

Announcement of Winners:

The names of winners of the Dove Awards will not be made public until released by the auditing firm and until the presentation event selected by the Board of Directors of the Gospel Music Association.

Limitations on Category Qualifications:

Album Categories: Albums released July 1 to June 30 preceding the presentation. This category includes cover photo, backliner; and graphic art.

Definitions of Album Categories:

Inspirational: Composition with lyrics, sacred in nature, performed vocally or instrumentally in a traditional church-oriented style and whose purpose is to exalt the mind and soul of listener.

Southern Gospel: Melodic music drawn from American fudamentalist culture with simple straight-forward-true-of-the-gospel lyrics performed in a free uninhibited style.

Contemporary: Message music in tune with the times, text with traditional religious and gospel overtones, performed in any modern style (rock, soul, jazz, folk) and designed to induce listner to "a new life".

Best gospel album by a non-gospel artist: Any recording of inspirational, contemporary or southern gospel music by any non-gospel artist.

Presentation Limitations:

Category II (Best Gospel Record Album Cover Photo or Cover Art) This award presented to the photographer or artist.

Category III (Best Graphic Layout & Design of a Gospel Record Album Cover) This award presented to the designer.

Category X (Best Gospel Record Album of the Year) Three "Doves" to be awarded to: album producer, artist and record company.

Category XI (Best Gospel Song of the Year) Individual "Doves" to be awarded to composers and/or authors.

In all other categories one "Dove" will be presented.

The Ambassadors Award:

The Ambassadors Award is presented by the Board of Directors of the Gospel Music Association to an individual who has contributed to the advancement of gospel music. Who has achieved the respect of the industry and is considered an asset to the industry whatever his gospel music activity may be.

The presentation of the Ambassadors Award is determined only by a unanimous vote of the Board of Directors. Consequently the Ambassador Award will be presented only when so voted.

Dove Award Winners, 1969-1975

and 1976

The Dove Award is the award for excellence presented by the members of the Gospel Music Association to those who have contributed to the ministry and growth of gospel music through the years. Following is a listing of those who have won the award.

BEST MALE GOSPEL GROUP

1969—Imperials
1970—Oak Ridge Boys
1972—Oak Ridge Boys
1973—Blackwood Brothers
1974—Blackwood Brothers
1975—Imperials
1976--Imperials

BEST MIXED GOSPEL GROUP

1969—Speer Family
1970—Speer Family
1972—Speer Family
1973—Speer Family
1974—Speer Family
1975—Gaither Trio
1976--Speer Family

BEST GOSPEL SONG OF THE YEAR
(title/composer/Publishing Co./Performance Rights affiliation)

1969—Jesus Is Coming Soon
　R.E. Winsett/R.E. Winsett Publishing Co./SESAC
1970—The Night Before Easter
　Don Sumner-Dwayne Friend/Gospel Quartet Music Co./SESAC
1972—The Lighthouse
　Ron Hinson/Journey Music/BMI
1973—Why Me, Lord?
　Kris Kristofferson/Resaca Music/BMI
1974—Because He Lives
　Bill Gaither/Gaither Music Co./ASCAP
1975—One Day At A Time
　Marijohn Wilkin-Kris Kristofferson/Buckhorn Music./BMI
1976--Statue Of Liberty
　Neil Enloe/Neil Enloe Music/BMI

BEST GOSPEL ALBUM OF THE YEAR
(Title/Artist/Label/Producer)

1969—It's Happening
　Oak Ridge Boys/Heartwarming/Bob MacKenzie
1970—Fill My Cup Lord
　Blackwood Brothers/RCA Victor/Darol Rice
1972—Light
　Oak Ridge Boys/Heartwarming/Bob MacKenzie
1973—Street Gospel
　Oak Ridge Boys/Heartwarming/Bob MacKenzie
1974—Big and Live
　Kingsmen Quartet/Canaan/Marvin Norcross
1975—I Just Feel Like Something Good Is About To Happen
　Speer Family-Doug Oldham/Heartwarming/Bob MacKenzie
1976--Between The Cross And Heaven
　Speer Family/Heartwarming/Joe Huffman

BEST MALE VOCALIST

1969—James Blackwood
1970—James Blackwood
1972—James Blackwood
1973—James Blackwood
1974—James Blackwood
1975—James Blackwood
1976--Johnny Cook

BEST FEMALE VOCALIST

1969—Vestal Goodman
1970—Ann Downing
1972—Sue Chenault
1973—Sue Chenault
1974—Sue Chenault Dodge
1975—Jeanne Johnson
1976--Joy McGuire

406

GOSPEL SONGWRITER OF THE YEAR

1969—Bill Gaither
1970—Bill Gaither
1972—Bill Gaither
1973—Bill Gaither
1974—Bill Gaither
1975—Bill Gaither
1976--Bill Gaither

BEST GOSPEL INSTRUMENTALIST

1969—Dwayne Friend
1970—Dwayne Friend
1972—Tony Brown
1973—Henry Slaughter
1974—Henry Slaughter
1975—Henry Slaughter
1976--Henry Slaughter

GOSPEL DISC JOCKEY OF THE YEAR

1969—J. G. Whitfield
1970—J. G. Whitfield
1972—J.G. Whitfield
1973—Sid Hughes
1974—Jim Black
1975—Jim Black
1976--Sid Hughes

BEST GOSPEL TELEVISION PROGRAM

1969—Gospel Jubilee
Florida Boys, Host
1970—Gospel Jubilee
Florida Boys, Host
1973—Gospel Jubilee
Florida Boys, Host
1974—Gospel Jubilee
Florida Boys, Host
1975—Gospel Jubilee
Florida Boys, Host
1976--Gospel Jubilee
Florida Boys, Host

ASSOCIATE AWARD

1975--Blackwood Brothers
1976--Statue Of Liberty/Neil Enloe/
Neil Enloe Music/BMI

BEST BACKLINER NOTES
OF A GOSPEL RECORD ALBUM
(Author/Album Title/Artist)

1969—No award given
1970—Mrs. Jake Hess
Ain't That Beautiful Singing/Jake Hess
1972—Johnny Cash
Light/Oak Ridge Boys
1973—Eddie Miller
Release Me (From My Sin)/Blackwood Brothers
1974—Don Butler
On Stage/Blackwood Brothers
1975—Wendy Bagwell
Bust Out Laffin'/Wendy Bagwell
1976--Sylvia Mays
Just A Little Talk With Jesus

BEST GRAPHIC LAYOUT AND DESIGN
OF A GOSPEL RECORD ALBUM
(Graphic artist/Album Title/Artist)

1969—No award given
1970—Jerry Goff
Thrasher Brothers at Fantastic Caverns/Thrasher Brothers
1972—Acy Lehman
L-O-V-E Love/Blackwood Brothers
1973—Bob McConnell
Street Gospel/Oak Ridge Boys
1974—Charles Hooper
On Stage/Blackwood Brothers
1975—Bob McConnell
Praise Him . . . Live/The Downings
1976--Bob McConnell/No Shortage/Imperials

BEST GOSPEL RECORD ALBUM COVER PHOTO
OR COVER ART
(Photographer/Album Title/Artist)

1969—No award given
1970—Bill Grine
This Is My Valley/Rambos
1972—Bill Grine
Light/Oak Ridge Boys
1973—Bill Grine
Street Gospel/Oak Ridge Boys
1974—Hope Powell
On Stage/Blackwood Brothers
1975—Spears Photos
There He Goes/Blackwood Brothers
1976--Bill Barnes
Old Fashioned, Down Home, Hand
Clappin', Foot Stomping,
Southern Style, Gospel Quartet
Music/Oak Ridge Boys

Artists/Musicians

ALL STAR QUARTET
Mike Powell
Box 9302
Ft. Worth, TX 76107

THE ALTERNATIVE SOUND
Ron Born
5024 Dogwood
Everett, WA 98203

AMBASSADORS QUARTET
J.D. Draper
311 Meadow Lane
Collinsville, VA 24078

AMBURGEY FAMILY
Glen Dye, Jr., Mgr.
446 Raleigh Ave.
Hampton, VA 23361

AMIGOS
Box 576
Duncanville, TX 75116

ANCHORS QUARTET
Bob Ray
499 N. Fulbright
Springfield, MO 65801

THE ANSWER
Tom McCormick
P.O. Box 4612
Albuquerque, NM 87106

APPLE FAMILY
Ken Apple
P.O. Box 35
Fayetteville, TN 37334

ASHCROFT and BACON
1447 E. Kearney
Springfield, MO 65803

THE BAILEY SINGERS
Tom Bailey
P.O. Box 6545
Charleston, WV 25302

BAXTER FAMILY
R.V. Baxter
1106 Fourth Street
Corning, AR 72422

BELIEVERS
P.O. Box 712
West Plains, MO 75775

BENTON'S
P.O. Box 657
Mokena, IL 60448

JERRY W. BERNARD
Box 90128
Houston, TX 77090

BERRY SINGERS
Allen Berry
705 So. Main
Fredericktown, MO 63645

BETTY and the STEPHENS
Betty Wills Stephens
P.O. Box 50
Nashville, TN 37202

ERNIE BIVENS
Rt. 2, Box 236
Moyock, NC 29758

BLACKWOOD BROTHERS
James Blackwood
3935 Summer Ave.
Memphis, TN 38122

BLACKWOOD SINGERS
Winston Blackwood
P.O. Box 1613
Nashville, TN 37202

BLAKELY SINGERS
P. O. Box 23042
Nashville, TN 37202

BLUE RIDGE QUARTET
Burl Strevel
P. O. Box 441
Spartanburg, S.C. 29301

BOB & JODI
Box 241
Carlsbad, NM 88220

BRIGHTEN AIRS
Bob Markcum
9903 Highcourt Slope
Brighton, MI 48116

SINGING BROWNS
Rt. 1
Bryant, AL 35958

THE CALIFORNIANS
Dale Peters, Mgr.
P.O. Box 1043
Glendora, CA 91740

CALVARY BOYS
Waylon Moore, Mgr.
P. O. Box 127
Tenaha, TX 75974

CALVARYMEN QUARTET
P.O. Box 7813
Flint, MI 48507

GLENN CAMP FAMILY
712 Loop Road
Hendersonville, NC 28739

CARPENTER CREW
9515 Monrovia No. 100
Lenaxa, KA 66215

EARL CARPENTER SINGERS
1822 Tenby Crt.
Charlotte, NC 28211

CATHEDRAL QUARTET
Glenn Payne
P.O. Box 1512
Stow, Ohio 44224

CHALLENGERS
Rodney Maples
Route 4, Box 906
Springfield, MO 65802

THE CHALLENGERS
Darrell Kennedy
4903 N.E. Sandy Blvd.
Portland, OR 97213

CHAPEL AIRES
George Green
Box 92
Lake Stevens, WA 98258

CHILDRESS FAMILY
Elmer Childress
440 N. Armour Drive
Wichita, KS 67206

CHORALIERS
Gordon Veale
P.O. Box 459
West Vancouver, BC

THE CHORDS
Dave Musselman
9810 United Rd.
Youngstown, OH 44514

CHRISTIAN TROUBADOURS
Wayne Walters
P.O. Box 4624
Nashville, TN 37216

WILLIAM CLAUSON
P.O. Box 166
Crestline, CA 92325

CONCORDS
Jim Black
Box 40096
Nashville, TN 37204

KENNETH COPELAND
P.O. Box 3407
Fort Worth, TX 76105

COUNTRY COUSINS GOSPEL SINGERS
Dale Schwartz
Star Route
Hartville, MO 65667

102

408

THE COUNTRY LIGHTS
Roger Smith
302 Med. Dent. Bldg.
Everett, WA 98201

THE COUNTRY VERSION
Bill Textor
P.O. Box U
Hendersonville, TN 37075

COURIERS
Dave Kyllonen
5221 E. Simpson Road
Mechanicsburg, PA 17055

THE CROFFORDS
Don Crofford
254 Southridge Dr.
Rochester, NY 14626

THE CROSSROAD
Al Vogt
409 Filbert Rd.
Alderwood Manor, WA 98036

ANDRAE CROUCH & THE DISCIPLES
P.O. Box 635
Pacoima, CA 91331

CRUSADERS
P.O. Box 59
Sedalia, OH 43151

THE CRUSADERS
Doug VanderBroek
Box 243
Firth, NE 68358

CRUSE FAMILY
Box 1899
Jacksonville, TX 75766

JIMMIE DAVIS
P.O. Box 2626
Baton Route, LA 70821

DESTINATIONS
James Pratt
1327 N. Clay
Springfield, MO 65802

DEWEYS
LaVoy Dewey
P.O. Box 1677
Nashville, TN 37207

TIM AND SHERYL DEWEY
P.O. Box 1677
Nashville, TN 37207

**SINGING DICKERSONS
AND JAMES DICKERSONS**
Fair Play, MO 65649

DIXIE ECHOES
Dale Shelnutt
2631 W. Cervantes Street
Pensacola, FL 32502

DIXIE MELODY BOYS
Ed O'Neal
513 Harding Ave
Kinston, NC 28501

THE DOSS FAMILY
Donald R. Doss
Route 2, Box 683-B
Trinity, NC 27370

SINGING DOUGLAS FAMILY
5905 Mayhews Landing Rd.
Newark, CA 94560

DOWNINGS
Paul Downing
131 Saunders Ferry Rd.
Hendersonville, TN 37075

CLAUDETTE DYKSTRA
6757 Nooksack Rd.
Everson, WA 98247

EASTMAN QUARTET
J. R. Damiani
P. O. Box 504
Lansdale, PA 19446

EINERT
Bill, Mary & Jim Einert
P.O. Box 552
Clarksville,AR 72830

CURTIS ELKINS
P.O. Box 635
Hurst, TX 76053

THE EMERALDS
P.O. Box 17039
Nashville, TN 37217

ENVOYS
Don Storms
P.O. Box 253
Rockaway, NJ 07866

ESQUIRES
Doyle Ankrom
3314 N. Stewart
Springfield, MO 65803

FARR FAMILY
P.O. Box 16
Middletown, PA 17057

FERGUSON TRIO
B. J. Ferguson
18029 13 Mile Rd.
Fraser, MI 48026

FLORIDA BOYS
Les Beasley
P. O. Box 12207
Pensacola, FL 32533

FOLLOWERS QUARTET
1105 N. Chandier Dr.
Ft. Worth, TX 76111

FOUNDATIONS
Don Gardner
926 E. Sayer
Springfield, MO 65803

THE FOWLERS
Jack Fowler
7402 Pineville Dr.
Jacksonville, FL 32210

BILL GAITHER TRIO
Bill Gaither
P. O. Box 300
Alexandria, IN 46001

THE GALATIANS
Wayne Queen
311 W. Highland Ave.
Elkin, NC 28621

GARY & THE SINGING CHRISTIANS
Gary Christian
6439 Trigg Rd.
Ferndale, WA 98243

GASKIN FAMILY
Dee Gaskin
Rt. 1
Battle Ground, IN 47920

GEMS
Teddy Huffam
P. O. Box 350
Nashville, TN 37202

GEM-TONES
Jim Wilmouth
606 W. Oak Ave.
Jonesboro, AR 72401

GLORY ROAD TRIO
1417 E. Lindberg
Springfield, MO 65804

THE GOSPELAIRES
Jim Foster
8217 Beverly Blvd.
Everett, WA 98203

GOSPEL BRASS
Charles Sizemore
P.O. Box 1644
Rome, GA 30761

THE GOSPEL ECHOES
Omer Reaves
12050 166th Street
Artesia, CA 90701

GOSPEL GENERATIONS
Curtis Barton
P.O. Box 53
Salem, AR 72576

GOSPEL HARBINGERS
Star Route, Box 179
Buffalo, MO 65622

GOSPEL LADS
P.O. Box 1177
Joplin, MO 64801

GOSPEL LIGHTS
Juanita Peters, Mgr.
4437 Langdon St.
Columbus, GA 31907

GOSPEL MELODIES
Ralph Plummer
Rt. 3
Hitchcock, SC 57348

GOSPEL MESSENGERS
Malvern Poor
Box 162
Boody, IL 62514

GOSPEL MESSENGERS
Jake Winter
2007 S. Fairway
Springfield, MO 65804

THE GOSPEL RELATIVES
Jerry Hunter
9823 Bilteer Dr.
Columbus, GA 31907

GOSPEL SONS
Stan Kirschsenmann
12218 N.E. 23rd St.
Vancouver, WA 98664

GOSPEL TROUBADORES
414 Dailey St.
E. Lansing, MI 48823

103

409

GOSS BROTHERS
P.O. Box 372
Atlanta, GA 30084

SAMMY HALL SINGERS
Rt. 8
Sevierville, TN 37862

HALLELUJAH MINSTRELS
Ray Lewis, Mgr.
P.O. Box 305
Hendersonville, TN 37075

HAMES FAMILY QUARTET
Rt. 5, Box 380
Gaffney, SC 29340

HAPPY GOODMAN FAMILY
Howard Goodman
P.O. Box 13
Madisonville, KY 42431

HART FAMILY
Mrs. Aileene Hart
6215 Harding Rd.
Nashville, TN 37205

THE HAWAIIANS
Everette, WA

HEMPHILLS
Joel Hemphill
P. O. Box 627
Nashville, TN 37202

HERITAGE SINGERS U.S.A.
John O. Musgrave
P.O. Box 1358
Placerville, CA 95667

JAKE HESS SOUND
Jake Hess
532 Whispering Oak Place
Nashville, TN 37211

HIGHER GROUND
Wayne Hilliard
P.O. Box 40139
Nashville, TN 37204

HINSON FAMILY
Ronnie Hinson
267 Spicer Ave.
Madisonville, KY 43431

HOLLYWOOD HARMONEERS
Richard Nueslein, Mgr.
P.O. Box 11
Hollywood, MD 20636

HOPPER BROTHERS & CONNIE
Claude Hopper
Box 525
Madison, NC 27025

SINGING HOSANNAS
Leon Smith
1942 E. Smith
Springfield, MO 65803

MIKE HUMPHRIES
Rt. 1, Box 177
Alexandria, LA 71301

HYMN MASTERS
Kenneth W. Etheridge
P.O. Box 436
Ashford, AL 36312

HYMNSMEN
Rt. 1
Ooltewah, TN 37363

IMPERIALS
Joe Moscheo
1508 Sigler Street
Nashville, TN 37203

INSPIRATIONALS
Bob Wills
Box 8006
Ft. Worth, TX 76010

INSPIRATIONS
Martin Cook
P.O. Drawer "JJ"
Bryson City, NC 28713

THE JACKSONS
Chuck Jackson
P.O. Box 17177
Nashville, TN 37217

JERICO SINGERS
P.O. Box 91
Lake Grove, NY 11755

JERICO WAY SINGERS
Richard Myers
P.O. Box 16
Jerico Springs, MO 64756

JERRY & THE JORDANS
Jerry Jordans
Box 792
Brownfield, TX 79316

JEWEL-TONES
Carl H. Scott, Director
150 Homeland Rd.
York, PA 17403

SINGING JONESES
P.O. Box 454
Springfield, MO 65801

JOYFUL NOISE
Box 328
New Knoxville, OH 45871

JOYFUL NOISE
Gary Winters
Rt. 3, Box 737A
Annville, PA 17003

JOYOUS CELEBRATION
Jan Lind
P.O. Box 33238
Seattle, WA 98133

THE JUBILAIRES
9210 Golondrina Dr.
LaMesa, CA 92041

JUBILEE QUARTET
Whitey Gleason
P.O. Box 5087
Topeka, KS 66605

KELLY FAMILY
Leonard Stephens
Rt. 2
Spring Hill, TN 37174

KEYNOTES
Bill Phillips
10711 Gloria
Cincinnati, OH 45231

KEYS QUARTET
Herman Richie
Fairfield, VA 24435

KINCAID SINGERS
Imogene Kincaid
919 Allen Street
Nashville, TN 37214

KING JAMES VERSION
John Lindstrom
P.O. Box 91, Station R
Toronto 17, Ontario, Canada

KING'S CHILDREN SINGERS
Frank Tulloch, Jr.
1506 W. 21st.
Houston, TX 77008

KING'S EDITION
Paul Fricke, Mgr.
P.O. Box 697
Gallatin, TN 37066

KINGS EDITION
Jerry Halcomb
Route 4, Box 246
Paragould, AR 72450

KING'S QUARTET
P.O. Box 11504
Station E
Albuquerque, NM 87104

KING'S WITNESS
Dan Duncan
224 Cherry Ave.
Meridian, ID 83642

KINGSMEN
Eldridge Fox
P.O. Box 2622
Asheville, NC 28002

KINSMEN
Dean Jaggers
1419 Laurel Avenue
Bowling Green, KY 42101

KINSMEN SINGERS
Jack Brattin
808 W. Village
Springfield, MO 65807

KLAUDT INDIAN FAMILY
Vernon Klaudt
P.O. Box 47397
Atlanta, GA 30340

LILLIE KNAULS
P.O. Box 5353
San Jose, CA 95150

KROWNSMEN
Buddy Craig
3242 Hetzel Drive
Parma, OH 44134

LAMB
7516 City Line Ave. #8
Philadelphia, PA 19151

THE LAMPLIGHTERS
Bobby Moxley
P.O. Box 5025
Roanoke, VA 23212

LAMPLIGHTERS
Joe McConnell
Route 1
Willard, MO 65781

LARRY & GOLDEN-HEIRS TRIO
P.O. Box 283
Chilliwack, B.C.
Canada V2P-6J1

THE LATINOS
Eddie Velasquez, Mgr.
P.O. Box 159
Baldwin Park, CA 91706

THE LEARNINGS
Sam Learning
215 Avondale Boulevard
Bramalea, Ontario
Canada L6J 1J1

**DANNY LEE & THE CHILDREN
OF TRUTH**
P.O. Box 6523
San Jose, CA 95150

LeFEVRES
Rex Nelson
P.O. Box 400
Atlanta, GA 30301

LESTER FAMILY
Hershel Lester
2008 S. 38th Street
St. Louis, MO 613116

ERV LEWIS
Box 41
Johnsonville, SC 29555

LEWIS FAMILY
Roy Lewis
Rt. 1
Lincolnton, GA 30817

LIGHTHOUSE QUARTET
816 South Vine
Mt. Vernon, MO 65712

LISEMBY FAMILY GOSPEL SINGERS
Mrs. Sue Lisemby
2114 Third Street
Lake Charles, LA 70601

THE LIVING WAY
Gary Griffith
8807 N.E. 161st Place
Bothell, WA 98011

LOCKLEAR TRAVELERS
Leon Locklear
Rt. 1, Box 186-F
Pembroke, NC 28372

MARK LOWRY
17403 Anvil Circle
Houston, TX 77090

LUNDSTROM TEAM
Lowell Lundstrom
Sisseton, SD 57262

LYNN GOSPEL ECHOES
Thad Winters
Smithville, AR 72466

MAGICAL HARRY
Harry Anderson
744 N. Kansas
Springfield, MO 65802

MANI STRING SINGERS
Dennis Chappman
2914 Overlook Drive
Huntington, WV 25705

MARANATHA SINGERS
Claude Childers
Route 1, Box 9
Fulton, MO 65251

THE MARINERS
Joe Alcorn
9500 Silver Star St.
Vancouver, WA 98662

MARK IV QUARTET
185 Deming Road
Rochester, NY 14704

MARKSMEN
Earl Wheeler
Rt. 1
Murrayville, GA 30564

JACK MARSHALL
832 W. Walnut Street
Springfield, MO 65806

MARTIN FAMILY
12112 Pearl St.
South Gate, MI 48195

DAVE MATHES
707 Toby Lynn Drive
Nashville, TN 37211

JOHN MATHEWS FAMILY
2011 Richard Jones Road
Apt. R3
Nashville, TN 37215

RANDY MATHEWS
807 Redwood Dr.
Nashville, TN 37220

SHIRLEY McCLUSKEY
1421 N. Campbell No. 204
Springfield, MO 65802

McDUFF BROTHERS
Roger McDuff
P.O. Box 190
Pasadena, TX 77501

MELODYAIRES
John Allen
Rt. 1, Box 194-A
Mt. Airy, GA 30563

BILL MICHAEL
P.O. Box 2334
Joplin, MO 64701

MID SOUTH BOYS
P.O. Box 695
Malvern, AR 72104

MID WESTERN GOSPEL SINGERS
Orville White
P.O. Box 3248
Enid, OK 73701

AUDREY MIER
Box 11
Duarte, CA 91010

MILLIONAIRE GOSPEL SINGERS
J.W. Austin
Box 102
Trion, GA 30753

SPENCE & DEANA MOORE
122 North Rosemont
Amarillo, TX 79106

MORLAN FAMILY
Dewey Pennell
1220 S. Tyler
Aurora, MO 65605

MORRIS FAMILY SINGERS
Richard Morris
Rt. 1
Cornelia, GA 30531

MURPHY BROTHERS QUARTET
Rt. 9, Box 234A
Glenco, AL 35905

MURPHYS
Don Murphy
Route 3, Box 158C
Strafford, MO 65757

NEW BIRTH SINGERS
Roger Provencal
5311 176th S.W.
Lynwood, WA 98036

NEW CAVALIERS
616 Stonewall
McKenzie, TN 38201

NEW CREATION
Larry Teague, Mgr.
5408 Whitnerville Rd.
Alto, MI 49302

THE NEW GENESIS
David Fulton
Rt. 4, Box 1044
Lakeland, FL 33803

NEW HORIZONS
Gene Beavers
14 Hanover Dr.
Little Rock, AR 72209

NEW HORIZONS
Danny Rhodes
L.C.S.R.
Lebanon, MO 65536

NEW LIFE DIMENSIONS
Denny Strand
10211 N.E. 139th
Kirkland, WA 98033

NEW LIFE SINGERS
Steve Garrison
Box 402
Licking, MO 65542

NEW REVELAIRES
Charles Suratt
Box 89
Locust, NC 28097

NEW SPIRITS
Ray Barnwell
Rt. 1
Seneca, SC 29678

OAKLAND QUARTET
Terry Smoak
Rt. 2, Box 343
Johns Island, SC 29455

OAK RIDGE BOYS
William Golden
920 19th Ave. So.
Nashville, TN 37212

DOUG OLDHAM
11039 Timberlake Rd.
Lynchburg, VA 24502

THE OLSONS
Grady Olson
P.O. Box 374
Enumclaw, WA 98022

THE DON OLSON QUARTET
Arnold Olson
P.O. Box 236
Kirkland, WA 98033

ONE ACCORD
Jerry McMahon
Box 1542
Maryland Heights, MO 63043

ORRELLS
P.O. Box 68
Allen Park, MI 48101

OZARKIANS
Jerry Adams
106 E. Jay
Ozark, MO 65721

THE OZARK QUARTET
Palmer Foley
P.O. Box 425
Mtn. Home, AR 72653

KENNY PARKER TRIO
1645 Wendy Circle
Soddy, TN 37379

DON PARKS FAMILY
Kevin Hauskins
1349 12th St.
Marion, IA 52302

PAUL G. PARR & SONGMASTERS
Paul Parr
P.O. Box 855
Decatur, IL 625254

PATHFINDERS QUARTET
P.O. Box 68
Covina, CA 91723

PAYNE FAMILY
P.O. Box 1515
Abilene, TX 79604

THE PHELPS BROTHERS
David Phelps
1115 Grant Street
Eldorado, IL 62930

PIEROT FAMILY
224 N. 11th
Durant, OK 74701

THE PIONEERS
110 Highland
Raeford, NC 28376

THE PREMIERS
Leyden Ingebrigtsen
P.O. Box 701
Seattle, WA 98107

PRISONERS OF LOVE
Freeman Borntreger
1930 Jasmine Dr.
Sarasota, FL 33579

THE PRODIGALS
P.O. Box 17373
Tampa, FL 33682

THE REAPERS
Billy Byrd
1839 Joy Circle
Nashville, TN 37207

VERN REEVES
12623 29th PL. W.
Everett, WA 98204

REFLECTIONS
Jim Kerr
P.O. Box 152
Auburn, WA 98002

REFLECTIONS
Wanda Neugent
P.O. Box 8607
Long Beach, CA 90808

REGENTS
Charles Novell
5695 Princeton-Glendale Rd.
Hamilton, OH 45011

REGENTS OF HUNTSVILLE
Bill Bowen, Mgr.
P.O. Box 5244
Huntsville, AL 35805

REVELATIONS
J.D. Greene
Route 3
Rogersville, MO 65804

REVELATORS
Bob Ball
P.O. Box 243
Clarksville, AR 72830

RHYTHM MASTERS
Carroll Rawlings
320 Mill Street
Cincinnati, OH 45215

RIDDLE FAMILY
Star Route
Marlow, OK 73055

ROBBERSON FAMILY
Grover Robberson, Mgr.
Route 2, Box 106
Ozark, MO 65721

ROSE OF SHARON GOSPEL
    SINGERS
1480 Flordawn Drive
Florissant, MO 63031

RUSS FAMILY
John Russ
907 N. Sunset Ave.
Rockfield, IL 61103

SALVATION SINGERS
Connie Vinton
Route 1, Box 89
Strafford, MO 65757

SAMUELSONS
Kjell Samuelson
BOX 200 751-04
Uppsala 1, Sweden

SAY FAMILY
Rev. Bob Say
1515 Pine Lake Drive
Orlando, FL 32808

SCENIC LAND QUARTET
Fay Sims
3215 Rossville Blvd.
Chattanooga, TN 37407

BOB SCOTT
4551 S. Whitepine Drive
Tucson, AZ 85730

SECOND COMING
Wendell West
7111 Canyon Rd.
San Bernadino, CA 92404

SEGO BROTHERS & NAOMI
James Sego
White House, TN 37188

LAMAR SEGO FAMILY
P.O. Box 7309
Macon, GA 31208

SENATORS
Ray Shelton
P.O. Box 622
Columbus, MS 39701

GEORGE BEVERLY SHEA
4068 Garden Ave.
Western Springs, IL 60558

REV. LAVERNE SHIFFER
209 Stryker
Joliet, IL 60436

THE SHINING LIGHT
Alan Skoog
19915 2nd N.W.
Seattle, WA 98177

SINGING APOSTLES
Route 1
Hartsville, MO 65667

SINGING BUTTERMORE FAMILY
Rt. 1, Box 267-C-1
Tarpon Springs, FL 33589

SINGING CHRISTIANS
Wayne Christian
P.O. Box 545
Tenaha, TX 7597

SINGING COMMODORES
Marvin Browder
Rt. 2
Fyffe, AL 35971

SINGING ECHOES
1615 Ridgeview Dr.
Cleveland, TN 37311

SINGING EVANGELIST
Mrs. Carol Robertson
5003 Selena Street
Winston-Salem, NC 27106

SINGING GOFFS
Jerry Goff
P.O. Box 15707
Nashville, TN 37215

SINGING LACEY FAMILY
Wayne Lacey, Mgr.
6916 Central Ave.
Tampa, FL 33604

SINGING LEDBETTERS
Glen Ledbetter
518 Hiram Street
Wichita, KS 67213

SINGING PROUSES
Jim Prouse
Rt. 6, Box 645
Salisbury, MD 21801

SINGING RAMBOS
Buck Rambo
2199 Nolensville Rd.
Nashville, TN 37211

SINGING REIDS
1038 Bank Street
Painesville, OH 44077

SINGING SNIDERS
Bernice Snider
Star Route, Box 431
Hollister, MO 65672

SINGING SOUL WINNERS
Ivan Wall
Route 1, Box 22A
Ulman, MO 65083

SINGING SPEARMANS
Rt. 1, Box 304
Blacksburg, SC 29702

SINGING TRAVELERS
4420 South St.
Marion, IN 46952

HENRY & HAZEL SLAUGHTER
P.O. Box 8073
Nashville, TN 37207

SMITH FAMILY SINGERS
Dan Smith
6046 Valley Drive
Bettendorf, IA 52722

SONG MASTERS
Joel Kelsey
P.O. Box 647
Milan, TN 38358

SONG OF CELEBRATION
Donn Clayton
32305 N.E. 8th
Carnation, WA 98104

SONS OF THE LORD
C.S. Taylor
118 So. McIlroy
West Terre Haute, IN 47885

SOUTH FAMILY
5830 W. Oakton
Morton Grove, IL 60053

SPEER FAMILY
Brock Speer
P.O. Box 40201
Nashville, TN 37204

STAKERS
Paul B. Durham
Rt. 3, Box 53
Walnut, MS 38683

STAMPS QUARTET
J.D. Sumner
Box 15532
Nashville, TN 37215

SUNDAY EDITION
Deon Unthank
1311 No. 51st St.
East St. Louis, IL 62204

SUNDOWN GOSPEL SINGERS
Darrell Phillips
4105 Shawnee Drive
Kansas City, KS 66106

SUNLITERS
Wendy Bagwell
4425 Ridge Road
Smyrna, GA 30080

SUNRISE SINGERS
Box 687
Alvin, TX 77511

SUNSHINE SISTERS
P.O. Box 2205
N. Hollywood, CA 91602

SUPERNALS
Paul Kittleman
2548 N. Main
Springfield, MO 65803

JIMMY SWAGGART
P.O. Box 66318
Baton Rouge, LA 70806

THE SWORDSMEN
Eddie Arnold
314 Shoreline Dr.
Hampton, VA 23369

THE TAFOYA SINGERS
2319 Pioneer Ave.
Cheyenne, WY 82201

TELLESTIALS
218 E. Palestine
Madison, TN 37115

TEMPLE TRIO
Norm Van Patten
P.O. Box 1756
Everett, WA 98206

THE TEMPOS
Bob White, Mgr.
P.O. Box 100
Rothesay, N.B.
Canada, EOG 2WO

THE TENNESSEANS
Willie Wynn
Rt. 1, Box 45A
Pleasant Shade, TN 37145

TEXAS AMBASSADORS
Emory Atkins
407 Cunningham Dr.
Rufkin, TX 75901

THOMPSON FAMILY SINGERS
Kemit Thompson
513 College St.
Henderson, NC 27536

TONESMEN
Randy Parker
Box 62361
Virginia Beach, VA 23462

TRAVELLERS
Ted Hampton
4329 Pratt
Springfield, MO 65804

TRIBUNES
Jay Kirkland
P.O. Box 10
Plant City, FL 33566

THE TRU DIMENSION
Jerry Baser, Mgr.
202 Lohman, Apt. 209
Miami, OK 74354

TUCKER FAMILY
3511 North West 63rd
Hollywood, FL 33024

UNITED QUARTET
3931 S. Compton
St. Louis, MO 63118

VALLEYAIRES QUARTET
Johnny Clowdus
P.O. Box 642
Oneonta, AL 35121

THE VANGELS
Burl Rogers
P.O. Box 357
Coppell, TX 75019

VELVET & THE EVANGELS
Edgar Williams, Jr.
Rt. 2, Box 956
Bryceville, FL 32009

THE VICTORY SINGERS
Love Turner
9 Hadley St.
East Wenatchee, WA 98001

VIKINGS
Don Burris
P.O. Box 609
Benso, NC 27504

VIRGINIANS
P.O. Box 1922
Roanoke, VA 24008

VOICES TRIUMPHANT
724½ Giley Street
Flatwoods, KY 41139

NEIL GRANT VOSBURGH
3729 So. "K" St.
Tacoma, WA 98409

THE WATCHMEN
John Abraham, Mgr.
P.O. Box 218
Clymer, PA 15728

WATCHMEN QUARTET
Don Yates
808 N. Marion
Springfield, MO 65802

WATERS FAMILY
Maynard Waters
Box 488
Eden, NC 27288

WEATHERFORDS
Earl Weatherford
Box 116
Poalia, OK 73074

107

413

WESLEY CHAPELAIRES
Ron Forsyth
P.O. Box 333
Winchester, OH 45697

TEEP WICKER FAMILY
P.O. Box 151
Huntingdon, TN 38344

WILLIAMS FAMILY
Monty Williams
Route 3, Box 251
Springfield, MO 65804

WILLS FAMILY
Calvin Wills
Box 211
Arlington, TX 76010

WISEMEN QUARTET
Bob Chambers
3451 Barbett
Springfield, MO 65804

LANNY WOLFE TRIO
P.O. Box 20407
Jackson, MS 39209

WORLD MINISTRY SINGERS
Jim Gross, Mgr.
1424 Northwest 6th St.
Gainesville, FL 32602

YOUNG APOSTLES QUARTET
Chip Huffman
P.O. Box 155
Steubenville, OH 43952

THE YOUNG CHRISTIANS GOSPEL QUARTET
Mitchell Granttaw
204 Woodbine St.
Goldsboro, NC 27530

YOUNG DEACONS
Richard Lee
Rt. 2, Box 350
Burlington, NC 27215

YOUNG GOSPELS
Darold Johnson
Rt. 1, Box 265
Alton, MO 65606

Talent Agencies

ASSOCIATED ARTIST AGENCY
118 East Second Street
Lexingto, KY 40508

BEAVERWOOD TALENT AGENCY
133 Walton Ferry Road
Hendersonville, TN 37075

BOLLMAN ENTERPRISES
P.O. Box 28553
Dallas, TX 75228

BOSS ATTRACTIONS
P.O. Box 11457
Columbia, SC 29211

CALIFORNIA ARTIST TALENT AGENCY
P.O. Box 6523
San Jose, CA 95150

CENTURY II
Sonny Simmons
P.O. Box 707
Nashville, TN 37202

DESIGNER GOSPEL ATTRACTIONS
P.O. Box 11286
E. Memphis Station
Memphis, TN 38111

FISHERS OF MEN OPPORTUNITIES, INC.
Suite 1004/3050 Biscayne Boulevard
Miami, FL 33137

BILL FORD AGENCY
P.O. Box 3322
Lynchburg, VA 24503

GOSPEL MUSIC WORLD TALENT AGENCY
3935 Summer Ave.
Memphis, TN 38122

GOSPEL ROAD AGENCY
Buddy Poe
P.O. Box 6865
Irondale, AL 35210

MARVE HOERNER
P.O. Box 99
Amboy, IL 61310

DON LIGHT TALENT
Herman Harper, Mgr.
1100 17th Ave. So.
Nashville, TN 37212

NASHVILLE GOSPEL
Lou and Howard Hildreth
P.O. Box 50
Nashville, TN 37202

LARRY RILEY AGENCY
Larry Riley, President
P.O. Box 59
Sedalia, OH 43151

SKYLIGHT TALENT AGENCY
1008 17th Ave. So.
Nashville, TN 37212

STARLIGHT PRODUCTIONS
Johnny Massengill
P.O. Box 127
Enville, TN 38332

SUMAR TALENT AGENCY
Don Butler
58 Music Square West
Nashville, TN 37212

TOP TEN CORPORATION
P.O. Box 5025
Roanoke, VA 24012

WADE STALEY TALENT AGENCY
P.O. Box 5712
High Point, NC 27262

WAYNE COOMBS AGENCY, INC.
655 Deep Valley Dr.
Rolling Hills Estates, CA 90274

WORLD WIDE TALENT, LTD.
P.O. Box 966
Oklawaha, FL 32679

TOP BILLING
Bob Bray
4301 Hillsboro Road
Nashville, TN 37212

Periodicals

AMUSEMENT BUSINESS
Walter Heeney
1717 West End Ave.
Nashville, TN 37203

ASSOCIATED PRESS
Nancy Shipley
1100 Broad
Nashville, TN 37203

BILLBOARD MAGAZINE
1717 West End Ave.
Nashville, TN 37203

BOOKSTORE JOURNAL
Mavis Sanders
2031 W. Cheyenne Boulevard
Colorado Springs, CO 80901

CASH BOX
Juanita Jones
7 Music Circle N.
Nashville, TN 37203

CHRISTIAN HERALD
27 E. 39th St.
New York, NY 10016

THE COMMUNICATOR
Bob Dixson/NISCO
20 Music Square W.
Nashville, TN 37203

CONCERT LIFE
Cheri Mummert
5252 Trindle Rd.
Mechanicsburg, PA 17055

COUNTRY MUSIC WORLD
L.M. Dodson
P.O. Box 3593
Arlington, VA 22203

CLAIRE COX ASSOC.
Towners Road/Route 3
Brewster, NY 10509

EVANGELICAL PRESS
Norman Rohrer
P.O. Box 707
LaCanada, CA 91101

GOSPEL BANNER
P.O. Box 458
Arnold, MO 63010

GOSPEL JOURNAL
Gene Gideon
P.O. Box 56
Branson, MO 65601

THE GOSPEL LISTENER
Steve Aune
1015 16th Ave. So.
Nashville, TN 37212

**GOSPEL MUSIC WORLD
NEWSPAPER**
3935 Summer Ave.
Memphis, TN 38122

GOSPEL TRADE
Steve Aune
1015 16th Ave. So.
Nashville, TN 37212

GOSPEL WEST
Mrs. Judy Spencer
P.O. Box 2205
No. Hollywood, CA 91602

GRIT
208 West Third Street
Williamsport, PA 17701

MID WEST GOSPEL NEWS
Dale Signs
P.O. Box 357
Vestaburg, MI 48891

MOODY MONTHY
820 LaSalle Street
Chicago, IL 60610

MUSIC CITY NEWS
P.O. Box 900
Nashville, TN 37202

THE NASHVILLE BANNER
Red O'Donnell
1100 Broadway
Nashville, TN 37203

NASHVILLE ENTERTAINER
812 16th Ave. So.
Nashville, TN 37203

THE NASHVILLE TENNESSEAN
Lynn Harvey
1100 Broadway
Nashville, TN 37203

NEW MUSIC MAGAZINE
1 Sherman Rd.
Bromley Kent, United Kingdom

PLAYTIME NEWS
Michael McGuirk
1697 Seamens Neck Road
Seafork, NY 11783

RECORD WORLD
John Sturdivant
49 Music Square West
Nashville, TN 37203

SAY IT WITH MUSIC
Phyllis Olsa
P.O. Box 1206
Flint, MI 48501

THE SHOWMAN
P.O. Box 35810
Huntsville, AL 35810

THE SINGING NEWS
Jan Cain
P.O. Box 5188
Pensacola, FL 32505

SOUND FORMAT
Bonnie Bucy
2407 12th Ave. So.
Nashville, TN 37204

SOUTHERN EXPOSURE
Sue Thrasher
88 Walton Street, N.W.
Atlanta, GA 30303

STARTIME NEWS
P.O. Box 410
711 E. Church Street
Batesburg, SC 29006

UNITED PRESS INTERNATIONAL
Duren Cheek
159 4th Ave. No.
Nashville, TN 37219

VARIETY MAGAZINE
154 West 46th Street
New York, NY 10036

WORDS
Mike Priddy
Stephens Bldg.
4436 Dixie Hwy.
Louisville, KY 40216

THE WORLD OF GOSPEL MUSIC
Gary Caudel
792 W. Main
Hendersonville, TN 37075

GMA

Radio Stations

ALABAMA

WABT   Box 668, Tuskegee, 36083 ....18 hrs. weekly
WACT   Drawer 126, Tuscaloosa, 35401 ....28 hrs. weekly
WAGC   P. O. Box Q, Centre, 35960 ....18 hrs. weekly
WAMI   Box 169, Opp, 36467 ....11 hrs. weekly
WANA   Box 609, Anniston, 36201 ....8 hrs. weekly
WANL   P. O. Box 597, Lineville, 36266 ....18 hrs. weekly
WAUV   WQSB P.O. Box 190, Albertville, 35950....12 hrs. weekly
WAYD   Box 1259, Ozark, 36360 ....15 hrs. weekly
WBHP   Huntsville, 35601 ....2 hrs. weekly
WBIB   Box 217, Centerville, 35042 ....25 hrs. weekly
WBSA   P. O. Box 597, Boaz, 35957 ....12 hrs. weekly
WBTS   P. O. Box U, Bridgeport, 35740 ....12 hrs. weekly
WCRL   Box 490, Oneonta, 35121 ....15 hrs. weekly
WCTA   p. o. box 8, Andalusia, 36420 ....21 hrs. weekly
WDJC   Box 58021, Birmingham, 35210 ....Full Time
WEBJ   Brewton, 36426 ....20 hrs. weekly
WEIS   Box 295, Centre, 35960 ....24 hrs. weekly
WELB AM   Box 467, Elba 36323 ....24 hrs. weekly
WELR AM-FM   P. O. Box 709, Roanoke, 36274 ....20 hrs. weekly
WERH AM-FM   Box 187, Hamilton, 35570 ....10 hrs. weekly
WETU   Box 60, Wetumpka, 36092 ....15 hrs. weekly
WFEB   Box 358, Sylacauga, 25150 ....14 hrs. weekly
WFHK   Box 606, Pell City, 35125 ....25 hrs. weekly
WFPA   Box 155, Ft. Wayne, 35967 ....18 hrs. weekly
WIPH   p. o. Box 6787, Birmingham, 35210 ....35 hrs. weekly
WJAM   P. O. Drawer 930, Marion, 36756 ....20 hrs. weekly
WJBY   P. O. Box 930, Gadsden, 35901 ....Full Time
WJHO   P. O. Box 710, Opelika, 36801 ....20 hrs. weekly
WJOH   P. O. Box 710, Opelika, 36801 ....20 hrs. weekly
WJMW   Box 386, Athens, 35611 ....10 hrs. weekly
WJOF FM   Box 386, Athens, 35611 ....10 hrs. weekly
WKLD   Box 490, Oneonta, 35121 ....15 hrs. weekly
WKLF   P. O. Box 110, Clanton, 35045 ....26 hrs. weekly
WLAY   Box 220, Sheffield, 35660 ....Full Time
WLPH   416 Woodward Bldg., Birmingham, 35203 ....Full Time
WMFC   Box 641, Monroeville, 36460 ....11 hrs. weekly
WMGY   Box 2271, Montgomery, 36103 ....49 hrs. weekly
WMOO   Box 1967, Mobile, 36601 ....35 hrs. weekly
WMSL   701 Bank St., Decatur, 35601 ....4 hrs. weekly
WNDA   2407 9th Ave., Huntsville, 35805 ....108 hrs. weekly
WNUZ   Box 974, Talledega, 36160 ....16 hrs. weekly
WPID   Box 223, Piedmont, 36272 ....25 hrs. weekly
WRAG   Box 71, Carrollton, 35447 ....7 hrs. weekly
WRCK   Box 517, Tuscumbia, 35674 ....10 hrs. weekly
WRFS AM-FM   Box 72, Alexander City, 35010 ....15 hrs. weekly
WROS   Box 966, Scottsboro, 35768 ....20 hrs. weekly
WRSA   Rt. 1, Box 203, Lacey's Spring, 35754 ....2½ hrs. weekly
WSHF   Martin Ave., Sheffield, 35660 ....15 hrs. weekly
WTUB   Troy, 36081 ....20 hrs. weekly
WULA AM-FM   Box 531, Eufaula, 36027 ....10 hrs. weekly
WVSA   Box 630, Vernon, 35592 ....17 hrs. weekly
WVSM   Box 161, Rainsville, 35986 ....14 hrs. weekly
WWWB   Box 622, Jasper, 35501 ....20 hrs. weekly
WWWF   Box 189, Fayette, 35555 ....15 hrs. weekly
WWWR   Box 518, Russellville, 35653 ....15 hrs. weekly
WYAM   Brighton Rd., Bessemer, 35020 ....11 hrs. weekly
WYLS   Box 687, York, 36925 ....17 hrs. weekly

ALASKA

KICY   Box 820, Nome, 99762 ....20 hrs. weekly
KJNP   Box 0, North Pole, 99705 ....Full Time

ARIZONA

KFMM FM   Box 4009, Tucson, 85717 ....99 hrs. weekly
KHCS   9827 N. 32nd St., Phoenix, 85028 ....40 hrs. weekly
KHEP   3883 N. 38th, Phoenix, 85019 ....43 hrs. weekly

ARKANSAS

KAMD   P. O. Box 957, Camden 71701 ....10 hrs. weekly
KAMO   114½ South 1st St., Rogers, 72756 ....8 hrs. weekly
KAMS FM   Box 193, Mammoth Springs, 72554 ....20 hrs. weekly
KBHC   Box 236, Nashville, 71852 ....15 hrs. weekly
KBIB   Box B, Monette, 72447 ....12 hrs. weekly
KBJT   Box 659, Fordyce, 71742 ....10 hrs. weekly
KBRS   Box 47, Springdale, 72764 ....10 hrs. weekly
KCCB   Pearl St., Corning, 72422 ....8 hrs. weekly
KCCL   24 S. Express St., Paris, 72855 ....12 hrs. weekly
KDDA   P. O. Box 215, Dumas, 71639 ....7 hrs. weekly
KDEW   Box 326, DeWitt, 72042 ....12 hrs. weekly
KDQN   Box 311, DeQueen, 71832 ....18 hrs. weekly
KDRS   Box 117, Paragould, 72450 ....8 hrs. weekly
KPBA   Box 5086, Pine Bluff, 71601 ....12 hrs. weekly
KENA   Box 1450, Mena, 71901 ....8 hrs. weekly
KFDF   711½ Main St., Van Buren, 72956 ....48 hrs. weekly
KGMR   Box 311, Jacksonville, 72076 ....34 hrs. weekly
KJBU   John Brown University, Siloam 72761 ....25 hrs. weekly
KPBA   Box 5086, Pine Bluff, 71601 ....Full Time
KSOH   4015 W. Capitol, Little Rock 72207 ....Full Time
KSUD   104 North 5th, West Memphis, 72301 ....Full Time
KWCK FM   Drawer 708, Searcy, 72143 ....25 hrs. weekly
KWAK   Box 907, Stuttgart, 72160 ....10 hrs. weekly
KWCB   P. O. Box 95, Searcy, 72143 ....13 hrs. weekly
KXOW   Box 579, Hot Springs, 71901 ....Full Time

CALIFORNIA

KAVR   Apple Valley, 92307 ....6 hrs. weekly
KBBL   P. O. Box 292, Riverside, 92501 ....19 hrs. weekly
KCHJ   Box 6056, Bakersfield, 93306 ....15 hrs. weekly
KDNO   Box 99, Delano, 93215 ....99 hrs. weekly
KECR   312 West Douglas, El Cajon, 92020 ....Full Time
KEWG   6013 Nort Libby Rd., Paradise, 95969 ....20 hrs. weekly
KEWQ   Box AA, Paradise, 95969 ....40 hrs. weekly
KGER   Box 7126, Long Beach, 90807 ....20 hrs. weekly
KHOF FM   Glendale, ...6 hrs. weekly
KLBS   Los Banos, 93635 ....14 hrs. weekly
KLRO   233 "A" St., Suite 205, Sand Diego, 92101 .....41 hrs. weekly
KMAX FM   3844 E. Foothill Bovd., Pasadena 91107 ....Full Time
KMGO   Box 637, Vista, 92083 ....12 hrs. weekly
KNGS   Box 49, Hanford, 93230 ....8 hrs. weekly
KOAD   15279 Hanford-Armond Rd., Lemoore, 93245 ....14 hrs. weekly
KPRL   P. O. Box 96, Paso Robles, 93446 ....8 hrs. weekly
KQLH FM   P.O. Box 5640, San Bernadino, 92412 ....Full Time
KREL   P. O. Box 100 Corona, 91720 ....Full Time
KRDU   110 North "L" St., Dinubia, 93618 ....22½ hrs. weekly
KSOM   Box 1510, Ontario, 91762 ....12 hrs. weekly
KVIP AM-FM   1139 Hartnell Ave., Redding, 96001 ....7 hrs. weekly
KWCR   Westmont College, Santa Barbara, 93108 .....30 hrs. weekly
KYNS   1601 No. Bristol, Santa Ana 92706 ....Full Time

COLORADO

KPIK   Box 24404, Colorado Springs
KPOF   Westminster, 80030 ....20 hrs. weekly
KQXI   P. O. Box 504, Arvada, 80002 ....38 hrs. weekly
KRIS   6535 Jewell Ave., Denver, 80226 ....40 hrs. weekly
KWYD   Box 5668, Colorado Springs, ...Full Time

CONNECTICUT

WIHS FM   P. O. Box 117, Middletown, 06457 ....27 hrs. weekly

DELAWARE

WKEN   Rt. 1, Box 302C, Hartly, 19953 ....10 hrs. weekly

110

416

FLORIDA

WAPG	Box 632, Arcadia, 33821	23 hrs. weekly
WAPR	P. O. Box 1390, Avon, 33825	12 hrs. weekly
WAUG	Box 936, Wauchula, 33873	11 hrs. weekly
WBIX	P. O. Box 16656, Jacksonville, 32216	47 hrs. weekly
WCNU	Box 518, Crestview, 32536	20 hrs. weekly
WCOF	Box 520, Immokalee, 33934	15 hrs. weekly
WEBY	P. O. Box 5008, Pensacola, 32505	18 hrs. weekly
WFIV	Drawer 5519, Orlando, 32805	18 hrs. weekly
WFIY	Drawer B, Kissimmee, 32741	36 hrs. weekly
WGLY	495 Baltimore Way, Suite 404, Coral Gables, 33134	Full Time
WGNB AM-FM	Box 888, St. Petersburg, 33708	60 hrs. weekly
WIII	Box 98, Homestead, 33030	8 hrs. weekly
WINQ	P.O. Box 1010, Seffner, 33584	Full Time
WJOE	P. O. Box 5008, Pensacola, 32505	18 hrs. weekly
WJSB	Box 267, Crestview, 32536	14 hrs. weekly
WKMK	P. O. Box 297, Blountstown, 32424	15 hrs. weekly
WNER	Box 130, Live Oak, 32060	8 hrs. weekly
WOMA	Box 1047, Tallahassee, 32302	20 hrs. weekly
WONN	Box 2038, Lakeland, 33801	20 hrs. weekly
WPAS	P. O. Box 508, Zephrhills, 33599	5 hrs. weekly
WPCV FM	P. O. Box 9205, Winter Haven, 33880	3 hrs. weekly
WPLA	Drawer J, Plant City, 33565	10 hrs. weekly
WPRV	Box 936, Wauchula, 33873	12 hrs. weekly
WQDI	507 N. W. 2nd St., Homestead, 33030	
WRTM	P. O. Box 197, Blountstown, 32424	15 hrs. weekly
WSBP	Radio Road, Chattahoochee, 32324	10 hrs. weekly
WSOR	P. O. Box 953, Ft. Myers, 33905	Full Time
WSWN	Box 786, Belle Glade, 33430	14 hrs. weekly
WTBJ	Box 519, Monticello, 32344	
WTBJ	Drawer AA, Apoka, 32703	25 hrs. weekly
WTMT	Box 1047, Tallahassee, 32302	20 hrs. weekly
WTWB	Box 7, Auburndale, 33823	35 hrs. weekly
WTYS	Box 777, Marianna, 32446	10 hrs. weekly
WVCF	Box 768, Windemere, 32786	20 hrs. weekly
WWAB	Box 65, Lakeland, 33802	10 hrs. weekly
WWBC	Box 493, Cocoa, 32922	7 hrs. weekly
WWQS	Box 1550, Orlando, 32803	23 hrs. weekly
WWSD	Box 519, Monticello, 32344	28 hrs. weekly
WXBM	P. O. Box 5008, Pensacola, 32505	18 hrs. weekly
WYRL	Box 508, Melbourne, 32901	10 hrs. weekly
WZEP	Box 387, De Funiak Springs, 32433	15 hrs. weekly

GEORGIA

WACL	P. O. Box 858, Waycross, 31501	9½ hrs. weekly
WACX	P. O. Box 746, Austell, 30001	14 hrs. weekly
WAFT	Box 338, Valdosta, 31601	16 hrs. weekly
WAUG	P. O. Box 669, Augusta, 30903	Full Time
WBHB	Box 100, Fitzgerald, 31750	10 hrs. weekly
WBIT	Box 538, Adel, 31620	24 hrs. weekly
WBMK	705 W. 4th Ave. West Point, 38133	24 hrs. weekly
WCHK	Box 1290, Canton, 30114	24 hrs. weekly
WCQS	Box 40, Alma, 31510	24 hrs. weekly
WCQS	Box 40, Alma, 31510	20 hrs. weekly
WDGL	Douglasville, 30134	24 hrs. weekly
WDMG	Box 860, Douglas, 31533	12 hrs. weekly
WDUN	Box 10, Gainesville, 30501	12 hrs. weekly
WDYX	Box 307, Buford, 30518	10 hrs. weekly
WEHK AM-FM	Box 1290, Canton, 30114	25 hrs. weekly
WGFS	Box 869, Covington, 30209	7 hrs. weekly
WGHG	Box 348, Clayton, 30525	10 hrs. weekly
WGRA	401 Mathewson, Pelham	15 hrs. weekly
WGSR	Box 869, Millen, 30442	7 hrs. weekly
WGTA	P. O. Box 20, Summerville, 30747	20 hrs. weekly
WGUN	Box 67, Decatur, 30031	14 hrs. weekly
WGUS	Box 1475, Augusta, 30904	24 hrs. weekly
WHIE	Box 971, Griffin, 30223	15 hrs. weekly
WHYD	Box 1537, Columbus, 31906	12 hrs. weekly
WISK	So. Lee St., Americus, 31709	12 hrs. weekly
WJEM	Box 368, Valdosta, 31606	16 hrs. weekly
WKIG	226 E. Bolton St., Glennville, 30427	7 hrs. weekly
WKUN	702 E. Spring St., Monroe, 30655	15 hrs. weekly
WLET	423 Prather Bridge Rd., Toccoa, 35077	21 hrs. weekly
WLOP	Box 647, Jesup, 31545	24 hrs. weekly
WLOR	Box 45, Thomasville, 371794	18 hrs. weekly
WLYB	Box 1624, Albany, 31702	15 hrs. weekly
WMAH	Martin Army Hospital, Ft. Benning, 31905	9 hrs. weekly
WMES	Box 32, Ashburn, 31714	15 hrs. weekly
WMGA	Box 549, Moultrie, 31768	11 hrs. weekly
WMGR	Box 706, Bainbridge, 31717	13 hrs. weekly
WMTM AM-FM	P. O. Box 788, Moultrie, 31768	30 hrs. weekly
WNEA	Box 405, Newman, 30263	20 hrs. weekly
WNEG	Box 907, Tocca, 30577	16 hrs. weekly
WNGA	Box 645, Nashville, 31639	10 hrs. weekly

WOKA AM-FM	Box 471, Douglas, 31533	30 hrs. weekly
WOWE	Rossville	
WPEH	Box 425, Louisville, 30434	10 hrs. weekly
WRIP	Rossville, 30741	Full Time
WRLD	P. O. Box 312, West Point, 31833	24 hrs. weekly
WRWH	Box 181, Cleveland, 30528	19 hrs. weekly
WSEM	Box 87, Donaldsonville, 31745	20 hrs. weekly
WSIZ	Box 186, Ocilla, 31774	14 hrs. weekly
WSNE AM	Box 609, Cumming, 30130	56 hrs. weekly
WSOJ FM	P. O. Box 1038, Jesup, 31545	Full Time
WSYL	Box 519, Sylvania, 30467	10 hrs. weekly
WTGA	Box 853, Thomaston, 30286	8 hrs. weekly
WTIF	Box 967, East Point, 30344	Full Time
WTJM	2146 Dodson Dr., East Point, 30344	20 hrs. weekly
WTTI	Box 216, Dalton, 30720	15 hrs. weekly
WTWA	Box 591, Thomson, 30328	4 hrs. weekly
WUFE	Box 389, Baxley, 31513	30 hrs. weekly
WUFF	Box 626, Eastman, 31023	20 hrs. weekly
WVLF	Box 1987, Alma, 31510	25 hrs. weekly
WVMG FM	P. O. Box 504, Cochran, 31014	Full Time
WVMG AM	P. O. Box 504, Cochran, 31014	14 hrs. weekly
WWCC	Box 397, Bremen, 30110	8 hrs. weekly
WXLI	Box 967, Dublin, 31021	15 hrs. weekly
WYNX	Smyrna,	Full Time

HAWAII

KAIM	3555 Harding Ave., Honolulu, 96816	12 hrs. weekly

IDAHO

KBGN	Caldwell, 83605	30 hrs. weekly
KCRH	Northwest Nazarene College, Nampa, 83651	Full Time
KGEM	Box 5278, Boise, 83705	12 hrs. weekly

ILLINOIS

WBBA	Radio Park, Pittsfield, 62363	8 hrs. weekly
WDDD	Route 37 N. Marion, 62959	13 hrs. weekly
WDLM	Box 87, East Moline, 61244	25 hrs. weekly
WEIC FM	Charleston, 61920	19 hrs. weekly
WETN	Wheaton College, Wheaton, 60187	10 hrs. weekly
WFIW	P. O. Box 310, Fairfield, 62837	7 hrs. weekly
WHOW	Box 160, Clinton, 61717	10 hrs. weekly
WJBM	Box 310, Jerseyville, 62050	10 hrs. weekly
WLCC	Box 178, Lincoln, 62656	15 hrs. weekly
WLNR	2915 Bernice Rd., Lansing, 60438	10 hrs. weekly
WMBI AM-FM	820 N. La Salle St., Chicago, 60610	70 hrs. weekly
WMOK	P. O. Box 720, Metropolis, 62960	14 hrs. weekly
WPEQ	121 N. Jefferson, Suite 204, Peoria, 61602	Full Time
WPOK AM-FM	P. O. Box 740, Pontiac, 61764	7 hrs. weekly
WTAQ	9355 W. Joliet, LaGrange, 60525	35 hrs. weekly

INDIANA

WBAT	Box 839, Marion, 46952	40 hrs. weekly
WBNL	Boonville, 47601	7 hrs. weekly
WCRD	Box 321, Bluffton, 46714	4 hrs. weekly
WHME FM	Box 12, South Bend, 46624	189 hrs. weekly
WCNB	406 Central Ave., Connersville, 47331	25 hrs. weekly
WHON	Box 1647, Richmond, 47374	8 hrs. weekly
WIFF FM	P. O. Box 551, Auburn, 46706	16 hrs. weekly
WMPJ	Box 270, Scottsburg, 47170	7 hrs. weekly
WQLK	1027 Abington Pk., Richmond 47374	28 hrs. weekly
WRIN	P. O. Box 282, Rensselaer, 47978	15 hrs. weekly
WSBT	300 W. Jefferson, South Bend, 46601	79 hrs. weekly
WSLM	Salem, 47167	Full Time
WSVL FM	Morristown Rd., Shelbyville, 46176	7 hrs. weekly
WVAK	Box 150, Paoli, 47454	20 hrs. weekly
WVHI	6621 Kratzville Rd., Evansville, 47708	90 hrs. weekly
WVTL	Box 570, Monticello, 47960	2 hrs. weekly
WWVR	Route 3, West Terre Haute, 47885	Full Time
WXUS	1000 Ortman Lane, Lafayette, 47905	12 hrs. weekly
WYCA	6336 Calumet Ave., Hammond, 46324	Full Time

IOWA

KDMI	2907 Merle Hay Rd., Des Moines, 50310	Full Time
KFGQ	924 W. 2nd, Boone, 50036	7 hrs. weekly
KNWS	4880 LaPorte, Waterloo, 50702	75 hrs. weekly
KSAY	Box 709, Clinton, 52732	96.1 Full Time
KSMN	P.O. Box 1446, Mason City, 50401	10 hrs. weekly
KTAV	Box 436 Knoxville, 50138	Full Time
KTOF	158 Collins Rd., Cedar Rapids, 52406	Full Time
KWKY	419½ Locust St., Des Moines, 50309	10 hrs. weekly
WMT	Paramount Theater Bldg., Cedar Rapids 52406	14 hrs. weekly

KANSAS

KCLO	335 Muncie Rd., Leavenworth, 66048	35 hrs. weekly
KFDI	Box 1402, Wichita, 67201	8 hrs. weekly
KFLA	Rt. 1, Box 6, Scott City, 67871	24 hrs. weekly
KJRS	Box 567, Newton, 67114	25 hrs. weekly
KSKG	Box 995, Salina, 67401	Full Time
WNIC	Suite 300, 1st National Bank Bldg., Winfield, 67156	50 hrs. weekly

KENTUCKY

WABD	Box 521, Ft. Campbell, 42223	20 hrs. weekly
WAIN	Box 77, Columbia, 42728	15 hrs. weekly
WANY	Box 158, Albany, 42602	20 hrs. weekly
WCTT	Kentucky Ave., Corbin, 40701	16 hrs. weekly
WDOC	Box 309, Prestonburg, 41653	20 hrs. weekly
WEKG	1138 Main St., Jackson 41339	10 hrs. weekly
WFIA	310 W. Libert, Louisville, 40202	Full Time
WFKY	Box P, Frankfort, 40601	7 hrs. weekly
WFTM	34 E. 3rd St., Maysville, 41056	20 hrs. weekly
WGOH	Box 487, Grayson, 41143	12 hrs. weekly
WGRK	Rt. 5, Greenburg, 42743	10 hrs. weekly
WHKK	100 Commonwealth Ave., Erlanger, 41018	89 hrs. weekly
WIXI	108-A Stanford St., Lancaster, 40444	18 hrs. weekly
WJKY	box 263, Jamestown, 42629	25 hrs. weekly
WJMM	1200 South Broadway, Lexington, 40508	Full Time
WJRS	Box 263, Jamestown, 42629	25 hrs. weekly
WKAY	P. O. Box 219, Glasgow, 42141	8 hrs. weekly
WKDO	Box B, Liberty, 42539	25 hrs. weekly
WKDZ	Drawer "D," Cadiz, 42211	8½ hrs. weekly
WKIC	Box 698, Hazard, 41701	12 hrs. weekly
WKKS	1106 Fairlane Dr., Vanceburg, 41179	20 hrs. weekly
WKWY FM	Box P, Frankfort, 40601	6 hrs. weekly
WKXO	p. o. Box 423, Berea, 40403	Full Time
WLBJ	Box 689, Bowling Green 42101	10 hrs. weekly
WLCK	Box 158, Scottsville, 42164	15 hrs. weekly
WLJC	box S, Beattyville, 41311	40 hrs. weekly
WLKS	129 College St., West Liberty, 41472	40 hrs. weekly
WLKS	129 College St., West Liberty, 41472	12 hrs. weekly
WLLS	Box 160, Beaver Dam, 42340	7 hrs. weekly
WMIK	North 19th St., Middlesboro, 40965	12 hrs. weekly
WMTL	Leitchfield, 42754	20 hrs. weekly
WPDE AM-FM	Box 440, Paris, 40361	10 hrs. weekly
WPHN	Middlesburg St., Liberty, 42539	18 hrs. weekly
WFSL	Box 237, Stanford, 40484	10 hrs. weekly
WRVK	Box 1460, Renfro Valley, 40473	23 hrs. weekly
WSIP	Box 591, Paintsville, 41240	14 hrs. weekly
WTKY	Highway 1049, Tompkinsville, 42167	16 hrs. weekly
WVHI	1030 N. Green St., Henderson, 42420	6 hrs. weekly
WYWY	Barbourville, 40906	35 hrs. weekly

LOUISIANA

KCIJ	Box 197, Shreveport, 71102	17 hrs. weekly
KDLA	Box 46, DeRidder, 70634	16 hrs. weekly
KDXI	Drawer 740, Mansfield, 71052	12 hrs. weekly
KLUV	p. o. Box 189, Haynesville, 71038	7 hrs. weekly
KMAR AM	Box 312, Winnsboro, 71295	18 hrs. weekly
KMRC	602 Brasher Ave., Morgan City, 70380	Full Time hrs. weekly
KNCB	P. O. Box 1072, Vivian, 71082	7 hrs. weekly
KREB	Penn Resort Hotel, Monroe, 71201	14 hrs. weekly
KTDL	Box 64, Farmersville, 71241	14 hrs. weekly
KTOC AM-FM	Box 550, Jonesboro, 71251	12 hrs. weekly
KTRY	Box 1075, Bastrop, 71220	15 hrs. weekly
KWCL	Box 1130, Shreveport, 71102	9 hrs. weekly
WBFS	Rt. 1, Box 306, Slidell, 70458	12 hrs. weekly
WBOX	P. O. Box 280, Bogalusa, 70427	6 hrs. weekly
WFCG	Box 404, Franklin, 70438	15 hrs. weekly
WLUX	p. o. Box 2550, Baton Rouge, 70821	Full Time
WVOG	125 No. Glavez St., New Orleans, 70119	Full Time
WYLD	2906 Tulane Ave., New Orleans, 70119	32 hrs. weekly

MAINE

WDHP FM	P. O. Box 969, Caribou, 04736	26 hrs. weekly

MARYLAND

WASA	P. O. Box 97, Havre De Grace, 21978	90 hrs. weekly
WBMD	5200 Moravia Rd., Baltimore, 21206	12 hrs. weekly
WHDG	Box 97, Harve de Grace, 21078	59 hrs. weekly
WOLC	Box 130, Princess Anne, 21853	Full Time
WRBS	1130 E. Cold Spring Lane, Baltimore, 21716	18 hrs. weekly
WTHV	Radio Lane, Thurmont, 21788	3 hrs. weekly

112

MASSACHUSETTS

WRYT	312 Suart St., Boston, 02116	14 hrs. weekly

MICHIGAN

WANG FM	Box 1590, Coldwater, 49036	5 hrs. weekly
WAOP	Box 980, Otsego, 49078	Full Time
WBFG	8009 Lyndon Ave., Detroit, 48238	75 hrs. weekly
WCBF	Box 75, Claire, 48617	Full Time
WCZN	Box 1600, Flint, 48501	6 hrs. weekly
WGPR	3908 W. Warren Ave., Detroit, 48208	42 hrs. weekly
WKPR	Box 667, Kalamazoo, 49005	25 hrs. weekly
WMPC	Box 104, Lapeer, 48446	20 hrs. weekly
WMRP	3217 Lapeer, Flint, 48503	28 hrs. weekly
WMUZ	12300 Radio Place, Detroit, 48228	Full Time
WSAE	220 Cottage, Spring Arbor, 49283	6 hrs. weekly
WUFN	Concord Road, Albion, 49224	Full Time
WUGN	Main Street, Midland, 48640	Full Time
WUNN	1571 Tomlinson Rd., Mason, 48854	Full Time
WVOC	Box 17, Battle Creek, 49016	10 hrs. weekly
WYFC	Box 1520, Ypsilanti, 48197	26 hrs. weekly
WYNZ	Box 1520, Ypsilanti, 48197	91 hrs. weekly
WZND	410 E. Main St., Zeeland, 49464	30 hrs. weekly

MINNESOTA

KNOF	1347 Selby Ave., St. Paul, 55811	99 hrs. weekly
KTIS	Northwestern College Radio, Rossville, 55113	50 hrs. weekly
WWJC	1120 E. McCuen, Duluth, 55808	40 hrs. weekly
WWJO	S. E. Lincoln Ave., St. Cloud, 56301	7 hrs. weekly

MISSISSIPPI

WABU	Box 507, Waynesboro, 39367	10 hrs. weekly
WACR	p. o. Box 1078, Columbus, 39701	30 hrs. weekly
WAML	Box 367, Laurel, 39440	12 hrs. weekly
WBFN	Drawer 70, Quitman, 39355	18 hrs. weekly
WBKH	Box 1503, Hattiesburg, 39401	8 hrs. weekly
WBKN	110 S. Main, Newton, 39345	16 hrs. weekly
WCPC	Box 569, Houston, 38851	24 hrs. weekly
WCSA	Box 435, Ripley, 38663	10 hrs. weekly
WECP	T. 3 Box 135, Forest, 39074	10 hrs. weekly
WEPA	P. O. Box 202, Eupora, 39744	12 hrs. weekly
WESY	Box 900, Leland, 38756	26 hrs. weekly
WFFF AM-FM	Box 569, Columbia, 39429	14 hrs. weekly
WFTO	Box 587, Fulton, 39843	12 hrs. weekly
WGOT	103 School St., Newton, 39345	21 hrs. weekly
WGVM	P. O. Box 1438, Greenville, 38701	28 hrs. weekly
WHOC	Box 26, Philadelphia, 39350	10 hrs. weekly
WIGG	Box 1420, Wiggins, 39577	12 hrs. weekly
WJFR	Box 8887, Jackson, 39204	Full Time
WJXN	Box 786, Jackson, 39205	20 hrs. weekly
WKCU	Hwy. 72 East, Corinth, 38834	16 hrs. weekly
WKFO	Box 445, Prentiss, 39474	14 hrs. weekly
WLSM	Box 111, Louisville, 39339	18 hrs. weekly
WMAG	Box 1539, Forest, 39074	12 hrs. weekly
WMSC	702 2nd Ave., N., Columbus, 39701	14 hrs. weekly
WMLC	Box 1270, Monticello, 39654	16 hrs. weekly
WNAU	202 Bankhead, New Albany, 38652	15 hrs. weekly
WORV	604 Gussie Ave., Hattiesburg, 39401	24 hrs. weekly
WOSM	Box 789, Ocean Springs, 39564	Full Time
WOSM FM	Ocean Springs, 39564	
WRKN	Box 145, Brandon, 39042	30 hrs. weekly
WASO	Box 68, Sentaobia, 38668	8 hrs. weekly
WSEL	Box 240, Pontotoc, 39963	18 hrs. weekly
WSJC	Box 426, Magee, 39111	39 hrs. weekly
WTUP	Box 258, Tupelo, 38801	8 hrs. weekly
WTYL	Box 447, Tylertown, 39667	8 hrs. weekly
WVYL	Drawer 511, Water Valley, 38965	11 hrs. weekly
WVGM	Box 279, Iuka, 38852	20 hrs. weekly
WWHO	168 Kilkenney Blvd., Jackson, 39209	24 hrs. weekly
WXTN	Drawer M, Lexington, 39095	16 hrs. weekly

MISSOURI

KALM	Box 15, Thayer, 65791	20 hrs. weekly
KBFL	Buffalo, 65622	12 hrs. weekly
KBOA AM-FM	Box 509, Kennett, 63857	20 hrs. weekly
KBTC	Star Route 8, Box 68 Houston, 65483	12 hrs. weekly
KCBC	c/o Central Bible College, 3000 N. Grant, Springfield, 65803	30 hrs.
KCHI	917 Jackson, Chillicothe, 64601	26 hrs. weekly
KECC	1111 N. Glenstone, Springfield, 65802	Full Time
KFTW	Box 71, Fredericktown, 63645	14 hrs. weekly
KLFJ	1030 Lander Bldg., Springfield, 65803	Full Time

418

WLYK   P. O. Box 222, Milford, 45150 ....14 hours weekly
WMGS   138 No. Main, Bowling Green, 43402 ....30 hours weekly
WMNI   So. Hotel, Main & High St., Columbus 43215 ....12 hours weekly
WMOH   220 High St., Hamilton, 45011 ....7 hours weekly
WOMP   Box 448, Belleaire, 43906 ....15 hours weekly
WPAY   1009 Galiia St., Portsmouth, 45662 ....25 hours weekly
WPBF   4505 Central Ave., Middletown, 45042 .....15 hours weekly
WPKO   Box 67, Waverly, 45690 ....20 hours weekly
WPOS   7112 Angola, Holand, 43528 ....15 hours weekly
WQMS   770 New London Rd., Hamilton, 45011 ....20 hours weekly
WSLR   mill St., and So. Main, Akron, 44308 ....10 hours weekly
WTGN   1500 Elida Rd., Lima, 45805 ....24 hours weekly
WTOF   619 Peoples Merchant Trust Bldg, Canton, 44702 ....46 hours weekly

WZIP AM 400 Oak Street, Cincinnati 45219

OKLAHOMA
KBJH   769 N. Elwood, Tulsa 74106 ....Full Time
KEBC   Box 94580, Oklahoma City, 73109 ....13 hours weekly
KELR   Box 1460, El Reno, 73036 ....45 hours weekly
KFMJ   Box 746, Tulsa, 74101 ....Full Time
KGOY   4032 Coronado Pl., Oklahoma City, 73122 ....Full Time
KJHN   Box 489, Antlers, 74523 ....10 hours weekly
KKMA   Box 55, Owasso, 74055 ....32 .... hours weekly
KLCO   Box 520, Poteau, 74953 ....24 hours weekly
KORV   7777 So. Lewis, Tulsa, 74105 ....99 hours weekly
KTJS   Box 311, Hobart, 73651 ....8 hours weekly
KTLQ   Box 497, Tahlequah, 74464 ....7 hours weekly
KVYL   Box 856, Holdenville, 74848 ....15 hours weekly
KWSH   Box 1260, Wewoka, 74884 ....4 hours weekly

OREGON
KBMC FM 2895 Hilyard, Eugene, 97405 ....99 hours weekly
KOHU   Box 145, Hermiston, 97838 ....7 hours weekly
KORE   Box 296, Springfield 97477 ....84 hours weekly
KWIL   P. O. Box 278, Albany, 97321 ....95% of Total programming

PENNSYLVANIA
WAVL   P. O. Box 277, Apollo, 15613 ....34 hours weekly
WAYZ   33 East Main St., Waynesboro, 17268 ....2 hrs. weekly
WBYO   Box 177, Boyerton, 19512 ....19 hours weekly
WDAC   P. O. Box 22, Lancaster, 17604 .....Full Time hours weekly
WFMZ   East Rock Rd., Allentown, 18103 ....15 hours weekly
WGCB   Box 88, Red Lion, 17356 ....15 hours weekly
WHGM FM Altoona, ...Full Time
WHYP   Box 112, Northeast, 16428 ....7 hours weekly
WISR   Box 151, Butler, 16001 ....8 hours weekly
WJSM   RFD 2, Martinsburg, 16662 ....Full Time
WKPS   Westminster College, New Wilmington, 16142 ....7 hours weekly
WLBR   Box 1270, Lebanon, 17042 ....7 hours weekly
WMSP   24 So. Second, Harrisburg, 17101 ....13 hours weekly
WPEL   Locust & High St., Montrose, 18801 ....40 hours weekly
WPGM   Danville, 17821 ....30 hours weekly
WKE-FM Box 187, Everett 15537 ....10 hours weekly
WTLN FM 3128 Glenview St., Philadelphia, 19149 .... 14 hrs. weekly
WXVR   526 Ridge Ave., Media, 19063 ....26 hours weekly

SOUTH CAROLINA
WAGI FM P. O. Box 1210, Gaffney, 29340, ...30 hours weekly
WAGS   Box 526, Bishopville, 29010 ....7 hours weekly
WAGY FM Box 1210, Gaffney, 29340 ....60 hours weekly
WAIM   321 Kingsley Rd., Anderson, 29621 ....12 hours weekly
WANS   Box 211, Anderson, 29621 ....14 hours weekly
WATP   p. o. BVox 1033, Marion, 29571 ....9 hours weekly
WAZS   Summerville, 29483 ....11 hrs. weekly
WBBR   Box 456, Travelers Rest, 29690 ....Full Time 1560kc
WBCY   Union, 29379 ....10 hours weekly
WBUG   Drawer "E," Ridgeland, 29936 ....15 hours weekly
WCAY   1303 State St., Cayce, 29033 ....8 hours weekly
WCKI   P. O. Box 709, Greer, 29651 ....18 hours weekly
WCMJ   P.O. Box 297, Chester, 29745 ....25 hours weekly
WCPL   P. O. Box 5, Pageland, 19718 ....24 hours weekly
WDKD   Box 525, Kingstree, 29556 ....7 hours weekly
WDSC   Dillon, 29536 ....14 hours weekly
WEAC   Gaffney, 29340 ....60 hours weekly
WEAC AM P. O. Box 1210, Gaffney, 29340 ....30 hours weekly
WELP   Box 667, Easley, 29640 ....18 hours weekly
WESC   Box 2447, Greenville, 29602 ....12 hours weekly
WFIS   Box 156m, Fountain Inn, 29644 ....40 hours weekly
WJOT   Acline Ave., Lake City, 29560 ....8 hours weekly
WKDK   Box 753, Newberry, 29108 ....10 hours weekly
WKHJ   Holly Hill, 29059 ....8 hours weekly

WKKR   Box 7, Pickens, 29671 ....10 hours weekly
WKMG   P. O. Box 698, Newberry, 29108 ....7 hours weekly
WLBG   Box 269, Laurens, 29360 ....7 hours weekly
WLCM   103 S. Catawba, Lancaster, 29720 ....4 hours weekly
WLOW   P. O. Box 2206, Aiken, 29801 ....10 hours weekly
WOIC   2012 Hydrick St., Columbia, 29203 ....8 hours weekly
WOLS   Box 789, Florence, 29501 ....9 hours weekly
WPCC   Clinton, 29325 ....9 hours weekly
WQIZ   Box 458, St. George, 29477 ....50 hours weekly
WRHI   p. o. Box 429, Rock Hill, 29730 ....14 hours weekly
WSJW   Box 30, Woodruff, 29388 ....30 hours weekly
WWMC FM Box 1337, Moncks Corner, 29461 ....99 hours weekly
WYCL   P. O. Box 398, York, 29745 ....7 hours weekly
WQXL   P. O. Box 3277, Columbia, 29230 ....5 hours weekly

SOUTH DAKOTA
KNWC   Rt. 3, Box 205-A, Sioux Falls, 57107 ....70 hours weekly
KVSR FM Box 15, Keystone St., Rapid City, 57701 ....Full Time

TENNESSEE
WAAN   Box 386, Waynesboro, 38485 ....25 hours weekly
WAEW   Drawer "W," Crossville, 38555 ....13 hours weekly
WAGG   950 Mallory Rd., Franklin, 37064 ....3 hours weekly
WAMG   P.O. Box 521 Gallatin 37066.......................... 20 hrs. weekly
WBFJ   Box 64, Woodbury, 37190 ....26 hours weekly
WBLC   Box 100, Lenoir City, 37771 ....20 hours weekly
WBOL   Box 191, Bolivar, 38008 ....28 hours weekly
WCMT   Box 318, Martin, 38237 ....12 hours weekly
WCOR   Box 549, Lebanon, 37087 ....12 hours weekly
WDBL   Box 729, Springfield, 37172 ....15 hours weekly
WDOD   Box 4232, Chattanooga, 37405 ....Full Time hours weekly
WDSG   Dyersburg, 38024 ....18 hours weekly
WDTM   Box 126, Selmer, 38375 ....18 hours weekly
WDXE   N. Military Ave., Lawrenceburg, 38464 ....9 hrs. weekly
WDXI   Box 489, Jackson, 38301 ....64 hours weekly
WDXL   Box 170, Lexington, 38351 ....18 hours weekly
WEAG   Box 127, Alcoa, 37001 ....7 hours weekly
WEEN   Box 160, LaFayette, 37083 ....5 hours weekly
WEKR   Box "M," Fayetteville, 37334 ....10 hrs. weekly
WENR   Box 190, Englewood, 37329 ....10 hours weekly
WFWL   Box 543, Camden, 38320 ....15 hours weekly
WGRV   Box 243, Greenville, 37743 ....9 hours weekly
WHAL AM-FM Box 696, Shelbyville, 37160 ....9 hours weekly
WHBT   Box 331, Harriman, 37748 ....2½ hours weekly
WHDM   Box 370, McKenzie, 38201 ....15 hours weekly
WHLP   Box 66, Centerville, 37033 ....18 hours weekly
WIRJ   2606 E. End Dr., Humboldt, 38343 ....21 hours weekly
WJFC   P. O. Box 271, Jefferson City, 37760 ....22 hrs. weekly
WJKM   Marlene St., Box 21, Hartsville, 37074 ....10 hours weekly
WJLE   Rt. 1, Smithville, 37166 ....20 hours weekly
WKBJ   P. O. Box 230, Milan, 38358 ....8 hours weekly
WKBL   Box 299, Covington, 38019 ....28 hours weekly
WKPT FM 222 Commerce Kingsport 37660 ....12 hours weekly
WKXV   844 N. Central, Knoxville, 37901 ....32 hours weekly
WLAF   N. 5th St., LaFollette, 37766 ....11 hours weekly
WLAR   Box 298, Athens, 37303 ....13 hours weekly
WLIJ   Box 7, Shelbyville, 37160 ....18 hours weekly
WLIL   P. O. Box 340, Lenoir City, 37771 ....32 hours weekly
WLIV   Box 359, Livingston, 38510 ....15 hours weekly
WLSB   Copperhill, 37317 ....11 hours weekly
WMCH   Church Hill, 37642 ....35 hours weekly
WMCT   1211 Church St. Mountain City, 37683 ......16 hours weekly
WMLR   Box 1540, Hohenwald, 38462 ....Full Time
WMOC   3661 Brainard Rd., Chattanooga, 37411 ....Full Time
WNAH   1701 West End, Nashville, 37203 ....Full Time
WNTT   Box 95, Tazewell, 37879 ....15 hours weekly
WOFE   Rockwood, 37854 ....15 hours weekly
WPHC   P. O. Box 368, Waverly, 37185 ....40 hours weekly
WPJD   Hwy. 27, Morton Bldg., Daisy, 37319 ....Full Time
WRGS   Burren Rd., Rogersville, 37857 ....20 hours weekly
WRIP   Chattanooga
WOWE FM Chattanooga ....Full Time
WSEV   Rt. 3, Box 192, Smithville, 37166 ....9 hours weekly
WSKT   Box 2310, Knoxville, 37901 ....12 hours weekly
WSLV   Box 96, Ardmore, 38449 ....20 hours weekly
WSMG   Box 737, Greeneville, 37743 ....20 hours weekly
WTCV   2265 Central Ave., Memphis, 38104 ....112 hours weekly
WTNE   205 College, Trenton, 38382 ....14 hours weekly
WTNN   6960 Bucknell Rd., Milington, 38053 ....Full Time
WTRB   Box 410, Ripley, 38053 ....12 hours weekly
WVRC   Crossville Rd., Sparta, 38583 ....24 hours weekly
WWGM   P. O. Box 1100, Nashville, 37202 ....Full Time
WYSH   Box 329, Clinton, 37716 ....10 hours weekly
WYXI   Box 645, Athens, 37303 ....25 hours weekly

113

KLTI Box 188, Macon, 63551 ....20 hrs. weekly
KAMA Box 191, Butler, 64730 ....7 hrs. weekly
KOBC 1111 No. Main, Joplin, 64801 ....20 hrs. weekly
KODE 3001 W. 13th, Joplin, 64801 ....7 hrs. weekly
KPCG FM Box 212, Joplin, 64801 ....Full Time
KPWB P.O. Box 50, Piedmont, 63957 ....14 hrs. weekly
KRMS P.O. Box 225, Osage Beach, 65065 ......35 hrs. weekly
KSIM 1501 W. Malone Ave., Sikeston, 63801 ..3 hrs. weekly
KSOA Box 386, AVA, 65608 ....12 hrs. weekly
KSWM 126 S. Jefferson, Aurora, 65605 ....8 hrs. weekly
KTCB Box 379, Malden, 63863 ....8 hrs. weekly
KTSR 1700 E. Myer, Kansas City, 64131 ....45 hrs. weekly
KTUI Box 151, Sullivan, 63080 ....10 hrs. weekly
KWFC Box 905, Springfield, 65801 ....Full Time
KWPM West Plains, 65775 ....10 hrs. weekly
KWTO AM-FM 1121 S. Glenstone, Springfield, 65801 ...10 hrs. weekly
KXEN Box 28, St. Louis, 63166 ....70 hrs. weekly
KXLW 2735 Bompart, St. Louis, 63144 ....Full Time
KYMO box 130, East Prarie, 63845 ....12 hrs. weekly

MONTANA
KGVW Rt. 1, Box H72, Belgrade, 59716 ....18 hrs. weekly
KIVE Box 931, Glendive, 59330 ....28 hrs. weekly

NEBRASKA
KBHL 2820 N. 48th St., Lincoln, 68504
KGBI 1515 S. 10th St., Omaha, 68198 ....53 hrs. weekly
KJLT Box 709, N. Platte, 69101 ....13 hrs. weekly
KJSK Box 99, Columbia 68601 ....15 hrs. weekly
WJAG Box 789, Norfolk, 68701 ....30 hrs. weekly

NEVADA
KNIS p. o. Box 1971, Carson City, 89701

NEW JERSEY
WAWZ Alma White College, Zarephath, 08890 ....30 hrs. weekly
WFME FM 290 Mt. Pleasant Ave., West Orange, 07058 ...99 hrs. weekly
WKDN FM 2906 Mt. Ephraim Ave., Camden, 08104 ...99 hrs. weekly
WLUP P.O. Box 102, Franklin, 07416 ....29 hrs. weekly
WNNN Box132, Salem, 08079 ....Full Time
WRLB 47 Hickory St., Metuchen, 08840 ....34 hrs. weekly
WWDJ AM 497 Hackensack Ave., Hackensack, 07602 .....Full Time

NEW MEXICO
KAVE Box 1538, Carlsbad, 88220 ....7 hrs. weekly
KCHS Box 351, Truth or Consequences, 87901 ...10 hrs. weekly
KDAZ 3403 Morningside N.E., Albuquerque, 87110 ...40 hrs. weekly
KENM P.O. Box 886, Portales, 88130 ....12 hrs. weekly

NEW YORK
CBN P.O. Box "G," Ithaca, 14850 ....Full Time
WBAB Route 109, Babylon, 11704 ....Full Time
WBIV FM Buffalo ....Full Time
WCBA Box 1427, Corning, 14803 ....9 hrs. weekly
WGNR FM Box 160, Oneonta, 13820 ....24 hrs. weekly
WHAZ Box 784, Troy, 12181 ....30 hrs. weekly
WHBI 80 Riverside Dr., 10024 ....40 hrs. weekly
WIZR AM-FM Box 307, Johnstown, 12095
WJIV Albany ....Full Time
WJSL Houghton College, Houghton, 14741 ....33 hrs. weekly
WKOP 34Chenango St., Binghamton, 13901 ......10 hrs. weekly
WMIV Rochester ....Full Time
WOIV Syracuse ....Full Time
WOUR FM 224 Genesee St., Itoca ....24 hrs. weekly
WYRD 3000 Erie Blvd. E., Syracuse, 13224 ....15 hrs. weekly

NORTH CAROLINA
WABZ Box 608, Albemarle, 28001 ....15 hrs. weekly
WADA Drawer 1390, Shelby, 28150 ....8 hrs. weekly
WADE Box 341, Wadesboro, 28170 ....36 hrs. weekly
WAGY Box 280, Forrest City, 28043 ....25 hrs. weekly
WAKS P.O. Box 588, Fuquay, Varina 27526 .....7 hrs. weekly
WATA Box 72 Boone, 28607 ....20 hrs. weekly
WBHN Box 820, Bryson City, 28713 ....10 hrs. weekly
WBLA Box 458, Elizabethtown, 28337 ....12 hrs. weekly
WBMA Box 668, Black Mountain, 28711 ....34 hrs. weekly

WBTE Box 509, Windsor, 27983 ....15 hrs. weekly
WCAB Box 511, Rutherfordton, 28139 ....26 hrs. weekly
WCEC P.O. Box 2005, Rocky Mount, 27801 ....15 hrs. weekly
WCOK P.O. Box 517, Sparta, 28675 ....7 hrs. weekly
WCSL P.O. Box 367, Cherryville, 28021 ....8 hrs. weekly
WDBM Box 1027, Statesville, 28677 ....10 hrs. weekly
WDSL Box 404, Mocksville, 27028 ....20 hrs. weekly
WEGO Box 128, Concord, 28025 ....3 hrs. weekly
WELS Box 3334, Kinston, 28501 ....10 hrs. weekly
WFCM Drawer 1, Winston-Salem, 27105 ....13 hrs. weekly
WFGW Box 158, Black Mountain, 28711 ....Full Time
WFMA Box 2005, Rocky Mount, 27801 ....15 hrs. weekly
WFSC Box 470, Franklin, 25734 ....Full Time
WGPL Box 598, Winston-Salem, 27101 ....99 hrs. weekly
WGWR FM Box 309, Asheboro, 27203 ....22 hrs. weekly
WHIT Drawer 1049, New Bern, 28560 ....20 hrs. weekly
WHKY AM-FM P.O. Box 1059, Hickory, 28601 ...12 hrs. weekly
WHPE P.O. Box 1819, High Point, 27261 ....13 hrs. weekly
WHRY 536 "M" Ave., S.E., Hickory, 29601 ......12 hrs. weekly
WHVL 717 Greenville Hwy., Hendersonville, 28739 ...25 hrs. weekly
WIFM Drawer 1038, Elkin, 28621 ....30 hrs. weekly
WJRM Box 549, Troy, 27371 ....22 hrs. weekly
WKBC Box 938, N. Wilkesboro, 28659 ....10 hrs. weekly
WKDX Box 826, Hamlet, 28345 ....16 hrs. weekly
WKGX Box 452, Lenoir, 28645 ....10 hrs. weekly
WKYK Box 744, Burnsville, 28714 ....10 hrs. weekly
WLLE 649 Maywood, Raleigh, 27602 ....28 hrs. weekly
WLOE Boulevard, Eden, 27288 ....12 hrs. weekly
WLTC Box 3927, Akers Center Sta., Gastonia, 28052 ...18 hrs. weekly
WMDE 311 Asheboro St., Greensboro, 27406 ...15 hrs. weekly
WMMH Box 528, Marshall, 28753 ....15 hrs. weekly
WMNC Box 969, Morgantown, 28655 ....22 hrs. weekly
WMNG FM Morgantown, 28655 ....Full Time
WMSJ Box 1044, Sylva, 28779 ....10 hrs. weekly
WNOS Country Club Dr., High Point, 27260 .....24 hrs. weekly
WPEG FM Box 128, Concord, 28025 ....10 hrs. weekly
WPET Box 950, Greensboro, 27402 ....48 hrs. weekly
WPGD Drawer N-1, Winston-Salem, 27105 ......Full Time
WPTL Box 471, Canton, 28716 ....13 hrs. weekly
WPYB Box 215, Benson, 27504 ....41 hrs. weekly
WQWX P.O. Box 68, Mebane, 27302
WRCM Onslow Broadcasting Co., Jacksonville, 38540 ...7 hrs. weekly
WRKB Kanapolis, 28081 ....37 hrs. weekly
WRNC P.O. Box 27946, Raleigh, 27611 ....Full Time
WRRZ P.O. Box 378, Clinton, 28328 ....35 hrs. weekly
WSAT Drawer 99, Salisbury, 28144 ....5 hrs. weekly
WSJS Box 3018, Winston-Salem, 27102 ....7 hrs. weekly
WSKY Box 1780, Asheville, 28802 ....3 hrs. weekly
WSTH Box 997, Taylorsville, 28681 ....20 hrs. weekly
WSVM Box 99, Valdese, 28690 ....12 hrs. weekly
WTIK Box 1571, Durham, 27702 ....9 hrs. weekly
WTLK Box 847, Taylorsville 28681 ....18 hrs. weekly
WTNC Box 250, Thomasville, 27360 ....25 hrs. weekly
WIOE Box 668, Spruce Pine, 28777 ....40 hrs. weekly
WTSB Box 393, Lumberton, 28358 ....12 hrs. weekly
WVCB 2304, Shallotte, 28459 ....21 hrs. weekly
WVOE RFD 2, Box 124-A, Chadbourn, 28431 ...21 hrs. weekly
WWIT P.O. Box 391, Canton, 28716 ....28 hrs. weekly
WWMO Box 1349, Reidsville, 27322 ....Full Time
WXNC FM P.O. Box 1240, 27536 ....13 hrs. weekly
WXRC 329 1st Ave., NW, Hickory, 28601 ....5 hrs. weekly
WYDK Rt. 1, Box 51-B, Yadkinville, 27055 ......14 hrs. weekly

NORTH DAKOTA
KBOM Box 1377, Bismarck, 58501 ....28 hrs. weekly
KFNW Rt. 1, Fargo, 58102 ....60 hrs. weekly
KGPC 312, Grafton, 53273 ....8 hrs. weekly
KHRT Box 1320, Monot, 58701 ....9 hrs. weekly

OHIO
WALR Box 1590, Akron, 44309 ....10 hours weekly
WAKW P.O. Box 24-G, Cincinnati, 45224 ....28 hours weekly
WBEX P.O. Box 224, Chillicothe, 45601 ....30 hours weekly
WBZI 989 Bellbrook, Xenia 45385 ....Full Time
WCNW Box 50, Fairfield, 45p14 ....30 hours weekly
WCHI 1022 Eastern Ave., Chillicothe, 45601
WCOL FM 22 So. Young St., Columbus, 43215 ...84 hours weekly
WEEC 48 Troy Rd., Springfield 45504 ....Full Time
WELX 44 Lonsdale Ave., Dayton, 45427 ....46 hours weekly
WGIC Box 99, Xenia, 45385 ....Full Time
WGGN Box 247, Castalia, Ohio 44834 ....Full Time
WIRO Box 292, Ironton, 45638 ....18 hours weekly

TEXAS

KBBB   Box 1478, Borger, 79007 ....8 hours weekly
KBUC   3259 East Commerce, San Antonio 78220 ....10 hours weekly
KBUK   Box 419, Baytown, 77520 ....6 hours weekly
KBUY   P. O. Box 2049, Fort Worth, 76101 ....10 hours weekly
KBWD   800 Hawkins St., Brownwood, 76801 ....10 hours weekly
KBYP   P. O. Box 21, Shamrock, 79079 ....13 hours weekly
KCAN   1605 5th Ave., Canyon, 79015 ....Full Time
KCAS   Box 276m, Slaton, 79364 ....18 hours weekly
KCLR   Box 669, Ralls, 79357 ....10 hours weekly
KCOM   Box 9, Comanche, 76442 ....10 hours weekly
KCTA   Box 898, Corpus Christi, 78403 ....28 hours weekly
KCYL   Box 886, Lampasas, 76550 ....10 hours weekly
KDOX   200 Interstate 20, Marshall, 75670 ....2 hrs. weekly
KDRY   Box 6628, San Antonio, 78209 ....45 hours weekly
KDTX FM   P. O. Box 7030, Dallas, 75209 ....Full Time
KEES   Rt. 4, Box 538, Longview, 75601 ....15 hours weekly
KFMK   Suite 1900, Medical Towers Bldg., Houston, 77025 ...84 hours weekly
KFRO   P. O. Box 792, Longview, 75601 ....10 hours weekly
KHCB   Box 45345, Houston, 77045 ....84 hours weekly
KHEM   Box 750, E. Hwy. 80, Big Spring 79720 ....12 hrs. weekly
KHYM   Rt. 4, Gilmer, 75644 ....Full Time
KIMP   Box 990, Mt. Pleasant, 75455 ....23 hours weekly
KIKZ   Box 308, Seminole, 79360 ....10 hours weekly
KIVY   Box 1109, Crockett, 75835 ....10 hours weekly
KIZZ   444 Executive Ctr. Blvd, El Paso, 79902 ...15 hours weekly
KKAS   Box 455, Silsbee, 77656 ....15 hours weekly
KLBK   7400 S. University, Lubbock, 79413 ....42 hours weekly
KLIS   Box 788, Palestine, 75901 ....10 hours weekly
KLKZ   120 S. E. Avenue B., Seminole, 79360 ......7 hours weekly
KLUF   114½ N. 1st St., Lufkin, 75901 ....2 hours weekly
KLUL   1406 Federal Rd., Houston, 77015 ....18 hours weekly
KMHT   P. O. Box AA, Marshall, 75670 ....10 hours weekly
KMIL   Drawer 832, Cameron, 76520 ....8 hours weekly
KMOO   Box 499, Mineola, 75773 ....12 hours weekly
KNOK   P. O. Box 7116, Fort Worth, 76111 ....18 hours weekly
KOLJ   Box 589, Quanah, 79252 ....20 hours weekly
KPBC   1401 S. Akard, Dallas, 75215 ....Full Time
KPDN   Hughes Bldg., Pampa, 79065 ....10 hours weekly
KPLT   Box 9, Paris, 75460 ....2 hours weekly
KRBA   Hughes Bldg., Pampa, 79065 ....10 hours weekly
KRBA   Box 1345, Lufkin, 75901 ....15 hours weekly
KSKY   Stoneleigh Terrace, Dallas, 75201 ....Full Time
KSTA   Box 432, Abilene Hwy., Coleman, 76834 ...12 hours weekly
KTAL FM   Box 1948, Texarkana, 755501 ....Full Time
KTBB   2638 Caldwell, Tyler, 75701 ....16 hours weekly
KTRM   Box 5425, Beaumont, 77702 ....Full Time
KVLL   P. O. Box 458, Woodville, 75979 ....14 hours weekly
KWBA   Box 419, Baytown, 77520 ....28 hours weekly
KWFA   Box 220, Merkle, 79536 ....9 hours weekly
KWGO   6125 Avenue "A," Lubbock, 79401 ....12 hours weekly
KZAK   Box 3367, Tyler, 75701 ....10 hours weekly
KZOL   Box 458, Farwell, 79325 ....25 hours weekly

VIRGINIA

WABH   Deerfield, 24432 ....15 hours weekly
WBBI   Box 190, Abington, 24210 ....10 hours weekly
WBDY   P. O. Box 509, Bluefield, 24601 ....21 hours weekly
WBZI   Box 889, Blackburg, Va. ....Full Time
WDYL FM   10600 Jefferson Davis Hwy., Richmond, 23234 ...Full Time
WEMC   Eastern Mennonite College, Harrisonburg, 22801 ....21 hours weekly
WEOO   Box 339, Smithfield, 23430
WESR   Tasley, 24441
WFAX   161-B Hillwood Ave., Falls Church, 22046 ...13 hours weekly
WFGH   Box 799, Bristol, 24201 ....16 hours weekly
WFIC   P. O. Box 475, Collinsville, 24078 ....42 hours weekly
WHBG   Box 392, Harrisonburg, 22801 ....10 hours weekly
WHEO   Rt. 1, Box 24, Wayside Rd., Stuart, 24171 ...12 hours weekly
WHHV   Box 648, Hillsville, 24343 ....7 hours weekly
WIKI   10600 Jefferson Davis Hwy., Richmond, 23234 ...99 hours weekly
WIVE   Ash Cake Rd., Ashland, 23005 ....Full Time
WJJJ   P. O. Box 30, Christian, 24073 ....10 hours weekly
WJJS FM   801 Main St., Lynchburg, 24504 ....31 hours weekly
WJLM   P. O. Box 6099, Roanoke, 24017 ....10 hours weekly
WKBA   204310th NE, Roanoke, 24012 ....50 hours weekly
WKBY   105A, Chatham, 24531 ....14 hours weekly
WKCW   Box 740, Warrenton, 22186 ....10 hours weekly
WKDE   P. O. Box 512, Altavista, 24517 ....8 hours weekly

WKJC   Box 509, Bluefield, 24605 ....25 hours weekly
WLCM   801 Main St., Lynchburg, 24504 ....7 hrs. weekly
WLSD   big Stone Gap, 24219 ....20 hrs. weekly
WORK   Norfolk, Va.
WRAA   Box 128, Luray, 22835 ....7 hrs. weekly
WRIS   P. O. Box 6099, Roanoke, 24017 ....10 hours weekly
WSIG   Box 425, Mt. Jackson, 22842 ....20 hours weekly
WSLS   Box 2161, Roanoke, 24009 ....11 hours weekly
WSVA   Harrisburg, 22801 ....7 hours weekly
WSWV   pennington Gap, 24277 ....13 hours weekly
WTZE   Box 69, Tazewell, 24651 ....12 hours weekly
WWOD   P. O. Box 1390, Lynchburg, 24505 ....126 hours weekly
WXGI   710 German School Rd., Richmond, 23225 ...10 hours weekly
WXRI   511 Oaklette Dr., Chesapeake, 23325 ....99 hours weekly
WYAL AM   10600 Jefferson Davis Hwy., Richmond, 23234 ...Full Time
WYTI   P. O. Box 430, Rocky Mount, 24151 ....11 hours weekly

WASHINGTON

KAYE   1520 E. Main St., Puyallup, 98371 ....24 hours weekly
KARI   Box "X," Blaine, 98230 ....55 hours weekly
KBLE . 114 Lakeside Ave., Seattle, 98122 ....35 hours weekly
KLYN FM   Front St., Lynden, 98264 ....17 hrs. weekly
KMO   Box 1277, Tacoma, 98401 ....64 hours weekly
KNCC   P. O. Box 579, Kirkland, 98033 ....18 hrs. weekly
KOQT   558 Sterling Dr., Bellingham, 98225 ....Full Time
KTEL   Box 948 Walla Walla, 99362 ....15 hours weekly
KTW   1505 Northern Life Tower, Seattle, 98101 ...84 hours weekly
KVDY   Box 8022, Spokane, 99203 ....50 hours weekly

WEST VIRGINIA

KBKW FM   WJLS Bldg., Beckley, 25901 ....140 hours weekly
WCST   Box 8, Berkley Springs, 25411 ....10 hours weekly
WELD   Fisher, 26818 ....10 hours weekly
WETZ   Box 249, New Martinsville, 26155 ....10 hours weekly
WHJC   Box 68, Matewan, 25678 ....15 hrs. weekly
WKJC   McDowell St., Welch, 24801 ....56 hours weekly
WKLC   Box 556, St. Albans, 25177 ....25 hours weekly
WMOV   Box 647, Ravenswood, 26164 ....23 hours weekly
WMUL FM   Marshall Univ., Huntington, 25701 ......10 hours weekly
WOAY   Oak Hill, 25901 ....40 hours weekly
WOVE   McDowell St., Welch, 24801 ....20 hours weekly
WPAR   Box 449, Parkersburg, 26101 ....10 hours weekly
WRDS   Box 8305, S. Charleston, 25304 ....10 hours weekly
WSGB   Box 514, Sutton, 26601 ....16 hours weekly
WVAF   Box 4318, Charleston, 25304 ....99 hours weekly
WVAR   Box 349, Richwood, 26261 ....12 hours weekly
WWHY   P. O. Box 390, Huntington, 25708 ....8 hrs. weekly
WWNR   1708 Harper Rd., Beckley, 25801 ....8 hrs. weekly
WWVA   Capitol Music Hall, Wheeling, 26003 ....8 hrs. weekly
WPNS   P. O. Box 454, Hurricane, 25526 ....13 hrs. weekly

WISCONSIN

WAWA   12800 W. Blund, Elm Grove, 53211 ....29 hours weekly
WDMW FM   321 Main St., Menomonie, 54751 ....20 hrs. weekly
WGEZ   2025 E. Ridge Rd., Beloit, 53511 ....13 hours weekly
WRVM   Box 212, Suring, 54174 ....28 hrs. weekly
WWIB   Box 44, Cornell, 54732 ....Full Time

CANADA

CHLO   133 Curtis St., St. Thomas, Ont. ....7 hrs. weekly
CJSN and
CKWS   P. O. Box 4, Swift Current, Sask.
CKTB   18 Kings Grant Rd., St. Catharines, Ont. ....Syndicated
CKWS   Kingston, Ontario ....15 hours weekly
VOAR   106 Fushwater Rd., St. Johns, Newfoundland ...14 hrs. weekly

PUERTO RICO

WCGB   Box 248, Juana Diaz, 00665 ....21 hours weekly
WIVV   Box A, San Juan, 00936 ....Full Time

GMA

Record Companies

ACCENT RECORDS
Scott Seely, President
6533 Hollywood Blvd.
Hollywood, CA 90028

ALBUM COMPANY OF AMERICA
P.O. Box 374
Morristown, TN 37814

AMERICAN ARTIST
Joseph Higgins
1763 E. Elm Street
Springfield, MO 65804

AVANT GUARDE
250 West 57th Street
New York, NY 10019

BEAVERWOOD RECORDING CO.
133 Walton Ferry Road
Hendersonville, TN 37075

BEE GEE
3104 South Western Ave.
Los Angeles, CA 90018

BENSON SOUND
Larry Benson
3707 South Blackwelder
Oklahoma City, OK 73119

BIG GOSPEL RECORDS
Harry McDowell
828 So. Lawrence Street
Montgomery, AL 36104

BLACKWOOD RECORDS
Mark Blackwood
3935 Summer Ave.
Memphis, TN 38122

BLUE ASH RECORDS
Don Spangler
1033 Kingsmill Pkwy.
Columbus, Ohio 43229

CALVARY RECORDS
Nelson Parkerson
P.O. Box 175
Fresno, CA 93700

CANAAN RECORDS
Marvin Norcross
4800 West Waco Drive
Waco TX 76703

CAPITOL RECORDS CO.
38 Music Square East
Nashville, TN 37203

CAPRICCIO RECORDS
Polly Grimes
P.O. Box 1387
Redondo Beach, CA 90278

CENTURY RECORDS
Bob Davis
P.O. Box 15501
Charlotte, NC 28210

CENTURY RECORDS
1429 Hawthorne Street
Pittsburgh, PA 15201

CHRISTIAN FOLK
Joel Gentry
1008 17th Ave. So.
Nashville, TN 37212

COLUMBIA RECORD CO.
34 Music Square East
Nashville, TN 37203

CRUSADE RECORDS
Flora, IL 62839

ECHO RECORDS
Joe Whitfield
P.O. Box 5657
Pensacola, FL 32505

FANFARE RECORD STUDIO
RONDELL AUDIO
  ENTERPRISES, INC.
120 East Main Street
El Cajon, CA 92020

GOOD NEWS RECORDS
8319 Lankershim
No. Hollywood, CA 91605

GOSPEL CITY RECORDS
P.O. Box 28553
Dallas, TX 75228

GOSPEL MUSIC WORLD
  RECORD CO.
Cecil Blackwood
3935 Summer Ave.
Memphis, TN 38122

GOSPEL TRUTH RECORDS
Div. Stax Record Co.
2693 Union Ext.
Memphis, TN 38112

HALL, JOHN RECORDS CO.
P.O. Box 13344
Ft. Worth, TX 76118

HALO RECORDS
Bob Edwards
P.O. Box 7004
Greenville, SC 29610

HARBOR RECORDS
Rusty Goodman
P.O. Box 13
Madisonville, KY 42431

HEARTWARMING RECORDS
1625 Broadway
Nashville, TN 37203

HERALD RECORDS
P.O. Box 41
Johnsonville, SC 29555

H.H. RECORDINGS
P.O. Box 113
Clinton, MD 20735

HORIZON RECORDS
P.O. Box 15477
Tulsa, OK 74112

HOUSE OF McDUFF
Roger McDuff
P.O. Box 190, 919 East Shaw
Pasadena, TX 77501

HYMNTONE RECORDS
Don Baldwin
5252 Trindle Road
Mechanicsburg, PA 17055

IMPACT RECORDS
1625 Broadway
Nashville, TN 37203

JEWEL RECORDING COMPANY
P.O. Box 31078
Cincinnati, OH 45231

KING DAVID RECORDS
P.O. Box 653
Nashville, TN 37202

KSS RECORDS
Joe Keene
P.O. Box 602
Kennett, MO 62857

LIGHT RECORDS
Ralph Carmichael
4800 West Waco Drive
Waco, TX 76703

LeFEVRE SOUND
Meurice LeFevre
1314 Ellsworth Industrial Dr., S.E.
Atlanta, GA 30318

LOVE/PEACE/SERVICE RECORDS
2140 St. Clair St.
Bellingham, WA 98225

MAJESTIC RECORDS
P.O. Box 253
Rockaway, NJ 07866

116

422

MARK V RECORDS
Joe Huffman
P.O. Box 7084
Greenville, SC 29610

MANNA RECORDS
Hal Spencer
2111 Kenmere
Burbank, CA 91504

MCA RECORDS
Owen Bradley
27 Music Square East
Nashville, TN 37203

McDOWELL RECORD CO.
828 S. Lawrence St.
Montgomery, AL 36104

MESSIANIC RECORDS
7516 City Line Ave. No. 8
Philadelphia, PA 19151

MT. NEBO RECORDS
Bill Textor
P.O. Box "U"
Hendersonville, TN 37075

NASHVILLE INTERNATIONAL
RECORDS
20 Music Square West
Nashville, TN 37203

NRS RECORDS
P.O. Box 653
Nashville, TN 37202

PHOENIX RECORDS
20 Music Square West
Nashville, TN 37203

PLATO RECORDS, INC.
Mr. Pat Wiseman
1169 Pike Street
Milton, WV 25531

PRAISE RECORDS OF CANADA
Paul Yaroshuk
P.O. Box 2307
Vancouver, B.C., Canada

PRESTIGE RECORDS
Jim Thrasher
P.O. Box 2806
Birmingham, AL 35212

PRINCESS RECORD CO.
P.O. Box 2221
Nashville, TN 37202

PRINCESS RECORD CO.
P.O. Box 5025
Roanoke, VA 24012

PROCLAIM RECORDS
P.O. Box 653
Nashville, TN 37202

PROMISE RECORDS
Ed Bosken
2632 Spring Grove Ave.
Cincinnati, OH 45225

PYRAMID RECORD COMPANY
296 Indian Lake Road
Hendersonville, TN 37075

QUEEN CITY ALBUM, INC.
Edward R. Bosken
2832 Spring Grove Ave.
Cincinnati, OH 45225

RAINBOW SOUND
Bob Cline
2721 Irving Boulevard
Dallas, TX 75207

REVELATION RECORDS
711 West Broadway
Minneapolis, MN 55411

ROUNDER RECORDS
Bill Nowlin
65 Park Street
Somerville, MA 02143

SACRED RECORDS
Kurt Kaiser
4800 West Waco Drive
Waco, TX 76703

SELAH RECORDS
Joseph Higgins
1763 E. Elm Street
Springfield, MO 65704

SINGCORD
Maury Lehman
Record Div. of Zondervan Publ. Co.
Grand Rapids, MI 49506

SKYLITE-SING
Joel Gentry
1008 17th Ave. So.
Nashville, TN 37212

SPECTRUM
P.O. Box 757
San Carlos, CA 94070

SUNWORLD RECORDS
P.O. Box 1893
Orlando, FL 32802

SUPERIOR SOUND INC.
Duane Allen
Rockland Road and Louise Ave.
Hendersonville, TN 37075

SUPREME RECORD CO.
Tom Wall
110 21st Ave. So.
Nashville, TN 37203

SWORD & SHIELD RECORDS
Calvin Wills
P.O. Box 211
Arlington, TX 76010

TEMPO
Jesse Peterson
1900 W. 47th Place
Mission, KS 66205

TRIANGLE RECORDS
824 19th Ave. So.
Nashville, TN 37203

VICTORY
Record Div. of Zondervan Publ. Co.
Grand Rapids, MI 49506

VISTONE RECORDS
Rue Barclay
6331 Santa Monica Boulevard
Hollywood, CA 90038

W.P.I.
Barbara Willis
P.O. Box 72
Farmington, MO 63640

WORD, INC.
Marvin Norcross
4800 West Waco Drive
Waco, TX 76703

WORLD CONCEPT RECORDS, INC.
1304 West Lake Drive
Fenton, MO. 63026

gma

117

AMERICANA RECORDING STUDIOS
Rogers W. Lawson, Jr.
P.O. Drawer L.
709 West California Ave.
Ruston, LA 71270

AMERICAN ARTISTS RECORDING STUDIO
Joseph Higgins
1763 E. Elm Street
Springfield, MO 65804

ARTIST RECORDING CO.
Michael McGuire
302 Mill Street
Cincinnati, OH 45215

ATWELL SOUND
Lorne Atwell
Lafayette, TN 37083

AUDIO MEDIA RECORDERS
P.O. Box 12384
Nashville, TN 37212

BENSON SOUND
Larry Benson
3707 South Blackwelder
Oklahoma City, OK 73119

BOB DAVIS SOUND PRODUCTIONS
P.O. Box 15501
Charlotte, NC 28210

BRADLEY'S BARN
Owen Bradley
1609 Hawkins Street
Nashville, TN 37203

CAPITOL RECORDING STUDIOS
38 Music SquareEast
Nashville, TN 37203

CENTRAL SOUND STUDIOS
Leonard Walls
401 Magnolia Ave.
Auturndale, FL 33823

CENTURY 21 PRODUCTIONS
494 Bethesda School Rd.
Lawrenceville, GA 30245

CHEROKEE SOUND RECORDING STUDIO
Ernest Spearman
Rt. 1, Box 304
Blacksburg, SC 29702

COLUMBIA RECORDING STUDIOS
34 Music Square East
Nashville, TN 37203

COUNTERPART & CREATIVE STUDIOS
Shad O'Shea
3744 Applegate Ave.
Cincinnati, OH 45211

CREATIVE SOUND
Sunset Boulevard
Los Angeles, CA 90069

FLORENCE SOUND
356 Woodland Ave.
Florence, SC 29501

GOODMAN SOUND
Rusty Goodman
P.O. Box 13
Madisonville, KY 42431

HALL OF FAME RECORD STUDIO
1012 17th Ave. So.
Nashville, TN 37212

HILLTOP STUDIOS
902 Due West Ave.
Madison, TN 37115

INTERPRO CANADA LTD.
Mrs. Roylene Corkum
P.O. Box 102
Fredericton, N.B.
CANADA

JACK CLEMENT RECORDING STUDIO
3102 Belmont Boulevard
Nashville, TN 37212

JEWELL RECORDING STUDIOS
Rusty York
1594 Kinney Ave.
Cincinnati, OH 45231

KENNETT SOUND STUDIOS
Joe Keene
P.O. Box 602
Kennett, MO 63857

KINGSMILL RECORDING CO.
Don Spangler
1033 Kingsmill Parkway
Columbus, Ohio 43229

LeFEVRE SOUND
Meurice LeFevre
1314 Ellsworth Industria Dr. N.W.
Atlanta, GA 30318

MARK V STUDIOS
P.O. Box 7084
Greenville, SC 29610

McDOWELL RECORDING STUDIOS
828 S. Lawrence
Montgomery, AL 36104

MERCURY RECORDING STUDIOS
12 Music Circle South
Nashville, TN 37203

MONUMENT RECORDING STUDIOS
Tommy Strong
114 17th Ave. So.
Nashville, TN 37203

NASHVILLE AUDIO RECORDERS
1307 Division Street
Nashville, TN 37203

NASHVILLE INTERNATIONAL STUDIOS
Reggie M. Churchwell
20 Music Square West
Nashville, TN 37203

NUGGET RECORDING STUDIO
Fred Carter, Jr.
400 Tinnin Road
Goodlettsville, TN 37072

PINEBROOK RECORDING STUDIO
Dan Posthuma
P.O. Box 146
Alexandria, IN 46001

PRESTIGE PRODUCTIONS
Jim Thrasher
P.O. Box 2868
Birmingham, AL 35212

Q.C.A. RECORDING STUDIO
2836 Spring Grove Ave.
Cincinnati, OH 45225

QUAD-EIGHT STUDIOS, INC.
Jose Bocanegra
Ave. 65 de Infanteria, KM.11
Carolina, Puerto Rico 00630

118

424

QUADRAFONIC SOUND STUDIO
1802 Grand Ave.
Nashville, TN 37212

RCA RECORDING STUDIO
Cal Everhart
30 Music Square West
Nashville, TN 37203

RAINBOW SOUND
Bob Cline
2721 Irving Boulevard
Dallas, TX 75207

ROME RECORDING STUDIO
Jack Casey
1414 East Broad Street
Columbus, OH 43200

SENSATION SOUND STUDIOS
Michael J. Schieman
2080 Peachtree Industrial Court
Chamblee, GA 30341

**RAY STEVENS SOUND
LABORATORY**
1708 Grand Ave.
Nashville, TN 37212

RICHLAND SOUND STUDIO
P.O. Box 283
Portland, TN 37248

RITE RECORD PRODUCTIONS, INC.
9745 Lockland Rd.
Cincinnati, OH 45215

RONDELL AUDIO ENTERPRISES
Fanfare Studio & Music Center
120 East Main Street
El Cajon, CA 92020

SONIC SOUND STUDIO
Crusade Enterprises
Flora, IL 62839

SUNCOAST PRODUCTIONS
P.O. Box 1893
Orlando, FL 32802

SUPERIOR SOUND, INC.
Duane Allen
Rockland Road and Louise Ave.
Hendersonville, TN 37075

TRC CORPORATION
Talun Midwest Recording
1330 North Illinois Ave.
Indianapolis, IN 46202

TRI-STATE RECORDING CO.
Tilford Salyer
1767 Ford Henry Drive
Kingsport, TN 37664

WHITNEY SOUND
Louis Whitney
1516 West Glenoaks Boulevard
Glendale, CA 91201

WOODLAND SOUND
Glen Snoddy
1011 Woodland
Nashville, TN 37206

WOOTEN RECORDING CO.
Style Wooten
3373 Park Ave.
Memphis, TN 38111

Performing Rights Organizations

ASCAP
1 Lincoln Plaza
New York, NY 10023

ASCAP
2 Music Square West
Nashville, TN 37203

BMI
40 W. 57th St.
New York, NY 10019

BMI
10 Music Square West
Nashville, TN 37203

SESAC
10 Columbus Circle
New York, NY 10019

SESAC
11 Music Circle So.
Nashville, TN 37203

GMA

Publishers

ARCHER MUSIC/ASCAP
P.O. Box 201
Tecumseh, OK 74873

BAVA MUSIC CO./SESAC
Davis, WV 26260

BEACON HILL MUSIC
P.O. Box 527
Kansas City, MO 64140

BEASLEY & BARKER
MUSIC, INC./BMI
P.O. Box 48
Pensacola, FL 32591

BEECHWOOD MUSIC CORP./BMI
1804 N. Ivar
Hollywood, CA 90028

BENSON PUBLISHING/ASCAP
1625 Broadway
Nashville, TN 37202

BLACKWOOD BROTHERS
PUB. CO./SESAC
3935 Summer Ave.
Memphis, TN 38122

BOSKEN MUSIC/BMI
2832 Spring Grove Ave.
Cincinnati, OH 45225

BRIDGE MUSIC/SESAC
P.O. Box 41
Johnsonville, SC 29555

BROADMONT PRESS/SESAC
127 9th Ave. No.
Nashville, TN 37203

BROAD RIVER PUBLISHING
CO. BMI
Rt. 1, Box 304
Blacksburg, SC 29702

BRUMLEY & SONS, ALBERT/SESAC
Powell, MO 65703

BUENA VISTA PUBLISHING CO./BMI
P.O. Box 28553
Dallas, TX 75228

BULLS-EYE MUSIC/ASCAP
6326 Selma Ave.
Hollywood, CA 90028

CANAANLAND MUSIC/BMI
825 19th Ave. So.
Nashville, TN 37203

CARTER MUSIC CO., ROY D./SESAC
4115 Vans Road
Fort Worth, TX 76118

CEDARWOOD PUBLISHING CO./BMI
39 Music Square East
Nashville, TN 37203

CENTERPOINT PUBLISHING CO./BMI
P.O. Box 15457
Nashville, TN 37215

COUNTRY SUN PUBLISHING CO.
Vernon Smith
403 Magnolia Ave.
Auburndale, FL 33823

CHAPPELL & CO., INC./ASCAP
47-55 58th Street
Woodside, L.I., NY 11377

CONCEPT MUSIC CO./ASCAP
1625 Broadway
Nashville, TN 37202

CRESCENDO MUSIC
PUBLICATIONS/BMI
2580 Gus Thomasson Road
P.O. Box 28218
Dallas, TX 75228

CROSSLINE MUSIC
PUBLISHING CO.
P.O. Box 1387
Redondo Beach, CA 90278

CROWN-BLACK MUSIC/SESAC
Paul Downing
131 Saunders Ferry Road
Hendersonville, TN 37075

CRUSADE ENTERPRISES/SESAC
P.O. Box 252
Flora, IL 62839

DA'PO' MUSIC/BMI
Dave and Polly Crawford
2553 Pineworth Road
Macon, GA 31206

DATELINE/BMI
P.O. Box 50
Nashville, TN 37202

DAVIS MUSIC CO., JIMMIE/BMI
P.O. Box 15826
Baton Rouge, LA 70815

DEBRA LYNN PUBLISHING
CO./BMI
P.O. Box 192
Forrest Park, GA 30083

DE GRANDE MUSIC CO./ASCAP
P.O. Box 99
Amboy, IL 61310

DIMENSION MUSIC CO./SESAC
1625 Broadway
Nashville, TN 37202

EDDIE CROOK MUSIC/SESAC
296 Indian Lake Road
Hendersonville, TN 37075

ELLIS PUBLISHING COMPANY
Harriet L. Ellis
1129 N.E. 92nd Street
Miami Shores, FL 33138

ETERNAL PUBLICATIONS/SESAC
P.O. Box 1693
Stow, OH 44224

FAIRER MUSIC/SESAC
112 Martin Drive
Hendersonville, TN 37075

FAITH MUSIC, INC./SESAC
P.O. Box 527
Kansas City, MO 64141

FARMHOUSE MUSIC/BMI
1015 16th Ave. So.
Nashville, TN 37212

FELLOWSHIP MUSIC/BMI
P.O. Box 50
Nashville, TN 37202

FIESTA MUSIC, INC./BMI
P.O. Box 2450
Hollywood, CA 90028

FOUR SEASONS MUSIC/ASCAP
20 Music Square West
Nashville, TN 37203

FOX MUSIC PUB., BAYNARD/BMI
P.O. Box 9741
Atlanta, GA 30319

FRICK MUSIC PUBLISHING CO.
Mr. Robert Frick
4551 S. White Pine Dr.
Tucson, AZ 85730

FUNKERBURK-SURRATT
PUBLISHING CO./BMI
P.O. Box 81
Locust, NC 28097

GAITHER MUSIC CO./ASCAP
P.O. Box 300
Alexandria, IN 46001

GOFF PUBLISHING CO./BMI
P.O. Box 15707
Nashville, TN 37215

GOLDLINE MUSIC/ASCAP
920 19th Ave. So.
Nashville, TN 37212

GOSPEL MUSIC WORLD
PUBLISHERS
3935 Summer Ave.
Memphis, TN 38122

GOSPEL PUBLISHING
HOUSE/SESAC
1445 Boonville
Springfield, MO 65802

GOSPEL QUARTET
MUSIC CO./SESAC
58 Music Square West
Nashville, TN 37212

GOSPELTONE MUSIC CO./BMI
P.O. Box 15826
Baton Rouge, LA 70815

HAMBLEN MUSIC CO., INC./BMI
P.O. Box 8118/3100 Torreyson Place
University City, CA 91608

HAPPY DAY MUSIC CO./BMI
P.O. Box 602
Kennett, MO 63857

HARTFORD MUSIC CO./SESAC
Powell, MO 65703

HARVEST TIME PUBLISHERS/SESAC
3217 Moorewood Dr.
Nashville, TN 37207

HEADLINE PUBLISHING CO/BMI
P.O. Box 1693
Stow, OH 44224

HEARTSTONE MUSIC/BMI
Renie Peterson
2140 St. Clair St.
Bellingham, WA 98225

HEART WARMING MUSIC CO./BMI
1625 Broadway
Nashville, TN 37202

HEMPHILL MUSIC/BMI
P.O. Box 637
Nashville, TN 37202

HOMEWARD BOUND MUSIC/BMI
P.O. Box 1386
Stow, OH 44224

HOPE PUBLISHING CO./ASCAP
5707 West Lake Street
Chicago, IL 60644

HOUSE OF CASH/BMI
P.O. Box 508
Hendersonville, TN 37075

HOUSE OF DAVID/BMI
P.O. Box 653
822 19th Ave. So.
Nashville, TN 37203

HALL, JOHN MUSIC/SESAC
P.O. Box 13344
Ft. Worth, TX 76118

HYMNSPIRATION/BMI
P.O. Box 5171
Madison, WI 53705

HYMNTIME PUBLISHERS/SESAC
4145 Kalamazoo, S.E.
Grand Rapids, MI 49508

HUFFMAN PUBLISHING CO./BMI
P.O. Box 7084
10 Michael Drive
Greenville, SC 29611

INGLES MUSIC/SESAC
P.O. Box 1924
Tulsa, Okla 74101

JIMMY KISH MUSIC/BMI
2-Dedham Dr.
Nashville, TN 37215

JOURNEY MUSIC/BMI
P.O. Box 13
Madisonville, KY 42431

JOE KEENE MUSIC CO./BMI
P.O. Box 602
Kennett, MO 63857

JOYSONG MUSIC
PUBLICATIONS/SESAC
803 18th Ave. So.
Nashville, TN 37203

LeFEVRE SING PUBLISHING
CO./BMI
P.O. Box 43703
Atlanta, GA 30336

LEXICON MUSIC/ASCAP
20135 Delita Dr.
Woodland Hills, CA 91364

LILLENAS MUSIC CO./SESAC
P.O. Box 527
Kansas City, MO 64141

LITTLE DAVID MUSIC/ASCAP
P.O. Box 653
Nashville, TN 37202

LORENZE PUBLISHING CO./ASCAP
501 E. 3rd Street
Dayton, OH

LOVELINE MUSIC/ASCAP
P.O. Box 50
Nashville, TN 37202

LYNN MUSIC CO./ASCAP
P.O. Box 153
Brewster, NY 10509

LYNWOOD SMITH
PUBLISHERS/SESAC
Route 1, Box 151
Wesson, MI 39191

MANNA MUSIC/ASCAP
2111 Kenmere
Burbank, CA 91504

MARK IV MUSIC/BMI
P.O. Box 441
Spartanburg, SC 29301

McDOWELL MUSIC CO./BMI
828 So. Lawrence Street
Montgomery, AL 36104

MILL RUN MUSIC
Don Spangler
1033 Kingsmill Pkwy.
Columbus, Ohio 43229

MYLON LeFEVRE MUSIC/BMI
1314 Ellsworth Industrial Dr. N.W.
Atlanta, GA 30318

NASHVILLE INTERNATIONAL
MUSIC/ASCAP
20 Music Square West
Nashville, TN 37203

NASHWOOD MUSIC PUBLISHING CO.
P.O. Box 2205
No. Hollywood, CA 91602

NEIL ENLOE MUSIC CO./BMI
506 E. Winding Hill Road
Mechanicsburg, PA 17055

NEW PAX MUSIC PRESS/BMI
803 18th Ave. So.
Nashville, TN 37203

PARAGON MUSIC CORP./ASCAP
Bob MacKenzie
803 18th Ave. So.
Nashville, TN 37203

PATHWAY PRESS/SESAC
1022-1080 Montgomery
P.O. Box 850
Cleveland, TN 37311

PENWORTHY PUBLISHING CO./BMI
Bill Textor
P.O. Box "U"
Hendersonville, TN 37075

PLEASANT RIDGE MUSIC/BMI
P.O. Box 7084, 10 Michael Dr.
Greensville, SC 29611

PROMISELAND MUSIC/SESAC
825 19th Ave. So.
Nashville, TN 37203

QCA MUSIC/ASCAP
2832 Spring Grove Ave.
Cincinnati, OH 45225

RAMBO MUSIC, INC./BMI
2199 Nolensville
Nashville, TN 37211

RAP MUSIC LIMITED
Rt. 6, Box 65
Edgewater, MD 21037

RAY OVERHOLT MUSIC/BMI
112 So. 26th St.
Battle Creek, MI 49015

ROGER HORNE MUSIC/SESAC
P.O. Box 17496
Nashville, TN 37217

RITELINE PUBLISHING CO./BMI
P.O. Box 50
Nashville, TN 37202

RODEHEAVER CO./ASCAP
P.O. Box 1790
Waco, TX 76703

RONTOM PUBLISHING CO./ASCAP
110 21st Ave. So.
Nashville, TN 37203

SACRED HARP PUBLISHING CO.
Hugh McGraw
P.O. Box 185
Bremen, GA 30110

SACRED SONGS/ASCAP
4800 W. Waco Dr.
Waco, TX 76703

SAM ROBERTS PUBLISHING/SESAC
514 2nd Ave. So.
Nashville, TN 37210

SATWIN MUSIC/SESAC
P.O. Box 11217
Knoxville, TN 37919

SELAH PUBLISHING CO.
Joseph Higgins
1763 E. Elm Street
Springfield, MO 65804

SILHOUETTE MUSIC/SESAC
P.O. Box 41
Johnsonville, SC 29555

SILVERLINE MUSIC, INC./BMI
920 19th Ave. So.
Nashville, TN 37212

SINGSPIRATION, INC./SESAC
4145 Kalamazoo Ave., S.E.
Grand Rapids, MI 49508

SKYLITE MUSIC/SESAC
209 N. Lauderdale Dr.
Memphis, TN 38105

SOMERSET MUSIC PUBLISHERS
Tradewind Shopping Center
Somerset, KY 42501

SONGS OF CALVARY/BMI
P.O. Box 175
Fresno, CA 93701

BEN SPEER MUSIC CO./SESAC
54 Music Square West
Nashville, TN 37212

STAMP-BAXTER MUSIC/BMI
P.O. Box 4007
Dallas, TX 75208

**STAMPS QUARTET MUSIC
CO./SESAC**
58 Music Square West
Nashville, TN 37212

STOKER MUSIC CO./SESAC
John Daniel Catalogue
4720 Benton Smith Road
Nashville, TN 37215

SUMAR MUSIC/SESAC
58 Music Square West
Nashville, TN 37215

SWORD & SHIELD MUSIC/SESAC
P.O. Box 50
Nashville, TN 37202

THROFF PUBLISHING CO./BMI
6900 2nd Ave. So.
P.O. Box 2868
Birmingham, AL 35212

TENNESSEE MUSIC CO./SESAC
1022-1080 Montgomery Ave.
P.O. Box 850
Cleveland, TN 37311

TIDWELL MUSIC CO./BMI
P.O. Box 168
Hermitage, TN 37076

TOWNSHIP GROUP, INC./BMI
P.O. Box 7084
Greenville, SC 29610

TRIUNE MUSIC/ASCAP
Elwyn C. Raymer
824 19th Ave. So.
Nashville, TN 37203

UPWARD BOUND MUSIC/SESAC
P.O. Box 1386
Stow, OH 44224

VANZANT & VANZANT/BMI
North Oak Trafficway and I-29
Kansas City, MO 64141

WINFRED PUBLISHING CO/ASCAP
1634 Spruce St.
Philadelphia, PA 19103

WHITE OAK PUBLISHING CO./BMI
7771 Cheviot Road
Cincinnati, OH 45239

**WHITE-WING PUBLISHING
HOUSE/BMI**
P.O. Box 1039
Cleveland, TN 37311

WHITFIELD MUSIC/BMI
P.O. Box 5657
Pensacola, FL 32505

WILLIS PUBLICATIONS/SESAC
P.O. Box 72
Farnington, MO 63640

WINONA MUSIC INC./BMI
Helen Weaver
7459 Davis Hill Circle
Harrison, TN 37341

WINSETT MUSIC CO./SESAC
128 E. Second Street
Dayton, TN 37321

WORD, INC./ASCAP
825 19th Ave. So.
Nashville, TN 37203

**WRONG WAY MUSIC &
PUBLISHING CO.**
P.O. Box 5025
Roanoke, VA 24012

**ZONDERVAN PUBLISHING
HOUSE/SESAC**
1415 Lake Drive, S.E.
Grand Rapids, MI 49506

CMA

The Gospel Music Association in selecting individuals to submit articles for this publication of our annual directory and yearbook, has endeavored to select only those persons whose lives or location caused them to be in a position to have first hand knowledge of the subject matter about which they write. We gratefully acknowledge this service and have attempted to publish the articles, despite some editorial review, in the spirit in which they were originally written. While the Gospel Music Association acknowledges editorial review by condensing we have tried to let each author speak.

Appendix D

Charts

GOSPEL LP's

BY LABEL

These listings are the best selling Gospel LP's as reported to Billboard by the leading manufacturers in this field.

COLUMBIA RECORDS

1. HE WALKS WITH ME, Chuck Wagon Gang, CL 2080 (M); CS 8880 (S).
2. GOD'S GENTLE PEOPLE, Chuck Wagon Gang, CL 1899 (M); CS 8699 (S).
3. CHUCK WAGON GANG SINGS SONGS OF HOVIE LISTER, CL 1592 (M); CS 8392 (S).
4. PRAYER IN SONG, Chuck Wagon Gang, CL 1396 (M); CS 8191 (S).
5. ALL PRAISE THE LORD, Chuck Wagon Gang, CL 1330 (M); CS 8137 (S).

HEART WARMING RECORDS

1. FIRESIDE HYMNS, Jake Jess and the Imperials, LPHF 1783 (M); LPS 1782 (S).
2. BLENDS AND RHYTHMS, Jake Jess and the Imperials, LPHF 1785 (M); LPS 1784 (S).
3. INTRODUCING THE IMPERIALS, Jake Jess and the Imperials, LPHF 1777 (M); LPS 1776 (S).
4. TIME FOR THE HYMNS, The Weatherford Quartet, LPHF 1789 (M); LPS 1788 (S).
5. BEST WISHES, Elmer and June and Pam Too, LPHF 1781 (M); LPS 1780 (S).

RCA VICTOR RECORDS

1. THE BLACKWOOD BROTHERS QUARTET, featuring their famous bass, J. D. Summer, LPM 2752 (M); LSP 2752 (S).
2. THE PEARLY WHITE CITY, The Blackwood Brothers Quartet, LPM 2397 (M); LSP 2397 (S).
3. ON STAGE—THE BLACKWOOD BROTHERS QUARTET, LPM 2646 (M); LSP 2646 (S).
4. A GOSPEL CONCERT, Statesmen Quartet, LPM 2647 (M); LSP 2647 (S).
5. THE MYSTERY OF HIS WAY, Statesmen Quartet, LPM 2546 (M); LSP 2546 (S).

SIMS RECORDS

1. THE BEST OF THE HAPPY GOODMAN FAMILY, SLP 117.
2. SWEET JESUS, The Frost Brothers, SLP 120.
3. MOTHER LEFT ME HER BIBLE, The Luttrells, SLP 116.
4. TOUCH THE HAND OF THE LORD, The Plainsmen Quartet, SLP 106.
5. MARTHA CARSON, SLP 109.

SING RECORDS

1. THE GOSPEL SINGING CARAVAN, Various Artists, MFLP 575.
2. LORD IT'S ME AGAIN, Le Fevres Quartet, MFLP 3211.
3. PASSING THRU, Blue Ridge Quartet, MFLP 457.
4. THE PROPHETS RELAX, The Prophets Quartet, MFLP 3003.
5. THE SEGO BROTHERS AND NAOMI, MFLP 9091.

SKYLITE RECORDS

1. THE OAK RIDGE BOYS SING FOR YOU, SRLP 6020 (M); SSLP 6020 (S).
2. WITHOUT HIM, New Stamp Quartet, SRLP 6021 (M); SSLP 6021 (S).
3. SONGS OUR FATHERS SANG, The Jr. Blackwood Brothers, SRLP 6016 (M); SSLP 6016 (S).
4. THE GARDEN OF MELODY, The Speer Family, SRLP 6013 (M); SSLP 6013 (S).
5. GOSPEL MOODS THAT THRILL, Wally Varner, SRLP 6006 (M); SSLP 6006 (S).

SONGS OF FAITH RECORDS

1. SING THE GOSPEL, Sego Brothers and Naomi, SOF 110.
2. THE AWARD WINNING SEGO BROTHERS AND NAOMI, SOF 121.
3. ON THE WINGS OF A DOVE, The Florida Boys Quartet, SOF 106.
4. MY GOD SO REAL, Wally Fowler and the Oak Ridge Quartet, SOF 100.
5. THE FLORIDA BOYS AT CARNEGIE HALL, SOF 112.

STARDAY RECORDS

1. GOLDEN GOSPEL MILLION SELLERS, The Sunshine Boys, SLP 156.
2. WALLY FOWLER'S ALL NIGHT SINGING CONCERT, SLP 112.
3. SINGING CONVENTION, The Lewis Family, SLP 252.

WARNER BROS. RECORDS

1. THE OAK RIDGE BOYS, W 1497 (M); WS 1497 (S).
2. NOTHING BUT—THE GOSPEL TRUTH, The Curriers, W 1514 (M); WS 1514 (S).
3. FOLK-MINDED SPIRITUAL FOR SPIRITUAL-MINDED FOLKS, The Oak Ridge Boys, W 1521 (M); WS 1521 (S).
4. WARNER BROS. PRESENTS THE GOSPEL ECHOES, W 1499 (M); WS 1499 (S).
5. INTRODUCING STAN AND DAN, Stan Bonham and Dan Howell, W 1498 (M); WS 1498 (S).

<u>Previous</u> <u>Winners</u>: <u>Best</u> <u>Inspirational</u> <u>Performance</u> (non-
Classical)

1975 JESUS, WE JUST WANT TO THANK YOU, The Bill Gaither
Trio (Impact)

1976 THE ASTONISHING, OUTRAGEOUS, AMAZING, INCREDIBLE,
UNBELIEVABLE WORLD OF GARY S. PAXTON, Gary Paxton (New
Pax)

<u>Previous</u> <u>Winners</u>: <u>Best</u> <u>Gospel</u> <u>Performance</u> (Other than
Soul Gospel)

1975 NO SHORTAGE, Imperials (Impact)

1976 WHERE THE SOUL NEVER DIES, Oak Ridge Boys (Columbia)

Information derived from <u>NARAS</u> 18 (New York: Pilgrim
Press Corp., [1976]), n.p.; and from <u>Good</u> <u>News</u> (March, 1977),
4.

NATIONAL QUARTET CONVENTION

[Schedule of Performances]

MONDAY, OCT. 4
8:00 p.m. GMA Dove Awards Presentation,
Regency Ballroom, Hyatt Regency Hotel

TUESDAY, OCT. 5
7:00 p.m. Municipal Auditorium

Blackwood Brothers	Lester Family
Speer Family	Jake Hess Sound
LeFevres	Singing Americans
Kingsmen	Kenny Parker Trio

WEDNESDAY, OCT. 6
7:00 p.m. Municipal Auditorium

Jerry and the Singing Goffs	Senators with Jim Hamill
The Hinsons	Curtis Elkins
The Hemphills	The Telestials
Roger Horne Trio	Stu Phillips
Dixie Melody Boys	Songmasters

THURSDAY, OCT. 7
12:00 noon — SESAC Luncheon, Hyatt
Regency Hotel (Invitation Only)
7:00 p.m. — Municipal Auditorium

Wendy Bagwell and the Sunliters	LeFevres
Oak Ridge Boys	Singing Canadians
Hopper Brothers & Connie	John Mathews Family
Willie Wynn & The Tennesseans	Imperials
Scenic Land Boys	Galileans
Sego Brothers & Naomi	Gordon Jensen & Sunrise

FRIDAY, OCT. 8
11:00 a.m. — GMA Annual General Membership
Meeting, Davidson Room, Hyatt Regency Hotel
(Members Only)
3:00 p.m. — Blackwood Brothers Banquet, Hyatt
Regency Hotel
7:00 p.m. — Municipal Auditorium

Florida Boys	Stamps Quartet
Blue Ridge Quartet	Wally Fowler
Cathedrals	Singing Christians
Jim Sunderwith	Anne Criswell Jackson
Blackwood Brothers	The Fowlers
Blackwood Singers	Hovie Lister & the Statesmen
Speer Family	

SATURDAY, OCT. 9
9:00 a.m. — DJ Appreciation Breakfast, Hyatt
Regency Hotel (Free to DJ's registered to the
convention)
9:00 a.m. — Municipal Auditorium, Talent Contest
2:00 p.m. — GMA Hall of Fame Groundbreaking
Ceremonies, Corner of 16th Avenue S., Demonbreun
and Division (Public Invited — Free)
7:00 p.m. — Municipal Auditorium

Annual Parade of Stars

Happy Goodman Family	Scenic Land Boys
Couriers	Sego Brothers & Naomi
Florida Boys	Willie Wynn & The Tennesseans
Wendy Bagwell & The Sunliters	Jake Hess Sound
Blackwood Brothers	Singing Americans
Speer Family	Songmasters
LeFevres	John Mathews Family
Jerry and the Singing Goffs	Singing Christians
Stamps Quartet	Anne Criswell Jackson
Wally Fowler	Telestials
Lester Family	

SUNDAY, OCT. 10
Municipal Auditorium
10:00 a.m. — Worship Service (No Ticket Needed)
Special Music
Speaker — Dave Kyllonen (of The Couriers)
1:30 p.m. — Concert

Stamps Quartet	Bill Baize
Speer Family	John Mathews Family
Blackwood Brothers	(and others)
Jake Hess Sound	

TWENTY-FIRST
ANNUAL NATIONAL
QUARTET CONVENTION

OCTOBER 4,5,6,7,8,9 – 1977

[should read: 1976]

MUNICIPAL AUDITORIUM, NASHVILLE, TENNESSEE

MAKE PLANS NOW TO ATTEND

TICKETS AVAILABLE AUDITORIUM BOX OFFICE TO-NITE!

Gospel Music World [Nashville, Tennessee], I (October,
1976), n.p.

433

Song title: "Oh What A Love"
Words and Music by David Reece
Publisher: Lynn Music Corp., 100 W. 42nd St. New York,
    N. Y. [No reply to letter of Sept. 18, 1975.] Also,
    P. O. Box 153 Brewster, N. Y. [No reply to letter of
    Oct. 11, 1976; no telephone listed according to
    Information Operator January 1, 1977.] Unofficial
    permission to use song received from David Reece
    January 12, 1977.
Performing Group: "The Trebles" (1) Bibb County
Accompaniment: Piano, electric bass, drums; improvisatory;
    skillful.
Amplification: Yes. Singers used hand-held microphones.
    [Performance took place in television studio, all
    instruments were "miked."]
Introduction: Piano and electric bass. Approximately
    four measures.
Key: Changed from Ab to Eb.
Melody: Uses all seven scale tones and one accidental
    (raised second degree).
Anacrusis: None.
Range of melody: One octave.
Harmony: I   II^7 IV   V^7 VII^7 In general: Several
            I^7 ii   iv6   v^7 complex chords
                  ii6   v6   within basic I   IV
                  ii^7 v9   II V^7 structure.
                  ii^9

                                          Harmony not performed
                                          exactly as written
                                          (simplified).
Tonality: Ab Major [changed to Eb Major].
Meter: 3/4.
Rhythm: Uncomplex; dotted half-notes, half-notes, quarter-
    notes, eighth-notes. Dotted quarter-note followed by
    eighth-rest used more for phrasing than for rhythm.
    Rhythm not performed exactly as written. Slight
    modifications toward more complexity.
Texture: Homophonic. Some movement of harmony parts when
    melody has sustained tones.
Form: Written as verse-and-chorus; in reality AA form
    with seven-measure coda. Second verse performed as
    solo with sung vowel background.
Dynamics: [This is the only song with dynamics indicated.]

434

Verse mp; Chorus mf; last four measures of coda f.
Dynamic indications not followed accurately in
performance.
Tempo: None indicated. Performed at approximately ♩=72.
Text: Christ identified as Master, He, His, throughout
the song. No specific reference to the Deity.
    Verse 1: Forgiveness, blessing, peace of mind
from knowing Master [i.e. conversion experience].
    Verse 2: Security and hope.
    Chorus: Love, peace, joy, cleansing, feeling of
completeness [from conversion experience].
    In general: Peace, love, joy from conversion.
Text not performed exactly as written; slight modifications.
Personal: Yes (intensely). Much use of the personal
pronouns I, me, my (especially "me").

Appendix E

Miscellaneous

	Same	Slightly Changed	More Complex	Simplified	Brief Description
Melody	(1) (4) (5) (8) (10) (12) (13) (14) (15) (23)	(2) (3) (9) (11) (16) (18) (19) (22) (24)	(7) (17) (21) (25)		
Harmony (Vocal)	(1) (4) (16) (23)	(2) (13) (18)	(5)	(22-Unison)	Harmony part not sung as written (3) (7) (8) (9) (10) (11) (14) (15) (17) (19) (21) (24)
(Instrumental)	(8) (14)		(3) (12) (25)	(1) (7)	
Rhythm	None Exact	(1) (2) (3) (4) (5) (7) (8) (9) (11) (12) (13) (14) (15) (16) (18) (19) (22) (22) (23)	(21)	(17) (25)	Meter changed 3/4 to 4/4 (10) (24) Addition or subtraction of beat (14+) (13-)
Texture	(3) (4) (8) (11) (14) (16) (18) (23) (24)	(1) (2) (9) (13) (19)	(7) (12) (21) (25)	(5) (22)	Solo verse (7) (10) (15) (17) (21) (22); solo verse (vowel background) (1) (2); solo chorus (7)
Form	(1) (2) (3) (11) (12) (16) (18) (24)	(4)	Coda not written (5) (7) (8) (9) (10) (15) (17) (19) (21)	Interlude (7) (9) (10) (14) (17) (25)	Verse omitted (3) (4) (16) (23) Chorus repeated (7) (9) (15) (17) (21) (22)

	Same	Slightly Changed	More Complex	Simplified	Brief Description
Form (continued)					Chorus omitted between adjoining verses (13). Began with chorus (21).
Dynamics	Forte (3) (4) (7) (9) (17) (18) (22) (23) (24) (25)	Mezzo-forte (5) (8) (10) (11) (12) (13) (14) (15) (16) (19) (21)	Modified by texture (1) (2)		Dynamic indications appear only in (1); not accurately observed
Tempo					Tempo indications appear only in (11). Metronomic tempi are listed in Figure 22, page 319.
Text	(4) (8) (9) (10) (11) (12) (13) (14) (15) (16) (17) (18) (22) (23) (24)	(1) (2) (3) (5) (7) (19) (21) (25)			
Accompaniment	Piano alone (2) (4) (8) (10) (11) (12) (14) (16) (17) (18) (21) (22) (23) (24)	Amplified guitar alone (5)	Acoustic guitar alone (15)	Acoustic guitar and piano (3); Piano, electric bass, drums (1); Electric guitar electric bass, drums (7)	Two guitars, tambourine (19); Piano, 2 electric guitars, electric bass (9); 2 guitars, electric bass (25); A cappella (13)

440

	Same	Slightly Changed	More Complex	Simplified	Brief Description
Amplification of voices					(1) (5) (7) (9)(10)(11) (21)(22)
Key changed					Change of key by Performers is presented as Figure 23, page 322.
Instrumental introduction	Piano alone four Meas. (2) (4) (8)(11) (14)(16) (17)(18) (22)(24)	Piano 2 meas. (10); 6 meas. (12); 8 meas. (23) Piano arpeggio (21)	Piano and bass 4 meas. (1) (9)	Guitar arpeggio (3)(15) (25) Guitar introduction (5)(19)	Guitar and drums (7)
Tuning	Half-step low (piano) (4)(11)	Half-step low (guitar) (5)(19) (25)	Half-step high (guitar) (7)		
Instrumental improvisation	Chordal piano (2) (3) (7) (8) (10)(11) (14)(16) (17)(18) (23)(24)	Chordal guitar (5)(15) (19)(25)	Expert (1) (9) (12)(21) (22)		

441

National Academy of Recording
Arts and Sciences
Grammy Awards

Previous Winners: Best Soul Gospel Performance

BEST SOUL GOSPEL PERFORMANCE
1968 THE SOUL OF ME, Dottie Rambo
1969 OH HAPPY DAY, Edwin Hawkins
Singers
1970 EVERY MAN WANTS TO BE FREE,
Edwin Hawkins Singers
1971 PUT YOUR HAND IN THE HAND OF
THE MAN FROM GALILEE, Shirley Caesar
1972 AMAZING GRACE, Aretha Franklin
1973 LOVES ME LIKE A ROCK,
Dixie Hummingbirds

1974 IN THE GHETTO, James Cleveland and
the Southern California Community Choir

1975 TAKE ME BACK (album) Andrae Crouch and the Disciples
(Light)

1976 HOW I GOT OVER, Mahalia Jackson (Columbia)

Previous Winners: Best Gospel Or Other Religious Recording

**BEST GOSPEL OR OTHER RELIGIOUS
RECORDING**
1961 EVERYTIME I FEEL THE SPIRIT,
Mahalia Jackson
1962 GREAT SONGS OF LOVE AND FAITH,
Mahalia Jackson
1963 DOMINIQUE, Soeur Sourire; (The
Singing Nun)
1964 GREAT GOSPEL SONGS, Tennessee
Ernie Ford and the Jordanaires
1965 SOUTHLAND FAVORITES, George
Beverly Shea and the Anita Kerr Singers
1966 GRAND OLD GOSPEL, Porter Wagoner
and the Blackwood Bros
1967 MORE GRAND OLD GOSPEL, Porter
Wagoner and the Blackwood Bros
1967 HOW GREAT THOU ART, Elvis Presley
(sacred)
1968 THE HAPPY GOSPEL OF THE HAPPY
GOODMANS, Happy Goodman Family
1968 BEAUTIFUL ISLE SOMEWHERE,
Jake Hess

1969 IN GOSPEL COUNTRY, Porter Wagoner
and the Blackwood Bros
1969 AIN'T THAT BEAUTIFUL SINGING,
Jake Hess
1970 TALK ABOUT THE GOOD TIMES, Oak
Ridge Boys

1970 EVERYTHING IS BEAUTIFUL, Jake Hess
1971 LET ME LIVE, Charlie Pride
1971 DID YOU THINK TO PRAY, Charley
Pride
1972 L-O-V-E, Blackwood Brothers
1972 HE TOUCHED ME, Elvis Presley
1973 RELEASE ME (FROM MY SIN),
Blackwood Brothers
1973 LET'S JUST PRAISE THE LORD,
Bill Gaither Trio
1974 THE BAPTISM OF JESSE TAYLOR,
Oak Ridge Boys
1974 HOW GREAT THOU ART, Elvis Presley

442

Billboard Gospel LPs

This Week	Last Report	Weeks on Chart	TITLE, Artist, Label & Number
1	1	31	WALTER HAWKINS & THE LOVE CENTER CHOIR Love Alive, Light LS 5686 (Word/ABC)
2	5	8	GOSPEL KEYNOTES Ride The Ship To Zion, Nashboro 7172
3	3	66	JAMES CLEVELAND & CHARLES FOLD SINGERS Jesus Is The Best Thing That Ever Happened To Me, Savoy SGL 7005 (Arista)
4	8	84	THE GOSPEL KEYNOTES Reach Out, Nashboro 7147
5	7	22	JAMES CLEVELAND & THE SOUTHERN CALIFORNIA COMMUNITY CHOIR Give It To Me, Savoy SGL 14412 (Arista)
6	10	8	JAMES CLEVELAND & CHARLES FOLD SINGERS, Vol. II Savoy SGL 7009 (Arista)
7	4	53	SHIRLEY CAESAR Be Careful Of Stones You Throw, Hob HBX 2191 (Scepter)
8	11	58	GOSPEL KEYNOTES Destiny, Nashboro 7159
9	2	48	ANDRAE CROUCH AND THE DISCIPLES The Best Of Andrae, Light LS 5678 (Word/ABC)
10			ANDRAE CROUCH & THE DISCIPLES This Is Another Day, Light 5683 (Word)
11	6	83	ANDRAE CROUCH & DISCIPLES Take Me Back, Light LS 5637 (Word/ABC)
12	9	147	ANDRAE CROUCH Live At Carnegie Hall, Light LS 5602 (Word/ABC)
13	12	36	REVEREND MACEO WOODS & THE CHRISTIAN TABERNACLE CONCERT CHOIR Recorded Live In Chicago, Ill., Jesus Can Work It Out, Savoy SGL 7007 (Arista)
14	15	4	EDWIN HAWKINS & THE EDWIN HAWKINS SINGERS Wonderful, Birthright BRS 4005
15	18	8	SHIRLEY CAESAR No Charge, Hob 2176 (Scepter)
16	15	143	HAROLD SMITH MAJESTICS James Cleveland Presents-Lord, Help Me To Hold Out Savoy SGL 14315 (Arista)
17	14	40	REVEREND W. LEO DANIELS What In The Hell Do You Want, Jewel LPS 0110
18	13	17	PILGRIM JUBILEE SINGERS Don't Close In On Me, Nashboro 7169
19	24	122	REVEREND ISAAC DOUGLAS WITH THE JOHNSON ENSEMBLE The Harvest Is Plentiful, Creed 3056 (Nashboro)
20			ARETHA FRANKLIN/JAMES CLEVELAND Amazing Grace, Atlantic SD 2-906
21	21	143	JAMES CLEVELAND & THE VOICES OF TABERNACLE God Has Smiled On Me, Savoy SGL 14357 (Arista)
22	17	31	GOSPEL WORKSHOP MASS RECORDED IN NEW YORK Savoy SGL 7006 (Arista)
23	26	84	JAMES CLEVELAND & THE SOUTHERN CALIFORNIA COMMUNITY CHOIR To The Glory Of God, Savoy SGL 14160 (Arista)
24	28	8	JACKSON SOUTHERNAIRES Down Home, Malaco 4350 (TK)
25	35	4	INEZ ANDREWS War On Sin, ABC/Songbird SZLP 266
26	27	4	SHIRLEY CAESAR Go Take A Bath Brother, Hob 2183 (Scepter)
27			THE BEST OF THE EDWIN HAWKINS SINGERS Buddah BDS 2 5616
28			REV. ISAAC DOUGLAS PRESENTS HOUSTON TEXAS MASS CHOIR Beautiful Zion, Creed 3072 (Nashboro)
29			REV. ISAAC DOUGLAS & HIS SINGERS You Really Ought To Get To Know Him Creed 3075 (Nashboro)
30			SOUL STIRRERS Heritage-Volume II, Jewel LPS 0111
31	31	4	THE CARAVANS Travel On, Birthright BRS 4003
32			SENSATIONAL WILLIAMS BROTHERS I Can't Get Tired, ABC/Songbird 267
33	34	3	WILLIE BANKS & MESSENGERS For The Wrong I've Done, HSE 1506
34	30	44	JESSE HILL Also Known For Soul
35	19	11	BROOKLYN ALL STARS He Touched Me, Jewel LPS

443

THE OFFICIAL SINGING NEWS TOP 40 GOSPEL HITS

GOSPEL MUSIC'S ORIGINAL AND MOST RECOGNIZED NATIONAL CHART

THIS MONTH	LAST MONTH	
1	1	LEARNING TO LEAN Blackwood Brothers - Skylite
2	3	THE TOUCH OF THE MASTER'S STRONG HAND Hinsons - Calvary
3	2	IT MADE NEWS IN HEAVEN Kingsmen - Skylite
4	8	SHOUTIN' TIME Inspirations - Canaan
5	4	BORN AGAIN CHILDREN Galileans - Calvary
6	10	OPEN MY EYES Kemphills - HeartWarming
7	29	I WON'T WALK WITHOUT JESUS Hinsons - Calvary
8	11	HERE THEY COME Florida Boys - Canaan
9	6	OPERATOR Downings - Impact
10	7	PLEASE SEARCH THE BOOK AGAIN Jerry & The Singing Goffs - Lighthouse & Songs of Faith
11	5	SMALL LONELY HILL Rusty Goodman - Canaan
12	12	I'VE MADE A COVENANT Kingsmen - Canaan
13	33	JESUS, THIS IS JIMMY Bobby Grove - QCA
14	9	ALL IN THE NAME OF JESUS Jimmy Swaggart - JIM
15		BETWEEN THE CROSS AND HEAVEN Speer Family - HeartWarming
16	28	THE SON IS SHINING Rambos - HeartWarming
17	13	JUST WHEN I NEED HIM Rambos - HeartWarming
18	14	JESUS IS MINE Inspirations - Canaan
19	25	STAND BY ME Senators - Supreme
20	22	TOUR THE GOLDEN CITY LeFevres - Canaan
21	20	MY SOUL HAS BEEN SET FREE Willie Wynn & The Tennesseans
22	31	I HAVE RETURNED Marijohn - Myrrh
23		WHEN I STAND IN THE PRESENCE Florida Boys - Canaan
24		ONE WAY FLIGHT Telestials - Calvary
25		I LOST IT ALL Sammy Hall - Impact
26	23	HE DIDN'T COME DOWN Cathedrals - Canaan
27		THE SEEKER LeFevres - Canaan
28		WITH HIM Cathedrals - Canaan
29	24	THE BRUSH Speer Family - HeartWarming
30	38	10-4 ON THE COTTONTOP Wendy Bagwell - Canaan
31	26	I'LL TAKE JESUS Dixie Echoes - Supreme
32		BEHOLD THE LAMB Songmasters - Calvary
33	17	THE SCARS IN THE HANDS OF JESUS Florida Boys - Canaan
34	18	I'M A KING'S KID LaVerne Tripp - QCA
35		I'VE GOT SOMETHING TO SING ABOUT Doug Oldham - HeartWarming
36	39	BETWEEN THE CROSS AND HEAVEN Bill Gaither Trio - Impact
37		HE WROTE MY NAME Kemphills - HeartWarming
38	36	THANK YOU LORD FOR YOUR BLESSINGS ON ME LeFevres - Canaan
39		THE SWEETEST HALLELUJAH Kenny Parker Trio - HeartWarming
40		I FEEL GOOD Lanny Wolfe Trio - Impact

444

THE OFFICIAL
SINGING NEWS
CONTEMPORARY
GOSPEL

THIS MONTH	LAST MONTH	MONTHS ON CHART	
1	1	5	OPERATOR
			Downings - Impact
2	2	5	JUST WHEN I NEED HIM
			Rambos - HeartWarming
3	7	3	I LOST IT ALL
			Sammy Hall - Impact
4	10	10	STATUE OF LIBERTY
			Couriers - Impact
5	4	3	HE MEANS ALL THE WORLD TO ME
			Dallas Holm - Greentree
6	16	2	SHOW A LITTLE BIT OF LOVE AND KINDNESS
			Renaissance - Singcord
7	3	11	NO SHORTAGE (OF GOD'S LOVE)
			Imperials - Impact
8	5	2	HE'S COMING BACK
			Imperials - Impact
9		1	LEARNING TO LIVE
			Truth - Impact
10		1	AIN'T GONNA FIGHT IT
			Daniel Amos - Maranatha
11	13	11	MY CHILD, WELCOME HOME
			Imperials - Impact
12	14	3	WALKING SINAI
			Dan Whittemore - Tempo
13	9	2	LULLABY
			Couriers - Tempo
14		1	DAVID'S PSALM
			Imperials - Impact
15	6	2	DIFFERENT WORLD
			Gary S. Paxton - NewPax
16		1	IT'S SO GOOD TO KNOW
			Gentle Faith - Maranatha
17		1	OPEN OUR EYES
			Joy Strange - Maranatha

THE OFFICIAL
SINGING NEWS
TRADITIONAL
GOSPEL

THIS MONTH	LAST MONTH	MONTHS ON CHART	
1	2	11	I HAVE RETURNED Marijohn - Myrrh
2	10	2	I'VE GOT SOMETHING TO SING ABOUT Doug Oldham - HeartWarming
3	3	8	BETWEEN THE CROSS AND HEAVEN Bill Gaither Trio - Impact
4	1	11	THIS IS THE TIME I MUST SING Bill Gaither Trio - Impact
5	7	11	HIS KIND OF LOVE Marijohn - Myrrh
6	4	3	PASS IT ON Evie - WORD
7	-	1	PEACE SHALL COME Bill Gaither Trio - HeartWarming
8	-	1	COME, LORD JESUS Nancy Grandquist - Freedom
9	-	1	I AM HEALED David Ingles - DIP
10	6	5	THERE'S A WHOLE LOT OF PEOPLE GOING HOME David Ingles - DIP

THE OFFICIAL
SINGING NEWS
COUNTRY
GOSPEL

THIS MONTH	LAST MONTH	MONTHS ON CHART	
1	1	3	JESUS, THIS IS JIMMY Bobby Grove, OCA
2	2	2	10-4 ON THE COTTONTOP Wendy Bagwell - Canaan
3	-	1	CLOSER TO GOD Grandpa Jones
4	5	2	EVERYONE'S SINGING FOR THE LORD Lewis Family - Canaan
5	9	3	THERE'S A HAND Grandpa Jones - CMM
6	-	1	DON'T WAIT FOR SUNDAY Ray Price - WORD
7	-	1	JUST A LITTLE TALK WITH JESUS Lewis Family - Canaan
8	(Return)		I LOVE YOU Tennessee Ernie Ford - Capitol
9	(Return)		DID YOU THINK TO PRAY? Charley Pride - RCA
10	(Return)		THERE'S A MAN IN HERE Statler Brothers - Mercury